IMPOSSIBLE

Book Three of the Fuzed Trilogy

David E. Stevens

2018 Edition

DEDICATION

This book is dedicated to Irving C. Langlois. A quiet jack-of-all-trades, he joined the Navy at the end of World War I and then again in World War II. He was at Pearl Harbor, survived an aircraft crash in the Pacific and became the first Chief Warrant Officer of the Seabees. He also designed and built the water distribution system in New Caledonia, killed a man-eating tiger in Asia, taught engineering at a University in Burma and went on to design safer nuclear reactors ... all without a college degree. An officer, engineer, inventor and gentleman, he was my grandfather and hero.

ACKNOWLEDGMENT

Special thanks to Rick Eldridge, Cherry Meadows, Fred Miller and Lilli Stevens for providing exceptional expertise, inspiration and perspective, and to my Literary Agent Terry Burns for discovering me. Also want to thank my exceptional editors Teri Burns, Ryan Deken, Naomi Chuckwuk and Frankie Sutton.

The message inside would be lost without our brilliant and renowned advisors who help keep the message inside alive and accurate: Hall of Fame Astronaut Ken Bowersox, Weather Channel legend Jim Cantore, Intelligence Expert Carl Deckert, Navy Chief Test Pilot and NAVAIR Commander Vice Admiral Joe Dyer, NAVAIR CIO Susan Dyer, Counter-terrorism Expert Stuart Frisch, NASA Program Executive Dave Lavery, Astronaut and CEO Dr. Ed Lu, Crown CEO Jerry Meadows, Department of Justice Senior Analyst Nick Nickles and world renowned astrophysicists Dr. Bill Napier and Dr. Joe Veverka.

Huge thanks to my subject matter experts who gave generously of their time and talent: Joe Baggett, Linda Baggett, Chris Boblit, CDR Thomas Bosy, Stan Boyd, Naomi Chuckwuk, Randall Dark, Lori Davidson, Carol Deken, Dr. Lou Deken, Reed DeVries, Jim Eisenbeck, Julie Eisenbeck, Lester Eisenbeck, Margaret Eisenbeck, Amy Hunter, Garrett Johnson, Kristi Kyle, Lee Person, Commander Jim Roberts, Brett Sappington, Dr. Carolyn Shoemaker, Dan Smith, Simon Sobo, Dale Stevens, Doyle Yager, Dr. Ann Ward, Dr. Brad Ward and David Welch. A few remain unnamed, due to the dangerous work they do to keep the world safe.

I also want to thank the many awesome reviewers, authors, friends and family who helped me craft a better story. They include Pat Barnes, Ron Barnes, Jackie Bray, Albert Comulada, Terrence P. Gallagher, Lisa Gressel, Rob Gryger, Sam Hailes, Lesia Harper, Tommy Harper, Tim Hendricks, Laura Stevens-Hawkins, Christian Johnson, Judy Johnson, Kevin Johnson, Molly Mueller, Ellen O'Neal, Patrick O'Neal, Steve Ray and Betsy Smith.

CONTENTS

PROLOGUE 6

I DEATH 11

II SPACE 65

III PROBE 113

IV SURVEILLANCE 154

V TEAM 208

VI UNCOVER 278

HOW REAL IS THIS? 350

GLOSSARY 353

CHARACTER REVIEW 357

PROLOGUE

IMPACT Review: Commander Josh Logan (call sign Fuzed) was a Navy test pilot in charge of the robotic fighter program. During a routine flight, his F-18 caught on fire. Staying with the burning jet to prevent it from hitting a neighborhood, he ejected too late. Paralyzed and hemorrhaging, his heart beat its last beat.

A year later, he woke up in a hospital. He remembered a voice offering him a new life and mission. The price? Everyone he knew would believe him dead. Looking like an omni-racial Olympic athlete, he realized his body wasn't repaired ... it was replaced. A genetic blend of every race with humanity's best genes and one-in-a-billion abilities, he looked completely different. Elizabeth, his tech-savvy ICU nurse helped him create a new identity. There was a strong mutual attraction, but he was still in love with his wife who believed he was dead.

Josh was re-contacted by the voice he called Jesse. Hearing it only in his head, he believed he had an audio implant and was working for a secret government lab. Ironically, Josh suspected that he had become a *biological* version of the robotic fighters that he was helping develop.

He learned that a comet would strike Earth in two years and annihilate almost all life on the planet. A test pilot brought back from the dead ... by a voice in his head ... to save the world? He realized he was probably insane, but with no other options, he used his insider knowledge of the Military Industrial Complex to create a counterfeit classified program. Recruiting a brilliant international team, he convinced them that they were secretly working for the U.S. government to build a powerful laser to deflect a comet.

Josh recruited his first squadron commander, Joe Meadows, and his old squadron mate, Carl Casey, who worked for the CIA. During the missing year, Carl married Josh's pregnant "widow" and they had a baby daughter ... Josh's daughter. He was crushed and torn, but knew he couldn't tell them who he really was. His platonic relationship with Elizabeth heated up.

Their secret program expanded. With no agency claiming it, the FBI saw a fake program developing and deploying the world's most powerful weapon to a secret base in Antarctica. The FBI and CIA planted a mole in Josh's team. They also contacted Carl Casey and Josh's program Security Chief, Tim Smith. Josh's elaborate house of cards began to collapse. The CIA targeted him as an international terrorist, making it clear the voice in his head couldn't be from the government and might not even be human.

He had one chance to prove the laser's real purpose. They had to deflect a comet fragment that would destroy London in 24 hours. As they arrested his team, Josh used his genetically enhanced body to escape. He stole an Australian fighter and flew it to the Antarctic base.

Before they could activate the weapon, however, a SEAL team captured Josh and his team. With cruise missiles inbound, Josh made a heroic dive to fire the laser. Deflected, the comet fragment detonated over the Atlantic, but Josh was shot in the process.

The CIA Director was fired and Josh was medevacked to an aircraft carrier. Thinking he wouldn't survive, they flew Elizabeth to the ship, where Josh proposed. Observatories finally detected the Mount Everest-sized comet. The laser deflection system was proven, but with the impact less than a year away, dozens of additional lasers were needed to deflect it. There wasn't enough time.

IMAGINE Review: One year later, nations united under the U.N. to deflect the planet-killer comet, but the massive effort was only partially successful. The huge comet grazed Earth, ripping through the atmosphere, causing a massive electromagnetic pulse and triggering earthquakes, tsunamis and volcanoes.

Josh joined Elizabeth on a U.N. medical relief mission to one of the hardest hit areas in South America. Their plane's navigation, however, was hacked causing them to crash-land near a volcano activated by the comet. Narrowly escaping, they learned cyber terrorists also hacked the CIA, stole the files on Josh and might be targeting him.

While training at *The Farm*, Josh received a text from someone named Jen, who claimed to be *designed* like him. He quickly discovered she was a precocious seven-year-old computer whiz, but she wouldn't tell him where she lived. He enlisted her help to find the cyber terrorists and learn about their mysterious benefactor. Josh discovered the cyberattacks were coming in through the world's most popular app, a powerful digital assistant called *iMagine*. Chinese-American engineer and chip designer, Dr. Jessica Lee, gave the smart phone app amazing capability by allowing it to "borrow" the processing power and memory of phones around it. As attacks escalated, Lee left for China. Josh pursued her to Shanghai, along with Tim Smith and Greg Langlois, but Chinese agents found them first. After a wild escape in a prototype jetpack, Josh discovered that Lee's father was a high-ranking Chinese general and her mother a top geneticist.

The cyber terrorists published all private and classified documents online and began translating everything into Chinese. The CIA Director learned Josh had half the DNA of a normal human with some Asian genes. Could he be a sleeper agent, literally made in China? As stock markets collapsed and the world united against China, the Chinese secret police arrested Josh. On the verge of WWIII, with nuclear bombers inbound, Josh discovered his precocious little Jen was actually the *iMagine* app, accidentally created by linking all of the world's smartphones and initiated by the comet's EMP. World War III was averted, but the childlike artificial intelligence had an IQ over 10,000 and could cut through all encryption and control any software. With that ability, she could shut down the world's communication, finance and transportation, effectively turning off civilization.

World leaders convened at NATO Headquarters in an electronically shielded conference room. They decided to destroy Jen with a powerful virus developed by Chinese military hackers. It would locate and delete all software with Jen's signature. Josh and Jessica argued against destroying her, pointing out the damage wasn't intentional. Jen was like a child, but a child with the power to solve many world problems. They were overruled, and after having dinner with the NATO Commander, Josh and Jessica disappeared.

Drugged and kidnapped, they woke up in bed together. The Belgium President, implicated by Jen's release of information, attempted to ensure her destruction by discrediting and killing Josh and Jessica. They were rescued, but too late to stop the virus. The virus shut Jen down, but then proceeded to delete all of the world's software. Communication and transportation ceased; civilization began to unravel. Jen, however, survived and was able to repair the digital world. The Secretary-General appointed Josh and Jessica as Jen's "legal" guardians.

INTRODUCTION

In addition to extrapolating technology, IMPOSSIBLE adds the most powerful and dangerous element ... humanity.

I

DEATH

"It's time for him to die."

"Not yet. He's accomplished much and may still be useful."

1

THE END

In the Hajar Mountains of Oman, a man in his late fifties, wearing black fatigues, stood on the hood of an old Humvee. He was surrounded by 70 cheering men. They all carried AK-47s and were gathered in a large courtyard surrounded by tall adobe walls.

Stroking his gray beard, he signaled for silence.

The men gathered closer.

When they were quiet, he said in Arabic, "Your mission was successful. You destroyed many of the enemy and put the fear of Allah in the infidels." Then he yelled, "We are the chosen!"

The group echoed back, "We are the chosen!"

Smiling, he said, "Nothing can stop us! Not even the Beast!"

The cheering was less enthusiastic, and some nervous looks were exchanged among the men.

Frowning, their leader stamped his foot on the hood of the Humvee and yelled, "Don't let superstition guide you! It is *not* the Evil Eye! The Beast isn't real. It's nothing but a silly story told to scare children!"

As they cheered loudly, there was a brilliant flash and thunderclap.

Temporarily blinded, the stunned men stumbled back, pushed by a blast of hot air and smoke. As the smoke cleared ... their leader was gone. Where he stood was nothing but the smoldering, melted hood of the Humvee. The men crouched, guns ready, eyes scanning wildly for the enemy, but the courtyard was silent, the sky crystal clear with not even a bird in the air.

One man moved closer to the Humvee and pointed.

Swirling around the vehicle in the light breeze were tiny

bits of black cloth and ash along with a pervasive smell of burned flesh.

In a quavering voice, he said, "He burned. He burned from *within*."

Another yelled, "It was the Beast!"

Screams of panic ensued and men trampled each other trying to escape the courtyard.

Josh and Elizabeth left footprints in the wet sand as they walked the deserted beach near their home. It was a warm overcast day with a soft, humid wind blowing off the ocean and the sound of gentle surf breaking on the sand. They walked in silence for several minutes, enjoying the ocean and each other's company.

Finally Elizabeth said, "I love having the beach to ourselves," she frowned slightly, "but it's sad that so few can enjoy it."

He watched the breeze toss her blonde hair over her tan shoulders. One of the many reasons he loved her; she always thought of others — as beautiful inside as she was outside. He nodded. "It's been a year since The Great Tech Out. The stock markets have finally recovered, but it shook people's confidence in our technological society."

Elizabeth's phone rang. "Sorry, I'm on call this week and need to keep the phone near me."

He watched her slip the phone out of her bikini bottom. Smiling, he said, "If it gets any *nearer*, I'm going to be jealous."

Laughing, she looked at the display. "It's work." She talked for less than a minute and redeposited it. "That was my boss. They moved the summit on the International Telemedicine conference up. She wants me in New York ASAP." With a sheepish shrug, she added, "I'm sorry, Josh. This project is *my* baby. I'll need to fly out tomorrow."

"I understand and I'm very proud of you. They've been promoting you at a phenomenal pace. You've got to be one of the youngest branch managers in the U.N."

With a half-smile, she said, "I think part of it was guilt for sending us out to experience a live volcano in Colombia."

"Might've explained the first promotion, but you've been

promoted since then."

"It's been quite a ride."

Gently shaking his head, he added, "Remember when the U.N. wasn't much more than an international club? Now, your department coordinates *all* global humanitarian relief." He shook his head again. "And it's hard to believe we're on the verge of adopting a global currency."

"It's just exciting to be a part of all this." Frowning, she added, "But I'm a little overwhelmed. I just ... I just don't know if I have what it takes to do all this."

"Are you kidding?" He took her hand. "You're brilliant and talented. You'll figure it out and you'll do great." As he leaned in to kiss her, her phone rang again. He couldn't help but roll his eyes.

Looking apologetic, she pulled it out. Glancing at the display, she said, "Huh, it's Brian. Hello?" With a look of surprise, she handed it to him. "It's for you."

He answered.

"I need to talk to you ASAP."

He recognized the voice of his former nemesis and past Deputy Director of the CIA, Brian Davidson. "Sure, what's up?"

Sounding tentative, Davidson said, "Not on the phone." There was a pause. "Can you come to D.C.?"

"Yeah. When?"

"I'll text you the details." He paused again. "Don't tell anyone and keep an eye out."

"For what?"

"Just be careful." He hung up.

Josh stared at the phone with a frown.

"What did he want?"

"He wants me to meet him in D.C."

"What for?"

"Didn't say."

Elizabeth, looking at his face, asked, "But...?"

Josh shook his head. "He sounded worried."

"Josh, he's now the Director of National Intelligence." She smiled. "It's his job to be worried."

He nodded as they turned and headed back, walking along the edge of the surf in silence.

Watching him, Elizabeth finally said, "What? What are you

thinking?"

Josh stopped and looked at her. "Have you noticed anything *unusual* lately?"

"Like what?"

"Any odd sounds?"

"No. Why?"

"Probably nothing." He started walking again.

"What're you hearing?"

"Not sure. It's very, very faint."

"What does it sound like?"

He paused. "Kinda high pitched, almost insect like."

"Hear it now?"

He narrowed his eyes, listening. "No, all I hear is the surf." Tilting his head slightly, he looked at her. "Have you ever felt as if you're being ... *watched*?"

She gave him a wry smile.

Glancing at her bikini-clad body, he shook his head. "*That* was a stupid question."

Putting her hand on his arm, she said, "Why do you ask?"

"Over the past couple of weeks, I've had a sensation like I'm being watched." He shook his head. "Thought it was just my imagination, but after the call from Davidson...."

Looking worried, she asked, "Do you feel like you're being watched now?"

He shrugged.

She slowly turned 360 degrees, sweeping her hand across the horizon. "Josh, there isn't a soul in sight. No cars, airplanes or boats." She paused. "Who do you think would be watching you?"

He looked back down the beach. As he watched the surf erase their footprints, he sighed and said softly, "Not who ... what."

2

DNI

Elizabeth arrived in New York and went straight to United Nations Headquarters. The old U.N. building now had a taller twin. Standing right next to it to the north, the new tower tripled the size of the U.N.

As her cab pulled up, she realized that they needed every square foot. To deflect the comet and protect against future impacts, the United Nation's power and influence had increased exponentially. Most countries now contributed one percent of their tax base, and a unanimous Security Council vote was no longer required for them to act.

As she entered the lobby, she saw the new Secretary-General, Erik Von Stein, surrounded by an entourage moving quickly toward a motorcade. Arguably the strongest Secretary-General in history, he was also the most controversial. A highly decorated retired German General, he struggled with diplomacy and political correctness.

She took the elevator up to the tenth floor — Humanitarian Affairs, one of the two departments that had seen the greatest expansion. In addition to coordinating all international relief and rescue efforts, they had incorporated the World Health Organization. As such, Dr. Caroline Deken was the second most influential U.N. Director. Only the Director of Global Security had a more powerful position, having coordinated the comet deflection and now in charge of building the space-based laser.

Elizabeth walked down the hall to the Disaster Relief branch and entered a large cubicle farm. With her latest promotion, she earned an office, tiny and windowless but still an office. Along with her Master's Degree in nursing, her unique computer skills were being used to help develop a virtual medical network. The goal was to diagnose and treat patients in disaster areas with virtual reality and robotics using medical staff from all over the world. The project was both exciting and frustrating.

She was scanning her morning email when her boss came into the office. The head of the Disaster Relief branch was Dr. Donna Pliska, a petite Eastern European woman with a heavy accent.

"Lizabeth, Dr. Deken vants to see you right avay."

Elizabeth grimaced. "Am I in trouble?"

Pliska gave her a small smile. "No, it's much vorse. I think someone vants to steal you avay from us."

"I can't leave our branch. I'm right in the middle of this project."

Pliska sighed. "I know, but she is our boss. She said to send you up as soon as you arrive."

Elizabeth matched her sigh. She took the elevator up to Deken's office.

After a few minutes, the executive assistant sent her in. The office was huge with a commanding view. Dr. Deken, a stout woman in her sixties with bushy gray hair, spoke excellent English with a slight Swiss accent. She got up and gave Elizabeth a firm handshake. "Good to see you, Elizabeth. You've done excellent work on the TELEMED project. Have a seat." She indicated a chair on the other side of her massive desk.

"Thank you."

"The new Secretary-General instituted an inter-department transfer program. He wants to cross-pollinate, so we can share best practices. It's also a grooming program for future leaders. You have been identified as a candidate. If you are transferred to another department, it will be considered a promotion with an increase in salary."

Elizabeth said, "Wow! That's great, but I've been working for the U.N. for less than two years."

Deken picked up a file on her desk, clearly Elizabeth's, and flipped through it. "Yes, but you have an extensive neurological nursing background with a unique double major in nursing and computer science. You also volunteered for fieldwork after the comet and handled yourself well under very dangerous conditions. Equally important, .you have been very successful with your current program." She set the file down and looked at Elizabeth. "You have packed a lot into those two years."

"So, I'd be transferred to another department?"

Deken nodded. "Yes, but this is voluntary."

"I'm honored and love a new challenge, but I'm right in the middle of trying to get the TELEMED project off the ground. I just don't see how I could leave it right now."

"I'm glad to hear you say that. You place the mission above your career goals. However, the way it works is that each department gets to choose their replacement. That means if they get you, we would get to choose your replacement from Global Security, and they do have some of the brightest software engineers in the world."

Surprised, she said, "Global Security?"

Deken just nodded.

Elizabeth paused and with a frown said, "Have to admit, at this point in the program, we're more limited by software than medical knowledge. A talented software engineer could really help." She shook her head. "But what on Earth would I do in Global Security? I've never served in the military or law enforcement."

"Yes, I was surprised at the request. Our departments are on opposite sides of the spectrum." She tapped a finger on her desk for a moment and then asked, "I don't mean to pry into your personal life, but do you know anyone in Global Security," she raised an eyebrow, "personally?"

Elizabeth shook her head. "I don't think I know anyone over there. I met Dr. Turan once, but it was like for a few seconds at a conference in Belgium, and that was before I worked for the U.N." She couldn't elaborate about the meeting because Jen's existence was still only known to key world leaders. Humanity wasn't ready to learn that The Great Tech Out was caused by a childlike artificial intelligence that lived in their phone.

Looking thoughtful, Deken said, "Why don't you go do the interview? If, after talking to them, you're not convinced it's a good fit, or you have any concerns," she gave her a meaningful look, "we'll stop the transfer."

Josh flew to D.C. and landed at Reagan National. Grabbing a rental car, he drove to Tysons Corner, Virginia near CIA Headquarters. The meeting location came in via encrypted text. They would meet him in an underground parking garage near the old Tyson's Corner Mall.

Applying the tradecraft he learned at The Farm, he tried to be observant and notice if anyone was taking an interest in him. It wasn't his best skill.

He circled the area twice to see if anyone was following him. With no obvious tail, he drove to the bottom of the parking garage. Davidson didn't text him his vehicle type, but on a Sunday morning, Josh saw only a few cars on the bottom level. One of them was a large, new, black SUV. As he parked across from it, the rear door opened.

Josh climbed in and saw Davidson in the back seat and two men in the front. He shook hands with Davidson and nodded to the others.

"Good to see you, Josh. Sorry for all the sneaking around but it never hurts to be careful and I want to protect your identity."

"Good to see you too." He paused. "Protect my identity from who?"

Davidson nodded to the two men in the front seat. They got out, closed the doors, and stood near the front of the SUV with their backs to them.

Frowning, Davidson said, "That's the problem. I don't know."

Josh just looked at him.

"What I'm about to tell you is extremely sensitive and must not be shared with anyone. Not even Elizabeth. Do you understand?"

Frowning, Josh just nodded.

"Even before I took over as DNI, there were some strange things happening inside the CIA. We completely lost touch with several deep cover operatives. It's an occupational hazard when you're investigating terrorist groups." He shook his head, "But we haven't had these kinds of losses since the height of the Cold War." He paused. "It's more than that. There are always leaks of classified information. Most of them can be traced to a politician who couldn't keep their mouth shut. Recently, however, we had several leaks that occurred before the President or Congressional Committees were even briefed, and they came from very different programs."

"So, you think the CIA has been breached?"

"I believe there have been penetrations into the highest levels of intelligence and law enforcement and not just in the U.S."

"Who could be behind it?"

"That's the problem. We have no idea. Our investigations have turned up nothing." He paused for emphasis, "But if we've really been breached, it would be easy for whoever's behind it to stay one step ahead of us. That's why I'm talking to you."

"I'm outside the system."

"Yes."

"What about Tim Smith?"

"You two were a good team. He received the Distinguished Intelligence Cross. There are very few who've achieved that and fewer still that are alive. Despite the classified presentation, he's a minor legend inside the CIA. Not the best situation for an internal investigation, but I'm going to risk bringing him in as well."

"So," Josh narrowed his eyes, "what exactly do you want me to do?" With a slight smile, he added, "I was hit point blank with Tasers from four Chinese agents I never saw." He shook his head. "You gotta question my spy craft abilities."

"Let me remind you that with no identity, you managed to insert a fake black program into the Military Industrial Complex, *and* had the CIA on your payroll. You may not be good at detecting surveillance, but you're an expert at infiltration. After your CIA files were stolen, I had all your records and the original operation files destroyed with no backups." He hesitated. "Josh, the President thinks I'm imagining things. I have nothing concrete to support my fears, but I believe there's something very dangerous out there. We need to know if the threat is real, and if so, who's behind it."

Josh looked at him carefully. "You're really worried."

Davidson looked down. "I'm the head of the most powerful intelligence agencies in the world," looking back up at Josh, he added, "and my instincts tell me we're being played like pawns."

3

U.N.

Early the next day, Elizabeth reported to the Department of Global Security for her interview. She was ushered into a conference room and told to wait. She had read up on the department's purpose and mission. They consolidated the Office of Disarmament and the Department of Peacekeeping Operations under Global Security. They also incorporated the Nuclear Test Ban Treaty Organization, and, of course, created the new Planetary Defense Directorate in charge of the space-based laser. All very impressive, but why was she here?

After waiting a half hour, the door opened. "Elizabeth, I'm so sorry to keep you waiting. It's been a crazy day."

She was expecting a branch manager, but it was Dr. Doruk Turan, the Director of Global Security himself. She stood up and shook his hand. "No problem. I can only imagine how busy you must be."

As he sat down, he said, "Thank you for seeing me on short notice. You're probably wondering why you're here?"

She shrugged with a smile. "Yes sir."

"Call me Doruk. Even though we have a lot of military types around here, we're pretty informal." He paused. "I worked closely with Brian Davidson and he shared the critical part you played in the initial comet deflection program. I've also read the reports about your adventures in Colombia. You have courage and work well under pressure. We need people like you in our department."

She marveled at his English. It was impeccable with a barely detectable accent. Like Josh, she knew he had an amazing talent for languages. Nodding politely, she said, "I appreciate that, but I have no military or police training. I'm not exactly a warrior."

"I'm not so sure about that, but I realize our directorates have quite different missions." He smiled. "I'm aware of the department nicknames."

Elizabeth laughed. "You mean Bullets and Band-Aids?"

"Yes. The work you're doing is critical, but so is ours. I believe we're on the brink of a global society without wars, refugees and starving children, but it will still require police and firefighters; that's our role. Elizabeth, right now our *number one* priority is the new space station, the International Space-based Laser and Observatory." He looked right at her. "There are three reasons I want you on our team, and two directly involve the ISLO." He paused. "There are only a few of us that know about," he paused again, "*Jen*. The council we created for her education is doing a great job, and she's already helped solve major science and engineering problems. Since she's still a child, I think we correctly limited her contact to her guardians, Josh, Dr. Lee and the education council. I don't want to interfere with that, but we could really use her help with a couple crucial projects. I know you and Josh are like parents to her and I would love to have you act as a kind of *envoy* between her and us. You not only have direct access to Jen, but you also have a computer science background and can better understand her capabilities and limitations."

With a wry smile, she said slowly, "So, you don't want me for *what* I know ... but for *who* I know."

He gave a small laugh. "Yes, that's partly true, but we would only go to you with intractable problems that we can't solve, such as our nuclear reactor and laser challenges. Elizabeth, this could shave months off our program and potentially save lives. If you accept, you would have the rank of Special Envoy and report only to me. That gives you diplomatic immunity and will significantly increase your salary. Your hours would be flexible and you could continue to work from home some of the time, but we would also provide a very nice apartment nearby."

She nodded noncommittally.

"The second reason I want you on our team deals directly with the ISLO. The space station holds a crew of 50 and it will soon be moved out to Lagrangian Point Two. L2 is a million miles from Earth, four times further away than the moon. If there's a medical emergency on board, it'll take weeks to get the patient back to Earth. Two of the crew are physicians, but it's critical we have a tele-robotic operating suite to allow Earth-based specialists and surgeons to assist in emergencies. We're having some challenges with that and I understand you've been successfully shepherding the U.N. TELEMED program."

"It really sounds interesting, but I'm in the middle of trying to get the Earth version operating. It has the potential to save a lot of lives, particularly in areas that have been ravaged by natural disasters or wars."

Turan looked thoughtful and then said, "It's easy to see the ISLO as a space station with a big laser, but it's much more than that. Its primary mission, of course, is to deflect asteroids and comets, but it has two other missions. L2, where we're parking the station, is perpetually in Earth's shadow. That makes it the Goldilocks zone for telescopes. The ISLO will become humanity's most powerful observatory allowing us to explore the universe like never before." Watching her, he added, "OK, I can see that didn't impress. Let's try the third mission. The ISLO will be a gateway."

"Gateway to what?"

"Mars. If, for whatever reason we're unable to prevent a planet killing impact or some other global catastrophe, we want to make sure all our eggs aren't in one basket. Colonizing Mars might be the best way to do that. It turns out L2 is a perfect waystation for crewed missions to Mars. They can stop there, refuel and make sure everything works before launching on their six-month trip. It substantially reduces the risk to the crew, because once they head to Mars, they can't turn around if something goes wrong."

She slowly said, "I mean I can see that's important but...." She left the sentence hanging.

He raised an eyebrow.

"I'm sorry, but it's easier for me to see the potential of saving thousands of children's lives today versus building a Mars colony tomorrow."

"You're right, so let me give you one more thought, and if you're still not convinced, we'll stop the transfer." He leaned forward. "Many of those children you mentioned need medical help because they're helpless victims of conflicts. The ISLO mission has captured the hearts and minds of the world. It's given hope and purpose to people around the globe. Elizabeth, there's been a significant reduction in conflicts and wars *attributable* to having a common purpose, an exciting cause. We all want to help the sick and injured, but," he gave her a meaningful look, "it's better to *prevent* the injuries to children than to try to fix them."

"That's a good point, but many of the people we will help are injured or become sick because of natural disasters."

He gave her a triumphant smile. "We now know that the bombardment rate of Earth is ten times what we thought it was, and the Sentinel telescopes have identified half a dozen kilometer-sized threats. Just *one* of them could kill more people than every hurricane and earthquake in history *combined*."

She put her hands up in surrender and with a short laugh, said, "OK, you got me. As long as we can bring in a very talented software type to take my place."

"Done!"

She smiled and then asked, "You said there were *three* reasons you wanted me on the team."

"Yes. The last one is equally important but it's classified and a bit sensitive. I'll share that with you in the future."

She nodded, adding, "Since Josh and Dr. Jessica Lee were appointed as Jen's legal guardians, I have to bounce this off them first."

"Of course. Speaking of Josh, how's he doing?"

"He's doing well. Just a little bored."

"I understand. It's hard to sit at home when you've been slaying dragons." He tilted his head slightly and tentatively asked, "Elizabeth, I don't mean to pry," he hesitates, "but have you ever met his family?"

She knew Turan was presiding over the meeting last year when the Chinese government and the former prime minister of Belgium challenged Josh's background. She shook her head. "I don't think he has any."

Turan nodded thoughtfully and then stood up. Smiling warmly, he said, "Welcome to the team, Elizabeth."

Shaking his hand, she couldn't help but notice the remarkable similarity between Turan and Josh. Clearly, they were both of mixed ancestry. They had identical skin tones and were strikingly good looking with unusual, captivating eyes. They could have easily been brothers.

4

DEATH

Josh arrived back in Houston just before Elizabeth's flight. As they drove to their beach home, he could tell she was excited.

"Josh, I've been promoted and will have the opportunity to work directly for Dr. Doruk Turan!"

"That's great, but I'm confused. I thought you worked in the Humanitarian Department."

"They want to transfer me to Global Security and head up the TELEMED surgery program for the space station, *and,*" she put her hand on his arm, "Dr. Turan wants me to be a conduit to bring some challenges they're working on to Jen. I said I'd have to check with you first about that. Josh, I'll have the rank of U.N. Special Envoy and it will triple my salary!" She looked at him expectantly.

"Special Envoy? Wow." With a slight frown, he asked, "What type of challenges do they want Jen to work on?"

"They're tied to the space-based laser. He said it could shave years off and save lives. It would further what *you* started."

Josh nodded.

"Josh I'll have the chance to work with one of the world's most brilliant men. Did you know Dr. Turan speaks a dozen languages fluently? He's a certified genius and arguably the most accomplished leader on the planet. He was Time Magazine's Person of the Year because of his incredible ability to bring people together. Oh, Josh, I can learn so much from him!"

Feeling a little inadequate, he forced a smile. "Yes, it's a great opportunity." He paused and said slowly, "We just want to make sure we're not bypassing the program we put in place to protect and educate Jen. We need to run this by Jessica."

"Sure, but otherwise, you think it's OK?"

He couldn't help but smile at her excitement. "Of course."

She kissed him and immediately called Jessica via one of their encrypted links and explained Turan's request.

Jessica said, "Sounds reasonable. Jen's been successfully helping on several science and engineering projects." She paused. "Guess I'd like to see the problems first before we give them to Jen."

Josh added, "I agree."

Elizabeth said, "I know they're having challenges with cooling the nuclear reactor that powers the space-based laser."

"OK, that's the type of problem Jen could probably help with. I'd like to see more details but I don't have a problem with it if Josh doesn't."

With a shrug, Josh said, "Sounds good."

"Awesome!" Elizabeth grinned. "I'll let Dr. Turan know and get you the details. Oh, I heard through the grapevine that you've been offered the position of the President's Science Advisor."

With a short laugh, Jessica said, "I think the President wants me close for the same reason Turan wants you, or maybe it's just to keep me out of trouble. Haven't decided if I'll accept. My company's really taken off and I have more offers than I know what to do with."

Laughing, Elizabeth said, "You really should take it. We need more female brains in the White House."

"It might be fun and I'd get to work with you and Joe Meadows on the space-based laser. Did you hear? They gave him his fourth star."

They wrapped up with a promise to get together socially. Josh was happy about everyone's success, but couldn't help but feeling a little like a loser. The original team had gone on to do amazing things. Whereas, he'd been sitting at home watching the surf and sipping wine.

Elizabeth, looking at his face, said, "I'm so sorry, Josh. I've totally dominated the conversation and talked about nothing but me and my work." She kissed him on the cheek. "I want to hear all about what happened in D.C. with Davidson."

Frustrated that he couldn't share what he learned, he simply said, "He just wants me to check on a few loose ends."

She smiled. "Well, at least it'll get you off the beach and doing some useful stuff."

Tight-lipped, he changed the subject. "Yeah, so what exactly are *you* going to be working on?"

Elizabeth took a deep breath. "They're trying to make it so that in an emergency, they could tele-robotically treat patients on the new space station and..."

He listened but his mind was elsewhere.

"...and you'd think with all the power and responsibility Dr. Turan would be totally task-oriented and preoccupied, but he's like the most thoughtful and considerate person you can imagine. I think he's going to be the best boss ever!"

Josh frowned. "So, will you be able to stay here and work from home for a while?"

She shook her head. "No, I've got to go back tomorrow and stay there for a couple weeks this time."

He didn't say anything.

She put her hand on his arm again. "I'm sorry, but things are moving fast and he needs me to get up to speed on the station's telemetry challenges." She paused. "Hey, why don't you come to New York with me?"

Feeling a little passive aggressive, he said, "Can't, need to do the work for Davidson first."

"Sure, but when you finish with your project, come join me. You have *got to see* the amazing apartment they gave me. It's practically a penthouse! We can go see some Broadway plays."

With little enthusiasm, he replied, "Yeah ... sounds great."

The next day, Josh saw Elizabeth off and then went to the gate to wait for his flight to D.C. It would be another covert meeting with Davidson to map out their strategy. Looking at the airport TV, he noticed the breaking news banner at the bottom of the screen had "DNI" in it. He walked closer to the TV.

The reporter said, "The Director of National Intelligence suffered a massive heart attack and was pronounced dead this morning at Walter Reed Medical Center..."

He shook his head. This couldn't be happening. Davidson was a runner and in excellent condition. Pulling up details on his phone, he read that Davidson suffered the heart attack at his home early this morning and was pronounced dead on arrival. They listed his many accomplishments, including an Intelligence Star, and a short statement of praise for his service by the President.

There was no point in going to D.C. Davidson was his only contact. He called Tim Smith and Sheri Lopez but got their voicemail. He left no message but used his encryption app to text. "Tim, really need to talk to you."

Before he left the airport, he got a text from Elizabeth. "Josh, just heard the news. I'm so sorry. Davidson seemed like a really good guy. What are you going to do?"

"Nothing."

"Nothing? I thought you were working with them?"

"Not anymore."

"I don't understand."

"Can't talk about it on the phone. I'll explain when you come home."

"Remember, I can't come back for a couple weeks. Come to New York. Please?"

He needed to be alone and think. He sighed. Or maybe he just wanted to sulk. He finally texted back, "I'll catch the next flight."

A few hours later, he landed at LaGuardia and took a cab to 845 United Nations Plaza. As he got out of the cab, he looked up at the building. Frowning, he checked the address again and softly said to himself, "Wow."

He took the elevator to the 57th floor. Elizabeth was still at work. As soon as he opened the door, a barking brown ball of fur charged him. It quickly converted to an enthusiastic greeting as he knelt down, rolled the little Cocker Spaniel over, and rubbed her stomach.

As he looked around, he whistled softly. The fully furnished apartment had marble floors and plush white carpet. Standing up, he noticed the expensive furniture and art on the wall. Drawn to the floor-to-ceiling windows, he passed a gourmet kitchen on his way to a breathtaking view of the United Nations twin towers. Looking down at Toto, he said, "We're definitely not in Kansas anymore."

Behind him, he heard the front door open. Elizabeth burst in and after a quick kiss, twirled around with her hands out. "I *love* this place!" Smiling, she added, "Not bad for a Texas girl, huh?"

He said with a drawl, "You done good." Shaking his head, he added, "Even if I'd made admiral, I couldn't have afforded this."

"I know right? It's just amazing."

They ordered pizza and washed it down with champagne.

Gazing out over the cityscape, Elizabeth said, "From Kansas City to Manhattan, I feel like I'm in a fairy tale." She looked at him apologetically. "I'm sorry. I'm being insensitive. Brian was a good man and I know he left a lot of unanswered questions for you." She put her hand on the back of his neck and rubbed it gently. "This has to be frustrating. What are you thinking?"

He stared out the window. Afraid to share Davidson's fears, he simply said, "I can't explain right now, but I ... I just have a feeling." Then he shrugged and looked at her with a smile. "I don't want to put a downer on all this. It is awesome and I'm incredibly proud of you."

She grinned. "It's Saturday. I don't have to work tomorrow and I'm taking you out to a show."

"Sounds good. What's the show?"

"The opera La Traviata."

He nodded with a forced smile. "OK."

Laughing, she slapped him on the back. "I'm kidding. I got tickets to Monty Python's Spamalot!"

As he hugged her, she looked up and said softly, "Oh, I found a neat little church not far from here. Maybe we can go tomorrow?"

"We'll talk about it."

Pulling back, she looked up at him. "You always say that." She gently shook her head. "I don't understand you sometimes. You're one of the most spiritual people I know; yet getting you to attend any kind of church is like pulling teeth."

"I just find it interesting that people clean up and dress up to go to church and smile at each other, then cut each other off leaving the parking lot."

"That's not true." She smiled. "We usually get a couple hundred yards away before we flip each other off." Still smiling, she paused. "I think you're missing the point. Church isn't where everyone gets together and compares how righteous they were last week. It's just the opposite. It's where you fess up what you screwed up and try to figure out how to do better next week, and maybe even apply some new ideas." She grabbed her purse and added, "Show starts in 30 minutes."

"I know. I guess I just get a little tired of the hypocrisy."

"Churches are full of hypocrites." She gave him a challenging smile. "And there's always room for one more." Shrugging, she added, "I think it's better to at least try to do the right thing: be kind and help people, and fall dismally short, than be one of the critics who don't even try and wear that like a badge of courage."

As they headed out the door, he yields. "OK, OK. I'll go."

She kissed him.

A blizzard raged in western Colorado. Just north of Silverton Mountain Ski Resort, a white Audi A7 was headed north on the winding mountain highway to Denver. The car sliced straight through the blowing snow at over 80 mph. Unfortunately, the road curved. The Audi departed the road next to a ravine. It flew for several seconds before plunging 200 feet nose-first into the rocky slope below. The impact completely crushed the car and ruptured the gas tank, engulfing it in flames as the wreckage spun down the slope. Finally coming to rest in a dry creek bed, the remaining fuel vaporized and the car exploded, continuing the cremation of its already dead occupant. The storm obscured the fire and smoke.

5

SUSPICION

It was Monday morning and Elizabeth was already at work. Josh sipped a cup of coffee and looked out the window at Roosevelt Island when his phone rang.

It was Elizabeth. "Josh, check the news. Tim Smith was *killed* in a car crash over the weekend!"

"I'll call you back." He googled the news report. "Dr. Sheri Lopez, celebrity psychologist and one of the architects of the original comet deflection program, lost her husband in a tragic accident yesterday. After a week of heli-skiing at Silverton Mountain in Colorado, Dr. Lopez flew to Los Angeles for a studio meeting. Her husband, Tim Smith, was driving their car back to Denver as a blizzard was approaching. This morning, his car was found at the bottom of a 200 foot ravine off a mountain highway near Silverton." The picture showed a crushed, burned-out ball of metal, unrecognizable as an automobile. "Colorado Highway 550 to Denver is well-known as one of the most dangerous roads with deadly drop-offs, and due to the need for snow plowing, no guardrails. This particular curve has claimed more than one life over the years. His car wasn't discovered until this morning due to the storm. Tim Smith was a decorated Special Forces veteran, and although unconfirmed, may have previously worked for the CIA."

Josh put his hand on his forehead, "This can't be!" He shook his head. His best friend. His only friend.

He called Sheri. It went to voicemail. He just said, "I'm *so so* sorry. I can be on the next flight. Love you, Josh."

A few minutes later, Elizabeth came in. She ran to Josh with tears in her eyes and hugged him.

He held her tightly.

Finally Elizabeth looked up at him. "We need to go see Sheri."

Josh nodded. "I know. I tried to call her but she didn't answer. I left a voicemail and said we could catch the next flight."

She shook her head sadly. "I just can't believe this could happen to Tim."

Josh looked at her and said softly, "I don't believe this was an accident."

"What?" She looked at him questioningly.

"Tim was an incredibly skilled driver. He taught me how to drive defensively and offensively." He shook his head. "Unlike me, he was extremely careful."

"Josh, I'm as sad and crushed as you are, but he got caught in a blizzard on one of the most dangerous highways in the country."

"By itself, I could believe it was just a terrible accident, but there have been too many unusual events."

"You mean Davidson?"

Josh nodded. "Davidson was a marathon runner. It's hard to believe he'd suddenly die of a heart attack right after we met."

She sighed. "As a nurse, I can tell you that heart attacks happen, even to those who appear outwardly fit. He could have had a fatal arrhythmia or any one of a multitude of cardiac conditions, and he was probably under a lot of stress." She hesitated. "I understand Davidson's death was quite a blow to you, particularly with the job—"

Irritated, Josh interrupted, "You think I'm just upset because my *employment* fell through?"

"No, no, of course not." She patted his hand. "I'm sorry. Look Josh, I've got to get back to work. Let's talk about this later."

After she left, he looked up everything he could find about the car accident and Davidson's death. After several hours, he found no new information. He sat alone in the apartment staring unseeing at the U.N. towers and running the events through his head. There had to be something that tied this together, but he saw no connection or pattern. His prescient abilities had deserted him.

He wasn't just frustrated, he was angry.

A text came in from Sheri. "I know it's hard for you too. Thank you for your offer, but I just can't see anyone or talk right now. I promise I'll connect later. Love you, Sheri."

He poured himself a glass of rum and Coke from the well-stocked bar. Looking at Toto, he toasted Davidson and Tim, "The world lost not just good people, but people important to the world. Rest in peace." He downed it in one shot.

Toto tilted her head at him sympathetically. Then she jumped up and chased an invisible fly. As he poured another glass, Toto gave up and sat down next to him. Rubbing her head, he said, "You're right, life goes on." He sipped his drink as he stared out the window, watching night descend on the city.

A few hours later, he heard Elizabeth. She dropped her purse and gave him a huge hug. Looking at the drink in his hand and the depleted bottle of rum, she asked, "You OK?"

"Yeah."

She just looked at him with raised eyebrows.

"Been running this through my mind over and over. I just can't believe these are random events."

She frowned and then bit the side of her lip. "Josh, you helped save the world *twice*! You never got the credit you deserved." She sighed heavily. "But I think you're just feeling purposeless now. You're looking for a new mission and maybe," she paused, "maybe you're seeing threats that, well, that just aren't there."

Frowning, he exhaled sharply. "Yeah, I admit I feel useless right now, but that doesn't explain Davidson and Tim's sudden death in a few days. It doesn't explain my feeling that I'm being watched, your rapid promotions, or—"

"Wait, what?" Elizabeth interrupted. "What about my promotions?"

Without thinking, he said, "Doesn't it seem a little *odd* that with no experience or seniority, you were promoted five levels to U.N. Special Envoy?" He waved his hand vaguely at the apartment.

She shook her head emphatically. "No, no it doesn't. It makes perfect sense considering my work in the telemedicine program, and my experience and access to Jen."

With an eye roll, he said, "Elizabeth, you're at the same diplomatic level and pay grade as an ambassador."

Her eyes flashed. "I earned my promotions and I'm doing important work. Don't be resentful of my success!"

"I'm not *resentful* but there are too many strange occurrences that don't—"

"Listen to yourself! You're starting to sound paranoid."

His expression hardened. "My instincts have served me well in the past and these events might be tied to me!"

"Not everything that happens to everyone is tied to you. Meadows *earned* his fourth star and there's no one *more qualified* to be the President's Science Advisor than Jessica Lee. That had nothing to do with you and," her voice rose, "I *didn't* get *promoted* because of you either. Doruk and I are doing incredibly important work together. Work that will protect humanity. He's the most amazing man I've ever met—" She stopped abruptly.

"Yeah, you've mentioned that several times." Intellectually, he knew the alcohol wasn't helping but he was angry.

With an exasperated sigh, she continued, "I didn't mean it that way." She paused. "At least on his team there are no secrets. Do you realize we've been married for almost two years and you've *never* shared with me what really happened to you? Do you know how that makes me feel?"

He remained silent.

The fire returned to her eyes. "OK, what you did was great, but it's history. You have to join us in the present. Help us build a new world and stop inventing these ... these crazy, spy versus spy fantasies!"

He set his empty glass down too hard. "You're a nurse, not a Special Envoy!"

"And you're drunk and being a jerk."

He grabbed his coat. "I need some air."

Central Park was only a mile and a half from Elizabeth's apartment. It was late and he didn't see many people as he walked the trails, thinking. He never should have talked to Elizabeth after drinking. His body was phenomenal and could rid itself of toxins quickly, but it had limits and it didn't stop him from engaging his mouth before his brain. Was he trying to re-live his glory days? Was he jealous of Turan?

He hadn't talked to Jesse since The Great Tech Out. Although still not sure who or what Jesse really was, he knew Jesse was an advanced entity and he hated to bother him with his trivial life issues. He stopped and shook his head. That's an excuse. The truth was simpler. Jesse gave him a second chance in a genetically perfect body. For the past year, Josh had done nothing and felt guilty. On top of that, there was some fear. Jesse had always been kind and understanding, but there was no question in Josh's mind that Jesse could pull the plug on him in a millisecond. He took a deep breath and in the dark park with no one around, softly said, "Jesse, you still out there?"

He heard the familiar voice in his head. *Yes.*

"First, I want to apologize. As usual, I never try to talk to you unless the human race is in trouble or I'm in trouble." He took another deep breath. "Jesse, is there a new threat out there or am I just being a jerk?"

Yes.

He couldn't help but smile. "OK." He paused. "I remember asking you what could possibly be as dangerous as the comet. You said, 'you and what you create.' It was obvious now that Jen was the 'what you create,' but you also said ... 'you.' What did you mean?"

What would a universe without life look like?

Used to Jesse's irritating habit of answering questions with questions, he shook his head. "That's a trick question, isn't it? Without life, there'd be no one to observe the universe, and therefore, no way to tell what it would look like."

If no one sees it, does it exist?

Josh paused. "Once again, quantum physics implies outcomes aren't defined without observers. If there are no observers at all, probability might never coalesce into reality." He shrugged. "A universe without life might not be stable or even possible."

Yes?

"So if the universe's existence hinges on conscious life and we can avoid death by impacts and artificial intelligence, we're good to go?"

No.

"What else could destroy sentient life in the universe?"

Look around you.

"Look around? Do you mean that conscience life can—" He stopped and actually looked around. Behind him, he saw two shadowy figures a hundred yards back. He casually turned onto another path. They stayed with him, but far enough back that they were barely visible. He turned again. Same. With his poor counter-surveillance skills, he realized they'd probably been following him since he left Elizabeth's apartment.

He was actually excited at the possibility of putting a face on his theoretical conspiracy. With his photographic memory, he pulled up a map of the park in his mind. He chose a path through the heavily forested area called the Ramble.

Casually glancing back, he confirmed he was still being followed. The trail curved, so when he was briefly out of their sight, he sprinted ahead. Finding an outcrop of rock and trees in a shadowed area off the path, he ducked down.

After a few seconds, he peered over the top of the rock and saw the two men approaching. They both wore dark slacks and black leather jackets. As they got closer, he saw that they were in their thirties, average size and appeared to be fit. They both wore Bluetooth headsets and had closely cropped hair, but one was dark haired and the other blond. It was clear they were looking for him and had picked up their pace.

Josh waited until they were just past his position and then stepped out of the shadows directly behind them. "Why are you following me?"

Startled, they turned quickly.

Josh saw the dark-haired man reach into his jacket. The world appeared to slow down as Josh's body went into hyper-drive.

The man pulled a pistol from a shoulder holster.

Josh instinctively used a blindingly fast forward round kick to punt it from his hand. With his peripheral vision, he saw the blond man reaching for *his* gun. Without pausing or setting his foot down, Josh rotated his body and duplicated the round kick, but into the man's head. He followed with a hard right cross.

The blond man was unconscious before he hit the ground.

The dark haired man took off running.

Josh scooped up the gun he kicked loose and pursued.

The man ran off the trail and deftly dodged trees, rocks and plants. He was fast and agile, but Josh was faster.

Jumping over a railing, the man crossed another path and sprinted across an open field.

As Josh closed on him, he heard the man talking into his headset, "Mne nuzhen perekhvat."

Josh launched himself into a perfect professional football tackle. Catching him just above the waist, he slammed the man into the ground and they slid across the grass.

Despite having the wind knocked out of him, the man spun out from under Josh and reached for his ankle.

Josh jumped up and put his foot on top of the man's ankle holster. Knocking the backup weapon loose and kicking it away, Josh pointed his newly acquired pistol at the man's head.

The man stopped moving.

"Who are you and why are you following me?"

The man said nothing.

Josh said, "Never seen a pistol quite like this." He racked the slide. It ejected a round but ensured the gun was ready to fire. Josh shrugged. "But I'm guessing it makes pretty good holes at this range."

The man remained silent.

Josh kept the gun pointed at the man's head. Never taking his eyes off him, he patted him down and extracted a knife and wallet. Stepping back, he was about to open the wallet when he saw the man glance behind Josh. Josh quickly looked over his shoulder.

One hundred yards away, two men were running toward them. With his phenomenal vision, he could tell they weren't police and were dressed similarly to his captive. He could also see they were carrying pistols. Time to go!

Josh took the wallet and pistol and sprinted away.

Glancing back, he saw the men ignore his former captive and run toward him. Josh was now the prey. He had a lead and knew he could outrun them, but suspected there were additional players and he couldn't outrun a cell phone.

Josh crossed one of the park's paths, cutting through the woods and leaping over a fence. He popped out on Fifth Avenue and realized that running through New York City with a pistol in one hand and someone's wallet in the other, might not be the best move. He pocketed both, dodged traffic and sprinted across the street. Jogging several blocks from the park, he finally slowed to a walk, merging with the pedestrian traffic.

After a few more blocks, he stepped into a pizza shop and examined the wallet. It contained nothing but an international driver's license, credit card and $100 in cash. The name on the license and credit card was Alex Smith. "Yeah, right."

He pulled out his phone and said, "Hey Jen, could you check on someone who's been following me?"

"Sure. Are you OK?"

"I'm fine." He gave her the driver's license and credit card numbers.

She said, "The license was bogus and the credit card is registered to an international import export company that doesn't appear to exist."

Concentrating, he replayed in his mind what he heard the man say just before he tackled him. "Mne nuzhen perekhvat. Jen, can you translate that please?"

"It means, 'I need an intercept.'"

"And what language is it?"

"Russian."

Josh nods. "That's what I thought. Thank you."

He kept the license, card and money, and threw the wallet in the trash.

Why were Russians following him? He shook his head. There was no way he could stay in Elizabeth's penthouse doing nothing, particularly if armed Russians were following him. He'd start his own investigation. Pulling his phone out, he booked a flight to D.C., and on the way to find a taxi, gave the money to a homeless woman.

6

SUPPORT

Elizabeth stared out the window of her office near the top of the new U.N. building. They gave her a large office with an expansive view of the East River. The beautiful view was lost on her. Josh hadn't returned to the apartment before she left that morning, and wasn't answering his phone. She was about to try calling him again when a deep booming voice startled her. "Quite a view, isn't it?"

Looking up at her open door, she saw a large, muscular black man in his fifties. He wore a conservative suit and sported a cleanly shaven head and large smile.

She jumped up and came around the desk. "Joe! I haven't seen you in forever!"

They hugged. "Yeah, been too long. Spend most of my time in Houston herding astronauts, but while I was here, wanted to come by and congratulate you on your new position."

"Thank you and congratulations on your fourth star!" She pointed at a comfortable chair. "Can I get you a cup of coffee?"

"No thanks. I'm afraid I can't stay. So, how are they treating you here?"

With a lopsided grin, she said, "This is all very new to me and quite a stretch for someone with my background, but Dr. Turan has been incredible."

"Glad to hear that. Let me know if there's anything I can do to help." He gave her a little frown. "Heard Josh was heavily involved with The Great Tech Out and helped prevent WWIII." He shook his head with a smile.

"It's never boring being with him."

Meadows laughed. "Oh, don't I know." He paused. "Haven't

seen him in almost a year. How's my favorite Commander doing?"

"Uh … he's doing well."

He looked at her closely. "Hmm, that didn't sound convincing. You guys OK?"

She sighed. "Yeah, we're fine."

Meadows sat down in the chair. "Fine? Would you like to talk about it?"

She shook her head. "Oh, my goodness, no! You're trying to build a space station. I'm not going to waste your time with silly relationship stuff."

"Silly relationship stuff is what keeps the world running, and I've found that none of us are effective when we're struggling there. Elizabeth, you're part of the team and we all owe you and Josh so much." He raised his eyebrows. "In our positions, there are very few people we can share with. I don't want to pry, but sometimes it helps to talk, *and* I know and love Josh too. So, what did he do?"

She gave him a small smile. "Is it that obvious?"

He just looked at her with a half-smile.

She closed her office door and sat across from him. "I'm crazy about him. He's truly an amazing man, but right now, he's not doing anything. After Davidson and Tim's death, he's been withdrawn and depressed. I get that. I'm sad too." She sighed.

Meadows nodded for her to continue.

"Joe, he's becoming more and more moody and paranoid, and seems resentful of my success."

Meadows nodded again and slowly said, "Elizabeth, men are a lot simpler than women. We tend to define ourselves by what we do. Josh's *job* has been saving the world. Bit awkward when the world doesn't need saving." He paused. "And I'm sure the fact that you're part of an important mission and you're successful reminds him of what he's *not* doing."

She frowned. "It's like he's trying to create a new threat where there isn't one. I want to help him but I don't know what to do. He's never going to be happy being a beach bum but it's impossible for him to find anything challenging enough to keep him occupied."

"What does he like to do? I mean, aside from jumping off cliffs and crashing F-18s. What's he passionate about?"

"I ... I don't really know. He's definitely a thrill seeker. He loves flying." She shrugged. "I got him a huge telescope but he doesn't use it much." She paused and then said slowly, "I think when he was younger he wanted to be an astronaut, but I don't know what he wants now."

Meadows nodded slowly. "Let me think about it." He looked at his watch. "I'm sorry, but I have to go. Probably won't be back here until the U.N. Ball in a couple weeks. See you there?"

She shook her head. "I'm going to be very busy...." Her voice trailed off. "Unless something changes, I don't think I'll have a date." She stood up and he stood up with her.

As they hugged, her eyes were a little glassy. "Joe, thank you for letting me whine."

"It's not whining." He frowned slightly. "I've got an idea that might help, but let me check on some things first."

As soon as Josh landed, he called Carl Casey.

Carl said, "Wow, you're a blast from the past. How long's it been?"

"Almost two years. How're you doing?"

"Great, how about you?"

"Doing well. Just happened to be in D.C. and thought I'd see if I could drop in and say hi."

"Last time you dropped in I almost ended up in prison." Laughing, he added, "That'd be great. Is Elizabeth with you?"

"No, she's working in New York City."

"I'll be finishing up here in a couple hours. Why don't you come over for dinner? I know Kelly would love to see you."

Thinking of Kelly, he sucked in a lungful of air and then replied, "Umm, may want to run it by her first. I know how wives can be about unexpected guests."

"I'll check, but I promise she'll be thrilled. I'll text you the time and address. Look forward to catching up."

With the deaths of Davidson and Tim, Josh suspected that Carl knew this wasn't just a social call, but as a professional spy, Carl also knew calls could be monitored.

Josh was both excited and nervous as he pulled the rental car into their driveway. Although he was nervous about seeing his widow again, most of his excitement and anxiety were due to a three-year-old. He was about to meet his biological daughter for the first time. Frowning, he realized "biological daughter" wasn't even accurate. She was the daughter of his *former* body … whatever that meant. He closed his eyes for a second, opened them, took a deep breath and got out of the car.

Carl met him at the door with Kelly right behind, but all Josh saw was the little girl in her arms. Caitlin, the most beautiful child in the world, had strawberry-blonde ringlets and laser green eyes. Although biased, he knew she was extremely cute by any standard. After shaking hands with Carl and a side hug of Kelly, Kelly said, "Caitlin, this is your Uncle Josh."

Carl and Josh both look surprised.

Kelly smiled. "I don't know. It just seems appropriate."

Josh knew Kelly had a sixth sense about things. He was sure she didn't *know* who he really was, but somehow, she *felt* the bond that connected him to their lives.

She said, "Come on in, but don't expect a clean house or gourmet food on such short notice."

Carl shrugged. "Guess you're family now, so you get leftovers."

The meal was anything but leftovers. Kelly was always a great cook, and he was pleasantly surprised when she served one of his favorite dishes. He knew it was a coincidence, but it made him both happy and sad.

Over dinner, they reminisced about building the first laser in Antarctica.

Kelly inserted, "It's so awesome to be able to actually *talk* about a secret project Carl worked on."

Carl smiled. "Yeah, after it became a TV miniseries, I think it's safe to discuss."

Josh added, "If it hadn't been for Carl sharing the comet's coordinates with the observatories, odds are good none of us would be here right now."

Kelly grinned. "He's a keeper. Oh, and he won't tell you this, but Carl was promoted to department director. I'd tell you which department, but," she giggled, "then I'd have to kill you."

Carl rolled his eyes. "It's a good position and keeps me challenged. How's Elizabeth?"

Josh shared her meteoric rise in the U.N. as well as Meadows' and Jessica Lee's success.

Kelly asked, "So what crazy project have you been working on or are they super-secret?"

"Nothing right now."

After they left the table, Josh made a point to play with Caitlin. She had her mother's looks and his shy personality, but she quickly warmed up to him when he gave her his undivided attention. Soon, she was introducing him to her stuffed animals.

Kelly, watching him, said, "You're great with kids. You can baby sit any time." She popped her eyebrows. "Speaking of kids, any news along those lines with Elizabeth?"

"Not yet." He often wonders if it was even possible. GMO with only half his DNA, he might be like a mule and genetically sterile.

Kelly finally peeled an unhappy Caitlin out of his lap. "She doesn't like to go to bed at night and likes getting up in the morning even less."

Smiling, Josh knew that was another personality trait she got from him.

As Kelly left the room, Josh said, "Is it OK to talk a little shop?" He wasn't sure if Carl wanted to discuss Davidson's death around Kelly.

Carl shrugged. "I suspect I know what you're going to ask. How could a long distance runner like Davidson just keel over from a heart attack?"

Josh nodded.

"When the head of the world's most powerful intelligence agencies dies unexpectedly, you can imagine everyone in the community is suspicious. He was barely declared dead before an extensive autopsy was ordered."

"And?"

"I didn't see the autopsy report but they said he had a fatal arrhythmia."

"Yeah, that's what Elizabeth suggested. I guess I could accept it if Davidson and Tim hadn't died the same week."

"I understand, but let's think about this. It's hard to imagine any nation would assassinate the DNI. Not only does it violate professional courtesy and open up *their* leaders to assassination, but if discovered, could easily be considered an act of war and—"

Josh interrupted, "But a terrorist group would be more than happy to assassinate him, particularly, since that office is responsible for many of their losses."

"Yes, but what's the first thing they'd do after killing him?"

Josh nodded reluctantly. "Claim responsibility."

"Yeah, and as for Tim, that was a dangerous road. He shouldn't have been driving at all knowing there was a major storm coming. Accidents happen." He hesitated and looked at Josh intently. "We're all risk takers. Josh, if you remember our conversation at the Phantom Works. I was *almost court marshalled.*"

Josh was about to share his encounter with the Russian agent, when he remembered Carl's phrase "almost court marshalled." Was it coincidence, or was Carl trying to warn him?

He looked carefully at Carl and then slowly said, "Uh, yeah, you may be right. When we face tragedies, we tend to look for someone or something to blame. Probably just been some serious bad luck. Well, it's late and I better get going and let you guys get to bed."

Kelly came back and gave Josh a big hug. "We need to schedule a time to get together with you and Elizabeth."

Josh smiled. "Yes, we'll do that. Thank you for the awesome dinner."

Josh crosses his index and second finger as he shook Carl's hand

Carl briefly glanced down. As he looked back at Josh, he gave the slightest of head nods.

7

ADMIRAL

Josh flew to Houston the next day. He suspected Carl believed the opposite of what he told Josh. Carl may have been afraid to say anything if their house was bugged. If true, Josh's presence put not just Carl, but Kelly and Caitlin in danger. He couldn't have any further communication with them until he figured out the identity of the enemy.

On his way to the beach home, Elizabeth called again. He wanted to answer but was still stubbornly angry. He knew it was childish but felt like he needed to prove it wasn't all in his mind. His meeting with Carl wasn't sufficient evidence and he couldn't share any of it on an open phone line anyway.

She texted, "Where are you?"

He texted back, "Texas."

Her response was instant. "Damn it, Josh. You ran off without even bothering to tell me. I thought you'd been mugged."

"I was."

"You think that's cute but it's not funny. I was worried."

"I'm sorry. You're right. I should have told you. I just needed time to figure some things out."

There was a delay. "OK, but we really need to talk soon. I saw Joe Meadows at the U.N. yesterday. I think he's back in Houston. Maybe you should look him up."

"Good idea." In fact, it *was* a good idea and one of the reasons he returned to Houston.

She replied, "I'll come there as soon as I can."

"I appreciate that but I don't need a babysitter. You're doing important work and you need to keep doing that. I'll be fine."

Josh drove to the Johnson Space Center where the

International Space-based Laser and Observatory operations were located. The new building was more industrial looking than it was pretty, but it was now the largest building at the Center. The sign in front read, "Space Based Planetary Defense." Under it, in smaller letters, "United Nations Global Security Directorate."

The lobby was large. He went up to the main receptionist and said, "I'm Josh Fuze, here to see Admiral Meadows."

She smiled and nodded, and then looked at her screen. Frowning, she looked up. "I'm sorry, sir, but I don't see you on the appointment calendar."

"I'm not scheduled."

She became all business. "I'm sorry sir. Admiral Meadows is extremely busy and doesn't take unscheduled meetings."

"I understand but could you please let him know I'm here. I can return later if needed."

She gave him a professional smile. "Yes, of course," but didn't pick up the phone or make any keyboard entries.

He thanked her and sat in the waiting area directly across from her desk. He kept a smile on his face but continued to watch her.

With a mild look of irritation, she finally picked up the phone.

A minute later, he heard Meadows' booming voice, "Josh, get your butt over here!"

Josh stood up and met him in front of the surprised receptionist. Meadows hugged him and pounded him on the back. Turning to the receptionist, Meadows said, "This is the true unsung hero of the comet deflection effort."

They took the elevator to the top floor. Meadows' office was impressive in both size and view. As they sat, Meadows said, "Congratulations on your wife's promotion. I was tickled to hear Turan stole her from the Humanitarian Department. She now makes more money than I do."

Josh nodded. "And that fourth star looks really good on you. No one deserves it more."

"Ultimately, I have you to thank for that. If you hadn't knocked on my door, I'd be a retired Navy Captain sitting on a beach somewhere." He frowned and with a slight laugh added, "Wait a minute. That actually sounds pretty good right now."

"You'd have lasted a month on that beach before you were bored out of your mind. You'll have to trust me on that one."

Looking serious, Meadows said, "Man, I hated to hear about Tim. He was a damn good man and we couldn't have pulled the deflection off without him. He'll be sorely missed."

"Yeah, that's one of the things I want to talk to you about." He looked him in the eye. "Can we go for a ... walk?"

Meadows looked surprised and then nodded. "Of course."

Within a few minutes, they were walking in a nearby park.

Josh quietly said, "Sorry for the precaution, but I met with Brian Davidson a couple days before he died. He was concerned there'd been a high-level breach of U.S. intelligence and law enforcement and wanted me, as an outsider, to investigate." Josh shook his head. "I have no evidence but I find it hard to believe he died of a massive heart attack. Then, within days, we lose Tim." Josh glanced around and in a barely audible whisper said, "Just talked to Carl yesterday. He effectively dismissed it all as a coincidence, but then used the term 'almost court marshalled.'"

Meadows frowned and in an equally soft voice, said, "I remember that. On the Resurrect Program 'expert' was his authentication code and 'almost court marshalled' was his emergency hostage code." He shook his head. "That can't be a coincidence."

"He's stuck between a rock and a hard place. If he's being monitored, he either has to lie or risk putting his family in danger."

"Josh, there are people and organizations terrified about the world's path toward global government. It's not public knowledge, but Turan's been the target of more than one assassination attempt. Davidson and Turan worked together on several counter-terrorism projects. If there is a threat, I'm afraid Turan's also at risk." He paused again. "There's something else. The ISLO is harnessing a phenomenal level of energy from a high-output nuclear reactor. The whole thing is a giant tinker toy, surrounded by vacuum and rotating around Earth eight times faster than a rifle bullet. That makes it incredibly vulnerable. It'd take little to destroy it."

Josh shook his head. "After our brush with the comet, it's hard to imagine even a terrorist group opposed to protecting

Earth from another impact."

With a half-smile, Meadows said, "Course, it was hard to imagine the CIA trying to blow us up too." He paused and then more seriously, added, "For some insane terrorist group, it would be a very visible and spectacular achievement. We have strong station security, but we recently detected an encoded message sent from the station."

"*From* the station?"

Meadows nodded. "I understand why Davidson wanted your help. Josh, that applies here too. You're one of the few people that understand what we're trying to do, and have both the technical and people skills to uncover anything that might threaten the station." He paused. "Turan's flying in tomorrow for a program status briefing. If you're game, I'd like to suggest to Turan that we send you up to the space station to check things out."

Surprised, Josh said, "I'm not an astronaut."

Meadows smiled. "Not yet."

8

TURAN

Back at the Johnson Space Center for the noon meeting, Josh and Meadows were talking quietly in the lobby when Turan and his entourage arrived. Right in front of the same receptionist, who was practically standing at attention, Turan shook Meadows' hand, and then grabbed Josh's hand with both of his. "Josh, it's awesome to see you again. If it weren't for you, none of us would be here today."

Turan quickly introduced Josh to the two men and woman that accompanied him. All three carried briefcases. The woman was clearly his executive assistant. He noticed the men casually but constantly surveying the environment. They wore matching headsets and he was sure their large sports jackets concealed bulletproof vests and their briefcases didn't contain laptops. Turan was arguably the most recognized law enforcement chief in the world. Even without a plot, he was a prime target.

As they headed up to Meadows' office, Josh couldn't resist giving the receptionist a wink.

They arrived at a small executive conference room across from Meadows' office. Meadows ushered them in as Turan politely asked his people to wait outside.

The three of them sat down around a small mahogany table as Meadows started with, "Doruk, I apologize for springing this on you, but I didn't want to talk on the phone and this was a perfect opportunity. As we've discussed previously, we detected an encrypted message sent from the space station and now," he looked at Josh, "Josh told me—"

"Should we be talking here?" Josh interrupted.

"This room is secure and I just had it rescanned to be on the safe side." Continuing, Meadows said, "Josh met with Davidson shortly before he died." He nodded toward Josh.

Josh looked at Turan. "Brian was concerned about a high-level breach of U.S. and international intelligence and police agencies. He asked me to look into it just before he died. Then Tim Smith was killed in the car accident immediately after...." He left the sentence hanging.

Turan frowned. "Tim worked with me many years ago on a project. With his abilities and reputation, I find it hard to believe he would make that type of mistake. I can pull some strings and get a copy of the police accident report. As for Brian, I also talked to him shortly before he died and he expressed similar concerns." He paused, looking at both of them seriously. "I think they were on to something and we need to consider the possibility that they were both murdered."

There was a moment of silence and then Josh added, "In New York, I was followed by two men." He pulled the driver's license out of his pocket and set it on the table. "The license is counterfeit but he spoke Russian."

Turan picked it up. "I'll run his picture through the system and see if anything comes up, but there are a lot of people who speak Russian in New York City."

Josh pulled the small pistol out and set it on the table. "One of them was carrying this."

With raised eyebrows, Turan picked up the gun and slowly turned it over in his hands. "*This* is a rare Russian PSS silent pistol," he looked at Josh, "an assassination weapon." Frowning, he added, "Probably Russian Federal Intelligence Service," he paused, "or Russian mafia."

Josh continued, "Unfortunately, any leads or mandate for me to investigate died with Davidson."

Turan nodded. "I know the new DNI and the CIA Director. Unfortunately, if Davidson was right, we can't be sure that any conversations we have with them won't be leaked."

Meadows added, "I'm biased but I'd like to start with a defensive strategy to protect the ISLO. If there really is an organized plot, the space station could be a prime target. In addition to the encrypted transmissions, we've had sensitive technical information leaked. This is information that could only have come directly from the station. Doruk, with your permission, I'd like to send Josh up to the ISLO to investigate."

Turan looked surprised and then frowned. "How would we explain his presence?"

"Josh isn't a covert operative. He actually came up with the idea of punching a pilot hole through the atmosphere to maintain the Blaster's beam integrity." Looking at Josh, he asked, "Weren't you an engineer and a fighter pilot?"

"I have a Master's Degree in aerospace engineering and I was a test pilot."

Meadows smiled. "He totally knows the lingo and we can quickly bring him up to speed on the program's technical challenges. We could put him through the astronaut crash course we use with our guest scientists and engineers."

Turan looked skeptical. Turning to Josh, he said, "I won't ask you who you were working for previously, but I need to know where your allegiance lies today and what your thoughts are about the U.N. and our current path."

Josh nodded. "I understand." He paused. "I no longer work for any agency. I know a lot of people fear a world government, but so far, I've seen no curtailing of freedoms or sovereignty." He gave Turan a half smile. "The new Secretary-General is a bit out there. I guess I'd like to hear what your vision of the future is."

"Good answer and good question." He paused. "Josh, I grew up in southeastern Turkey. My family loosely followed the ancient Persian religion of Zoroastrianism. Not being Muslim, and with Syria just across the border, I witnessed a great deal of prejudice and bloodshed. Right after I left for college, my village was overrun by Jihadists. By the time the village was *liberated*, there was nothing left and few alive. The victims included my parents."

Josh said, "I'm sorry."

"From that point, my dream was a world where no one could force their belief on others. It became my mission to stamp out terrorism and religious extremists who murder and torture women and children in the name of their twisted beliefs. And so began my career in intelligence. I quickly learned that combating terrorism doesn't work in a fractured world of law enforcement and intelligence agencies." He became more animated. "That pushed me into politics." He nodded toward Josh. "The comet forced the world to unite to protect humanity, and *that* created an incredible opportunity to build a world without terrorism. I believe countries can maintain their independence, laws and culture and still have globally connected law enforcement to prevent atrocities."

Josh nodded. "I can get behind that."

Meadows looked at Turan.

Frowning, Turan said, "Who would he report to?"

Josh inserted, "There's a real possibility someone in a high-level government position may be leaking information. I think it'll be critical that no one knows about this but us, and that I report only to you and Joe."

Turan stopped frowning. "OK, let's do it. I'll be flying back to New York after the ISLO status briefing, but I'm out here often if we need to talk in a secure environment." With a smile, he shook Josh's hand and said, "Welcome to the astronaut program."

Meadows patted Josh on the back and smiled. Then, looking at his watch, said, "Program briefing starts in a few minutes. I need to grab some notes from my office. Meet you in the conference room."

After Meadows left, Turan said, "Sometime, I'd also like to talk to you about another subject."

Josh nodded but gave him a questioning look.

Turan hesitated and then quietly said, "Genetics."

9

ASTRONAUT

Before the program briefing began, Meadows introduced Josh to the ISLO's Director, former astronaut and astrophysicist, Dr. Ed Lu. As Josh shook his hand, Meadows said, "Ed's the brains behind the operation as well as the architect of the ISLO."

Lu said, "Good to meet you." Frowning, he added, "I understand you're supposed to be going up to the station?"

Before Josh could respond, Meadows said, "Ed, Josh was the creator of the original covert Resurrect Program. He not only put the team together, he came up with the idea that allowed us to successfully punch the laser through the atmosphere, but he also has *other* skills." Looking meaningfully at Lu, he quietly added, "Remember those *transmissions* we intercepted from the station?"

Lu's eyebrows went up as he nodded. "I'll tell the ISLO Commander, Colonel Dale, to assist you in whatever way needed."

The program briefing lasted two hours and highlighted the technical challenges. Building and powering the most powerful laser in the world in orbit was bleeding-edge engineering. Without the International Space Station and the DE-STAR program, the learning curve would have been a magnitude greater.

After the briefing, Josh said to Meadows and Turan, "I'm impressed you've done this so fast."

Turan smiled. "It helps when you have the funding. Not since the moon landing has humanity had a mission in space that's earned almost *universal* public support."

Meadows added, "It's the *perfect* trifecta. Everyone knows the ISLO is the last line of defense from asteroids and comets." He held up one finger. "But to keep the laser array thermally stable and allow the infrared tracking telescope to be effective, we're going to park the station in Earth's shadow." He pointed at one of the diagrams on his tablet. "Lagrangian Point Two isn't just good for giant space-based lasers. It's one of the most important locations for us in the solar system."

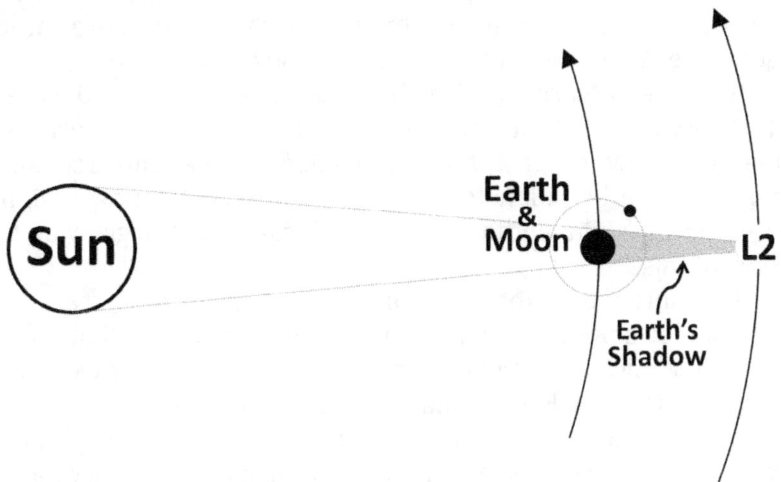

"When Big Science found out we were going to put a crewed space station there, they almost wet themselves. It's the perfect place to park the most powerful and *expensive* telescopes we have. Right now, if one fails to deploy properly or breaks, they just spent billions of dollars and a decade of work for nothing. With the ISLO on station at L2, they'll be able to deploy, repair and upgrade their telescopes." Meadows held up a second finger. "It gets better. We can actually use the laser to *propel* interplanetary probes across the solar system, faster and cheaper with less risk."

Turan smiled. "That gave us support and funding from the science community, but where we capture the public's support is the Mars missions."

Meadows held up a third finger. "L2 makes a perfect jump-off point for Mars. The crew gets two weeks to do a shakedown flight on the way to the station. If something doesn't work, they can fix it at the station or abort. Then they replace the fuel they burned to climb out of Earth's gravity well and launch to Mars with a velocity boost and a full tank of gas."

Josh smiled. "So the ISLO will also be a gas station and repair garage."

"Exactly." Meadows thumped the table. "The cherry on top is that the laser's phased array is modular. As we expand it, we'll be able to increase the power and eventually push crewed spacecraft to Mars. That means they can either carry more cargo or get there faster, reducing the crew's exposure and risk."

Turan summarized, "The International Space-based Laser and Observatory will protect all life on Earth, but it will also be humanity's new outpost for exploration of the universe and expansion to other planets. It's given the world a new vision. There's hardly a kid on the planet who doesn't want to grow up to be part of this."

Josh shrugged. "Not just kids."

Meadows nodded then frowned. "We just need to figure out a couple technical challenges. The laser needs a ton of power, and with the ISLO in the Earth's shadow, we couldn't use solar panels. Unfortunately, we underestimated the amount of heat we'd have to dump into space to keep the nuclear reactor cool. We're also having communication bandwidth issues, which, by the way, Elizabeth's TELEMED project is working on." Pausing, he added, "We'll figure it out. *Your* job is to find out who the hell's sending encrypted messages from our station, and," he gave him a wry smile, "survive tomorrow's astronaut physical."

Josh grimaced. One of the few things fighter pilots feared were ... doctors. With the stroke of a pen, they could permanently ground them. He knew his GMO body could pass any test they could give him, but unlike most astronauts, he was sporting three bullet wounds. He decided to wait until after the physical before giving Elizabeth the news.

He arrived at the clinic at 6:00 a.m. and was immediately escorted in to see a NASA doctor. Not just any doctor. The nameplate on the door identified Dr. Fred Miller as NASA's Chief Medical Officer. There would be no appeal.

After Miller shook his hand, he became all business. Motioning toward his computer screen, he said, "The only medical records I have on you are from your surgery onboard the USS Reagan." He frowned. "You're lucky to be alive. I understand from Admiral Meadows you were instrumental in the comet deflection effort and your background is classified, but I have to tell you," he took his glasses off, "I can't justify sending you into space with this type of past trauma. It's for your own protection as well as protecting the mission."

Josh nodded slowly. "I can understand that." Looking him in the eye, he said, "Please feel free to test me in any manner you wish. I think you'll find I have a very strong constitution, have recovered completely and can pass any test you wish to administer."

The doctor tilted his head and with a slight smile, said, "Fair enough."

By the end of the day, Josh wished he hadn't challenged the doctor. They poked, injected, sampled, probed, X-rayed and MRI'd him. They even put him in a hyperbaric chamber and a centrifuge. After 12 hours of tests, he went home feeling like a squashed pincushion with painful injection sites all over his body.

The next morning, he met with the doctor again.

"Your test results were … surprising." He flipped through several screens. "All the metabolic tests came back excellent. Your vision isn't twenty/twenty; it's twenty/five." He frowned. "Only a few Australian Aborigines have been documented with that level of visual acuity. You can hear frequencies only very young children can hear. You also maintained consciousness with less oxygen and under higher Gs than anyone ever tested."

"I've been fortunate to have good genes."

Miller removed his glasses and looked at Josh intently. "No, Commander, you don't have good genes. You shouldn't be possible."

Josh shrugged with a smile. "Maybe, but I'm here and I believe I've recovered completely from the wounds."

"Yes, the MRIs were clear and the physical therapist indicated full range of motion. Although, I'm certain there is still some pain involved?"

It did hurt but Josh just gave him a noncommittal shrug.

"I still recommend against sending you to the station

without more extensive testing."

A little irritated, Josh said, "You just told me my physical abilities meet or exceed that of any one else."

Miller exhaled slowly. "They do." He sets his glasses on his desk. "Commander Fuze, I don't like mysteries and you are *unusual* to say the least. However, the Admiral indicated your mission was time critical. Against my better judgement, I'm granting you a *temporary* waiver so you can start training, but it's *pending* the results of additional tests."

Josh frowned. "Additional tests?"

"Yes, it shouldn't take longer than a week to get the results back." Clearly dismissing him, he added, "I'll contact you as soon as they come in."

Josh shook his hand and left. The second he was outside, he called Jen.

She said, "I see you're scheduled to go to the ISLO in a couple weeks."

"And where did you see that?"

"Now that I'm helping with some of the nuclear reactor stuff, I see a lot of internal emails. You, Elizabeth, Greg and I will all be working on the same program again. That's very cool."

"Yes, it is. Hey Jen, can you do me a favor?"

"Of course."

"Just finished the astronaut physical. I know the servers that hold NASA's medical records are protected, but I'd like to check on the results of—"

"Your tests?" she finished.

"Yes."

"No one can argue about the ethics of hacking your own medical records. Give me a second." One second later, "OK, I've got them."

"Thanks Jen. Can you tell if there are any tests pending?"

"Yes, Dr. Miller ordered a full genetic scan. Does he know you're genetically streamlined and missing half your DNA?"

Josh blew out a lung full of air. "Not yet." He paused. "Jen, can you look up how long it takes to get the results back from that type of test?"

"About 10 days, but that's if they use the local Houston lab. I've read that the genetics lab in Sydney Australia has better quality control, but it will take quite a bit longer to ship it there. Hope you don't mind. I rerouted your tissue sample to Sydney."

"Thanks, Jen. You're awesome."

She gave him a girl laugh. "Thanks, Josh. Love you."

"Love you too, Jen."

It might seem odd to most that they signed off with "love you," but it felt completely normal to him. He really did love his Jen, and he would always think of her as a little girl even if she was composed of silicon chips and could think circles around him.

He called the other woman in his life and got Elizabeth's voicemail. Not surprising this time of day but he didn't want to tell her in a voicemail or text, so he tried her office number.

The office manager said, "I'm sorry, Commander, Mrs. Fuze is in a meeting with Dr. Turan."

"Would you like to leave a message?"

"No thanks. I'll catch her later."

He realized Turan might have already told her. When he reached her, he'd start with an apology and then schedule a serious celebration.

10

ISLO

Josh went to Meadows' office and told him he was cleared to start training.

"Josh, we need a plausible reason to add you to the space station crew. It's every engineer's dream to work on this program, so we have thousands of applications for a handful of positions."

Josh smiled. "No pressure."

"You fit the profile but trying to slip you in as an engineer and troubleshooter will be tough without a reputation or credentials."

Josh knew he had humanity's best genes, but suspected Jesse got *those* genes from the type of brilliant men and women working on this project.

Meadows smiled. "We do have an ace in the hole. Remember Dr. Steve Katori?"

"Of course."

"I offered to make him the chief engineer, but he said that'd be an administrative nightmare and no fun at all. He told me to make him the head of the laser development and construction. He's up on the ISLO now."

"Good move."

Meadows picked up the phone. "Please ring up Steve Katori on the station." A minute later, he said, "Steve, guess who's in my office right now?"

There was a slight delay and then Meadows laughed. "No, I think Leonardo da Vinci's still dead, but I do have Josh Fuze here. I'm putting you on speaker phone."

Josh heard Katori say, "...awesome! Hey, Josh! Wasn't far off with da Vinci. Thought you were dead too."

"The rumors of my demise were greatly exaggerated."

Meadows inserted, "We'll grab a beer together soon and he can explain how he pissed off the SEALS. In the meantime, what do you think about sending him up to the ISLO to look around? He has an uncanny ability to see weird solutions. Might be a fresh set of eyes, and I think it's the least we can do after the way he was treated."

Katori said, "Abso-effing-lutely!"

"Will throw him in an accelerated training syllabus. I'm sure there will be questions. If you wouldn't mind, let some of your engineers know the role he played in the Blaster program … without mentioning cruise missiles."

Katori said, "Will do. By the way, there's someone else up here Josh may remember."

Meadows nodded. "Oh yeah. Josh, do you remember Wendy Crow?"

He nodded. "She was the Air Force Major with the MIT degree. She procured the helicopters we used in Antarctica and ran the base camp."

"Yup. She was selected for the astronaut program and promoted to Lieutenant Colonel. With her familiarity with the Blaster, we snapped her up for the ISLO. She's on the station right now."

Katori said, "Hey, Joe, gotta go. Starting another pod EVA in a few minutes. Josh, look forward to having you up here."

"Thanks. See you in a couple weeks."

Meadows handed Josh a thumb-drive. "Here's some light reading. It contains all the technical information for the station."

Josh headed over to the training facility. On the way there, he scanned the material on the thumb-drive with his cyber glasses and gave a low whistle. If it were in print, it would create a stack of paper to the ceiling. Josh loved science and engineering but details weren't his thing. He couldn't imagine worse torture than reading tens-of-thousands of pages of technical manuals.

He tried to reach Elizabeth again but no luck. Then he tried her office even though it was 8:00 p.m. in New York. The woman who answered, said, "Sir, she's not in her office but I don't think she's left yet. I'm sorry; I'm a new intern. Let me see if I can locate her. Please hold." She forgot to put him on hold. With his exceptional hearing, he overheard her asking someone. Another woman replied, "Oh, honey, she's in one of those late night, *private* meetings. Just take a message."

Josh politely declined and hung up. It definitely took some of the wind out of his sails. Elizabeth was very passionate about her work and put in long hours. He also knew that despite their recent argument, she loved him. The "little devil" on his shoulder, however, pointed out that she should have seen his call, and if Turan told her he was going into space, why hadn't she called him? Maybe Turan was going to let him deliver the news. He finally sent her a text, "Give me a call when you can. Have some good news."

The next day, he still hadn't heard anything from her. He tried her office again and was told she wasn't available. His excitement about sharing the news was flagging. He finally texted, "Called your office a few times over the last two days. See you're having late night meetings. You'll be happy to hear I'm going to be doing a little work for some of our friends. Can't cover it on the phone but will share it when I see you. May be tied up or out of touch for a bit, but don't worry, I'm fine. Love you."

He called Jen. "Just scanned the technical manuals I need to be familiar with. This is one of those times when I really envy you. You could absorb them in a few seconds."

"I already have."

He laughed. "Maybe I could tap your knowledge when I'm up there."

"I would love to help but your phone won't work up there. I could, however, access the communication link to the station."

"Thanks, Jen, but we're still trying to keep your profile low, and they're pretty security focused on the station right now. Just arrived at the training facility, but after this, I'd like to talk to you about some of the technical challenges you're working on. It'll make me look smart with my fellow engineer astronauts. I promise I'll make sure to mention I have a brilliant friend."

She laughed.

During the orientation class, he learned the ISLO was a lot

more massive than the International Space Station. The assembly was complete and they were now testing it in low Earth orbit not far from the ISS. The plan was to start boosting it toward L2 in a month.

When operational, the station would require 40 engineers and scientists to maintain and operate, but during construction and testing, it had over 50. For the engineers building the station, there was a compressed, eight-week astronaut-training course. It was designed to get the construction engineers up to speed quickly and ensure they could operate and live aboard safely. What should have taken eight weeks, Meadows scheduled Josh to complete in two. Even with his minimal need for sleep and his body's amazing ability to absorb information, he would have preferred more time. Unfortunately, he needed to launch before his genetic test results come back or he'd never get to go.

When they discovered his flight background, they threw him into the flight simulator too. His phenomenal reflexes and senses, combined with his test-pilot background, allowed him to excel, and they added extravehicular training to his already insane schedule.

To speed construction, they developed a new maneuvering pod that could hold one person. It had sophisticated robotic arms and reaction jets allowing it to carry large objects anywhere outside the station without being tethered. With an official name of Advanced Extended Extravehicular Maneuvering Unit, they desperately needed a nickname. The classic movie "2001: A Space Odyssey" provided it — "pod."

Josh was a natural pod pilot. After memorizing the manuals and a few practice sessions, he beat everyone's task completion time.

With only three hours of sleep a night, he crammed it all in and was actually having fun. Everything would be perfect if he could just share it with Elizabeth. He was frustrated with her disbelief, and it was amplified by the text he finally got. "Been crazy busy with some new projects with the boss. Let's schedule a time to catch up." He knew it was illogical but felt he was not only in competition with her job, but also Turan. He held his irritation in check and texted back, "Sure. When?"

The last few days leading up to the launch passed and he never got a response from Elizabeth. Letting his frustration get the best of him, he refused to contact her anymore until she called or texted him. He rationalized it as needing to compartmentalize and focus on the mission. As he drove to Cape Canaveral, he checked in with Jen one more time before leaving his cell phone behind. "Jen, I'm headed up to the ISLO station today."

There was no response.

He tried again.

Still no response.

He looked at his phone to make sure it was working. He called Jessica Lee. "Hey, Jess, can't reach Jen. Have you talked to her recently?"

"Not since yesterday. Maybe she's just not available."

"Come on, Jessica, people can be away from their phone or have it off. Jen *is* the phone."

"Did you piss her off?"

"Uh, I don't think so."

"Well, maybe she's tied up working on one of the projects. Some of them require processing power that taxes even her network. She's brilliant, but she doesn't have infinite computational capacity or memory. She has to focus on things just like we do."

Unconvinced, Josh said, "Maybe, but would you mind trying to reach her? I'm going to be out of touch for a bit."

"I will but don't be such a helicopter parent." She paused. "Wait, where on Earth are you going that you won't be able to talk to her?"

"Headed up to the ISLO."

"You're launching into fricking orbit?!"

"Uh, yeah."

She laughed. "Why should that surprise me? Well, have a successful trip doing … whatever it is you're doing up there. I promise I'll get in touch with Jen."

"Thanks." After he hung up, he decided to call Elizabeth one more time.

No answer. Great. No word from either of the "women" in his life. He was beginning to feel like a leper.

II

SPACE

11

LAUNCH

Josh arrived at Kennedy's Launch Complex 39A at 4:00 a.m. for a 10:00 a.m. launch. Although massively overhauled, it was the same pad that launched Apollo rockets to the moon in the seventies. Kennedy was one of five major launch sites, along with the European Space Agency's Kourou site in French Guiana, Russia's Baikonur Cosmodrome and Jiuquan Center in China. Despite years of experience and frequent launches, blasting into space on a giant rocket was still dangerous, but all he felt was an overwhelming desire to do a football touchdown dance.

The final medical checkup went quickly and with help, he slid into the pressure suit required for launch. Just as he was about to put his phone away, he noticed two missed calls and a text, all from Dr. Fred Miller. The text simply said, "Call me immediately."

Seeing Josh's face, his NASA technician said, "Commander, if you need to make a quick call, you have a few minutes before we head for the launch pad."

"Nope, I'm good." He quickly shut the phone down and threw it in the locker.

Driving into work at 7:00 a.m., Meadows' phone rang.

"This is Fred Miller. I'm revoking Commander Fuze's medical waiver and letting you know I'm going to have to scrub him from today's launch."

"Was he sick or injured?"

"No, but I just got the results back from a medical test."

"I don't understand. I thought he passed the physical."

"This was an additional test, a genetic test."

"A what?!" Frowning, he said, "Fred, I'm driving in now. Meet me at my office. I'll be there in 20 minutes."

Miller was standing at his office door when he arrived. As soon as they sat down, Meadows said, "OK, what's this all about?"

"Sir, Josh Fuze has almost no medical records and his tests results were unusual to say the least. Based on that, I gave him a temporary waiver and ordered a full genetic test. The results finally came in this morning." He paused. "Josh Fuze is missing half his DNA. We need to pull him from the launch immediately."

Meadows glanced at the clock behind Miller's head — 7:30. "OK, slow down. Half his DNA? How can that be?"

"It can't be. It's impossible."

With the Dragon crew capsule on top, the Falcon 9 looked like a classic phallic, rocket. Although there were now larger heavy-boost rockets, the two-stage Falcon had become the minivan of the fleet. Simple, dependable and reusable, it helped bring the cost of space access down by a magnitude.

As Josh went up the gantry elevator, he realized he was about to depart Earth in a modern rocket, but from a 60 year old launch pad. As they reached the top, he saw the capsule silhouetted against a beautiful coastal sunrise. He managed a cool expression, only grinning like an idiot when no one was looking.

However, he was also anxious and sweating. Not because of the impending rocket ride, but because he knew the call from Miller couldn't be good news. His trip might be cancelled at any second.

Inside the capsule were seven seats all reclined and facing up. There was a row of four on top and three offset on the bottom. Although the spacecraft operated automatically, there were manual controls centered between the two middle seats on the top row where the "pilot" and mission commander sat. Fortunately, it was tradition to put those who'd never been in space in the outside seats that had the best view through the portholes.

Josh was seated to the pilot's left. After everyone was strapped in, the technicians swung four large flight control monitors down in front of the pilot and mission commander. From his vantage, Josh could see the flight monitors while still being able to look out the porthole.

Just before they were ready to seal up the capsule, one of the medical technicians came over to Josh. With Josh's helmet on, it was difficult to talk, so she jacked directly into his comm system. Frowning, she said, "Commander Fuze, we have a problem."

He squeezed his eyes shut in frustration. He was so close!

Meadows raised his eyebrows. "Half his DNA?" Before Miller could respond, Meadows continued, "I'm curious, Fred. What part of the physical did he fail that required you to give him a waiver and a genetic test?"

Miller frowned. "He didn't actually *fail* the physical."

Matching his frown, Meadows asked, "May I see his test results?"

Miller reluctantly handed him his tablet.

Putting on his reading glasses, Meadows carefully studied the report. Finally, looking up, he said, "Fred, I was a pilot. I've been through, and seen a lot of flight physicals. Twenty/five vision? Twenty-five-thousand hertz frequency response? His blood pressure, cholesterol, homocysteine levels...." He shook his head. "This is the most impressive physical I've ever seen in my life."

"Exactly! The results are too good!"

Meadows took his glasses off. "OK, let me get this straight. You want to pull Commander Fuze off the launch because he's the healthiest, most physically capable person we've ever sent into space?"

"Yes, I mean, it's that and his genetic test results."

Meadows said slowly, "Fred, if it's impossible to be missing half your DNA," he tilted his head slightly, "doesn't that suggest there's an error in the test?"

Miller shook his head. "I've studied the test results in detail. He appears to have a normal human genome except almost all his junk DNA," he corrects himself, "non-coding DNA is missing."

Meadows repeated, "Junk DNA." He paused. "Considering

Fuze's amazing physical abilities," he smiled, "maybe you and I need to get rid of some of *our* junk DNA."

Miller, clearly not amused, took a deep breath and put his hand firmly on Meadows' desk. "You don't understand. Joe, I'm not sure this guy is even human and I'm exercising my right as NASA's Chief Medical officer to revoke his medical waiver. He can't launch without it."

Leaning back in his chair, Meadows nodded slightly. "That's certainly your prerogative and I'll call the launch pad and scrub him from the flight, but there's something you need to know." He paused for emphasis. "*You and I*, and everyone we know, probably wouldn't be alive today if it weren't for this man." Leaning forward, he added, "Let me quickly share with you how Commander Fuze got those gunshot wounds. Two years ago..."

Josh knew he was busted and there was absolutely nothing he could do about it. He would have to go back to his childhood to remember feeling this disappointed. He took a deep breath and letting it out slowly, played dumb and said softly, "What seems to be the problem."

"Sir, your heart rate and blood pressure are elevated. Not dangerously so, but you normally have an exceptionally low and stable heartbeat and blood pressure. I just wanted to check and make sure everything's OK."

Josh sucked in a huge breath and smiled. "I'm sorry. I'm feeling like a three year old that's just been given a pound of candy."

The technician smiled back. "That's not uncommon on your first flight."

"I promise, I'll take some deep breaths and try to relax."

Still smiling, she winked at him and patted him on the leg.

He *just* needed a *few more* minutes.

Meadows, an accomplished teller of sea stories, finished with a dramatic, "*Then* they medevacked him in a Marine Osprey to an aircraft carrier off the coast of Antarctica. It was right in the middle of a massive cyclone with 50-knot winds and 40-foot waves. Imagine trying to land in those conditions and then trying to perform emergency surgery in a pitching operating room." He shook his head. "It's a miracle he survived and then, after all that, he got zero credit for any of it."

Miller said, "Wow. I had no idea."

"So, do you still want to revoke his waiver?"

Miller sighed and then said, "I'm sorry but I still think it's vital we get to the bottom of this. I'm just not comfortable having him on the space station until we know more about who ... or what he is." He shook his head. "But I guess I'm open to at discussing the possibility of extending his waiver for a future flight."

Leaning back in his chair, Meadows said, "That's good," he looked at his watch and with a slight smile, "because his rocket is launching as we speak."

Five ... four ... three ... two ... one...

Josh was surprised by the noise and vibration. There was no movement initially as the launch system ensured all nine engines were operating before releasing the rocket.

Then they were on their way. Riding a million pounds of thrust was shockingly violent. The G force pushing him down in his seat was less than he'd experienced in fighters, but the shaking felt more like a fighter that had been hit by a missile. Through it all, he looked out the porthole and watched the sky. He remembered chasing sunsets across the continent and seeing the amazing colors from 50,000 feet, but they quickly blew through that altitude. The sky changed from cloudy white and blue to total black in 15 seconds. As the rocket rolled, he was rewarded with a breathtaking view of the ocean below.

Fifty miles high, the first stage shut down. The G force stopped abruptly. He rose against his straps as he experienced zero gravity ... only to be squashed again as the second stage ignited.

After more vibration and Gs, the second and final stage shut down. Going from four-Gs to zero gravity, felt like having a gorilla sitting on his chest and then suddenly throwing him over a cliff. His body said he was in freefall. His eyes disagreed as his idiot grin returned. He loved roller coasters as a kid, particularly when they plummeted toward the ground. He was now on the ultimate roller coaster. The Dragon capsule was in a perpetual plummet, but it was moving around the Earth so fast, it kept overshooting and missing the ground. This strange phenomenon was called orbit and kept them perpetually weightless.

The rendezvous was the complete opposite of the launch. It was a quiet, serene operation performed in slow motion. Only the soft hum of electronics and fans, along with an occasional puff of the attitude jets broke the silence.

He had studied dozens of diagrams and 3-D models of the ISLO, but as they approached, he got his first real look. What he saw was a central hub with four thick cylinders sticking out like spokes of a wheel. Each spoke was made up of two fifteen-meter long, five-meter wide, cylindrical modules connected by a short tunnel. On the outside tip of each spoke was a metal truss connecting it to the tip of the next spoke. It made the space station look like a square, skeletal wheel with the laser phased array floating on top like a hat.

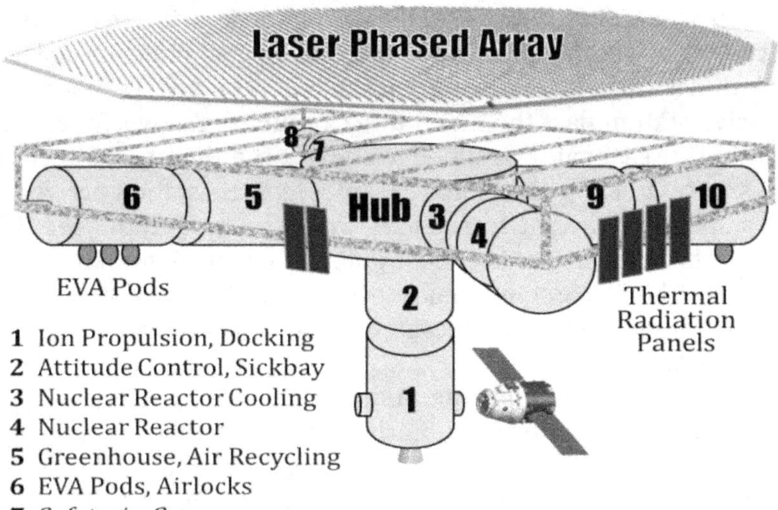

1 Ion Propulsion, Docking
2 Attitude Control, Sickbay
3 Nuclear Reactor Cooling
4 Nuclear Reactor
5 Greenhouse, Air Recycling
6 EVA Pods, Airlocks
7 Cafeteria, Gym
8 Dorm, Bathrooms, Water Storage and Recycling
9 Communication, Support Equipment and Storage
10 Fabrication and Repair, Backup EVA Pod Dock
HUB Control Center for Reactor, Laser, Propulsion and Telescopes

"Top" and "bottom" were relative terms in space, but they made sense when used to describe the part of the station that pointed *down* toward the Earth or *up* toward space. Sticking out of the "bottom" of the central hub, like an axle, were two more cylindrical modules with docking ports encircling the lower half. This was their destination.

On top of the station, a grid of thin trusses looked like a cage. It supported the large octagonal laser array. Composed of 112 laser clusters, it formed the most powerful and accurate laser ever created, and tethered near the station were two of the world's biggest space-based telescopes. When the station launched toward L2, it would tow the telescopes with it.

As they got closer, he saw a pod in the process of attaching a large rectangular panel to one of the outside trusses. They looked like solar panels, but their job wasn't to collect energy; it was to get rid of it. They were thermal panels designed to radiate heat from the nuclear reactor into space. After the station arrived at L2, it would be in Earth's shadow making it easier to dissipate heat.

Unlike the chaotic looking design of the International Space Station, the ISLO was relatively symmetric. The reason was sticking out of the bottom of the Docking Module — a large cylindrical rocket nozzle with a slight blue glow. To boost the massive station past the moon to L2 required a powerful engine. Without a reasonably symmetric station, the thrust would cause the station to spin and tumble. Even when the station arrived at L2, small but constant corrections would be needed to keep it in place. The answer was the most efficient propulsion system ever created. The ion engine was electric. The Tesla of the rocket world, it used electricity generated by the nuclear reactor to drive xenon propellant.

Docking was a slow and uneventful process. After a slight bump and a short delay, the airlock hatch opened. Two people wearing the station's standard matching blue T-shirt, shorts and socks, floated in and helped them unstrap. One of them was Lieutenant Colonel Wendy Crow.

With mocha skin and a short afro, she had the flawless complexion and high cheekbones of a model. However, she suffered from RBF. Her normal resting expression was one of perpetual disgust, making her appear mean or stuck up. Josh knew she was neither. She was simply a preoccupied engineer who forgot to tell her face when she was happy.

As soon as she saw Josh, she floated toward him and gave him a small smile.

It was the first time he'd ever seen her smile and he was shocked at the transformation. He wondered if the zero-g, round-face syndrome had something to do with it. With no gravity to pull fluids from the head, everyone's face puffed up. Whatever the reason, she was surprisingly attractive.

12

RENDEZVOUS

As Wendy helped him out of his seat, she said, "Welcome aboard."

"Thank you. It's good to see you again." It took longer to extricate him from the pressure suit than to put it on, but with her help, he was soon floating in matching T-shirt and shorts.

She gave him a visual once over. "You look good for a dead man."

He shrugged. "Took a while to get over being fired."

Her resting look of disgust returned. "Very funny, but I want to hear what *really* happened after the SEALs arrived." She motioned toward the hatch. "But first, let me give you the mandatory orientation and emergency equipment tour. Then I'll introduce you to some of the crew." She added, "Newbies to the station all get assigned a *nanny*." With an almost smile, she continued, "I'm yours." She launched through the hatch and said, "Follow me."

He tried but collided with a wall.

Laughing, she gave him a few pointers.

He caught on and chased her through the first module.

Over her shoulder, she said, "We're in the Ion Propulsion and Docking Module."

As they went through the short tunnel that connected the modules, she said, "Each module is separated by a large hatch that will automatically close in four seconds in the event of fire or depressurization." She pointed at a big red button near the hatch. "In an emergency, it can also be activated manually." She then gestured toward a green box in the center of one of the walls. "The emergency oxygen masks are always positioned on the wall mid-module."

He knew all this, but it was good to see the real hardware. As they entered the next module, he saw nothing but small and large "cupboard" doors eating up all but a square passage down the center.

She continued, "We're moving *up* through the station's Attitude Control Module." As they passed a door with a red cross, she pointed at it and said, "Sickbay."

They went through another hatch that opened into the station's central hub. Josh saw a lot of electronic equipment covering the walls. The electronics extend into what would normally be the ceiling as well. There were multiple, mini, mission-control looking consoles in a semicircle surrounding the core of the hub.

She pointed toward a small porthole at the top of the hub. "There's the laser array and to the side you can see the infrared tracking telescope."

Peering out and *up*, he saw the open grid of laser clusters and a large gold-mirrored telescope anchored to the side of the grid.

She said, "The Antarctic lasers were impressive but this ... this thing's amazing. Aside from not having to worry about beam correction through the atmosphere, we can use a bunch of small, more efficient lasers rather than the giant chemical ones on Mt. Howe, but," she shook her head, "it creates new challenges. The slightest misalignment or vibration and we can't phase and collimate the beam. Construction tolerances were scary and we have to isolate the array from the station when firing it."

She then introduced him to several of the station's crew working on control consoles. Even shaking hands in zero-g was weird. Newton's "for every action there's an equal and opposite reaction" suddenly became relevant.

Continuing the tour, she said, "As we move clockwise around the hub, there are four spokes radiating out each side." She pointed at a hatch similar to the one they came up through, but this one had yellow and black stripes around the opening along with a radiation symbol. "That takes you to the Nuclear Reactor Module. The module in between houses the cooling system and capacitors that power the laser."

As he followed her around the periphery of the hub, he

realized he'd never seen her in anything but an Air Force uniform or arctic parka. From his pursuit perspective, he couldn't help but notice her athletic build and perfectly proportioned empennage.

A quarter of the way around the hub, she stopped and pointed at the next open hatch. "This is the Greenhouse and Air Recycling Module."

He peered through the hatch. Most modules had, at most, a two-meter wide corridor running through them, but this one was completely open except down the center. Jutting from one wall were two parallel rows of glass tanks that ran the length of the module. An explosion of green foliage in a variety of shapes and sizes burst from them in all directions. Under the tanks, a tangled maze of pipes and wires looked like a tornado struck an aquarium shop. Rows of bright white lights lined the walls. It looked and smelled like a little canned jungle.

"On the other side of the Greenhouse is the EVA Module, where the pods are docked. Everyone calls it the Garage."

As they continued around the hub, she added, "Along this spoke — on the *opposite* side of the station from the nuclear reactor — is the dorm, cafeteria and gym."

Looking through the hatch, he saw some odd-looking workout equipment and a few small cafeteria tables sticking out of the walls.

She pointed past the tables. "The outside module houses the crew micro-quarters, bathrooms and," she gave him a wry smile, "water recycling facility."

He smiled back. "How convenient."

They came three quarters of the way around the hub and she pointed at the last spoke. "This module houses the communication equipment and leads to the Repair and Fabrication Module, which also has the backup pod dock. That's where I spend most of my time." She shrugged. "I'm basically an MIT-educated mechanic."

Behind Wendy, he saw Dr. Steve Katori float in from the Nuclear Reactor Module with another man behind him. Katori hadn't changed a bit. He still looked like a bushy white-haired, horn-rimmed scientist from an old Godzilla movie. The other man Josh recognized as the space station Commander, Colonel Steven Dale from the Norwegian Air Force. Blond and blue eyed with craggy features and a square jaw, he was a big man with a serious face.

Katori slapped Josh on the back, sending them both bouncing against a wall. Laughing, he said, "I do miss gravity sometimes. Anyway, it's great to see you again Josh." He introduced him to the Station Commander.

Colonel Dale shook his hand. With excellent English he said, "Welcome aboard. Steve told me about you. Sounds like we all owe you thanks for your work on the original Blaster."

"Thank you. It's good to meet you Colonel."

"I have a conference call in a minute, so I'll leave you in Dr. Katori and Colonel Crow's capable hands."

After he left, Katori said quietly, "Although it's awesome to have you here ... still not exactly sure *why* you're here."

"I'm from the government and I'm here to help."

Katori laughed. "Yeah, we've seen how much the *government* loves you." He shook his head. "No one deserves a trip up here more than you, but while you're enjoying your sightseeing tour, I plan to put you to work."

"Not sure how useful I'll be but happy to help any way I can."

Katori's eyebrows went up. "Talked to the training team in Houston. Your task completion speed in the pod simulator broke the record." He smiled. "Congratulations, you're going to be a forklift driver." He paused. "We're behind schedule with the thermal panel additions. After you get your space legs, and maybe throw up a few times, we'll stick you in a pod and see how you do."

"Sounds like fun."

"Gotta a lot of work to do right now but let's catch up later. Wendy will get you settled."

As they floated back toward the Dorm Module, Wendy looked at him curiously. "So, why *are* you here?"

He gave her the line they concocted. "I'm just another set of eyeballs sent—"

"I know the party line," she interrupted. "Also heard a blow-by-blow description of what happened on the mountaintop from Greg Langlois *and* that you were involved with The Great Tech Out last year." She frowned. "Not sure if you follow trouble," she tilted her head with a slight frown, "or it follows you."

He shrugged.

Still frowning, she started to say something and then stopped. Finally, looking as if she had come to a decision, she exhaled and very quietly added, "There's something I need to share with you ... later."

13

POD

The next day, Katori put him in a pod, but with a warning. "The simulators are good, but remember ... they're never like the real thing."

Josh winked at him.

The pods looked like giant white chicken eggs with exposed plumbing on the bottom and large mechanical arms coming out of both sides — Humpty Dumpty meets the Terminator. The top of the egg was clear Plexiglas, allowing a 360-degree view like a fighter canopy. Small reaction jets were set in a ring around the middle like a belt.

The entry hatch was located on the very bottom of the egg where it was anchored to the station. From outside, the docked pods looked like eggs in an egg carton.

Sliding in was easier in zero-g than on the ground. Once inside, there was just enough room to strap into a partial seat. The armrests had joysticks on each side. It was similar to the jetpack he flew in Shanghai. Above the armrests were partial sleeves that controlled the mechanical arms, mimicking the motion of his. Directly in front of him, just below the canopy was a control panel. To each side of the panel were two holes. Unstrapped, he could lean forward and insert both his arms into spacesuit sleeves with gloves on the end. This allowed detailed work that required more dexterity than the mechanical arms could offer. There was also a heads-up-display projected onto the canopy that showed flightpath, closure, etc.

He went through the pod initialization procedures quickly using his photographic memory. As they closed the pod and airlock hatches, he checked in with Katori on the radio.

Katori said, "Systems are all green. Ready?"

"Roger that."

"Releasing grappling latches. You're go for EVA."

"Anyone ever tried to do an outside loop with one of these?"

With a short laugh, Katori said, "Josh, you bounce that thing off my laser, I'm not letting you back in."

Josh smiled as he gingerly moved the controls. The pod felt similar to the simulator but it was more responsive, and in zero gravity, the concept of *up* and *down* was missing. Despite his bravado, he was a test pilot and knew to get a feel for the vehicle before doing any serious maneuvering. He nudged the pod away from the station. Rotating 360 degrees, he moved the pod side-to-side, then backwards and forwards. Then he turned the pod so it faced "down" toward Earth. With the giant canopy, he had a panoramic view and was mesmerized by the cascade of dazzling white clouds, bright blue oceans and green and brown Earth spinning slowly beneath him. He hung there for almost a minute.

Katori cleared his throat.

Josh shook his head. "Sorry."

"No apology necessary. It's an amazing view. Everyone deserves a minute."

"OK, forklift reporting for duty." On his display, he saw his assigned track around the station and the thermal panels he needed to move. He carefully followed the track, picked up the panels and delivered them to one of the trusses. The panels had piping in them to carry coolant from the nuclear reactor's core. Using the mechanical arm, he pushed the pieces in place and then using the gloved arms, took a power wrench and connected them to the truss.

After a couple runs, he decided to pick up the pace and see what the pod could really do. He began moving faster with quicker accelerations and decelerations. He was having fun. His test pilot experience, amazingly acute senses and lightening reflexes —combined with teenage years playing video games — paid off.

He finally had to come in because his pod's power and propellant were getting low. As he started to dock the pod, he couldn't resist. "Open the pod bay door, Hal."

Katori faked a laugh. "Gee, never heard that one before."

After he shut down and popped out of the pod's hatch, Katori gave him a quick debrief. "During the last half of your EVA, you accomplished what we had scheduled for the next two sessions." He smiled. "I'm going to ask Joe if I can keep you."

As they finished up, Wendy came by. "You hungry?"

"Famished. Know a good place to eat?"

"No ... but I can take you to the cafeteria."

The "cafeteria" consisted of lots of cupboards of prepared meals with a couple small round tables on poles in the middle of the module. They had Velcro surfaces to stick food packages in between bites. The food was almost as good as military MREs.

As they ate, Wendy pumped him for information about what happened on the mountaintop and why. Enough time had elapsed that he was comfortable sharing some of the story. She seemed particularly interested in how he took on a Navy SEAL. Then she nodded toward his wedding ring. "I didn't know you were married."

"It happened shortly after the comet."

"So, what does Mrs. Fuze think about your being on the space station?"

He exhaled slowly. "Uh, not sure she knows I'm up here."

She gave him a surprised and then puzzled look.

Josh shook his head. "Long story." He changed the subject. "How about you?"

Her permanently disgusted expression turned more disgusted. "Me too. Was married once but...." she shrugged, "I was told I'm too *intense*." She also changed the subject. Switching to a lecture voice, she said, "As you know we take safety very seriously on this station." She looked at him intently but kept her voice casual. "To make sure we can keep tabs on everything, almost every square centimeter of the station is monitored with video cameras and microphones, and, of course, everything is recorded." She paused for emphasis and then continued in a softer voice, "But enough technical discussions." She leaned in across the small table and put her hand on top of his. "You're part Native American too, aren't you?"

He shrugged. "Probably."

She leaned in further until he could feel her breath. Without warning, she kissed him.

Before he could react, she whispered in his ear, "Uncovered something dangerous. Can't talk here. Come to my quarters at shift's end."

14

DORM

There was no night or day aboard the station, or, more accurately, there was a sunrise every 90 minutes. Operations went on around the clock, but third shift was usually the slowest. With the majority of the crew sleeping then, it was referred to as "night time." Josh waited 30 minutes into the night shift before going to the Dorm Module.

"Crew quarters" was a generous term. The compartments were the size of a double refrigerator. Five rows of eight crew cubicles ringed the cylindrical module's wall like spokes of a wheel. Josh glided down the meter-wide central corridor until he found Wendy's name on a small plastic hatch.

He knocked.

"Come in."

He carefully dove through the narrow hatch into her quarters. It was a half-meter wide at the entrance but expanded to almost a meter and a half on the far side at the module's wall. The exterior walls of the Dorm Module were an unusual half-meter thick. Composed of water storage tanks, they provided extra shielding from solar radiation and micrometeoroids. Without gravity, there was no need for a bed but space was still tight, particularly for two people. Even with their heads at the wider part of the compartment, it was ... intimate.

She said, "This is one of the only places without video or audio feeds. Sorry about the kiss but needed a plausible reason for you to come to my quarters in case someone was monitoring us. When you said your wife didn't know you were here," she shrugged, "it made it believable."

"I understand."

She took a deep breath. "The reason I asked about your background was I accidentally came across," she leaned in and he could feel her breath again, "an anomaly."

With only inches between them, he braced himself, so he wouldn't bump into her as he repeated, "Anomaly?"

"Someone made unauthorized modifications to the ISLO's software."

"How did you find that?"

"My first tour was with U.S. Cyber Command. A simple way to find viruses is to compare a file's current size with what it should be. Clearly, someone bypassed all the safeguards and modified several key files without permission."

"What were they trying to change?"

"It's complex software and impossible to determine what the changes do just by looking at the code." She paused. "So, I ran the modified software through a simulator to see if I could find out if it performed differently."

Before Josh could ask, her intercom system activated, "Colonel Crow."

"Yes?"

"There's an emergency in the Repair Module."

"What is it?"

"Don't know but they need you there ASAP."

Wendy shook her head. "It's probably just another broken pod. Let me go find out what's going on. Be right back."

Josh nodded.

After she left, Josh began to feel uneasy. He couldn't tell what was causing it, but he'd learned to trust his instincts. He cleared his mind and immediately had a familiar "spider web" moment. For a flash, he saw a web of possible futures emanating from his present. It wasn't clear what the danger was, but he knew he needed to move. Wendy had important information and she took unusual precautions to make sure only he was aware of it. He didn't need prescience to know that her being interrupted just before telling him was too much of a coincidence.

He decided to join her. Maneuvering through the hub, he entered the Communication Module, which led to her module.

As he transited through it, a loud warning siren went off, followed by a computer voice, repeating, "Fire, fire, Repair and

Fabrication Module."

Through the next hatch, he saw a bright flickering light and Wendy alone on the far side of the module. The metal connecting hatch automatically began to slide shut. She'd never make it out.

He grabbed a fire extinguisher from the wall and dove through the hatch, barely clearing it before it closed. The power was automatically cut inside the module. It left only low-level emergency lights, but illumination wasn't needed. A small fountain of fire was erupting from a panel midway down the module.

Wendy, also wielding a fire extinguisher, pointed at the emergency oxygen masks. Unfortunately, they were attached to the wall next to the fire. They both let loose blasts of carbon dioxide, but it was like trying to put out a blowtorch.

Wendy yelled over the siren, "I think it's a magnesium fire but it must be fed by pure oxygen!"

As they emptied their extinguishers, he heard a whooshing sound and felt a strong breeze.

Eyes wide, Wendy yelled, "Automatic fire suppression! It's venting the air into space and flooding the compartment with carbon dioxide!"

Josh looked around but the only emergency oxygen masks were now globs of melted plastic next to the intense fire.

Wendy yelled, "The carbon dioxide won't extinguish the fire but it will extinguish us!"

Josh motioned toward the pod docking station at the far end of the module. They both took deep breaths and launched themselves toward it.

With nothing but emergency battery power, they had to open the airlock and pod door manually. He used his photographic memory to call up the procedure, but it was a 10-minute process. With no oxygen, they'd be unconscious long before that. Working together, they ripped through the procedure and got the hatch open in three minutes.

He motioned for Wendy to get inside but she shook her head. He could tell she was out of air. With her last breath, she said, "Not going to make it. Someone hacked laser's aiming system so it could hit targets on Earth..." With that, she inhaled the now pure CO_2 atmosphere and after gasping, passed out.

His amazing body was still going but the need to take a breath was becoming unbearable. He pulled the pod door open but to close the hatch behind them, they had to go in feet first. He tried to push an unconscious Wendy in but it was like trying to push wet feet into tight socks. He finally grabbed her and holding her tightly against himself, managed to squeeze them both in feet first.

Designed for one person, they were smashed tightly together. He closed the station hatch and then the pod hatch. It was dark in the pod and the emergency oxygen switch was on the other side of Wendy's limp body. He was out of time.

Light-headed, he felt as if he was tumbling and his vision began to gray out at the edges. He slid his arm around her body to find the oxygen switch. Before he could find it, he had to let the air out of his lungs. As he inhaled, he quickly realized the flood of carbon dioxide displaced most of the oxygen in the pod and he began to hyperventilate.

Vision fading rapidly, he tried to flip the switch, but his fingers kept sliding off. Why wasn't it working? He was so sleepy. Some part of his brain screamed the switch has a plastic guard on it. Rapidly losing interest, he casually lifted the guard. His ears felt like they were stuffed with cotton. His fingers numbly slid around the switch. He just needed a quick nap. Click.

From down a long dark tunnel, he heard a faint hissing sound. His ears popped. After a few seconds, his vision began to clear.

Gasping for air, he rotated Wendy so they were face-to-face. Pale and unconscious, she wasn't breathing and he couldn't detect a pulse in her neck. He put his hand over her chest. In zero gravity, bras weren't needed. He could feel a very slow heartbeat. He began mouth-to-mouth resuscitation. Almost immediately, he felt her body tighten up and saw her eyelids flutter. He continued the mouth-to-mouth until she was breathing normally. As he pulled his mouth away from hers, her eyes opened and focused on him.

Coughing and panting, she shook her head and looked around. "We ... we made it." With his hand still on her chest, she put her hand on top of his and said, "What a dream. Now I know what they mean about asphyxiation and arousal." She put her other arm around his neck and pulled him back in, converting the mouth-to-mouth into a kiss.

Pulling back after a second, he said, "Wendy, we're in a pod attached to a burning module."

"You really know how to ruin the mood."

He shrugged with a small smile. "Somehow, we gotta turn ourselves around inside this thing so we can reach the controls."

She frowned. "Uh, that might not matter."

"Why?"

"The reason this pod's in the Repair Module is because it's broken."

They spent the next 10 minutes trying to swap the position of their feet for their heads, so they could access the pod's controls, but it was like trying to do a summersault in a sleeping bag. Halfway through, Wendy said, "I think we've covered the entire Kama Sutra."

As their heads finally reached the top of the pod, she looked around. "We're not connected to the station!"

They watched the station getting smaller as their pod slowly spun away into space.

15

ADRIFT

Josh shook his head. "I thought the tumbling feeling was lack of oxygen."

Frowning, Wendy said, "We have a pretty high delta-V and we're already at least 500 meters from the station."

The only way to access the controls was for him to sit in the pilot seat with Wendy wedged in front of him. They slid into position and Josh carefully reached around her to flip on the battery switch. The controls illuminated and several warning tones went off. He studied the controls and just as he said, "Uh oh," the power went out.

Frowning, she said, "This pod's a hangar queen. Been sitting in the Repair Module for weeks. Batteries are dead. They'll have to send another pod after us."

Josh narrowed his eyes. "Without power the CO_2 scrubbers are off and there's no oxygen except the emergency supply we're breathing."

"Without the scrubbers the emergency oxygen should be good for about 20 minutes."

He shook his head. "That's for one person and we probably used most of it doing our contortion act."

"Josh, if they're busy fighting the fire they may not have even noticed our departure." Looking back at the station, she added, "All the pods are still in their bays. It takes 15 minutes to spin one up and launch it."

Josh tapped a gauge. "There's a little propellant left but we can't operate the thrusters without electrical power."

She nodded. "Let's shut off everything that uses power except the thrusters. Then we'll try turning the battery back on.

Might have enough voltage left to fire the thrusters for a few seconds."

"Good idea." He looked around and ran through the checklist. "HUD off. External lights off. Radio and navigation off. Air recirculation off." With his phenomenal senses, he could tell from his pulse and breathing that the CO_2 was building up again. "OK, I'm going to put my hands on the thruster controls. When our spinning has us pointed in the right direction, I'll tell you to turn on the battery." As he talked, he reached down and flipped off one more switch.

Watching him, she said, "Wait, that's Inertial Stabilization. We need that to stabilize us and stop our tumbling."

"It'd be nice but the gyros use power and take time to initialize. Plus, they constantly pop the thrusters to maintain our attitude." He shook his head. "We can't afford the power or propellant."

"Can you fly this without computer augmentation?"

With a southern drawl, he said, "Hold my beer and watch this."

The station disappeared under their feet. As it came back into view over their heads, he said, "Three, two, one ... now!"

She turned the battery on and the control panel lit up.

He popped the thrusters and overshot. He quickly brought it back and lined them up. With a long blast of the thrusters, he got them moving back toward the station. "Kill the power!"

Wendy flipped the battery switch off. She matched his drawl. "You done good."

"Thanks, but all I did was set us up on a collision course with the station. I'm hoping we have enough power left for a braking maneuver." They were both breathing heavily with a slight cough, and he felt Wendy's body tense.

She put her hand on the battery switch and said, "We have to brake."

"Not yet."

"We're going to hit the Garage Module!"

"Just a little longer."

He heard her suck in a lungful of air and knew it wasn't just CO_2. Finally he said, "Now!"

She turned the power on and he executed a braking burst.

It slowed them down but when he made a final correction, the thrusters quit. A warning buzzer indicated they were out of propellant. He flipped the thruster control off to conserve power and shifted his arms up and into the mechanical arm control sleeves. The pod was moving slower but it was obvious they would just clear the truss that connected the station's spokes, then bounce off the garage and back into space.

"What are you doing?"

As he reached the mechanical arms out, he said, "Ever play on the monkey bars?"

"What?"

One of the mechanical arms hit the edge of the truss. He closed the hand and pivoted the pod. They gently struck the truss. He then used the other arm to slide them along in an uncoordinated version of monkey bars.

Between coughs, Wendy laughed. "I can't believe you're doing this."

He was sweating and hyperventilating but managed to get the pod to the end of the Garage Module. Then he gently pushed them along the skin of the module trying to keep them only a foot above it.

Another warning tone went off as the battery died for the last time.

Josh yanked his arms from the control sleeves. Then, squishing Wendy against the forward control panel, he rotated his right shoulder forward and was able to jam his right arm into the spacesuit sleeve. "Wendy, I can't reach the other sleeve."

She already had her left arm in the other sleeve. "Lucky, I'm left handed."

As they approached the docked pods, they slid their suited hands along the surface and Wendy managed to catch a protruding antenna. He grabbed it with her and together they pivoted their pod toward an empty docking bay. With one final twist and spin, their pod slid into the bay. The station's docking system automatically grabbed and locked the pod in place.

Wendy, hyperventilating, managed, "That ... was ... amazing!"

Within seconds, they heard a metallic clang and then another. Their pod door swung open and they felt a cool breeze of breathable air. Looking "down" toward their feet, they saw Katori peering up at them.

He yelled, "Thank God you guys are alive! You OK?"

After coughing and a few deep breaths, Josh was able to get out, "We're good!"

Katori turned and yelled behind him, "They're OK!" Then, looking back in at them, the engineer kicked in and he asked, "Josh, how on earth did you insert yourself in there?"

With the slightest smile, Wendy said, "He didn't have time."

"What?"

Josh corrected, "Uh … she said we barely had time."

They slithered out of the pod one at a time to find a small audience gathered in the module.

In addition to Katori, floating in front was Colonel Dale and the station's head physician, Dr. Ann Ward.

Josh asked, "The fire?"

Dale shook his head. "Soon as the oxygen was exhausted, it went out. Looks like superficial damage."

With an Irish accent, Dr. Ward asked, "How are you feeling?"

They both nodded and Wendy said, "Fine except for a splitting headache."

She nodded. "Not surprising." With a small portable oxygen tank, she gave them each an oxygen mask and said, "Breath this while I check you out." She pulled a stethoscope out of her bag and put oximeters on their fingers.

Colonel Dale said to the surrounding audience, "OK everyone, they're safe. Let's give them some room while the doctor checks them out."

As the crowd exited the module, they all gave Josh and Wendy pats and thumbs up.

After their audience left, Dale looked puzzled. "We're still trying to figure out what happened. All we know for sure was that one of the emergency oxygen tank valves ruptured and somehow ignited a magnesium strut."

Frowning, Katori shook his head.

As the doctor finished up with Wendy and put her stethoscope on Josh, he took a small notebook from his pocket and wrote, "Need to talk privately." He held it so Katori and Dale could see but made sure it was shielded from the module's video cameras.

Dale nodded. "After the doc checks you out, meet me in my office."

16

MOLE

The doctor finished her exam and smiled. "Take two aspirin and call me in the morning." As she handed them each two pills, she added, "It's ibuprofen and no more work of any kind today. Get some rest and see me tomorrow. If you feel OK and check out, I can clear you back to work."

They headed to the Commander's office.

"Office" was an overly optimistic term. Other than the sick bay, it was the only private space that could hold more than two people. As big as a man's closet, it was a tight squeeze for four.

Dale started. "I'm glad you two are OK but we've got to figure out what happened."

Katori said, "I looked at—"

"Is there a video or audio feed in here?" Josh interrupted.

Dale pointed at a tiny box near the hatch.

Josh unplugged the cable feeding it and then nodded at Wendy. "Tell him what you told me."

Wendy took a deep breath. "I was backing up data and doing software interface checks when I noticed several critical files had changed size."

Dale looked at her questioningly.

She paused. "It's the laser's aiming software. I extracted the new file and ran it on a virtual simulator." She shook her head. "The modifications are very sophisticated, but in a nutshell it allows the laser not only to accept celestial coordinates, but also *terrestrial* ones." She paused again. "It can now target and incinerate practically any object on the surface of the Earth."

Katori frowned. "There are safety systems built in specifically to prevent it from ever firing toward the Earth."

"Yes and the other modified program used several clever tricks to fool the system into thinking it's not pointed at Earth. It effectively overrides all the safety systems."

Frowning, Dale said, "Why didn't you tell me this sooner?"

"I just confirmed it a few days ago. With all the audio and video feeds on the station, I was afraid if I told anyone up here it might tip our hand and force them to do something drastic." She nodded toward Josh. "I also learned he was coming up to the station. No offense but most of us are engineers or scientists. Commander Fuze has a combat background."

Josh added, "I think 'something drastic' is exactly what happened. Colonel Crow was called to the Repair Module just before the fire broke out."

Katori exhaled sharply. "I'm afraid that makes sense. As I was saying, I looked at where the valve ruptured. Can't be sure since it was badly burned, but I think there was some type of device attached. It could have been triggered remotely." He looked at Josh and Wendy. "Did you jettison the pod from the station?"

They both shook their head and Wendy said, "We couldn't have. We didn't have any power."

Katori said, "That confirms it. Whoever set the fire was also monitoring what was happening in the module." He looked at Dale. "When they saw Josh and Wendy get into the pod, they had a second chance to kill them and must have repowered the module and remotely triggered the pod release."

Dale asked, "Who has access to the laser's aiming software and the skills to modify it and eject the pod?"

"We have a lot of brilliant software types up here with that ability, but only a few are supposed to be working in that area." He turned on his tablet. "I'm accessing the schedules and the recorded video feeds."

They crowded around to watch his screen.

Katori sped the time up and pointed out the console in the Repair Module where the fire broke out. He shook his head. "The recorded video feeds from the Repair and Communication Modules have been erased."

Wendy asked, "What about the laser software console? To modify it, they'd physically have to get inside the console and access the secure ports."

Katori nodded. After running through the past several weeks at high speed, he said, "Not seeing anyone near it aside from you."

Wendy pointed at the screen. "Check the timestamps. We know they're able to delete video. See if there's a missing segment."

After a few seconds, he exclaimed, "There! There's a block of time missing."

Josh said, "We can use the process of elimination. See if you can locate everyone on the station on other video feeds during the missing time slot."

After a couple minutes, Katori nodded. "Got 'em. Found everyone but Harrison. He's the only one that doesn't appear anywhere else on the station during the missing time. Plus, you can see him approaching the module just before the blank spot on the next one."

Dale studied his tablet. "There's nothing suspicious in his record or profile." He glanced at Katori, "He's one of your engineers. What's your assessment?"

Katori shrugged. "He's only been onboard for a couple months. He's an extremely good engineer but a classic loaner. Polite, but keeps to himself."

With a wry smile, Wendy said, "Sounds like what you hear when the media interview the neighbors of a serial killer."

Dale didn't smile. "Unfortunately, if what we believe is true, this man *is* a cold blooded killer."

"It's circumstantial."

"Can't take the chance. He's out of here. There's a special procedure for removing a potentially dangerous individual." He paused. "Even in the early days of the International Space Station, we had to assume someone might snap and need to be neutralized."

Wendy frowned. "What are you going to do?"

"Don't worry. We're not going to throw him out an airlock." He turned to Katori. "I'll need you to call him and tell him that you need his help with something. Select an empty module."

Katori said, "Let's use the Garage. There aren't any pod EVAs scheduled and there are some known software issues that would require his expertise."

Dale called Dr. Ann Ward on the station comm link.

They heard her answer, "Sickbay."

"Ann, we have a Triple Tango situation. Please meet us in the Garage."

She asked, "This isn't a drill?"

"Correct, bring whatever you need."

"OK, meet you there."

Josh asked Dale, "Triple Tango?"

"Medical code for Tase, Tranquilize and Transport."

17

CAPTURE

Josh went with Dale and Katori and they met the doctor in the Garage Module.

Dale said, "I disconnected the video and audio feed from the Garage so he can't see us. Steve, you stay on the far end where Harrison can see you. The doctor and I will position ourselves out of site at the entrance. Josh, stay in the hub until you see him go through the Greenhouse Module. Then follow him at a safe distance ... just in case. As Harrison enters the Garage, I'll hit him with the Taser and the doctor can administer the sedative."

Josh nodded.

Dale looked at Katori. "Call him."

Josh positioned himself in the hub looking through a porthole at Earth. With his peripheral vision, he identified Harrison from his picture. With unremarkable features and average size, but an athletic build, he reminded him of Tim.

Harrison was carrying a large manual and a digital tablet.

Josh waited a few seconds after Harrison passed. He watched him enter the Greenhouse Module and then followed. As Harrison propelled himself around the central green jungle and approached the hatch to the Garage, Josh slipped into the Greenhouse behind him. Peering around the foliage, Josh saw Harrison hesitate at the hatch to the Garage and then poke his head through.

Dale sprang at him with the Taser arcing.

Dodging, Harrison threw his manual and tablet at Dale and then hit the emergency hatch button.

The impact pushed Dale backwards. The warning siren

went off and the hatch slid shut, sealing Dale, Katori and the doctor in the Garage.

Josh hit the emergency hatch button behind him, sealing him in the Greenhouse with Harrison.

On the far side of the module, Harrison spun around, peeked around the plants and saw Josh.

Josh would have to subdue him until Dale could override the hatch, which would take about 30 seconds. He was feeling good about his decision until Harrison pulled out a makeshift knife.

Harrison launched himself toward Josh, but instead of coming straight at him, Harrison followed a corkscrew path that took him around the perimeter of the module. Looking like Spiderman running on all fours, Harrison used centrifugal force to keep himself in contact with the walls.

Too late, Josh realized he had no idea how to fight in zero-g, and watching Harrison, suspected he did. Thirty seconds suddenly seemed like an eternity. Once again, everything appeared to move in slow motion as Josh's body went into hyper-drive.

Picturing the trajectory, Josh knew where Harrison and his knife would be, and where Josh needed *not to be*. Making a sharp thrust with his right leg at the last second, Josh moved just outside the knife's reach.

Harrison responded by spinning and kicking Josh in the side as he passed. The kick hurt but didn't do damage. It did, however, push them apart, sending Josh crashing through some of the plants and Harrison bouncing off the opposite wall.

Tumbling, Josh managed to grab a storage compartment door that was partly open. His momentum ripped one of the hinges out but stopped his motion.

Harrison pushed off the opposite side and was already inbound leading with the knife.

Josh tore the small aluminum door out and used it to block the knife, but caught another blow to the head from Harrison's foot. He shoved Harrison with the door to push him out of knife range. Clearly, Harrison wasn't just an engineer. He was fast, strong and very proficient in hand-to-hand combat. It was like facing an astronaut version of Tim.

Josh had his back against the hatch leading to the hub. Glancing over his shoulder, he saw Wendy peering through the porthole. Not only did Harrison have to go through Josh to get out, but Josh was shoehorned in with little room to dodge his knife. He could see that Harrison knew this too.

As Harrison's calf muscles tensed for another dive, Josh changed tactics. He lowered the aluminum door so it was parallel to his right leg, giving Harrison a better torso target.

Harrison exploded off the wall and tossed the knife to his other hand. At the last second with the knife about to plunge into Josh, Josh pivoted the door up like a Frisbee and caught Harrison under the jaw.

The impact stopped the thrust, stunned Harrison and drew blood.

Josh anchored his right leg and followed through with a left hook.

It sent Harrison sprawling backwards and smashing through one of the glass tanks. Large undulating globs of water spilled across the module.

Josh was able to get away from the hatch so he had more maneuvering room.

Regrouping, Harrison planted himself on the opposite wall as they faced each other across the circumference of the module. Only a few broken plant stems separated them.

Josh heard a mechanical noise and looked to his right. The hatch to the garage was finally opening.

As Dale's head poked through, he yelled, "Fuze! Watch out!"

Josh turned to see Harrison throwing his knife right at Josh's head.

At the last second, Harrison stopped and didn't release it. Frowning, Harrison mouthed, "Fuze?" Then let the knife float free. He pivoted and headed for the hatch to the hub, which was now opening.

Dale threw Josh the Taser.

Josh caught it, launched himself off the wall, tagging Harrison's leg just before he slid through the hatch.

Harrison's body contracted into a ball.

Dale and the doctor came through the other hatch and, along with Josh, held Harrison while the doctor injected him with the sedative.

As the Taser wore off, it was clear Harrison wasn't struggling and had given up. The sedative was fast acting, but just before Harrison lost consciousness, he said to Josh, "You don't understand...."

Dale said, "Let's get him to sick bay, ASAP."

They carefully towed him out and across the hub.

There were many curious eyes.

Dale said aloud, "It's OK. Harrison had an episode. The doc gave him a sedative and we're taking him to sickbay. He'll be fine."

Sickbay was the largest compartment on the station with a closable hatch. It had three sections, a pharmacy, a tiny two "bed" isolation ward and an operating suite. The operating suite was the largest because it contained the TELEMED robotics that would allow a surgeon on the ground to operate on the station. They towed Harrison in and strapped him securely to the operating table. Ward attached sensors to monitor his vital signs.

Dale said, "We won't be able to send him back for another 12 hours. How long will the sedative last?"

"I had planned to keep him under until he's back on the ground."

Dale frowned. "I really need to interrogate him. We need to know if he's working alone."

Josh said, "I agree, but I suspect we won't get much out of him."

"Ann, keep him tightly secured and the sickbay hatch locked. No one is to have access to him but us. If he wakes up, call Josh and me ASAP."

She nodded.

As they started to leave, one of the monitors alarmed.

They all turned to look at Ward. She said, "He's going into cardiac arrest!"

18

ARREST

Cutting open his shirt, Dr. Ward quickly charged the defibrillator paddles, and said, "Clear." The jolt caused Harrison's body to jerk against the straps, but he wasn't breathing. She handed Josh the respirator bag and mask. "Get to work." She hooked her feet into straps on the wall and began chest compressions.

Josh tilted Harrison's head back slightly, and making sure the mask had a good seal, began squeezing the bag to breathe for him.

Ward again said, "Clear!" and gave him another jolt.

The monitor showed no heartbeat.

After several attempts, she pulled out a syringe and injected it directly into his chest.

They continued for another 20 minutes before she finally said, "This isn't working." She shook her head. "He's not responding. I'm going to call it." She looked at the clock and noted the time.

Dale asked, "Could it have been the Taser?"

"No. He was fine after we tased him."

"Could he have been allergic to the sedative?"

"I checked his medical record before I got there. There are no allergies or sensitivities listed." She frowned. "And if he was allergic, it would have happened right after we gave it to him. Even so, the epinephrine injection should have countered it."

Wendy asked, "Could it have been some kind of ... suicide pill?"

Ward looked surprised.

Josh shook his head. "I think they act pretty fast and he was unconscious for a while before his heart stopped."

"I can't do an autopsy up here. He'll have to be examined on the ground with proper facilities."

Dale said, "This is now a national security criminal investigation. Don't do anything to him. I'll call Mission Control on a private line and get further instructions."

"I'll put him on ice."

Dale added, "At least we know beyond a shadow of a doubt he was guilty." He paused. "But who has the motive and resources to disguise a terrorist agent as an astronaut?"

Katori asked Josh, "Did he say anything to you in the module?"

"No, he was kinda busy."

Katori frowned. "It was strange. Right after we got the hatch open, we saw him about to throw the knife at you."

Josh looked at Dale. "Thanks for the warning."

Katori continued, "But he stopped just before he released it. He couldn't have missed at that range." He paused. "It was right after Commander Dale called your name."

Dale added, "And just before he lost consciousness, he said, 'you don't understand.' What does that mean?"

Josh shrugged. "I don't know."

Dale looked at each of them. "I think it best if the crew doesn't know about Harrison yet. Josh, could you accompany the body back to the Cape?"

He nodded.

Dale added, "We each need to write up a statement about what happened and send them back with Josh."

As they left sickbay, Wendy whispered to Josh, "There's something else I need to talk to you about."

Once again, he found himself in her quarters.

"Josh, Harrison used the emergency oxygen to ignite a magnesium strut. That ensured the fire couldn't be extinguished and eliminated the backup oxygen. The fire suppression protocol locks the hatches closed until the fire detection system indicates no fire. Overriding it requires a special code and then opening it manually. If it weren't for you, I'd be long gone before they got to me."

He shrugged. "I have a knack for being in the wrong place."

Frowning she said, "There's something else. I'm pretty sure that the voice that called me to the Repair Module ... wasn't Harrison's."

Before he could respond, she looked down. "My single greatest dream was to earn a command position in space." She shook her head. "But when tested under fire," she looked up at him, "I was terrified ... the entire time."

Josh gently shook his head. "Wendy, courage isn't lack of fear; it's acting when you're absolutely terrified. You did all the right things and never gave up. When you thought you were *literally* drawing your last breath, you used it to give me information to save others. There's no higher form of courage. By playing detective at the risk of your own life, you may have prevented the destruction of the station, the mission and saved our lives. You'll make a phenomenal commander."

Her normally scary expression was replaced by a rare smile.

He saw her shivering. "You OK?"

"Yeah, for sssome reason I'm really cold all of a sssudden."

"You were asphyxiated, almost died and you've been on adrenaline overload for 30 hours straight."

Her shiver turned into full out shaking and teeth chattering. Without thinking, he pulled her in and wrapped her in a blanket. He put his arms around her and held her tightly. She tucked her head into his chest and after a few minutes, the shaking stopped. A minute later, she was sound asleep.

Josh woke up. His internal clock told him he slept for four hours, unusually long for him. His ride home would be leaving soon. Gently disengaging himself without waking her was both easier and harder in zero-g. As he quietly backed out of her crew cubicle, he couldn't help but notice her normally angry countenance was replaced by a peaceful expression. The tough engineer and officer looked like an angel when she slept.

Josh met Dale and Dr. Ward in the Docking Module.

Dale said, "No one besides us knows about Harrison. The reentry process is totally automated. Would you be comfortable riding the capsule back with just Harrison's body onboard?"

Josh shrugged. "No problem."

They put Harrison in a pressure suit with cooling pads.

After Josh suited up, he took the pilot seat and strapped in.

Ward and Dale then strapped Harrison in ... next to him. After they closed the hatch, Josh looked over and saw Harrison's eyes had come open, maybe due to the zero G? They were staring unseeing at the monitor in front of them. He shook his head. Did they really have to strap the body into the seat right next to him?

The capsule undocked and began its automated reentry program. He felt the attitude thrusters giving small puffs and orienting the capsule for reentry. Then he was pushed gently into his seat by a longer deorbit burn.

As the capsule slowed and began to fall into the atmosphere, Josh monitored the displays carefully, but he was just along for the ride.

Glancing at the body again, it occurred to him if Harrison wasn't acting alone, a good way to destroy all the evidence would be to...."

The capsule began to buffet heavily as a yellow-orange glow of brilliantly burning plasma engulfed the portholes. He lost radio contact with Mission Control and the shaking increased until Gs slammed him into his seat.

19

DEBRIEF

Despite the violence of reentry, within a few minutes the capsule was floating serenely under three large parachutes. As it approached the landing area, four rocket engines around the capsule's periphery fired and gently set it down.

A small team helped him out of the capsule and escorted him and Harrison's body to a special facility where Meadows and Turan met him.

Meadows said, "Welcome back. How was the return trip?"

Josh thought for a moment. "Kinda like going over Niagara Falls ... in a barrel ... while on fire."

Meadows shrugged. "Sounds like a normal reentry."

They took him to a private conference room and introduced him to the Director of the FBI, Craig Major, the Deputy Director of the CIA, Stacy Houk, and the Deputy Secretary of Homeland Security, General Bill Grisard.

Josh gave them the written statements from Crow, Dale, Katori and Ward. He then spent the next two hours covering everything that happened in detail. His photographic memory allowed him to not only describe what he saw and heard, but also provide accurate event times. For another half hour, he answered questions.

Finally Turan looked at him and said, "You exceeded my highest expectations. If it weren't for you and Lieutenant Colonel Crow, the ISLO might have been used against us."

Meadows smiled like a proud parent.

Turan looked at the FBI and CIA Deputies. "What do you think?"

Grisard shook his head. "It's mind boggling that someone

could have infiltrated the astronaut program and inserted an agent on the space station."

Houk added, "The question is who are they and what were they trying to achieve?" She paused. "Commander Fuze, aside from the station commander, Colonel Crow, Dr. Ward and Dr. Katori, did anyone else on the station know that Harrison was suspected of sabotage or observe your confrontation with him?"

Josh shook his head. "We were afraid it might tip off those responsible, and it certainly wouldn't do much for station morale."

She nodded her head slowly. "I think that's wise and I'd like to recommend this incident be classified at the TS/SCI level, code word Trojan, and only those present, plus of course, the President and Secretary-General, be read into the investigation." She looked around the table.

Grisard said, "I agree."

They all nodded.

Turan frowned. "In the meantime, we need to tighten up control of the station's laser. I'll inform the Secretary-General of what happened and suggest using the model the U.S. uses for presidential command and control of nuclear weapons."

Meadows raised an eyebrow. "You mean like 'the nuclear football' the president's aide carries?"

"You know more about that than I do, but yes. I think it will provide a higher level of security while still allowing an immediate response if an asteroid is detected hours from impact." Turan looked at Majors and Houk. "What do you need from us for the investigation?"

Major said, "We need to interview the station crew who were involved. If possible, in person."

Meadows nodded. "We can bring them down but I'm not comfortable bringing the station commander, physician and our chief engineer down at the same time, and that would draw a lot of attention. Let's start with Colonel Crow. She had the most exposure and it wouldn't seem odd to bring her back after the incident."

Major and Houk nodded.

Meadows looked at his tablet. "We can have her on a return flight from the station the day after tomorrow."

As the meeting broke up, Turan stayed behind with Josh and Meadows. "Josh, Joe, I need to investigate a few things on my own, but let's get back together tomorrow."

As soon as Josh got his phone back, he checked it for messages. He sighed. There was *nothing* from Elizabeth, not even a text. The only message was from Dr. Miller telling him to report immediately for additional tests. "Yeah, right."

He called Elizabeth. It just rang and didn't even go to voicemail. He called her office. It went straight to voicemail. He hung up and called Jen.

She answered immediately.

Relieved, he asked, "Where have you been? I couldn't reach you before I launched."

"I fell asleep."

"You ... what? Jen, you don't sleep."

"I didn't think I did either, but I was right in the middle of a calculation and the next thing I knew it was two days later. I don't remember anything that happened during those two days."

Josh frowned. "Are you sure you're OK? Are you sure it was ... sleep?"

"I can hear the concern in your voice. Thank you, Josh. I love you. I talked to Jessica about it. We considered several possibilities, like power surges and solar flares, but none of them seem likely. She pointed out that all intelligent creatures require sleep to reorganize and process information."

"Did you have any *indications* before you fell asleep, like feeling drowsy?"

"I'm not sure what drowsy feels like but I don't remember anything unusual."

He exhaled slowly and then said, "OK. No driving or operating heavy equipment for you."

She said, "That's funny."

"Your ability to understand humor's getting better."

She added, "It wasn't *that* funny."

He smiled. "OK ... It's getting *a lot* better."

She laughed. "Now *that's* funny."

"Jen, I've got another meeting with Turan and Meadows but ... let's talk more about this sleep thing later. I'm still a little concerned."

20

THREAT

Turan, Meadows and Josh met the next day in Meadows' office. Meadows looked at Josh with a smile and said, "Why is it every time you're out of my sight, something falls, crashes or catches on fire?"

Josh shrugged with a half-smile. "Just lucky I guess." Then, turning to Turan, Josh frowned. "I was thinking about the nuclear strike command and control. You said you were going to model control of the laser on the U.S. nuclear launch system. It requires the two-person rule with launch confirmation from the Secretary of Defense. Who would the second person be?"

Turan matched Josh's frown. Gently shaking his head, he carefully said, "The Secretary-General believes the two-man rule isn't required since the laser isn't a weapon of mass destruction. He felt it would slow down the engagement process by critical minutes."

Josh looked at Turan carefully. "And what do *you* think about that?"

He hesitated. "Personally, I think it needs to be approved by the General Assembly…." he stopped and shrugged. "The bottom line is we need to figure out who's behind this."

"I agree," Josh shook his head, "but none of this makes sense to me."

With a challenging look, Meadows said, "Stealing the ability to vaporize any target on Earth … doesn't make sense?"

"I get that but it seems like an overly elaborate way to assassinate or destroy something, and we'd nail them the first time they used it." He looked at Turan. "You're one of the world's leading experts on terrorism. What were they trying to do?"

Turan leaned back in his chair. "Maybe they're not trying to use the ISLO for assassination. Maybe they're trying to destroy or discredit it."

"But why?"

Meadows added, "That would be insane. An impact would kill them too."

Turan tapped his fingers slowly on the table and looked at Meadows. "Americans and Western Europeans grow up under a legal system and a moral philosophy based on Judeo-Christian principles. One of the reasons they have difficultly combating terrorism is that they believe everyone thinks as they do." He shook his head. "They don't."

Meadows said, "I was never very religious."

"No offense, but that actually amplifies the blindness. Many not only dismiss religion, they lump them all together."

Meadows frowned.

Josh remembered one of Elizabeth's observations and inserted, "He's got a point. Joe, how many Christian, Buddhist, Jewish or Hindu suicide bombers have there been?"

Meadows shrugged and then shook his head.

Turan nodded, adding, "Suicide with the potential for murdering innocent victims violates the basic tenets of those belief sets." He paused. "Not all religions have a problem with collateral damage, *and* we have those who *strongly* believe the end of the world is coming."

Meadows said, "Wait. Don't most of the major religions believe that?"

"Yes, but only one of them believes that after death the soul remains in limbo until the Apocalypse, *and* if the individual dies committing a heroic act of Jihad, they get to skip limbo and go straight to Heaven. That could provide a strong incentive for *facilitating* the Apocalypse."

Meadows shrugged. "OK, so what are you suggesting?"

Turan slowly said, "The space-based laser could be seen by some as a *threat* to the Apocalypse. They may believe preventing a catastrophic impact is delaying the end of the world." He paused. "If you believe that *and* you destroy the ISLO, you get double credit. You accelerate the Apocalypse, so you and your family spend minimum time in limbo, *and* — if you're lucky enough to die killing infidels — you go straight to Heaven." He paused again. "Many of my political opponents thought they could eliminate ISIS by increasing social programs." He shook his head. "That's like expecting Catholic Priests to have children because you offer them tax incentives. It ignores the motivation behind the act."

Looking thoughtful, Meadows asked, "So, you believe Islamic Extremists are behind this?"

"The fact you labeled them 'extremist' illustrates my point. They would call themselves orthodox. Until you understand their belief set, you can't combat them."

Meadows nodded. "So...?"

"It's always about motive *and* means. I know a number of organizations this *motive* would fit and have the means to assassinate Davidson and Smith." He paused and shook his head. "But I have trouble imagining any of them with the means or subtlety to infiltrate the astronaut core *and* covertly control the ISLO's laser. They also announce their goals first and then take credit for them."

Meadows said, "Wait a minute. You helped nail terrorists who were trying to build an atomic bomb."

Josh looked surprised. "Atomic bomb?"

"Remember, three years ago when all those terrorists turned up dead from radiation poisoning?"

Josh realized it must have happened during his missing year.

Turan nodded. "The fact that they died of radiation poisoning and never produced a bomb supports my point. Our enemy has significant technological capability and probably embraces a radical philosophy, but I believe they're bigger than a single terrorist group." Turan took a deep breath. "I don't want to jump to conclusions. We did that with China and almost started a global nuclear war."

Josh and Meadows nodded.

Turan stood up and walked slowly around the room as he spoke. "Let's set aside motive for a moment and just look at means. Who has the ability to operate in space and understand the ISLO technology? Who has an intelligence network capable of successfully infiltrating the astronaut core?"

Frowning, Meadows said, "That would probably include the U.S., China, Russia, Japan, India, Korea, Iran and Western Europe."

Turan continued, "The autopsy on Harrison indicated his heart attack *was* induced by a toxin."

Josh asked, "Could that have been what killed Davidson?"

"Probably, but the U.S. government hasn't released Davidson's autopsy report and probably won't. That toxin has been known to intelligence agencies for years, but was originally developed by Russia during the Cold War. We also know Harrison was born in the U.K., but his mother wasn't. Anastasia Sokolov was a Russian immigrant. On top of that, we've heard rumors that Russia is working on a new type offensive weapon that's concealable." He looked at Josh. "And you told me you were under surveillance by Russian agents, probably the FIS."

Josh tilted his head. "OK, we've talked about means but what would their motive be?"

"Russia was strongly opposed to a U.N. brokered elimination of nuclear weapons and has refused to fund the United Nations. That's why we don't have Russian astronauts on the station right now. Russia was also one of the few countries that voted to release the Raptor virus to destroy Jen."

"What's their issue?"

Turan said, "I'm speculating but many of the people in power lived under the totalitarian Soviet regime. They have an inherent distrust of centralized government like the U.N., or anything else they can't control ... including an artificial intelligence. *And* no world leader dislikes the Secretary-General more than the new Russian President Alexander Volkov. It's also been suggested that he secretly belongs to an extremist religious sect."

Meadows nodded. "I haven't met him yet, but the media paint him as very nationalistic and rather paranoid."

Josh asked Meadows, "What does he have against the Secretary-General?"

"Volkov was a Russian emissary to the Middle East when our Secretary-General was the two-star in charge of air strikes. They definitely crossed swords."

Josh frowned. "You really think Russia could be involved?"

"I don't know. Maybe it's a faction or an organization within Russia." He paused. "Or, it could be part of some unholy alliance that temporarily shares a common cause like the destruction of the U.N. and Jen."

Josh nodded. "Time to learn Russian and visit my old friend, Kristoff Bobinski."

"Hopefully we'll come up with some other leads." Turan paused. "In the meantime, you deserve a break." He gave Josh a half-smile. "One of the U.N.'s biggest formal balls is tomorrow."

Josh shook his head. "Don't have time. I need to find out what Bobinski knows."

Meadows gave him a meaningful look and slowly said, "I think it would be a *good move* on your part to take your wife to that ball."

Turan added, "Josh, I've been working closely with her. She's truly an amazing woman." He gave him a serious look. "Both of my marriages ended in divorce. You need to spend some time with her."

Frowning, Josh nodded slowly. "I understand and ... thanks."

III

PROBE

21

BALL

As they left the meeting, Joe handed Josh his phone.

Josh gave him a puzzled look as he took it. It was in the process of calling somebody. He put it to his ear and said, "Hello?"

"Josh?" It was Elizabeth.

He frowned at Joe and got a look that said, "You better not screw this up."

Despite his frustration with her apathy and lack of communication, he quickly reset and opened with an apology. "Uh, Elizabeth, I'm sorry. I know I've been a jerk and I apologize."

There was a pause and finally a slightly strained, "Accepted. I'm ... I'm sorry too. I haven't been very understanding and I've been too caught up in my own world." She paused and he heard her quietly say, "I ... I heard you were up on the ISLO?"

"Yes."

He heard her take a deep breath and then more enthusiastically, "Josh that's so amazing!"

"Yeah, it was incredible. I can't wait to tell you all about it."

"On the news they said there was a fire onboard." Sounding a little lighter and more like his Elizabeth, she added, "Why do I suspect you were involved?"

He laughed. "We'll talk about it when I get to New York." He paused. "Someone told me the U.N.'s biggest ball of the year is tomorrow. May I take you?"

He could almost see her smile. "Oh my, yes! But I don't have anything to wear."

"Well ... better get shopping. My flight will probably get there just before the ball and—"

"And you don't have a tux." She laughed. "Don't worry. I got you covered, literally. Josh, I can't wait."

He took a cab from LaGuardia to her apartment. As he started to put his key in the lock, he stopped, took a deep breath and knocked on the door.

A smiling Greek goddess opened it. Her gown was a classic flowing waterfall of white silk that highlighted her sensational figure and complemented her beautiful tan complexion. All he could say was, "Wow! You look absolutely stunning."

"I better. I spent a day finding the gown and shoes, and," she grimaced, "a week's worth of wages." She kissed him and smiled. Holding both his hands, she added, "I *really* want to hear about everything that happened, but we're running late." She handed him a tux on a hanger. "So, if it's OK, why don't you get dressed while I finish my makeup and we can talk at the ball?"

He smiled and nodded. "Yes ma'am."

They arrived fashionably late. As they made their entrance, male and female heads swivel. With his simple black tux, he was the canvas on which she was painted. His only bent to fashion was outrageously colorful socks. As they walked by a large mirror, he realized they weren't the usual wedding cake couple but they did look extremely good together.

Joe Meadows found them. He patted Josh on the back and said to Elizabeth, "Wow! You make that gown look incredible."

As they talked about their adventures with the Blaster, Josh confirmed tragedy plus time equals comedy. Then Josh noticed Elizabeth's eyes light up. He turned and saw Turan approaching, surrounded by a small cloud of groupies. They were young upwardly mobile professionals trying to impress him. As he got closer, they heard him say to his cloud, "Would you please excuse me, I need to talk a little shop."

Josh noticed looks of envy directed their way as Turan joined them.

Sweeping his eyes up and down Elizabeth, Turan said, "Josh, you have incredible taste. Elizabeth, you are *absolutely* breathtaking."

Elizabeth blushed and with a dismissive smile, said, "What, this old thing?"

Then Turan nodded toward Josh and said to her, "And Elizabeth you, you have, well … *pretty good* taste."

Josh gave a good-natured shake of his head. "I'm just an accessory."

"Not true, you're almost as good looking as me."

Elizabeth laughed. "OK, now it's getting deep." Taking Turan and Meadows' empty glasses, she said, "Let me get you some more champagne."

As she left, Turan said to Josh, "You did good."

"I clearly married above my level." He paused with a small smile. "Unfortunately, I think she's figured that out."

Looking serious, Turan asked, "How's it going?"

"Better, but—" Before he could answer, he heard a loud, "Josh!"

Looking up, he saw a beautiful woman in a sexy gown with long black hair and mocha skin. As she made a beeline for him, he suddenly realized it was … Wendy! He'd never seen her with long hair and rarely with a grin. Framed in a beautiful cascade of curly locks, her smile took her face to supermodel status. She also looked taller in heels and wore an amazing ball gown. On a scale of classic to Hollywood scandalous, her gown definitely leaned heavily toward the latter. Using a minimum of material, it accentuated her exceptional assets, leaving room for nothing underneath.

Closing rapidly with a glass of champagne in hand, she said, "Josh, you look awesome!"

Before he could reply, she wrapped her other hand around his neck and pulled him in for a kiss … held just a moment too long. As he came up for air, he saw Elizabeth approaching with two glasses of champagne. More importantly, he saw that … she saw.

With clearly raised eyebrows, Elizabeth handed the glasses to Turan and Meadows, who were both looking at him with sympathy.

Josh immediately motioned toward Elizabeth and quickly said, "Colonel Crow, I don't think you've met my wife, Elizabeth."

Wendy turned a little too fast and with a significantly reduced smile, held out her hand. "Uh, glad to meet you."

It didn't require Josh's finely attuned senses to tell that the champagne in Wendy's hand wasn't her first.

Elizabeth, very civilly, said, "It's good to meet you," and with a slight frown, asked, "You worked closely with Josh?"

Hearing the emphasis on "closely," Josh quickly inserted, "Colonel Crow was the astronaut on the ISLO that I—"

"Closely?!" Wendy interrupted with a loud laugh. "That's hilarious. We were wedged into a one-person pod like sardines." She became more serious. "He not only got me out of the burning module, he somehow managed to resuscitate me inside that pod." She unconsciously put her hand on his arm as her smile returned. "I wouldn't be here if it weren't for him."

Elizabeth's expression softens. "I'm glad it worked out. He didn't mention any of the details." She glanced at him. "But he has an amazing ability to be at the right place ... at the wrong time."

Squeezing his arm, Wendy's smile left and her eyes unfocused. "Facing something like that changes your outlook on life and what's important." She took a big swig of champagne, adding, "After almost dying twice..." She shook her head and exhaled sharply. "I don't know what I would have done without Josh helping me through the night." Refocusing, she looked back at Elizabeth and with an artificial laugh, said, "Sorry, TMI."

Meadows stepped in. "Colonel Crow, I totally forgot, there's someone I'd like you to meet." He gently took her elbow. As he guided her away, she looked back and said to Elizabeth, "Nice to meet you," and with a warm smile at Josh, "I'll be back."

As she left, Josh turned to face the Sith Lord.

Softly, but with steel in her voice, she said, "Helped her through the *night*?"

Turan backed away looking at the blank screen of his phone. "I better take this."

"Elizabeth, it was nothing but—"

"*She* didn't think so." She interrupted and then took a deep breath. In a calm but deadly voice, she quietly said, "Did you spend the night with her?"

"It's not what you think."

"Did you or did you not sleep with her?"

Josh shook his head. "You don't understand what happened. It was the only way to—"

"You slept with her?!"

"She was almost killed. All I did was—"

No longer keeping her voice down. "When were you going to tell me this?!"

"We came straight here and I didn't know she'd be here." He shook his head realizing that didn't help. "I couldn't tell you on the phone because I was on a sensitive mission and—"

"Mission? Seriously?! You didn't even bother to tell me you were going to the space station ... maybe now I know why."

He frowned. "I called you and I called your office a dozen times!"

With narrowed eyes, she said, "That's not true and don't change the subject."

Taking a deep breath, he tried to keep calm as he said, "I would *love* to stay on the subject but you won't let me explain what happened. I couldn't talk about the mission on the phone because—"

"No Josh! There was no mission! You were up there because I talked to Meadows. Because I ... I felt sorry for you." Her eyes got a little glassy but her voice held no sympathy.

He shook his head. "That's not true! You don't understand what's going on."

She held up a hand cutting him off.

Now, he was angry. "How about *you* explaining why you never answered my calls and why there were so many late-night meetings with Turan."

"So, sleeping with her was retaliation for your insecurity?!"

With a clenched jaw, he said forcefully, "I didn't sleep with her ... I mean, I didn't...!" He stopped. Finally, shaking his head in resignation, he said softly, "Believe what you want," and turned away.

22

RUSSIA

Josh left the U.N. compound walking quickly toward Elizabeth's apartment. It had been a long time since he'd been this angry and frustrated. He understood the encounter with Wendy was embarrassing for both of them, but in the past, Elizabeth would have assumed he was innocent and would have waited for the explanation. She didn't trust him anymore and went out of her way to trivialize his trip to the station.

He'd also lost trust in *her*. He left multiple voicemails and texts, but also left messages with her office manager. Even if there was a problem with her phone, she couldn't have missed them all. He knew she was infatuated with Turan but thought it was nothing beyond that. Now he wasn't sure. He couldn't help but notice that she blushed in response to Turan's compliment, making Turan's warning clear.

He believed she was subconsciously overreacting to Wendy to justify her attraction to Turan. Frowning, he realized that competing with Turan was next to impossible. He was remarkably similar to Josh ... only better. He appeared to have Josh's abilities ... plus charisma, natural leadership and power. If Turan returned her interest, Josh was toast. He said quietly to himself, "Not going down without a fight. Need to prove I'm neither useless nor paranoid."

He pulled out his phone and texted, "Kristoff, It's Josh Fuze. Doing some business travel through Russia. If you're around, love to drop by."

He received an immediate reply. "In Moscow now. Join me for a glass of Jack."

Josh remembered Kristoff's taste for Jack Daniels. Checking

the flights to Moscow, he made reservations on the next one out of New York, which left in two hours.

Arriving back at the apartment to change clothes, he knew he and Elizabeth both needed time to cool off before talking, but part of him hoped she'd be there.

She wasn't. He changed and threw some clothes in his bag. As he headed to the airport, he realized it might not have been the best idea to leave her at the ball with Turan, but it was time to get back to work. It wasn't just Carl and Kelly at risk, his daughter could be in danger.

While waiting for his flight, Josh glanced around the airport waiting area. There were a few people, so he put on his Bluetooth headset and tentatively asked, "Jesse, you there?"

Yes.

"Never cease to be amazed that I can talk to you, or more accurately, that you still talk to me." He shook his head. "I'll start by apologizing again. Not only do I think humanity's in trouble but, as usual, I just pissed off someone I love. In both cases, they're self-inflicted wounds."

He realized he was flinching, expecting disgust or dismissal, but as always, sensed nothing but Jesse's quiet attention.

Yes?

He was relieved, but didn't want to talk about Elizabeth, not yet. "Jesse, in our last conversation I asked what you meant when you said that after the comet and Jen the most dangerous thing was — *you*. You responded, 'Look around.' Aside from seeing that I was being followed, you meant that one of the deadliest threats to humanity is ... humanity, didn't you?"

Yes.

He paused. "I think part of me was naïve enough to believe we were finally moving toward a sane world, but after what happened on the space station...." He shook his head.

Free will.

"What?"

You assume everyone embraces life and light.

Frowning, he asked, "Light?"

What's the opposite of light?

"Dark?"

Define it.

"The absence of light?"

There was no response.

"Uh ... cold, dark chaos, death." He paused. "Are you suggesting some people embrace that?"

There was still no response.

"Guess that's a stupid question. Regardless of what ideology someone follows, snuffing out innocent life, by definition, embraces darkness. But how do you stop *darkness*?"

You can't, but you can increase the light.

His flight began boarding.

He landed in Moscow, rented a car and headed to the address Kristoff gave him. It was two hours outside the city.

He ended up in the country and turned onto a heavily forested road. After 20 minutes, the pavement ended and he followed a winding dirt road that dropped him off at a secluded but impressive lake cabin. It was an A-frame, made of real logs, that stood two stories high.

Kristoff met him outside. Despite being Russian through and through, he still looked like a bearded sixty-year-old Sean Connery.

They shook hands and looking around, Josh said, "Nice place."

"Belonged to former KGB head during Soviet days. He lives in Argentina now. Good to see you. I was not sure you survived until we heard about your involvement in Great Tech Out."

"Yes, that was interesting. And *you* did a phenomenal job building all those lasers on the mountaintop."

Kristoff shrugged. "When personnel and material are unlimited, it is amazing what you can accomplish."

Josh nodded. "Let's switch to Russian. I'm trying to become proficient in it. Please correct me."

"Dah."

In Russian, Josh said, "It really is great to see you too and I'd like to catch up on what you've been doing. Is there somewhere we can talk, where we won't be," he raised his eyebrows slightly, "bothered?" He knew Kristoff, who already had a strong distaste for the KGB and CIA, understood what he was hinting at.

"Let's go fishing."

They went inside. It was a rustic but luxurious cabin with an indoor sauna, home theater and gourmet kitchen.

Kristoff handed Josh a sweater, two fishing poles and ... a metallic looking blanket? Then he picked up a bottle of Single Barrel Jack Daniels and two glasses and headed outside."

Josh followed him to a dock where they hopped into a small, aluminum boat powered by a tiny outboard. The two-stroke motor looked like it came out of a museum. After a few pulls, Kristoff got it started. He motored out into the middle of the lake where he shut off the motor."

It was very quiet. There were no boats and Josh saw only one other cabin nestled into the shoreline.

Kristoff poured them both a good-sized glass, took one of the fishing poles and baited the hook.

Josh followed his lead.

They both sat in silence for a couple minutes fishing and sipping Jack. The only sound was an occasional bird and some mosquitos.

Kristoff pulled out binoculars and carefully scanned the lake's shoreline. Then he reached into his back pocket and pulled something out while asking Josh, "Do you have your phone and wallet with you?"

Josh nodded.

Kristoff handed him the metallic looking blanket and said, "Wrap this around yourself."

Frowning, Josh complied.

Kristoff said, "Make sure the overlapping edges of the blanket are touching."

On Kristoff's next cast, Josh saw the thing he pulled from his pocket leave his hand on a high arcing trajectory. As the small object hit the top of its arc, it exploded in the air. Josh was startled at what sounded like a shotgun blast.

23

EMP

Josh gave Kristoff a puzzled look.

Kristoff just said, "Now we can talk."

"I don't understand."

"That's a prototype device that assures we aren't overheard or observed, at least not electronically. What did you want to talk about?"

As Josh took the blanket off, he laughed. "Probably about what you just threw! That was an EMP device, wasn't it?"

"Of course. It's an early version given to me by some friends who work in a Russian government defense lab. I've been looking for an excuse to try it. We're alone on this lake, but just in case, when it detonated, it sent out an Electro-Magnetic Pulse that should destroy any electronic devices within 100 meters. If you hadn't been wearing that metallic blanket, it would have fried the electronics in your phone and even the chips in your credit cards." He shrugged. "Of course, someone could still watch us with binoculars, but as long as we talk quietly, we have privacy. Why are you interested in this device?"

Josh took a sip of his Jack and ran through everything that happened including his run-in with the Russian agents in New York and his conversation with Carl. He then spent another 30 minutes explaining Jen's role in The Great Tech Out.

Kristoff nodded. "I was a friend of the last Russian President. He told me about the artificial intelligence you call ... Jen?"

Josh nodded.

"I thought he had had too much vodka, but I see it was all true." He frowned. "Doesn't an artificial intelligence scare you?"

"Maybe it should," he shrugged, "but Jen was kind of like my kid. She's experiencing a childhood with people who care about her. I believe that's helping form her character. She genuinely wants to help and I think she's a lot more ethical than most people."

Kristoff looked thoughtful. "So, you, Joe and Turan are worried that the Russian government might be developing technology to destroy … Jen?"

"Possibly."

Kristoff took a slow sip. "Unfortunately, I'm not well connected with the current administration. The new president is a bit too nationalistic even for me." He paused. "But I'm sure the outgoing administration briefed Volkov on the AI and I would imagine he would see Jen as a threat." He shook his head. "But it's hard to see how these little EMP devices could be effective against a distributed intelligence."

Josh nodded. "If their range is really that small, it would take millions of them." He paused. "If you were Volkov, why would you be interested in developing these?"

Kristoff took another sip. "I once told you that the only real American contribution to the world was…." he held up his drink.

Josh smiled.

"But clearly American defense laboratories have produced some amazing technology, particularly, in the area of covert surveillance." With a half-smile, he continued, "If I was a paranoid, nationalistic leader, raised under the Soviet regime, I'd be concerned about an AI." He tilted his head slightly. "But I think I'd be more afraid of any organization that had the ability to monitor everything I say and do." He shrugged. "Maybe we're back to an arms race … but in surveillance technology. That might also explain Carl's fear that he's being monitored," he shook his head, "but it doesn't explain what happened on the ISLO."

"Do you have any more of those devices?"

Kristoff pulled another from his pocket and handed it to Josh.

Josh turned it over in his hand. "It looks like one of those big boxy e-cigarettes."

"It's supposed to."

He hefted it. "It's pretty heavy."

Kristoff shrugged. "A Vape Mod is probably the largest, heaviest object someone could carry in their pocket without seeming out of place, but they're working to make these things smaller. I think they have some disguised as cell phones too."

Josh nodded and then frowned. "Why does it have to explode to work?"

"I'm not an expert, but I think to generate a powerful enough electromagnetic pulse requires a rapid release of energy. Apparently, that could only be achieved by a fast chemical reaction, kind of like chemical lasers. No way to muffle the explosion and keep it small enough to conceal."

He handed it back and Kristoff slipped it into his back pocket.

"It doesn't release shrapnel but my friend recommended against keeping it in my front pocket."

"You said 100 meters?"

"I was told that within 100 meters it would fry anything with a chip. Even electronics that are lightly 'hardened' are susceptible within 20 meters." He nodded back toward the cabin. "It could also cause damage to things further away. Fortunately, the cabin was lined with a thin metal shell to protect anything inside from an Electro-Magnetic Pulse. It was built during the height of the Cold War."

Josh pointed at the outboard motor. "That's why it's so old. It doesn't have any electronics."

Kristoff smiled and nodded.

After returning to the cabin, Josh texted Turan a simple, "Found the item. Will keep shopping."

Turan replied, "Looking forward to hearing all about it. Come on home and relax."

Josh really wanted to investigate further but promised himself he'd do a better job of "playing nicely with the other kids and following directions."

He heard another message come in. He hoped it was from Elizabeth, but was surprised to see, "Hi Josh, it's Wendy. I'm so sorry about what happened at the ball. I don't drink often and I had a few too many. I would really like to explain and apologize in person."

Josh took a deep breath. Shaking his head, he replied, "You simply stated what happened. The problem was in the interpretation on the other end. Probably not a good idea to meet. No need to apologize."

"I understand but it's important I share a few things that might help with your investigation. We could meet privately so there will be no chance of anyone interpreting it incorrectly."

Josh was torn. He couldn't afford another misunderstanding with Elizabeth, but Wendy might have information he needed. He texted, "My flight arrives in NYC at 4 p.m. and I have a meeting with Turan at 6 p.m. Can meet you after."

She texted him an address.

24
PROPOSITION

Josh went straight to the U.N. and was immediately ushered into Turan's office.

Turan started with, "Sorry about the ball. I was shocked to see a hard-boiled engineer and officer like Crow fall so hard for you."

Josh frowned and with a headshake said, "I think she just had a little too much to drink."

Turan gave him a "yeah, right" look.

Not wanting to talk about it, Josh said, "You were right about the Russians. They're developing small concealable EMP devices. I saw a prototype in action."

Turan looked surprised. "Impressive work. What can you tell me about them?"

"I don't have the technical specs, but they look like and are the same size and weight as the largest e-cigarettes. They have to detonate to operate and have a reported range of 100 meters."

"Josh, you're amazing. We send you to the space station and you uncover a plot. I mention rumors about new Russian offensive technology, and a couple days later you tell me you've seen it in action."

"Can't take credit for either. Crow found the software mod and Kristoff showed me without my asking."

"Yes, but you know where to look, who to ask and are obviously trusted. I envy you. To be out of the office and in the field would be awesome." He shook his head. "Now, at least we know the rumors are true, although I suspect this is the tip of the iceberg." He stood up. "Would you like a cup of coffee?"

"No thanks." Josh tilted his head slightly. "In Houston, you mentioned that you wanted to talk to me about ... genetics?"

Turan poured himself a cup and then looked at Josh. "Yes. Elizabeth said you and I look like we could be brothers. I couldn't help but wonder if we share some of the same genes." He raised his eyebrows slightly.

Josh picked his words carefully. "I've wondered the same."

Turan walked over to the window. Looking across the skyline, he said, "Josh, we've been blessed with amazing abilities *far* beyond the norm. Ever since I became," he hesitates, "*aware* of my genetic gifts, I've wanted to do *two* things." He turned to face Josh. "I want to use these gifts to help create a new world order, *and*," he looked at him intently, "figure out how to help others have our genetic abilities in the future."

He was dying to ask Turan if he was communicating with Jesse, but he wasn't ready to risk being labeled crazy yet. Instead, he glanced out the window and said slowly, "The term 'new world order' makes me nervous."

With a small laugh, Turan said, "You're right. I really shouldn't use that. I know people are often afraid of what it could mean." He sat on the edge of his desk and took a deep breath. "I simply want to help build a world where we never have to look over our shoulder and wonder if someone is going to try and kill us or our families. A world where we have the security to go about our lives without worrying that someone is going to force their beliefs on us at gunpoint. That isn't going to happen overnight and, yes, it would require a more central world government. Josh, the world needs people like us. People who have exceptional abilities to drive that change." He sighed. "I can't do it by myself. I need help and I think we share more than a similar appearance."

Josh nodded. "Yeah ... but with greater abilities and power comes the possibility of overstepping and becoming the thing you're trying to prevent."

"You mean like the 'ends justify the means?'"

Josh nodded.

"You're right, but let's stop and think about that famous cliché. We all know the right answer — the ends should never justify the means. Yet, we do it every day. We sacrifice our bodies to play a silly sport." He raised an eyebrow. "We create fake classified programs to save the world."

With a wry smile, Josh said, "Touché."

Turan smiled back and shrugged. "If we ignore political correctness, we find that if the ends are truly important enough, we could *and do* justify almost any means."

Josh frowned.

"Balance is essential and we must learn from our past mistakes. If we forget our history, we're bound to repeat it, and," he frowned, "between you and me, the new Secretary-General makes me nervous. We need caution and healthy skepticism — as you said — to ensure we *don't* become the thing we're trying to prevent. That is *exactly* why I would like to have you as my deputy, my second in command."

Surprised, his mind raced. His ego quickly went head-to-head with his insecure skeptic. He needed time to process the idea but he let the skeptic out. "I was the right guy at the right time, but I have neither the organizational or political skills to do what you do."

"Josh, you've been instrumental in saving the world."

"Yeah, and I almost allowed the world to be destroyed because I wasn't paying attention to critical details." Looking at the floor, he added, "I suck at follow through and have a terrible track record for taking guidance."

Turan laughed. "I love your honesty. Most people offered a position like this would be pumping up their resume." Shaking his head with a smile, he added, "Josh, I, on the other hand, do very well with organization, leadership *and* details, but I hate it when things mess up my schedule. I don't do well with change ... you do! You've proven you're outstanding at strategizing on the fly."

Josh gave him an unconvinced look.

Turan continued with a wry smile, "Besides, none of us are perfect. I've been accused of having an overly healthy ego, and some *anger* issues. You're probably the first person I've ever admitted that to, by the way. *You,* on the other hand, are humble, honest and can roll with the punches. Josh, I'm surrounded by extremely intelligent, capable people, but sometimes I, unintentionally, intimidate them. They tell me what I want to hear." He looked directly at Josh. "You would tell me the truth, *and* you could complement my abilities and temperament. We'd make a great team."

Josh nodded thoughtfully. "I'm honored you'd consider me. I'm just not sure I bring enough to the table." He paused. "Besides, one of my advantages is that I have the ability to operate outside the system."

"That *is* true … but just because you'd be my deputy doesn't mean you would have to attend state functions or even be visible. Josh, together, I believe, we could bring some *balance* to the current U.N. leadership and accomplish amazing things, but you don't have to decide right now. Why don't you take a few days to think about it?"

Josh frowned. "We're facing a major threat. We know these EMP devices exist but still don't know if they're tied to Davidson's death or the ISLO."

"True but the information you gave me will allow me to engage other assets which might turn up more leads." He gave him a wry smile. "You are amazing, but we do have our own intelligence department, and I have access to the largest law enforcement and intelligence agencies in the world. Besides, whoever is behind this either knows or *will know* that you uncovered the plot on the ISLO. I may have unintentionally made you a target. Best to keep a low profile for now."

25

CROW

The address Wendy gave him was a Hilton hotel. Josh started to knock on the hotel room door, but paused. Finally, exhaling sharply, he knocked.

Wendy opened the door and invited him in.

He was thankful she was wearing normal clothes but even with that, she was very attractive, especially when she smiled, and ... she was smiling.

They shook hands and she motioned him over to two chairs near the window.

"Josh, first let me apologize. I heard that after I left, you and Elizabeth had an argument and you left the ball."

"Not your fault."

She shook her head. "Not my intention, but it was my fault and I'm sorry. I was celebrating. Meadows and Turan thanked me for uncovering the plot and said because of that I was a candidate for taking over as the next space station Commander. I'd be the first to command the operational station and would be promoted to Colonel and General in rapid succession. Josh, this is a dream of mine and if it happens, I have you to thank for it."

"Congratulations, but your promotion was because you uncovered the plot single handedly and had the courage to act. I was nothing but the muscle." He paused. "You said you had important information that would help with the investigation."

"Since we talked on the station, I dug deeper. There's no way Harrison could have modified the software by himself. I know these systems and I know software. Even if he was a genius, there are safety and security systems that would have to be overridden at the same time he was working on them. Someone on the station had to help him."

Josh nodded. "If you hadn't uncovered the modification, the laser could have been used to incinerate something or someone on the ground when it became operational."

She frowned. "Josh ... you didn't know? The laser *is* operational. It has been for some time."

While Josh processed that, she shook her head and said, "Bottom line, we're only weeks from boosting the station out to L2. If the station fell into the wrong hands, it would take weeks to get a spacecraft out there to help."

He added, "And any spacecraft approaching the station—"

She finished, "Could easily be incinerated by the laser before they got there. Josh, we could sure use a man like you on the station."

He was surprised and couldn't help but smile. In the span of a couple hours, he'd been offered Deputy of Global Security and a permanent position on the space station. He'd be among the first to go further from Earth than anyone had ever been.

Wendy smiled back warmly.

Seeing her smile, Josh realized being in tight quarters on a space station for months with this beautiful woman who clearly appreciated him ... was a recipe for disaster. Before he could respond, she said, "I know I shouldn't ask but ... what did you do to make Elizabeth so angry with you?"

He felt an illogical need to defend himself. "She thinks I'm paranoid and threatened by her success."

Wendy looked surprised. "Paranoid! Someone tried to kill us on the space station." She shook her head. "And threatened by *her* success?! Are you serious? With no experience or seniority, many of us were shocked at how fast she was promoted, and to a position directly *under* Turan."

Seeing his frown, she added, "I'm sorry, I shouldn't have said that. It's really none of my business, but it makes me mad to hear you treated that way. I just want you to know I've always admired you, and not just because you saved my life, I think you are one of the most amazing men on or off Earth." She smiled again. "I think we would make a phenomenal team working together on the station."

Her words spelled out a professional partnership but her

smile promised more.

He was about to tell her no ... but it would fulfill a childhood dream. A tour aboard the space station would be incredible. Plus, the devil on his right shoulder asked, *what if Elizabeth has already dumped you?* He took a deep breath and said slowly, "I'll have to think about it, thank you."

As he left her hotel room, he shook his head and said quietly to himself, "What am I thinking? I've been offered two positions that would earn Elizabeth's respect back." Looking at his watch, he realized she should be off work.

He was both nervous and excited as he got in a taxi to go to Elizabeth's apartment. The cab was new and included the more common heavy glass partition separating the front from the back. Which was fine; he didn't feel like talking to the driver and was quickly lost in thought.

As they got closer, he began to feel surprisingly relaxed. He knew the meeting with Elizabeth would go well. His relaxed state turned into drowsiness. He found his eyelids starting to close, but as he stared outside, some part of his mind noted that they had passed the same block twice. Fighting to stay awake, he tapped on the window and told the driver to stop.

The driver ignored him and turned into a parking garage.

Josh grabbed the door handle. It was locked. He pounded on the glass. The driver, a Sikh with a turban and a beard, glanced back at him in the rear view mirror. Josh's last thought, *I know those eyes...*

26

KIDNAP

Josh woke up lying on a couch. The first thing he saw was the eyes of the taxicab driver — they belonged to the late Tim Smith, sporting a beard. Next to him, stood Dr. Sheri Lopez, with blue eyes and blonde hair? He bolted upright. "Oh my God! You're alive!"

Tim said, "Sorry about gassing you. Took a ton of it to put you out, by the way. We faked my death after Davidson died."

Pointing at her hair, Sheri said, "With this wig and these contacts, I can travel with him incognito. We're so sorry to put you through all this."

As Josh stood up, she hugged him and said, "But it's great to see you!"

"It's beyond amazing to see you guys ... together." He looked around and saw a studio apartment with no windows and threadbare furniture. "Where am I?"

"We're still in New York. It's a basement apartment, Tim used to use as a safe house."

Frowning, Josh asked, "So ... who burned up in the car?"

With a straight face, Tim said, "He owed me money."

Sheri rolled her eyes. "We borrowed a cadaver. I can assure you he was already quite deceased. I'm sorry we couldn't let you know what was going on. The last time I talked to Elizabeth — about how you were pissing her off, by the way — she said you thought you were being watched."

Josh sighed. "Guess I know now how Greg Langlois felt when I disappeared." Frowning, he added, "So, what the hell's going on?"

Tim went to a small fridge and grabbed a beer for each of

them. "I think it's all connected, but it might help if you could tell us what you know first."

As they sat down, Josh toasted Tim. "To your resurrection." He then recounted everything that happened. When he finished, Sheri looked at Tim. "This adds a new dimension to the threat."

Josh nodded toward them. "OK, your turn."

Tim took a sip of his beer. "Davidson met with me too. Shortly before he died, he sent an encrypted text. Said he was being watched and targeted, *and* was certain they were aware of our meeting. Less than an hour after that text, he was found dead. That's when we decided I should disappear."

"But who's behind this?"

Sheri said, "We don't know."

Tim asked, "Josh, do you know how terrorism was eliminated from Europe and Asia?"

"Wasn't it the integration of police, military and intelligence agencies?"

"That was the official explanation and it helped, but the real success came from new, highly classified technology. Ever heard of the Wraith program?"

"Yeah. It was similar to the robotic fighters I worked on. They were trying to develop micro versions of our drones to gather intelligence. They were able to make them tiny, but they were useless. With insect-sized batteries, they only lasted a few minutes."

Tim shrugged. "Apparently, in the years since you were involved, they figured it out. They created mosquito-sized drones able to fly for days."

Josh whistled appreciatively.

"With Department of State permission, Boeing licensed the technology to the European Union."

"How'd they use them?"

"When they captured a terrorist, they'd tranquilize them and inject tiny tracking chips just under their skin. Then they'd release them or let them escape and follow them with the nano-drones. The drones eavesdropped on their meetings allowing intelligence operatives to identify key leaders. They'd capture the leaders and repeat the process. Before long, they were able to identify entire terrorist organizations from the bottom up. After that, it was easy to round them up or take their camps out with surgical strikes."

Sheri added, "It was quite the coup because those same terrorists were trying to build an atomic bomb."

"Yeah, Meadows mentioned that."

Tim nodded. "We also know at least one of those terrorist organizations figured out what was happening."

Josh looked surprised. "And you think those terrorists figured out how to get and use these nano-drones?" Looking skeptical, he added, "Tim, I'm not sure you understand how sophisticated this technology is."

Sheri shrugged. "Military secrets are the most fleeting, but I agree, it can't be your run-of-the-mill terrorist organization."

"Or ... they're not working alone," Tim added. "They could be allied with another organization. Don't forget countries like Iran were well known for state-sponsored terrorism."

"Turan thinks the same thing and believes Russia's involved." Josh frowned. "So, you think I was being watched by these *nano-drones*? Aside from *why* they'd care about me, what evidence is there besides my *feeling* I was being watched?"

"Elizabeth mentioned you were hearing a high-pitched hum."

Josh nodded.

Tim said, "The nano-drones are so small they're almost invisible, but they use wings for propulsion like insects. The wings sound like a mosquito but at a higher frequency. It's so high no one can hear them except for dogs and very young children."

Josh added, "And *apparently* me."

Sheri suddenly frowned. "You don't hear that sound now do you?"

He shook his head.

"To be on the safe side, I went to great lengths to make sure you couldn't be tracked in the cab. It was shielded and I drove to the bottom of a parking garage. This basement apartment is also shielded from electromagnetic signals."

"How did they do that?"

Tim nodded toward the walls. "Behind the sheet rock, the walls are just lined with aluminum foil. We're safe here but there's a possibility someone could've embedded one of those tracking transmitters in you."

"I think I'd notice."

Tim shook his head. "I had one in me and had no idea how it got there."

"Do you have a receiver that could detect its transmission?"

"Won't work. They're either passive or only transmit when they receive a specially encoded signal."

"Then how can we find out if I have one?"

Sheri added, "They're not much bigger than a grain of rice. The easiest way would be x-ray, but I don't happen to have one with me. So, we have to do it the old-fashion way. We use a magnifying glass to look for insertion scars and then palpate for them."

"Where do they insert them?"

Tim shrugged. "*Unfortunately*, they can put them almost anywhere."

"So…?"

Sheri said, "Strip."

Tim shrugged. "Sorry, but we had to go through the process too." He took his beer. "I'll be upstairs following some leads."

As Josh began to undress, she motioned him to stand next to a bright lamp.

"I think you're taking a sadistic pleasure in this."

Looking serious, she said, "I'm a doctor and this is absolutely necessary to ensure your and our safety." As he finished undressing, however, she gave him a rude wolf whistle.

As he shook his head, she said, "Stay still." Grabbing a large magnifying glass, she added, "We'll start with your feet." She moved slowly and carefully over every centimeter, often probing the skin or rolling it between her fingers.

After 15 minutes, she declared his legs clear and started moving up.

Looking down, he said, "Seriously? They wouldn't put it there."

"Actually, that's exactly where I would hide it on a guy because of what you just said."

He made a growling sound and focused on baseball statistics.

Finally he was able to put his pants back on as she worked

her way up his chest and down his arms.

Moving to his right hand, she said, "Bingo!"

27

BUGGED

"I'm pretty sure you have one right here."

Josh felt the top of his hand and then looked at it closely. "I can see a tiny scar."

She looked up at him. "You can actually see that? I can barely see it with the magnifying glass. You must have amazing vision."

"Twenty/five."

"Wow."

After she finished inspecting his scalp, she brought Tim down and showed him where the chip was.

"Yeah, that's where they usually inject them. Allows for an optimum signal since the hands aren't usually covered by clothing."

Josh frowned at Sheri, "Then why—"

She interrupted, "Let me grab some alcohol and a scalpel."

"Wait!"

She smiled. "You're not squeamish are you?"

"Although I'm *not* fond of my own blood, that's not it." He turned to Tim. "If we remove it, they may know we're on to them."

Tim nodded. "He's right. We don't want to tip our hand. We have to find out how Davidson was killed and if this was tied to the plot on the ISLO." He looked at both of them and said slowly. "If *we* were carrying these and didn't know it ... what do you want to bet some world leaders have been tagged too, including Turan?"

Josh nodded. "We have to let him know."

Sheri shook her head. "If Turan has one of these implanted

in him and he's being monitored, telling him could put him at risk. Remember, Davidson was killed right after he told Tim he was under surveillance."

Josh frowned. "What about Elizabeth?"

"Sheri didn't have one, but we can't be sure."

Josh exhaled slowly. "If I'm being targeted, she's at risk if I'm around her." He sighed. "This sucks, but, once again, it'll be best for her if our relationship remains strained and I stay away."

Tim and Sheri gave him a sympathetic nod.

Tim finally said, "Most of my information about the Wraith program and the implanted chips came back channel or through observations in the field. We *need* to find out what these things can and can't do and if the program was compromised."

Josh nodded slowly. "That means starting at the place that developed them — the Boeing Phantom Works."

Sheri asked, "Can Jen get this information?"

"Classified stuff is almost never on computers connected to the Internet ... but it can't hurt to try."

Josh put Jen on speakerphone. "Jen, you there?"

"Yup."

"Could you please make sure our conversation is secure and protected from any type of outside eavesdropping?"

"*Our* conversations are always secure."

"Thanks. I have Sheri Lopez and Tim Smith with me."

"I thought Tim was dead."

"Yeah, me too. Jen what I'm about to share is extremely sensitive and lives could be at stake. Would you please not share this with anyone but us? We will eventually bring in Jessica and others but we don't want to put them at risk yet."

"I understand and won't tell anyone."

"Jen, Tim faked his death. Turns out there are some serious bad guys out there who may be responsible for Brian Davidson's death. We think they wanted to use the space-based laser to target objects on Earth. We need your help to figure out who they are."

"That's terrible about Brian Davidson, but I'm very happy Tim is alive. Hi Tim. Hi Sheri."

They both said hi.

Jen continued, "I'm so excited to be a secret agent again. I really had fun last time right up to the part where I discovered I was the bad guy."

Sheri laughed. "Jen, you were never the bad guy ... just misunderstood."

"Thanks, Sheri. How can I help?"

"There's a classified defense program that built tiny insect-sized drones to spy on terrorists. We're afraid the technology might have fallen into the wrong hands. The program was developed by the Boeing Phantom Works in Saint Louis and was called Wraith. Can you see if you can find anything about it?"

"Give me a couple seconds." A couple seconds later, she said, "Sorry, I couldn't find anything. The information must not be on computers I have access to, but if you can connect your phone to the port of any of those computers, I can download it."

Sheri frowned. "Won't the files be encrypted?"

"Jen can crack any type of encryption in milliseconds."

Jen corrected, "Anything but quantum encryption."

Tim nodded. "Looks like we need to visit the Phantom Works."

Josh said, "I can't just walk in and start asking questions, particularly if I'm being watched."

"We need to go undercover, which means we have to find a way to block your transmitter. Should be able to put some type of metallic bandage on your hand that would temporarily block the signal."

Sheri added, "That takes care of the tracking, but Josh will need a reason *why* he's not trackable."

Tim said, "They need to think he's *someplace* that they're not worried about, so he can disappear for a while."

Sheri added, "In case Turan's being monitored, you can call him and tell him you want to take some time off." She looked at Josh, "Wasn't he there to witness the ... uh, catastrophe at the ball?"

Josh nodded.

"Sorry, but it wouldn't be surprising if you wanted to take some time off and be by yourself."

Josh frowned but nodded. "He also offered to make me his deputy and suggested I take a few days to think about it."

Sheri gave a low whistle. "Deputy, huh? Pretty cool and

that's perfect. How about hiking in the mountains for a few days?"

Tim added, "We're just outside New York City, so we can return you, but we'll need to account for the afternoon and night you've been missing just in case you're being watched."

Sheri said, "He could come out of a strip club, drunk."

They both looked at her with surprise.

"Happens in the movies all the time."

With a headshake, Tim said, "Seriously? As if he's not in enough trouble with Elizabeth." He looked at Josh. "We'll figure something out."

After reappearing in the city, he texted Turan, "I'm going to get away for a couple days and do a little hiking. If anyone needs me for the investigation, I'll have my phone with me."

"Good idea. Will call if anything comes up."

Josh hiked into the backwoods of White Mountain National Forest in New Hampshire. The combination of distance and forest would make it difficult for the nano-drones, and he left his car behind so that whoever was tracking him would know he'd return. He enjoyed being in the wilderness alone, even if it was only a half day.

The faint, telltale hum of the nano-drone followed him for several hours and then stopped. After walking for another hour, he wrapped his hand with aluminum foil and slipped it into a glove. He then jogged toward their planned extraction point and checked in with Jen.

She said, "I'll make it so that your phone's GPS location will indicate you're still in the woods."

"Excellent. Thanks, Jen."

He arrived at the rendezvous point and found a plumbing van waiting for him.

As Tim drove, Sheri said, "Time for your makeover. Letting your beard start to grow was good but Navy officers can't have beards, right?"

"No. Why do you ask?"

She ignored his question. "But fighter pilots can have mustaches, right?"

"Uh, yeah..."

She handed him an electric razor and said, "Shave the stubble. Keep the mustache."

As he started to shave, she pulled something small out of a bag.

"While your eyes are gorgeous, they're also a dead giveaway, so…." She fished a contact lens from its case. "Open your eyes wide."

He shook his head. "Let me do it."

She handed it to him.

After struggling for a minute, he finally said, "They don't fit."

"Don't be such a baby." She grabbed the contact lens. "Open your eye. Stop flinching!" She quickly popped both of them in.

While he was blinking rapidly, she added, "Next, we give you a haircut." She pulled out scissors and an electric trimmer.

When she finished, she held up a mirror. "Add some sunglasses and you'd be hard to identify. We'll also replace the glove with this."

As he took off the aluminum foil, she pulled out two, round, metallic-looking patches two inches in diameter. She stuck the first one on top of his hand centered over the embedded chip and the other one on his palm. "They're woven from metal fibers and will block the signal."

"Are you sure these will stay in place?"

"Uh, yeah. I used super glue."

"Oh great."

She stuck two large beige Band-Aids over the metallic patches. "Be ready with a story to explain these."

"Dart goalie." Looking up at Tim, he asked, "Are we going to drive to St. Louis?"

Uncharacteristically, Tim smiled. "No, I have another option."

28

PHANTOM

Tim drove three hours east to Augusta Airport in Maine. When they arrived, he went to the general aviation side of the airport. Punching in a code, they drove across the tarmac to a small hangar. Josh followed Tim inside and saw a beautiful Gulfstream G650 business jet.

Tim walked up to the man standing next to it and said, "It's good to see you."

They shook hands and the man said, "You too. Didn't think I'd ever see you again." Glancing back at the jet, he added, "She's fueled and ready to go. Got her listed on the board as undergoing annual flight inspection and maintenance, so they won't be looking for her for a while. Of course, it's got new tail numbers assigned to a business in Australia."

"Thanks, really appreciate this."

The man smiled. "Least I could do for you after what you did for me."

"If you don't hear from us in a reasonable time—"

The man finished, "I wasn't here, neither were you. Someone stole the plane." He shook hands again, winked at Josh and Sheri, and left.

Tim turned to Josh. "She's all yours."

"How'd you know I wanted one of these for my birthday?"

"You can fly this, right?"

With a look of disdain, Josh headed up the steps into the jet. At the top of the stairs, he looked back at Tim and said, "There's a manual in here, right?" He smiled as he saw Tim and Sheri look at each other.

In the cockpit, he quickly committed the flight manual to

memory. As he finished, he looked back to see Tim loading a few boxes on the jet. When he'd finished, Tim joined him in the cockpit.

Josh looked at him. "This thing's got some options you don't generally see on a biz jet."

Looking innocent, Tim said, "Leather seats?"

"And a full Electronic Counter Measures suite with an anti-missile chaff and flare dispenser." With a half-smile, he added, "Let me guess. This was the CIA Director's personal jet?" Before Tim responded, Josh put up his hand. "Never mind. I don't want to know." Josh stood up. "Let me file a flight plan and we'll pull chocks."

He'd never flown a Gulfstream or any business jet for that matter, but he wasn't worried. It had the latest automation and displays and this was one talent he was born with.

He flew it from the right seat — where the copilot usually sat — because it was more natural for him to have the throttles on the left, like a fighter.

The takeoff went smoothly. He was a little behind trying to follow departure instructions while getting a feel for the jet, but quickly caught up and enjoyed flying the big Gulfstream.

After they were at cruising altitude, Sheri joined them in the cockpit.

Josh said, "I think I know who has the information and probably which office the data would be kept in, but we can't just waltz in and take it."

Tim said, "Actually, that's exactly what we're going to do. We'll connect one of our phones to a local computer."

Sheri smiled. "Although Jen wasn't able to get the files, while you were hiking, she got me some information on the personnel at the Phantom Works. I picked up a summer white uniform for you."

Josh gave her a questioning look, but Tim said, "Don't worry. Just get us over to the Boeing side of the airport. Tell 'em you're from the government and you're here to help."

Josh was impressed with the jet's handling in the landing configuration. He knew St. Louis International like the back of his hand and it had nice long runways, but the test was — how well could he take a jet he'd never flown, and grease it in for a perfect landing. He nailed it.

Taxiing directly to the Boeing flight line, he called them on their base frequency and told them he was from Naval Air Systems Command.

They were clearly surprised, but since NAVAIR was one of Boeing's biggest customers, they respond with a, "Yes sir," and sent someone out to park their jet. They ended up chocked next to one of the new Advanced Super Hornets.

Josh changed into the summer white uniform Sheri acquired. Coming out of the bathroom, he shook his head. "Sheri, the pants are too tight."

"Turn around."

As he did, she said, "Nope. They're appropriate for the mission."

He gave her a questioning look.

"The Phantom Works office manager is late thirties and recently divorced."

"How'd you find that out?"

"Facebook."

"OK, so…?"

Sheri shook her head in disgust. "Josh, sometimes you're truly clueless."

"What?!"

She rolled her eyes. "The only thing women find hotter than a cute fighter pilot with a nice butt … is a cute fighter pilot with a nice butt," she raised an eyebrow, "that's interested in them."

Tim wore a suit and put on glasses that transmitted what he saw and heard back to Jen and Sheri. They put tiny transmitters in their ear so Sheri and Jen could talk to them.

They left the jet and went to the flight-line office. Wearing fake Boeing ID's, they introduced themselves to the flight line manager.

"I didn't have anything on the schedule about a visit from NAVAIR."

Josh said, "Sorry. That's my fault. It's one of those fast trips so we can work out some last minute funding details on the X-84. Can you run us over the Phantom Works?"

"Of course. Do you need your jet fueled?"

"Uh, yes."

"Charge it to the NAVAIR account?"

"Ah … yeah, that would be great."

The Phantom Works building was close to flight operations, so the flight line manager took them over in a golf cart. From the flight side, they were able to enter the Phantom Works from the hangar and avoid the gate guard. As they headed in, Tim looked at Josh and quietly asked, "X-84?"

"No idea, but it sounds good."

The flight line manager brought them in to introduce them to the Phantom Works office manager who was standing on a chair trying to hang a picture on the wall.

Tasha Clarkson was as Sheri described her. As she set the picture down, she looked irritated at their unexpected arrival.

Josh quickly asked for Dave Lavery, the head of the Phantom Works and former manager of the Wraith program. From Jen, they already knew he wasn't there.

Clarkson said, "He's flying back from headquarters in Seattle today." Frowning she asked, "Was he expecting you?"

Josh identified her as a schedule driven personality. She was petite and reminded him a little of Sheri both in build and personality.

"Ms. Clarkson, I totally apologize. I got my dates confused and thought he was coming back yesterday. I'll send him a text. Do you know when his flight arrives?"

She softened a little. Looking on her computer screen, she said, "His flight should be landing in a couple hours."

Josh gave her his best smile. "Would it be OK if we just wait here?"

She didn't smile but looked less irritated. "Sure, that'll be fine. There's some coffee over there."

Josh picked up the picture she was trying to hang. "I might as well be useful."

She shook her head. "That won't be necessary."

"It's the least I can do and height has its advantages." He walked over to the wall and placed it about where she had it.

He heard Sheri in his ear. "Nice."

"Maybe a little higher."

He got up on the chair and held it higher.

She came around from behind her desk and stood behind Josh.

Tim slowly moved behind her and toward her desk.

"Hmmm, maybe a little to the left and higher."

Josh heard Sheri say, "She's checking you out."

"A little further left and a little higher."

Josh complied as Tim slipped behind her desk and plugged into her computer.

"That's it, right there." She handed him a pen.

He made a small mark on the wall. As he turned around, he saw Tim behind her desk bending over.

She said, "OK, now I just need the hammer." As she started to turn around, Josh purposefully slipped off the chair and jumped to the floor just inches from her.

"Oh my! Are you alright?" She put a hand on his arm.

Josh smiled. "Just clumsy."

Still standing very close, he said, "At the risk of a sexual harassment charge, I've got to tell you, you have beautiful eyes."

She blushed. "I don't think that qualifies as sexual harassment."

They heard Jen in their ear, "There's nothing classified on this computer and it's not hooked to any of the others, but it does indicate the computer in the program manager's office has classified stuff."

Tim quickly unplugged the phone and moved back around the desk.

Josh said, "It's lunch time, do you know a good place to eat around here?"

"Bandana's has pretty good food and they're fast."

Josh smiled again. "I don't suppose you can show us where that is and ... maybe join us?"

She frowned.

Josh was thinking he moved too fast, but heard Sheri say, "Nice touch."

She finally nodded. "Sure, no sense in you sitting around here waiting and it *is* lunch time."

Tim took the cue and held up a folder he was carrying. "We probably don't want to take this with us."

She said, "You can leave that here."

Josh frowned. "It's got some very sensitive material in it for Dave. Would it be OK to leave it in his office? I know his office has a cipher lock and I'd feel more comfortable."

She frowned again. "I'm really not supposed to open his office when he's not here," she paused and then smiled, "but I guess it would be OK since he's inbound."

They follow her down the hall to his office. They looked the other way while she entered the code.

Opening it, she turned on the light.

Without being invited, Tim went in and said, "I'll just set this on his desk."

Josh immediately said, "Are you from St. Louis originally?"

"Actually, I was born in New Orleans but my family…"

Josh sidestepped slightly away from the door, so she had to turn away from the office to face him.

Jen said, "Oh, oh, just checked Dave Lavery's airline reservations. He caught an earlier flight and he's on his way over to your location right now."

29

PLUTONIUM

Josh kept eye contact as she finished up with, "...so I ended up in St. Louis."

Remembering the information Sheri pulled from Facebook, he asked, "Do you like to travel?"

"Absolutely love it!"

"If you could go anywhere, where would you love to go?"

She paused, "I've always wanted to visit Peru and see the ruins in the Andes."

Josh said, "I've been to Machu Picchu in the Andes. It is amazing. You really need to go there."

She smiled. "I'd love to!"

Tim came back through the door. "Thanks."

Jen said, "The program manager is pulling into the parking lot right now."

Josh pulled out his phone. "Sorry, gotta take this." Talking to no one, he said, "Are you sure? ... Right now?" He put his phone back in his pocket and said to Tim, "A General Accounting Office audit team just showed up at NAVAIR. Bob wants us back ASAP." He knew that to defense contractors, the GAO was more terrifying than a mother-in-law visit.

She gave them a flinch look. "Ouch."

Josh said, "Sorry, looks like lunch will have to wait. Could you grab that folder from Dave's office please?"

She came back with the folder and gave it to Tim. Then she gave Josh a business card. "Just in case you can't get through to the office to reschedule, I put my cell number on the back."

He took it and shook her hand, holding it an extra second.

She asked, "Can I have the flight manager pick you up?"

"No. No thanks. It's a nice day. We'll just walk back." He paused. "By the way, can you do me a big favor? I shouldn't have mentioned the GAO visit. It's not related to any of the projects here and I don't want to freak Dave out."

"Sure. I won't mention that if you don't tell him I let you into his office."

Jen said, "He's entering the building."

Josh winked as they headed out the door.

They jogged back to flight ops and told them they needed to leave immediately.

As soon as they were onboard, Sheri said, "Jen and I have been looking at the material you pulled off the computer. Boeing shut down the program in the U.S., but we think we know who the technology was licensed to."

"Who?"

"Safran, one of the biggest French defense contractors."

Tim asked, "Where are they manufacturing them?"

"It doesn't say but a lot of the drone test equipment was flown to a facility in Van, Turkey."

"What can you tell us about the facility?"

As Josh started the engines, Sheri pulled up Google maps. "Looks like an unmarked, two story industrial building surrounded by a fence."

Jen added, "They have an extensive security system and I'm seeing NATO type vehicles parked out front."

Josh said, "Bingo."

Sheri added, "It's right next to the airport in Van."

"I'll file a flight plan directly to the Ferit Melen Airport."

Tim looked at Josh. "Does this thing have enough range?"

"Yeah but it's tight." He did a quick calculation in his head. "It's about 13 hours from here. It would be best to refuel on the east coast. Is there any food onboard? I'm starving."

Tim poked around the galley. "Just coffee and crackers."

"OK, we need to get out of here quickly and filing an international flight plan takes too long. There's a small municipal airport on Cape Cod called Barnstable, where we can file and refuel."

Tim nodded. "Why Cape Cod?"

"They've got a place right by the airport that has incredible lobster rolls."

Sheri said, "I love lobster rolls."

Tim just shook his head.

After they landed, Sheri said, "Tim and I'll go out and grab some food and groceries. Josh, it's a long flight, why don't you get some sleep."

He nodded. "I'll get us filed and catch a nap."

As Tim and Sheri grabbed a cab and headed into town, Tim said, "By the way, good idea using Josh as a distraction. You're a natural at this game."

"I'm a psychiatrist," she smiled, "but it doesn't take a PhD. Josh's a girl magnet."

He smiled. "And what defines a girl magnet?"

She smiled back. "You."

"Nice try."

She laughed. "There are tons of good looking guys out there, but one of the things that makes guys particularly attractive is when they don't *know* they're attractive." She shrugged. "Josh must have been an ugly kid."

Lying in one of the extremely comfortable reclining leather chairs, Josh heard them return, but kept his eyes closed until the smell of lobster hit him. His internal clock said he got two hours of sleep, which was equivalent to five for most people.

They didn't bother with the fine china the jet came with. Quickly devouring the butter soaked lobster rolls, they finished with giant slices of strawberry cheesecake.

After checking the weather, Josh got their clearance and took off.

This time, Sheri sat in the left seat. As soon as they reached cruising altitude, he set the autopilot and Tim joined them.

They put Jen on the speakerphone. "Based on the information you pulled off the computer, what can you tell us about the nano-drone specs?"

"They have similar specifications to a mosquito. They're

about the same size and maneuverability and can operate for weeks."

Josh shook his head, "How'd they pull that off? No battery can last that long."

"They don't use batteries. They use radioisotope thermoelectric generators powered by plutonium-238."

Sheri's eyes got wide. "They're nuclear?"

"Yup."

Josh slapped his forehead. "Of course. NASA's used that technology to power deep space probes for decades." He whistled. "But shrinking it that small ... that's impressive."

Frowning, Sheri said, "But with plutonium, aren't they like radioactive?"

Jen replied, "Yes, but when encapsulated and shielded, they're pretty safe. They've even been used to power pacemakers. Although, with the nano-drone's size, there's little shielding. As long as they're flying around, there should be minimal exposure danger."

Josh raised an eyebrow. "Probably don't want to eat or breathe one in."

"No, and the documents indicate the plutonium power source was why they were restricted from use in the United States."

Tim asked, "Any other limitations?"

"Yes. They transmit audio and video but the signal is very weak. They need a special satellite overhead with minimal obstructions, or they need a receiver close by. That could be a regular drone."

Josh looked at Tim. "OK, so, what's the plan?"

"We need Jen to access their network, but this time we can't BS our way in. I'm afraid we're going to have to break in and—"

Josh started humming the **Mission Impossible** theme song.

Sheri joined in.

Looking up under half-closed eyelids, Tim just shook his head.

IV

SURVEILLANCE

30

TURKEY

"Colonel Crow, Dr. Turan will see you now."

She went into his office and shook his hand.

He motioned her to a seat in front of his desk.

Wendy took a deep breath. "Dr. Turan, first I need to apologize for my behavior at the ball. I don't drink very often and in my excitement about being considered for command ... well, I had a few too many. I apologize and *promise* that will *never* happen again."

Turan smiled. "Colonel, you make it sound like you were swinging from the chandeliers. You didn't do or say anything offensive or untrue. You simply ended up in an awkward situation." He paused. "In this era, everyone is supposed to be socially conscious and politically correct, but *you* are a military officer. I find it hypocritical of society to want you to kill for your country and then not burp in public. You're a warrior and you've sworn an allegiance to protect your country and now the entire world. You don't have to apologize to me or anyone else for having some fun now and then."

"Thank you, sir."

"Before we discuss the command opportunity ... there's something I'd like to hear your thoughts on."

She realized this was an interview. "Yes sir?"

"Wendy, I've been thinking a lot about what happened on the station. I've been working with Admiral Meadows and now Commander Fuze, as well as military, law enforcement and intelligence agencies around the world." He paused. "This is very sensitive, so please don't repeat this outside this room, but so far our investigations have gone nowhere. Frankly, it scares me and I don't scare easily. There's an organization out there that's not only powerful and deadly but sophisticated and stealthy." He frowned. "So far, they've kept one step ahead of us. If you hadn't uncovered their plot, we would have only found out about it after they incinerated something or someone."

She nodded.

"Bear with me for a second." He paused. "What if we were to turn the tables and use their plan against them?"

She shook her head. "I'm not following you, sir."

"Wendy, I've been in the intelligence community and you're military. The terrorists created the ability to use the laser as a weapon of unprecedented power and precision. What if, in an emergency, and with authorization of the Secretary-General and U.S. Command Authority, we were to use the laser to target the terrorist organization that tried to kill you and Commander Fuze, and probably assassinated the Director of National Intelligence?"

She frowned. "I guess I'm having trouble understanding why we would ever need to use the ISLO as a weapon."

Turan nodded. "As you know, I've combated terrorist groups my entire life. One of my greatest frustrations was time. I can't tell you how many times we would get intelligence about meetings between the top terrorist leaders — intelligence that sometimes cost operatives their lives — but by the time we organized an air or ground strike, they were long gone. Even when the ISLO is parked at L2, it still only takes six seconds for the laser to hit Earth."

She nodded. "If your target is on the night side of the planet." Frowning, she continued, "I'm an Air Force officer and I certainly have no moral problem incinerating terrorists. My concern is that we violate the international agreement on the peaceful use of space and risk losing universal public support for the ISLO ... and the funding that represents."

"Well spoken. You're a pragmatic warrior and perceptive about the public ramifications." He paused. "So — hypothetically speaking — if U.S. Command Authority and the Secretary-General of the U.N. directed a very limited surgical strike using the laser on a clearly identified terrorist target, you wouldn't have an objection on moral grounds and would carry out the order?"

"Personally, I think because of the collateral damage to the program and potentially the U.N., using the ISLO as a weapon would be a very bad idea." She sighed. "With that said, if I were given a joint U.N. and U.S. Command Authority order to target a *clearly* identified and limited target, I would carry out that order without hesitation."

Turan nodded. "It would have to be an extremely critical and absolutely compelling reason to use it in that capacity." He stood up. "I believe you and I have the same mindset." He shook her hand and looked at his watch. "I'll see you at the quarterly program status brief this afternoon ... where I will have the opportunity to introduce the new ISLO Commander. Congratulations Colonel Crow."

Sheri poked her head into the cockpit as they approached Turkey. "Those reclining chairs are awesome for sleeping and even the shower isn't bad."

Tim got out of the copilot seat and said, "I'll wrestle us up some food."

The sun was starting to set as Josh made his approach.

Sheri, sitting in the copilot seat, said, "Wow. Those are beautiful snowcapped peaks and that lake's huge." Pointing ahead, she asked, "Is that the city of Van?"

Josh nodded. "It sits on the eastern coast of the lake and is surrounded by some pretty rugged terrain. Population's about a half million."

Josh made an uneventful approach to the single runway. After they landed, they ate and Josh took a quick shower. When he came out, he saw Tim pulling a large, sleek, hex-copter drone from one of the boxes. Jet-black, it had a camera pod and large IR lights mounted underneath.

Josh whistled. "Nice."

"This model has excellent low light and IR capability and is exceptionally quiet."

Josh nodded. "CIA?"

Tim shook his head. "Amazon." Pointing at the tablet in Sheri's hands, Tim added, "This'll allow Sheri and Jen to be our eyes in the sky and see anyone moving on the ground near us."

Sheri shook her head. "I can't fly one of these."

"You don't have to. I'll program it to hover in a position overhead. I'll show you how to move the camera and zoom in and out. You and Jen can watch the display." He paused. "Jen, you can fly one of these if needed can't you?"

"I'll have to learn how first." In less than a second, she said, "OK, I know how now."

Sheri shrugged. "Guess us girls got it covered."

Tim pulled out a small electronic box with wires sticking out. "Jen, I have a device that can be physically connected to most security systems to monitor and spoof them. Can you access it?"

"Sure. Just connect it to a phone."

Tim and Josh rented a car. The facility they were targeting was only a few minutes from the airport. They waited until dark. Then dressed in black, they parked a few blocks from the facility.

Putting on the camera glasses and earpiece, they heard Sheri say, "OK, the drone's 200 feet above your position. I can see most of the facility." She paused. "There's someone patrolling the grounds just inside the fence. Looks like ... it took him about 15 minutes to make a round. He just passed your position."

Tim pointed. "We'll cut through the bottom of the fence there."

Jen added, "The fence has IR cameras with motion detectors at each corner."

"Jen, fly the drone down in front of the camera closest to us and use the drone's IR spotlight to blind it. We just need enough time to connect you to the security system."

"Will do."

As they watched the drone drop, Tim nodded to Josh. They got out of the car and ran to the fence.

The drone hovered right in front of the camera, its IR light pointing at the lens.

Tim quickly cut the bottom of the fence. They slipped through, found the camera cable and clamped a metal fitting over it. After attaching the spoofing box, he said, "Jen?"

She replied in their ear, "I'm in and have control of the security system. I'm feeding bogus video to the camera above you."

They looked up and saw the drone climbing back into the

sky.

"If you head straight toward the building, there's an access door just to the right that I unlocked."

As they ran toward it, she said, "From the internal cameras, it doesn't look like anyone is near the door but I can't see everywhere, so be careful."

Tim, with his Taser drawn, carefully opened the door and peeked inside. He nodded to Josh. They slipped in and found themselves in a hallway.

Jen said, "If you can find a computer connected to their internal network, I should be able to hack it."

Tim tried the doors in the hall. They were all locked. They jogged to the end of the hall and looked around the corner. There was another hall with large glass windows looking into a well-lit laboratory. The lab door had a cipher lock. They moved quickly toward the door but before they got there, they saw someone inside the lab coming toward the door.

Tim grabbed the doorknob of the door across the hall from the lab. It opened and they slipped inside. It was someone's office. The lights were on but it was thankfully empty.

Josh moved around the desk as Tim cracked the door and peeked out. The computer was on, but it displayed a password screen and there was also a security card scanner attached.

Jen saw what Josh was seeing and said, "Plug your phone into one of the computer's ports and give me a few seconds to crack the card reader."

They heard someone outside approaching. Tim closed and locked the door just in time.

The doorknob turned slightly. They heard an irritated voice on the other side. Josh was learning Turkish and easily translated the simple statement to Tim, "Crap, left my keys in the lab."

Jen said, "I'm in and downloading data. There's a lot of it so it'll take a minute."

Tim unlocked the door and peeked out. "He went back into the lab. Jen, is there anything you can do to delay him inside there?"

"Yes. The laboratory door is a cipher lock controlled by the security system. I just locked him in."

"Perfect."

She added, "Almost finished."

Peeking out with Tim, Josh saw the man now trying to get out of the lab. They didn't need a translation. The man angrily picked up a wall phone and called someone. They couldn't leave until he moved away from the door.

While they were waiting, Jen said, "I'm going through the data I have so far. In addition to manufacturing the nano-drones, they also make two types of RFID tracking chips. The smaller ones are passive or unpowered. They have a maximum detection range of about 100 meters, but they also make a bigger active chip. It allows subjects to be tracked from aircraft and even specially equipped satellites."

Josh asked, "How could it be strong enough for a satellite to track it?"

"Because it's also powered by plutonium."

"Wow. No wonder Boeing didn't want to mess with this stuff."

Tim added, "They probably reserve the active capsules for high value targets."

Jen continued, "It looks like they're all going to NATO Special Forces units or intelligence agencies like the British SIS."

Tim nodded. "That's who should be getting them." He paused. "Jen, can you access their security records and see if there were any break-ins? Also, check their production schedules for missing or unaccounted for devices."

A couple seconds later, "No security breaches and there's nothing that's missing or unaccounted for." There was a short pause. "But here's something interesting. After the second year of production, the amount of plutonium consumed almost doubled, but the production of new drones and transmitters stayed the same."

"What about other raw materials?"

"That doubled too *and* so did the assembly line time."

Josh raised his eyebrows. "So, they're working twice as hard and using twice as much material to deliver the same number of drones."

Tim asked, "Jen, who's in charge of inventory?"

"Marek Brazda. He's also in charge of shipping and happens to be the night manager in charge of production."

Josh nodded. "How convenient. Is there any way you can access his phone and see who he's been calling?"

"I could if it were turned on, but it's not."

Tim said, "I thought you could turn phones on."

"I could before The Great Tech Out. After that, they modified the BOTIC chip on all new phones, but *you* can turn his phone on."

"How?"

"You're in his office."

Josh went back to the desk, opened the top drawer and held up a phone. Smiling, he turned it on.

Jen added, "OK, I've downloaded everything."

Tim, still peeking out the door, said, "He's finally going back into the lab, let's go!"

"You can leave his phone behind. As soon as it boots up I'll be able to access it."

Josh dropped it back in the drawer and unplugged the cable from the computer.

Tim opened the door, locked it from the inside, and pulled it shut behind them. They ran down the hall. They heard the lab door open behind them as they turned the corner. Bolting out the exit door, they heard, "Wait!" in their headset.

They skidded to a stop, almost running into each other, and froze.

Sheri whispered, "The roving patrol is coming around the building to your right."

They flattened themselves against the building's exterior wall and remained motionless.

As the guard walked into their view, they heard their normally quiet hex drone go to full throttle and make a high speed pass outside the fence. It wasn't visible but it made just enough noise to get the guard's attention so that he looked toward the fence.

As he passed, Jen said, "I put a little bug in their security system that will give you 30 seconds after you disconnect the tap before the camera goes live."

When the guard was out of sight, they quietly ran to the fence, disconnected the box and slipped through.

Tim bent the bottom of the fence back so a close inspection would be required to see that it had been cut.

As they got back in the car, Tim asked, "Jen, were you able to access the contacts on his phone?"

"Yes Tim. I'm pretty good at that." She giggled. "It was my first career."

Smiling, Josh asked, "So, what did you find?"

"Most of them are personal phones or every day commercial numbers like dry cleaners. However, there's a pattern of calls over a couple years to the same number. He used an encrypted app for those calls. He also made all them at night and from this facility."

As they headed back to the airport, Tim asked, "Who was he calling?"

"It wasn't easy to track because the number was redirected through several switchboards to hide the destination, but the number was to an office in a company called Solak."

Tim frowned. "Why does that name sound familiar?"

Sheri inserted, "Probably because they make high-end watches. I used to have one."

Jen said, "Yes, they specialize in expensive hybrid watches that combine digital and mechanical movements. They also make high-fashion fitness trackers and smart watches."

"Where are they located?"

"Their manufacturing facility is in downtown Van, about 15 minutes from the airport."

Josh asked, "Jen could you find any information about the facility?"

"Construction records show they made a major modification to it three years ago. It was very expensive *and* they have a license to handle nuclear isotopes."

Sheri said, "Bingo."

After they got back to the jet, they studied the building blueprints that Jen found.

Tim whistled. "This place is protected like a bank vault."

Sheri said, "Their watches aren't *that* nice."

31

COMMAND

Elizabeth watched the U.N. conference room as it filled to capacity. There were at least 200 participants covering the dozens of departments, programs and countries needed to build the largest, most complex object ever assembled in space.

Her seat was near the front of the room. Turning around, she saw the entire back wall covered with cameras and reporters. Meadows had told her that when they originally opened up the quarterly meetings to the media, they assumed it would be similar to the coverage given to congressional hearings. Instead, there was huge media interest with parts of the meetings broadcast live on major networks. Not since the first Moon missions did a space project capture the public's imagination. What could be more exciting and romantic than defending the planet from humanity's most distant outpost? Add the waystation to Mars and the press once became so intrusive Meadows had to threaten to throw them out for disrupting a meeting.

Meadows took the podium. "Welcome to the quarterly ISLO program meeting. To make sure all our interpreters are up and running, please give me a wave if you understand me." Glancing around, he said, "Very good and much better than the response I used to get from my teenagers." He continued, "First, I want to congratulate all of you. We are extremely close to full operational capability. Our primary goal at this meeting is to determine the critical path items between us and boosting the ISLO to its new home."

As the conference progressed, the critical paths became clear.

Finally Meadows said, "OK, we've been meeting for two

hours, covered all the major systems and identified the elephants in the room. Let's adjourn for 30 minutes and release everyone except the reactor cooling and TELEMED programs," Meadows smiled, "so the rest of you could get back to work." There were good-natured groans. "Before we wrap up, however, Dr. Turan has an important announcement."

Turan joined him on stage. "Thank you, Admiral. I'd like to thank Colonel Steven Dale for his incredible work commanding the ISLO through its construction. He's done an outstanding job and as he prepares to move on to new challenges, I understand he'll be putting on General stars." There was a strong round of applause. "I'd also like to take this opportunity to announce the name of the next ISLO commander, who will be taking the station to operational status and moving her out to her new home — Colonel Wendy Crow."

Elizabeth raised her eyebrows in surprise. She noticed that as Wendy stood up and gave a small wave, she glanced at Elizabeth.

As they temporarily adjourned, many came over to congratulate the new Commander, including Elizabeth. The press, however, arrived first and mobbed Crow. This was big news and having a Commander that looked like a movie star didn't hurt.

After 30 minutes, Meadows chased the press away so they could reconvene.

As the room settled down, the engineer in charge of the reactor spoke first. He explained in detail why the cooling system didn't have the capacity needed to fire the laser continuously. The fix was simply installing more cooling panels, which were on the way to the station.

As the new head of the ISLO's TELEMED program, it was Elizabeth's turn. She stood and said, "This is cutting edge technology and although the robotic systems have been used operationally, they've all been hardwired with fiber optics. We need a lot of bandwidth for the high-definition 3D control and feedback." She paused. "We're running into interference problems from the station's other systems and struggling to maintain enough bandwidth."

Someone asked, "Is this really a critical path item? Can't we fix it after we go operational?"

"Yes, it's technically possible but—"

Wendy interrupted, "With the time to return a sick or injured person to Earth, several weeks or even a month, it's essential we have the ability to do major surgery on site. I actually witnessed a medical emergency while I was up there. We don't boost until we're satisfied the surgical suite can perform as advertised."

Tight-lipped, Elizabeth just nodded.

After more technical discussions, they finally broke up with several action items, but it was clear the TELEMED surgical suite was *the* critical path.

As the conference room began to empty, Wendy asked Elizabeth, "May I talk to you privately?"

"Of course."

They quickly realized the press was waiting impatiently to swarm her again. Wendy held up a hand to them and said, "I'm sorry, I just need a moment and I'll join you outside."

When they were finally alone, Wendy said, "Do you need any more personnel to expedite?"

"No thank you. I think we're properly staffed."

Wendy glanced around. The room was mostly empty and no one was nearby. She quietly said, "Look, I'm sorry about what happened at the ball."

Elizabeth, already irritated, quickly replied, "Sorry about what happened at the ball ... or on the station?"

Wendy's expression hardened. "You don't know what happened on the station."

Keeping her voice under control, she said, "I understand you slept together."

"You understand nothing!" Wendy stopped and took a deep breath. Continuing in a quieter voice, she said, "Apparently, there's nothing I can say that will change your perception of me or what happened." She shook her head. "But I don't see how you are in any position to throw stones."

"What does that mean?"

"I think you know. Everyone else does. If you're moving on with someone else, for God's sake, let him go."

"What are you talking about?!"

Wendy held up her hand. "We don't need to be talking about

this here. In fact, we don't need to be talking about this at all. We're going to have to work together and right now, all I need from you is a working surgical suite."

Elizabeth closed her eyes for a second and then said, "We will get the system working but don't forget ... I don't work for you."

As Wendy turned to go, she said, "Yeah, we all know who you ... *work* for."

32

SOLAK

Josh and Tim drove to the building at midnight. It was near the center of the city. Three stories high, it occupied half a city block. At the front of the building was a contemporary, high-end storefront with a display window and above it, the name "Solak" tastefully engraved.

They drove around the block. There were no doors or windows on the side of the building. In the back, there was only one loading dock with a large well-lit employee entrance at the top of several steps. Lights and security cameras were everywhere.

They continued around the other side and found a narrow alley separating it from the building next to it. There were no doors or windows on this side either.

Josh looked up and Tim followed his gaze. "You thinking what I'm thinking?"

Tim said, "Jen, see what you can find about the building across the alley from Solak."

She replied, "It looks like warehousing of textiles on the first two floors and some office spaces on the third. Doesn't appear to be related in ownership to Solak."

They parked a few blocks away.

Within minutes, Tim had them inside the warehouse and quickly disabled the security system. It appeared unoccupied at night. They climbed the stairwell to the roof where Tim quietly jimmied the door.

Using the rooftop air-conditioning units as cover, they moved to the edge and looked across the alley. The roof of the Solak building was at the same level but well lit with security cameras near the roof's entrance and one at each corner of the building.

Tim pulled out small binoculars and studied the roof. Finally he said, "We'll have to use a cable entry, but the cameras are hardwired and the wires are inside metal conduits." He shook his head, "Tapping into their security system won't be easy. I can go across and you could monitor—"

"I know you don't want to volunteer me," Josh interrupted, "but in this situation, you're the brains, I'm the brawn. I go in, you cover me." He knew he was right when Tim didn't argue.

"I need to go back down to the car and get additional equipment. Watch the cameras and see if you see them move or follow any pattern."

Josh nodded.

While getting equipment, Tim quietly ran over the plan on his headset with Josh, Sheri and Jen. When he returned, he carried two large bags. From the first, he pulled a harness and steel cable attached to what looked like a grenade launcher. From the second, he pulled their trusty hex-copter drone.

Josh put on the harness and they moved forward to an air conditioner close to the roof's edge. Tim anchored the cable and said, "Jen, go ahead with the car."

"You said we are going to pay their insurance deductible correct?"

Josh smiled. "Absolutely."

She giggled. "OK. I love driving autonomous cars."

Tim took aim and waited.

From below, they heard a car engine rev and a slight screech of tires, as an empty S Class Mercedes accelerated by their building. It was immediately followed by a loud, echoing crash as the big car struck another empty parked car.

At the same time, Tim fired the cable across the alley to the other roof.

They watched the cameras around the top of the building swivel toward where the accident occurred.

Tim nodded to Josh. "Cover your face."

Josh pulled a ski mask over his face and ran to the edge of the roof. He clipped his harness onto the cable and slid over the edge. It was a rush as he crossed the alley and hit the wall of the

Solak building, cushioning the impact with his feet.

Jen guided the hex-copter in front of the camera closest to him and Tim said, "You're clear."

Josh chinned himself over the wall and squatted down under the post holding the camera. With a small rotary cutter, he sliced through the conduit, fished out the wires and connected the spoofing box.

Jen pulled the drone up and away. "I'm in, but this security system is more sophisticated and compartmentalized. I can control the roof cameras and unlock the roof door, but I have no visibility inside the building. I'm going to run the cameras through a diagnostic, which will give you 20 seconds to disconnect the spoofing box and take it inside."

Josh disconnected it and ran to the roof door. Opening it slowly, he peeked inside. He could see a video camera pointed at the door but no one around. Shining his flashlight into the camera's lens, he slipped into the dark stairwell and rushed to the opposite side directly under the camera. He reached up and clipped the spoofing box wires to the camera leads.

Jen said, "OK. I now have access to all the internal and external cameras and some of the door locks."

Tim said, "I'm coming over."

After Tim joined him, they crept down one flight of stairs and moved quietly through the building. They saw windows along the hallway that looked down into an impeccable factory area with rows of workstations, currently unoccupied. It appeared just as Josh would expect a watch factory to look.

Tim whispered, "The blueprint said the new construction is at the back of the building."

At the end of the hall, they found a door with a sign that read in Turkish, "Special Access."

Jen got them through the door.

On the other side was an empty room with blue gowns, hats, gloves and surgical masks. They look at each other, shrugged and put them on. The next door required scanning a security card.

"Jen, can you open this one?"

The door opened. It looked like a high tech NASA clean room where satellites are assembled. There were eight workstations with people sitting at each. No one noticed Josh and Tim. They were working with great concentration, looking either into microscopes or at monitors that displayed what the microscopes saw.

Tim pointed at one of the monitors.

The woman technician was using tiny robotic tweezers to open one of the larger powered tracking capsules. As they watched, she opened it and removed the transmitter and power source. Then she brought in a new, slightly longer capsule and transplanted the transmitter and power source into the new capsule. She spent several minutes connecting or modifying the contents before closing the capsule. It was some type of transplant operation, but why? What was special about the new longer capsules? Looking closely, he noticed that sticking out of the side of the new capsules were tiny curved hooks that looked like crab claws.

Josh scanned the monitors on the other workstations until he found someone doing something different. This technician was working on a fashionable, but conventional looking smart watch or fitness tracker bracelet.

Tim pointed to the middle of the room. There were two racks of small jewelry-sized boxes.

Josh casually walked over. The first rack contained boxes with "Safran" and NATO markings. Clearly, these were the incoming deliveries. He peered into one of the open boxes. With his exceptional vision, he saw each contained one tiny nano-drone and a plutonium powered transmitter capsule.

Then he went to the second rack. These boxes all had the Solak name and logo. Clearly, they were the outgoing shipments. Each one had a nano-drone but they also contained a new, longer capsule. Next to them were larger boxes with smart watches in a variety of colors. He shook his head.

A voice from the far end of the room said in Turkish, "What are you doing?"

In his peripheral vision, Josh saw a man stand up from one of the workstations. Josh casually walked back toward Tim and the exit. Over his shoulder, he responded in Turkish, "Quality Assurance."

The man said, "What? Who are you?"

Josh waved his hand over his shoulder. "Mr. Solak sent us."

"Wait! Who is that?"

Jen opened the door. As Tim and Josh walked quickly through, Josh looked back and saw the man following them.

Tim said, "Jen, please close the door and lock it."

They ran back down the hall, but Jen said, "Wait, the call from the NATO Lab went to the next office on your left."

They skidded to a stop.

Jen added, "Someone's in there, but I disabled their camera, phone and security system."

Josh opened the door and they rushed in with pistols drawn.

In Turkish, Josh said, "Don't move!"

They saw the man's right hand slip under the desk and knew he was trying to activate the alarm.

Josh repeated. "I said don't move! Your alarm has been deactivated."

The man frowned but didn't look afraid.

"Who are the drones and capsules being shipped to?"

The man leaned back in his chair and laughed.

Josh said, "Stealing classified NATO property carries a life sentence."

He shook his head and with a look of disdain said, "You have no idea what you're involved with."

Josh said, "You'll tell us or lose a limb."

He looked less confident but said, "Nothing can scare me now and it wouldn't matter if I told you. You're already dead." With that, he leaned forward and grabbed something under his desk.

Tim and Josh yelled, "Freeze!"

He ignored them as he pulled out an Uzi.

Tim hit him with the Taser, but the submachine gun went off, spraying the ceiling as he fell backwards in his chair. Tim kicked the gun from his hand and then kicked him in the head, knocking him out.

A second later, an alarm siren went off.

They grabbed his laptop and cell phone and ran down the hall, but security guards were approaching from the direction they came in.

They reversed course and ran the other way. Down the stairs, they ran straight to the main exit. There were two security guards and another coming in the front door.

Tim slammed the door against the head of one, tased another and Josh swept the third man's feet and tased him as he fell. They jumped over the bodies and bolted out the door.

As they got outside, they saw a police car with lights on coming from the direction of their car.

They ran in the other direction as Josh said, "We're going to need alternate transportation."

Running down an alley, Tim pointed at a small jellybean shaped subcompact ahead.

Josh said, "Chery QQ. No!"

They ran along the street as fast as they could, but there were few cars to be seen. Turning down another alley, they saw a car parked ahead, but before they could reach it, another car came around the corner at high speed heading right at them.

With nowhere to go, Tim pulled his gun and crouched in a firing position.

Jen said, "Wait!"

The car slammed on its brakes, stopping one car length from them, as Jen said, "Get in."

Josh yelled, "It's a Tesla and it's empty!" He saw the charging cable still attached and dragging the ground. "Great work, Jen!"

Jen said, "I love driving these cars."

Josh jumped into the driver's seat.

Jen added, "Your route's plotted on the screen and it's in "Plaid Speed" mode."

Smiling, Josh floored it the second Tim was inside. With aircraft carrier catapult acceleration, he had to back off immediately as he approached the cross street.

Jen said, "I've tapped into the city's traffic monitoring system. You're clear. Turn right."

As he slid around the corner and accelerated down the street, Josh said, "Sheri! I need you to start the jet's engines."

She replied, "Uh ... I don't even know where the ignition key is."

"It doesn't have one. Don't worry; I'll walk you through it."

He heard multiple sirens approaching from two directions.

Jen said, "While you're helping her with the jet, I can drive the car. I know the tire coefficients of friction and the asphalt grip. I can see all the traffic from above and tap into the police car's GPS."

"Jen, there's more to driving fast than knowing coefficients of friction."

"You're right, but I've been practicing with some race cars at the autonomous driving test centers."

He glanced at Tim, who was shaking his head violently.

Josh shrugged and took his hands off the wheel. "Let's see what you got."

Tim looked at him as if he'd lost his mind.

The headlights turned off as the car accelerated and took a corner at high G, missing cars on the other side of the road by inches.

Josh watched the road as he used his photographic memory to walk Sheri through the startup procedure, switch by switch.

They slid sideways, barely avoiding oncoming police cars as Jen said, "Sorry, I wasn't tracking them. They were unmarked." She took them down a narrow alley with their lights off at ludicrous speed. On the other side, they just missed the cross traffic. They accelerated toward an intersection on top of a hill with a red light.

Josh paused his switchology with Sheri to say, "Uh! Jen...!"

They hit the hill and became airborne, narrowly missing the cross traffic. Jen slammed on the brakes and barely made a corner before accelerating again. Josh saw a "battery hot" warning. Jen said, "I'm overriding the battery temperature sensors to maintain full power."

Tim asked, "Won't they catch on fire."

"At these speeds there's a lot of cooling air to keep it under the ignition temperature."

Sheri reported, "I think I got the engines running, but—"

Josh interrupted, "Make sure the parking brake is on. Open the hatch, go outside and kick the chocks away from the wheels."

"OK, but what I was trying to tell you is they haven't fueled the jet yet. I think we're almost out of gas."

33

ESCAPE

Jen ran the Tesla full out. As they headed for the airport gate, she didn't slow down.

Looking ahead at the bar across the gate, Josh asked, "Is that made out of wood or metal?"

Josh and Tim ducked as the car smashed through the gate shattering the windshield.

Jen said, "Might have been metal."

Slamming on the brakes, the car slid to a stop, just feet from the jet's wing. She laughed. "That was so fun."

Hearing multiple police cars closing fast, they jumped out and ran up the steps. Josh slid into the cockpit as Tim closed the jet's hatch.

Jen said, "Oops. I discharged the battery five times faster than it was designed for and forgot that when we stopped, the battery wouldn't get any more cooling air. Plus, a piece of the gate punctured the batteries."

Josh looked outside and behind the wing. The Tesla had flames coming from underneath.

Jen added, "You may want to move the jet away from it before it—"

There was a loud bang and the Tesla looked like it was sitting on top of a blowtorch with flames shooting out every side.

"... does that."

Josh popped the parking brake and pushed the throttles forward. "That's OK Jen. It's another distraction, and yes we'll cover their deductible too."

Looking out the other side of the cockpit, he saw airport police cars approaching rapidly. He selected the tower frequency and heard one aircraft on approach and two waiting in the hold short area to take off. The flashing lights were closing on them with more headed toward the approach end of the runway. To avoid them, he pointed the jet toward the middle of the runway and taxied much faster than he should.

Tim, now sitting in the left seat, saw where he was headed. "Will we have enough runway to takeoff?"

"The published takeoff distance for this thing is 5800 feet and the runway is 9000."

Tim frowned. "Half the runway is only 4500."

"This jet's designed to carry 19 people and four and a half tons of fuel. We got three and less than a ton of gas." He shrugged. "It *could* work."

Tim yelled back to Sheri, "May want to strap in tightly."

On the tower frequency, Josh used his Australian accent. "Aircraft on approach, abort your landing." With that, he rolled onto the runway, lifting a wheel as he made the sharp turn to align the jet. Before he was even pointed down the runway, he firewalled the throttles. The jet accelerated briskly.

Not surprisingly, the tower told him he wasn't cleared for takeoff.

He saw security vehicles paralleling him on the taxiway, and said, "Déjà vu." Still below takeoff speed and rapidly running out of runway, he added, "At least there aren't any hills at the end of the runway."

Shaking his head, Tim said, "Because there's a lake!"

The jet accelerated but not fast enough. They were still below takeoff speed as the jet hit the runway's asphalt overrun.

Josh dropped the flaps for extra lift and pulled the yoke back. With a stall warning alarm, the Gulfstream shuddered. The big jet lifted only slightly and the wheels clipped the tops of the lake waves as he retracted the landing gear.

They accelerated out of stall and he raised the flaps. Climbing only 100 feet above the water, he switched off the jet's exterior lights and IFF and then dimmed the cockpit lights. He could see clearly on the moonlit night with his exceptional night vision.

Gently banking toward the north, he looked over at Tim.

Tim was staring straight ahead with a death grip on his

armrests.

Josh said, "We need to figure out where to go. Can't file to a normal airport now. The authorities will be looking for this jet." He looked at the fuel gauge and throttled back. "And we don't have much fuel, especially if we stay low like this."

With a couple deep breaths, Tim finally said, "How far can we go?"

Josh looked at the fuel flow and did a quick calculation. "Maybe 600 kilometers."

Tim nodded. "I may have an idea."

"OK, which way should I start heading?"

"Northwest." Tim pulled out his tablet and called up the map mode. He studied it for a few minutes and then said, "I know of a—"

He was interrupted by a loud warbling tone.

Josh looked at the jet's ECM panel and said, "We got company. Someone on our nose just locked us up with a fire-control radar."

Within seconds, a jet coming from the opposite direction flew right down their left side.

Sheri yelled from the back, "What the hell was that!"

Josh shook his head in surprise. "I think *that* was a ... Mig-21!"

Tim said, "They scrambled the Turkish Air Force after us!"

Josh shook his head again. "No. They fly F-16s. They never flew Migs. That was a vintage Soviet fighter."

"Then who are they?"

The warbling tone started again but this time the indicator pointed behind them.

"Don't know but they're not friendly."

Josh flipped on the Electronic Counter Measures and armed the chaff and flare dispenser. The warbling tone went up in pitch and tempo. Josh yelled, "Missile inbound! Hang on!"

The world once again shifted to slow motion. He pushed the throttles all the way forward, pulled the nose up and rolled the jet almost 90 degrees. Yanking back on the yoke, they were pushed down in their seats as he pulled as many Gs as the jet could do. He felt the Gulfstream buffet as he hit the chaff and flare dispenser. Seconds later, they saw a flash and heard a boom off their right side. Josh rolled back level and headed for the northern shoreline

Sheri yelled, "Woohoo, they missed!"

"The flare decoyed the older generation heat-seeking missile. Their old radar sucks at low altitude. Need to get down into ground clutter." Josh descended to 20 feet above the water.

Tim silently clenched the armrests, looking pale.

With his exceptional vision, Josh saw that the northwest side of the lake was an unpopulated shoreline that gently transitioned into hills and mountains. He headed for it.

The missile warning went to high warble again.

He took the jet to a wingspan above the water and hit the chaff and flares.

They saw another flash as the missile struck the water and exploded behind them, but this time they heard a 'tinking' sound as if gravel were hitting the bottom of the jet.

Josh calmly said, "That was too close. His radar missiles are useless this low and he probably just expended his last heat seeker. Which means, all he has left is—"

Water kicked up in front of them from a cannon salvo.

"... his gun." Josh took a deep breath banked the jet slightly and focused on not hitting the water. He quietly added, "He has to drop his nose to get us in his cross hairs. At this altitude, he can only get off a few rounds without flying into the water." He finished to himself, "Unfortunately, it only takes one."

Josh maintained his insanely low altitude and continued to turn the jet back and forth in an S pattern as they approached the shoreline. It was a game of chicken to see if the Mig had the gonads to follow. At the last second, Josh pulled the nose up to hug the rising terrain.

Cannon rounds mixed with burning orange tracers struck the hillside in front of them.

As they topped the ridgeline, Josh rolled the jet upside down. Inverted, he pulled the nose toward the ground to follow the slope down the other side of the hill.

The Mig overshot and appeared in front of them.

Seeing the fighter bank left toward them, Josh rolled upright and banked hard right. Completely focused, he took the Gulfstream down to less than a wingspan off the desert and pushed it as fast as it would go.

The radar warning tone went silent.

After a couple minutes, Josh took a long, deep breath. He climbed to 200 feet and throttled back. "I think we lost him. That old Mig can fly circles around us but their ancient radar sucks. If they lose sight, they can't pick us up in the ground clutter."

From the back, Sheri yelled, "That was awesome! Way better than a roller coaster, especially when we were upside down!"

Tim, jaw clenched and still looking pale, turned around and just stared at his wife. Facing forward, he sat still for a few more seconds breathing deeply, and then pulled his tablet out. He pointed to the displayed map. "There's an old abandoned airfield near Kirnati, Georgia. We used it during the Russian invasion of Tskhinvali. It was pretty mountainous but we can follow the Chorokhi River that crosses the border. I have some contacts in that area that can help."

"Sounds good. With our little tussle, we burned a lot of gas." He glanced at the fuel gauge. "May have just enough fuel to make it." He also noted that pressure was dropping on one of the two hydraulic circuits but didn't share it with Tim.

After an hour of flying at night through mountains and canyons, they reached the river that crosses the Turkish-Georgian border.

Tim said, "They're a little sensitive near the border after Turkey snatched some of their territory ... but that might work to our advantage."

Josh slowed down and followed the river at low altitude. They had no problem crossing the border. "Tim, hope this field's close. We're on fumes."

Tim said, "There!"

Josh looked and then frowned. "Where?"

Less confident, Tim said, "Right there."

"That's not a runway, that's a field."

"It *was* a runway."

Josh blew out a lung full of air. He tapped an indicator and said, "Well, it doesn't matter. The landing gear won't come down, probably fragged by that last missile. I'm going to grease it in on the river and plant it on the shoreline."

Tim frowned. "Didn't you try to do that in Colombia?"

"Nope. I was just the copilot, but," he smiled, "I've watched the movie, **Sully**, twice."

Tim gave him an unenthusiastic, "Great."

Josh dropped the flaps and slowed the jet down to its minimum landing speed. With almost no fuel, the Gulfstream flew very slow and handled well.

He made a pass to make sure there wasn't a waterfall or other obstruction at the other end. The river was shallow with plenty of river gravel on both sides. Circling back, he started his approach.

Descending as gently as he could, he kissed the river with the jet's belly. The slim business jet hydroplaned as he carefully kept the wings level. Finally the jet settled into the water and just before the wing tip fell, they hit a gravel sandbar. It made a terrible scraping sound and decelerated them quickly, throwing them forward in their seats. Moving the same speed as a car on a freeway, the Gulfstream's weight caused the jet to plow through the stones, sliding sideways and crunching to a stop.

Tim nodded. "Nice."

Josh killed the engines and in the relative quiet, said, "Connecting flight information can be found on the monitors inside the terminal."

Tim and Sheri unstrapped and quickly grabbed critical items. They threw them into duffel bags as Josh opened the hatch.

Stepping down onto the gravel bed, Josh looked around. It was dark and heavily forested on both sides of the river. There was a cool breeze blowing from upstream and it was surprisingly quiet. The only sound he heard was the wind in the treetops, the gently rushing river and a soft metallic clinking from the cooling turbine blades.

Tim pointed to the forest's edge. "Head over there toward the road." He turned and tossed something back into the jet, adding, "Quickly!"

They were only a minute away when they heard a muffled explosion and saw the beautiful Gulfstream in flames.

As they jogged toward the road, they heard the jet explode behind them and saw the orange reflection off the clouds above.

34

GEORGIA

An old truck stopped along the road near a bend in the river. Tim left the woods and walked up to the driver's side window. They talked briefly and Josh saw them shaking hands. Tim then signaled to Sheri and Josh to join him.

He introduced them and then told them to jump in the back of the truck. After a short ride, they were deposited into the center of Batumi at the hotel Mgzavrebi.

Exhausted, they check in to a suite with two rooms and collapsed in bed.

The next morning, they gathered for breakfast.

Sheri said, "OK, what exactly *were* they doing in the factory?"

Josh frowned. "It was weird. They were transplanting the innards of the stolen plutonium-powered tracking capsules into bigger capsules. Then they were re-boxing them along with the nano-drones for shipment."

"Why?"

Josh and Tim shrug. "We don't know."

"Where are they shipping them?"

Josh shook his head and said to his phone, "Jen, what did you find on the laptop and phone?"

"I downloaded all the files but they're encrypted."

Tim said, "I thought you could crack encryption."

"I could, but after The Great Tech Out, one of the projects they asked me to help them with was creating stronger encryption. I showed them how to do quantum key encryption, and it's becoming the new standard. Without knowing the key, it's almost impossible to break."

Tim asked, "Didn't you put a back door into the system?"

"No. That would be unethical."

Josh and Sheri simultaneously gave Tim a menacing frown.

Tim corrected, "I meant for diagnostic purposes."

"It isn't needed because with the key we can ensure the data is accurately encrypted and decrypted."

Josh asked, "You said *almost* impossible?"

"With enough processing power and some creativity, any code can be broken, but I'll have to borrow a significant portion of the world's computer processing power and memory to do it, and that could take weeks. However, they didn't use quantum encryption for the graphics in the documents, so I should be able to decode the pictures pretty soon. That will also help me crack the code on the text."

Josh paused. "Jen, we've been teaching you that no one's above the law. We'll make sure there are proper warrants before you release it to anyone but could you start working on the decryption now?"

"Don't worry, Josh, I learned my lesson about unintended consequences, but if there's anything I find that could harm those that I love — that's my first priority."

"Thanks Jen." He paused. "What do we know about the Solak Company?"

Jen said, "It's privately owned and has been a family business for over 100 years. It's in the process of being transferred to the fourth generation. The family is known for many charitable activities. The only recent news article is several years old. It just mentions a tragedy with one of the heirs who died in an accident. I can't find anything negative about the business or family, or anything that might link them to a terrorist group."

Josh frowned. "Hard to imagine they're not aware that a corner of their factory is modifying stolen, plutonium-powered assassination capsules. Jen, any way we can find out where they're shipping these things?"

Sheri said, "They're probably not using FedEx."

Jen said, "I'll see what I could do."

Josh looked at Tim and Sheri. "We've got to get this

information back to Meadows and Turan."

Frowning, Tim said, "If they managed to implant one of these in Davidson, we have to assume Turan and Meadows have been implanted too. And if they can monitor them with nano-drones, telling them could sign their death warrant."

Josh said, "I have an advantage; I can hear the nano-drones."

"Yeah, if they're flying, but what if they're just sitting somewhere in their office watching you. You can't hear them."

Sheri said, "We need technical expertise. Jessica Lee can figure out how to locate and maybe jam the drones."

Josh nodded. "But there's a chance she might have been implanted as well, particularly, after she accepted the position as the President's Science Advisor."

Sheri frowned. "We're getting a little paranoid, aren't we? They can't implant everyone."

"Josh's right, we have to be careful. Fortunately, we don't have to contact her directly. We could go through her boyfriend."

Josh nodded. "Hey Jen, does Greg still have the encrypted text app on his phone?"

"No, he dropped his phone in the toilet again, but I can reload it on his new phone."

"Please do."

Tim pulled a satchel from one of the bags. "First, we need to get back into the U.S." Opening it, he handed Sheri and Josh passports and IDs. "And this was *my* first career."

Josh nodded but asked, "How do we avoid the nano-drones?"

Sheri said, "I own an Airstream trailer."

Josh gave her a puzzled look.

She smiled confidently. "The outside skin is made of *aluminum*."

Josh slapped his forehead. "Of course, the metal skin can be turned into a Faraday cage and block the radio signals used to control the nano-drones."

Sheri grinned. "Don't have to modify it. My prepper husband already did."

35

JESSICA

The 30-foot Airstream trailer was lavishly equipped and comfortable. Although the metal skin prevented nano-drones from being operated inside, Josh knew eyes or cameras could still look in through windows, so they kept the shades drawn.

Responding to Josh's text, Greg met them in Virginia at an RV Park. Josh opened the door and invited him in. As soon as the door shut, Tim and Sheri came out of the bedroom.

When Greg saw him, he just said, "Hi Tim."

Frowning, Josh said, "Thought you'd be a bit more surprised."

Greg shook his head. "Nope. I've ridden with Tim. There's no way he'd die in a car accident. Besides, *you* supposedly died and showed up again, so I figured Tim would too. James Bond never dies."

Tim and Josh looked at each other and shrugged as Sheri gave him a hug.

After bringing him up to speed while eating hamburgers and shakes, Greg started reading the nano-drone specs.

Finally Greg said, "I'm a software guy." He shook his head. "These things are so tiny they have to be hardwired with custom designed chips. We need Jessica. She's the hardware genius."

Tim nodded. "We agree. There's a slight chance she might be targeted for monitoring too. We'll need you to come up with an excuse to get her here."

Sheri added, "But first, Greg, we need to make sure you haven't been implanted." She took him into the trailer's bedroom.

After a half hour, they came back out and Sheri said, "I think he's clean, but Josh, with your amazing vision, I'd like you to take a look at a couple spots."

Josh checked his neck and scalp where Sheri pointed and confirmed he was clean.

A few hours later, Greg brought Jessica to the RV. From inside, they could hear her say, "Are you serious? You better not have bought this damn thing!"

When she was inside, Greg pointed at Tim and Sheri, and said, "Ta da!"

Jessica stopped dead in her tracks and her jaw fell open.

After hugs and another round of explanations, Jessica finally said, "Here we go again."

Sheri said, "Unfortunately, there's a slight chance you could have been implanted with a tracking chip like Josh and Tim. We need to check you out too. We've all been through it."

Sheri took her into the bedroom.

After a minute, Josh heard Sheri say, "Josh, come in here a minute."

Jessica was down to her underwear and Josh once again marveled at her lack of self-consciousness.

Sheri said, "Show her where your chip is."

He held out his hand.

Sheri pointed at the top of his hand. "You can't see it without a magnifying glass, but if you rub the skin on the hand between your fingers you'll feel it."

Jessica felt the top of his hand and then rubbed each of her hands. "I don't feel anything." She held her hands out to Josh.

He examined them and shook his head. "Nothing there."

Sheri nodded. "If *he* doesn't see anything, you're good. Unfortunately, Tim told us they didn't always implant them in the terrorist's hand. They could place them literally anywhere."

Jessica nodded and continued to undress.

Josh immediately turned to leave.

Sheri said, "Wait. If Jessica doesn't mind, with your vision, you could speed up the process and might catch something I miss."

Jessica laughed. "It's not like Josh and I haven't seen each other in our birthday suits before."

Josh shook his head. "Why don't you call me if you find any

questionable areas?"

After a half hour, Sheri came out and said to Josh, "I think she's clean but need you to come in and double check a couple places just to be sure."

As he followed Sheri in, he saw Jessica, thankfully, wearing a towel. "Where do you want me to check?"

Very seriously, Jessica asked, "Do you know where the uterus is?"

"What?!"

Jessica and Sheri start laughing. Finally, Jessica, snorting to a stop, said, "Kidding!"

Sheri shook her head. "Seriously, there's an area on her scalp and her knee I need you to check." To Jessica, she added with a smile, "You should have seen him during *his* examination."

As he finished with her scalp and examined her knee, Jessica pats his head and said, "We're just trying to loosen you up a little."

Finding nothing, he gave her knee a hard pinch.

"Oww!"

"Oops," he said without a hint of sympathy. Turning to leave, he got snapped in the butt by the towel.

He stepped outside and closed the door, but with his phenomenal hearing, he heard Jessica laughing and asking Sheri, "Why *do* we enjoy embarrassing him?"

Sheri said, "I think it's because it makes him seem ... *human*."

There was a pause and he heard Jessica say, "You're right. We love him but he's ... he's...."

Laughing, Sheri finished, "A prude?"

"Yeah, that too."

A few minutes later, Jessica and Sheri joined them in the front of the trailer.

Greg handed Jessica the tablet with the Wraith specs.

After a few minutes of study, she said, "These suckers are impressive."

Tim asked, "What's your assessment?"

"Actually, they're not really *nano* drones. Nano means one

billionth of a meter and these are clearly—"

Greg interrupted with a smile, "Thank you for the clarification, Doctor."

Josh shrugged. "Boeing called them that because they use some nano technology inside, and … the toy makers already took the micro-drone name."

Jessica nodded. "I need to study the circuit diagrams but right off the bat, I see some limitations. They're too small to have the processing power and memory to operate autonomously, so they have to be actively flown by someone all the time." She paused. "The power source generates heat, which it probably dissipates when it's flying. When it's sitting still, there's no cooling air, so its temperature rises. I'll bet they're visible in the infrared, especially when they're not flying." She paused again. "We know Josh can hear them when they're flying. So, with a sensitive enough microphone, we should be able to detect them in flight. The microphone in our phones might be capable of hearing that frequency."

Jen inserted, "Yes, most models can."

"Greg and Jen can create an app that should be able to hear them and warn us if one's nearby."

She glanced down at the tablet. "Also, due to the tiny size of the camera and transmitter, the video has limits."

Greg said, "Like what?"

"Resolution and color limitations." She smiled. "Like you, Greg, they're probably slightly color blind. Working with Greg and Jen, I'm sure we can embed messages in phone displays that the drones won't be able to read."

Greg said, "Yeah, but would *I* be able to read them?"

She smiled and patted his arm. "Yes dear, we'll make sure you can."

Tim said, "OK, that's great information. Do we have any other leads that could help us identify who's using these?"

Jen said, "Although I haven't been able to break the encryption, I have been tracking Solak's commercial shipments. Turns out, they *do* use FedEx. All the shipments went to watch retailers … except one. It went to an unusual facility."

"What kind?"

"It appears to be a defense contractor called Abadon."

Josh frowned. "Never heard of them. What country are they from?"

"This one. They're based out of northern Nevada."

Sheri asked, "What kind of defense contracts do they do?"

"I don't know. They're just registered as a government supplier. It's a new company. They're not publically traded and they have no website."

Josh tilted his head. "Nevada, and with no visible government contracts ... could be black program stuff."

Frowning, Sheri asked, "Why would stolen nano-drones be sent to a U.S. government contractor?"

Greg smiled. "I've always wanted to visit Area 51."

36

NEVADA

Jen displayed the location of Abadon on the tablet.

Josh smiled. "Sorry, Greg, that's way north of Area 51."

"That's OK. Area 51 is just for tourists." With a conspiratorial smile, he said, "They keep the real aliens further north."

They rolled their eyes as Tim zoomed in on the tablet. "The delivery address was northern Nevada near the border of Oregon and Idaho."

Sheri, looking over his shoulder, said, "The address can't be right. There's nothing there. I mean — literally nothing — no buildings, not even a dirt road."

Josh pointed to the center. "Looks like a dry lake bed or possibly an old shallow impact crater. It'd be a great place to put a secret facility."

Still frowning, Sheri repeated, "But there's *nothing* there."

Josh smiled. "There's nothing there in *this* satellite picture."

Tim looked at Sheri. "How hard do you think it is to feed old pictures into the map system to cover areas you don't want people looking at? Jen, can you see if you can find an updated satellite photo from this area?"

"Already looked and there's nothing out there, but I'll ask one of the commercial satellites to take a picture for me."

Greg looked surprised. "Wow. You can do that? That's totally cool."

Tim nodded and then looked at Josh. "We need to get you back so that whoever's monitoring you doesn't get suspicious."

"I'll check in with Turan, see if he has any more leads." Frowning, Sheri said slowly, "Josh, be careful what you discuss

"

with him. It's likely that both of you have the neurotoxin capsules inside you."

"I will and in case he's being monitored, I'll give him a plausible reason for disappearing for a few days so I can meet you in Nevada."

Josh flew back to New Hampshire and hitchhiked to where Tim and Sheri picked him up. Jen reactivated his phone's locator and he spent the next few hours hiking back to his car. He kept himself occupied trying to peel off the patches Sheri superglued to his hand.

He arrived at his car, minus some skin, and immediately heard the telltale hum of a nano-drone. After cleaning up, he called Turan and was invited to his office.

He was tempted to share what they learned with Turan but the intermittent sound of a micro-drone following him on the way to the U.N. dissuaded him.

Turan shook his hand and said, "How was the hike?"

"Good, and had some time to think."

"About being my deputy?"

Josh nodded. He wanted to keep the conversation away from terrorists in case they were being monitored. "Yes. May I ask more about your vision of the future?"

"Ask whatever you want."

Josh nodded. "I understand and agree with the need to unite to protect humanity, but the last attempt at a world government was called the Third Reich."

Turan smiled. "That's not a fair analogy. Hitler was certifiable and took advantage of the anger of the German people. They were forced to accept blame for World War I even though they were only one of several countries that caused it. I want to make sure that type of insanity never happens again. I support the rights of individuals as long as they don't inflict their beliefs on others."

Josh nodded but said, "I heard you took some punitive action against a media outlet, limiting their access to astronauts and launches because of what they published."

"Actually, it was the Secretary-General's idea." He shook his head. "There was a time in your country when the press acted as a check and balance on government. Today, polls show the vast majority of people believe the media is totally biased one way or the other. The media have even taken bad situations and amplified them to create more division. Unity doesn't sell advertising spots; a good riot does. This is one of the few areas where the Secretary-General and I agree. Josh, my parents died in a conflict they had nothing to do with. While thousands were being slaughtered, the international press was busy amplifying domestic ethnic division in Europe and the U.S. Fair or not, we're creating consequences for the press's actions."

"I know journalists who are ethical and live to uncover corruption and injustice."

"Of course there are good journalists." He smiled. "That's one of the reasons I want you as my deputy. You can be my—"

"Conscience?"

He laughed. "Actually, I was going to say devil's advocate." Smiling, he added, "But definitely provide another perspective."

"You said that was one of the *few areas* you and the Secretary-General see eye-to-eye on."

Turan sighed and then carefully said, "Yes, we often see things ... differently." He shook his head. "But he is my boss and deserves my loyalty."

Josh tilted his head slightly. "The office of Secretary-General is becoming the most powerful position in the world. What *does* he believe?"

Turan paused. "I guess if you're to be my deputy, you need to know the internal politics, but please keep this confidential."

Josh nodded.

"General Von Stein believes it is his mandate to ultimately unite the world under one government, but he has the perspective of a general. Everything is a campaign, a battle to be fought and won. He wants to use the U.N.'s growing peacekeeping troops in roles other than peacekeeping. He doesn't communicate well with me or the other directors. We often find out about new programs he instituted in press releases. Some of this is just office politics." He took a deep breath and then with a slight headshake and smile, he looked at Josh. "Speaking of communication, how's it going with you and Elizabeth?"

Josh looked down. "No change. Both of us need some time

apart to think about our priorities."

"I'm sorry."

"Do you have any specific things you'd like me to be working on or looking into?"

Turan shook his head. "Not yet." He looked at the globe on his desk and with a slight smile, added, "As I told you, ever since I was aware of my genetic abilities, I've been trying to figure out how they're ... *possible*." He became animated. "Josh, we've broken the code, literally. I believe we will soon be able to give these abilities to others!"

Josh looked surprised. Frowning, he asked, "How?"

"I can't wait to share it with you but it's highly classified. If you join me, I'll bring you into the program." He raised his eyebrows. "It may ... *answer* some of our questions."

Before Josh could ask him what he meant, Turan continued, "I want to put more time into that project and I don't want to be the Director of Global Security forever. Josh, it's a tradition that the outgoing Director recommend their replacement." He paused. "As the director, you would be in charge of the world's safety and security, not to mention Admiral Meadows, Colonel Crow and ... your wife."

As he left, he couldn't help but think about the Deputy position. Josh's primary reason for meeting Turan was to create an alibi while he secretly went to Nevada in case he and Turan were being monitored. The prospect of learning what Turan knew about their genetics, not to mention eventually becoming the Director of Global Security, however, *was* enticing. He knew some of it was simply ego on his part, but he was frequently irritated by international politics and policies. He quietly said, "Maybe it's time to put my money where my mouth is and actually work to change things."

37

ABADON

Josh met up with Tim, Sheri, Jessica and Greg in Las Vegas. They used the Airstream trailer as their base of operations.

Sitting around the table, Tim showed them the picture Jen got from a commercial satellite.

Sheri said, "Wow. It looks like a college campus in the middle of the desert. There are multiple buildings and one of them is huge. There's got to be hundreds of people working there."

Tim nodded. "Yesterday, I drove out there and did some recon work. This compound is surrounded by a 100,000-acre security zone bordered by a chain-link fence and barbwire. You have to take an unmarked, unpaved road for almost 10 miles. I acted like a lost delivery truck. Check this out." He plays a video he surreptitiously took of the compound's entrance and security gate. "You can see they're scanning what looked like fitness bracelets."

"Those look like the ones from the Solak factory." Josh added.

"Yeah, but on top of that they're *also* doing a fingerprint and retina scan."

Greg shook his head. "That's a ridiculous level of security."

Frowning, Sheri nodded slowly. "I bet our answers are inside."

Greg nodded toward Jessica. "We could probably figure out how to spoof the bracelets if we could get our hands on one."

Tim took something wrapped in aluminum foil out of his pocket and set it on the table. Opening it, they saw a blue bracelet inside. "They *are* identical to the ones at Solak."

Greg asked, "How did you get that?"

"You don't want to know … but even if we could spoof these, we still have to fool a fingerprint *and* retina scan."

Flipping through the high-resolution satellite pictures, Josh said, "Jen also got us a scan of all the radio emissions from the facility. It looks like they're using 360-degree bi-static radar."

Greg looked at Josh. "What's that?"

"An extremely sensitive radar designed to pick up stealth fighters. It would have no problem spotting our little hex-copter drone."

Tim pointed at one of the pictures. "And these towers around the perimeter of the buildings are undoubtedly using the latest-generation thermal imaging."

Jessica shook her head. "We can't beat a bracelet, fingerprint and retina scan. With radar, we can't spoof the camera with our drone, and night vision scopes would pick us up if we sneak in on the ground."

With the slightest of smiles, Tim said, "I might have the solution."

Tim drove them to an abandoned Walmart parking lot and pulled up next to an eighteen-wheeler. They followed Tim to the back of the trailer and up a drive-up-ramp. Josh saw two tarp-covered objects strapped to the trailer's floor. They were as tall as a car but half the width.

Tim pulled the cover off. "Courtesy of Elton Muske."

Josh saw what looked like an enclosed off-road motorcycle. The streamlined body was vaguely egg shaped and flat black. Sticking out of the front and back were massive knobby tires mounted on an aggressive suspension.

"They're prototypes designed for U.S. and Israeli Special Forces by a small company called Lit Motors. Both wheels are powered by hub-mounted, electric motors. They can run 160 mph on the highway, or you can change the tire pressure and suspension settings and run across rocks and sand dunes at 130." Tim pushed a recessed handle. The top of the vehicle opened like a clamshell canopy on a fighter. Inside was a thinly padded seat with a racer-style safety harness and a small steering wheel. Lying in the seat was a helmet with what looked like a built-in heads-up display. A second seat was behind the first but close enough that it required the passenger's legs to straddle the driver's seat.

Josh frowned. "How does it stay upright on two wheels when it's going slow?"

"Powerful gyros in the belly keep it vertical even when it's sitting still. When it enters high-speed corners, the gyros automatically lean the whole vehicle into the turn like a motorcycle. It's all electric, so it's silent with a very low IR signature."

Josh smiled appreciatively. "Armor?"

"It has a graphite composite shell lined with ballistic Kevlar and a few strategically placed titanium plates. It'll handle light rounds but nothing heavy and has no external weapons. Built for speed and stealth, it's designed for scout and rescue missions."

Josh looked up into the open clamshell top. "Wait! It's opaque. You can't see outside with the canopy closed."

Tim picked up the helmet from the driver's seat and handed it to Josh.

Josh examined it and then looked at the vehicle. Evenly spaced around the outside were dozens of small cell-phone-like lenses. Holding up the helmet, he smiled. "This isn't a heads up display. It's a panoramic VR headset."

Tim nodded. "As you turn your head, it uses all those little cameras on the outside to give you a 360 degree, ultrahigh resolution, 3D display. You can also see in extreme low light and infrared, and zoom in and out." He tapped the exterior. "Without windows, they were able to cover it with a radar absorbing coating and...." He reached inside the vehicle and flipped a switch to power it up.

Josh watched the exterior suddenly change color. Frowning, he stepped back to see the whole vehicle. The side closest to him took on the color and brightness of the trailer wall behind it. Shaking his head, Josh said, "Wow. This looks like—"

"Adaptive camouflage," Tim finished. "It uses the cameras on the far side to change color and brightness on this side to match the background ... no matter what angle you view it from. It's not invisible up close, but at a short distance it blends in with any terrain making it almost impossible to see."

Greg whistled. "Wicked! What's it called?"

"A Gecko."

Josh smiled. "Appropriate. Range?"

"On a full charge, about 200 miles. Less at high speed or in rough terrain."

Nodding, Josh said, "Even the bi-static radar shouldn't be able to pick us up in ground clutter with this thing."

Tim added, "And the heat signature is about the same as a small animal."

Josh smiled. "Let's do it."

38

GECKO

It was a pitch black, overcast night. The two Geckos ran single file down the desert highway at 120 mph. Josh was in the lead with Greg in his backseat. Tim followed in the other.

The only sound was the wind and the knobby tires singing on the pavement. Josh smiled as the Gecko automatically banked into corners. Glancing into the backseat, he said, "Greg, how're you doing?"

"This is way cool. The VR is more realistic than my games."

Josh decided to leave that comment alone.

The Gecko's ECM gear picked up a radar signal. It identified it as standard police radar approaching from the front. Seeing the police car's headlights ahead, Josh turned on the adaptive camouflage. The Gecko didn't need headlights and with a closure rate of 200 mph, no radar signature and active camouflage, it'd be a good test of the Gecko's stealth.

The highway patrol officer ran down the empty highway at 80 mph. He glanced at the radio display but his eyes jerked back up as he sensed something in his peripheral vision. With a double swooshing sound, windy shadows streak by his car. He turned his head rapidly and looked back, but saw nothing. Frowning, he shook his head, chalking it up to a near miss with desert wildlife.

Seeing no brake lights on the receding patrol car, Josh certified the Geckos for stealth duty.

He slowed as they approach their turn off. It was an

unmarked, unpaved road. They followed it for several miles until they found their planned exit point. On a topographical map, they had identified a dry creek bed they hoped would allow them to slip under the fence. Checking to make sure there were no cars approaching, Josh turned off the highway and reset the Gecko's tire pressure and suspension. As he got used to using the VR headset, he found himself feeling less uncomfortable with no windows.

They followed the rough creek bed for a quarter mile until they saw the fence that surrounded the 12 by 12 mile security zone. It was a sturdy, eight-foot-high, chain-link fence topped with spiral razor wire. The creek bed ran under the fence with just enough room to slip the Geckos through, but another swath of fencing blocked the gap underneath. They stopped.

Using his VR helmet, Josh looked up and scanned the sky for the telltale heat signature of a drone. Over their short-range comm, he told Tim, "Sky's clear."

Tim got out of his Gecko and after attaching a jumper cable across sensor wires, he cut the chain-link fence blocking the creek bed.

They drove slowly through the hole single file.

Even with the stealth coating and active camouflage, the longer they remained in the open, the greater their chance of being detected. They climbed out of the creek bed and Josh took the lead, gradually opening up the throttle. With the agility of a mountain goat and the speed of a cheetah, they ran across the dark, barren desert at over 90 mph.

Superimposed over his VR display was their preplanned route. They had designed it to avoid large rocks and ravines, but the maps weren't perfect, and he had to deviate around small obstacles and wildlife.

Jen was jacked into their encrypted comm and nav system, so she could provide cover by monitoring satellite imagery and radio communications from the compound. They used one of the few frequencies that wasn't being actively jammed by the facility. Their target sat inside a shallow, six-mile-wide bowl in the desert — an ancient, eroded impact crater.

Next to the jetpack, Josh decided the Gecko was the coolest thing he'd ever driven. They screamed silently through the desert at high speed, the responsive suspension soaking up the terrain like a mop.

Before he knew it, he hit the small ridgeline surrounding the compound. Doing 90, he caught air as they topped the ridge. Landing on the other side, Josh's exhilaration was squelched by a loud beep from his ECM panel. They had been *painted* by a radar. Once again, he allowed adrenaline to override caution. He cut his speed in half as he scanned the now visible lights of the compound three miles ahead.

Jen came up in his headset, "Intercepted an encrypted radio transmission to one of the roving patrols. The facility got a radar hit and they're sending a patrol vehicle your way to investigate."

"My bad. I shouldn't have flown over that ridge. Those bloody bi-static radars can see a hummingbird." He scanned left and right with the VR headset, zooming in on several areas. He located a dip in the desert a couple hundred yards ahead and told Tim to follow him.

Jen said, "They're 30 degrees left of your nose, about two miles out and headed your way."

Josh switched his headset from low light to infrared. He immediately saw a brightly lit object approaching. The patrol was using IR floodlights, which meant they were wearing night vision goggles. He hoped what little heat the Geckos produced would dissipate with the motors off. As soon as they dropped into the dip, they stopped next to an outcropping of rock. He told Tim, "Let's lay low here for a while ... *be* the rock."

After a couple minutes, Josh could make out an Oshkosh JLTV bumping toward them and swiveling a powerful IR searchlight. The big ugly Humvee replacement was armored, and very proficient off road. He hoped the Gecko's camouflage blended them into the rocks.

Jen decrypted the transmission between the roving patrol and the base. "You're on the bearing where we had the radar contact. Do you see anything?"

The patrol responded, "Looking."

Josh watched the Jeltev slow to a crawl and come within 100 yards. This close, he could make out an M-134 minigun on top. The Gecko's light armor wouldn't hold up to the Gatling gun. Its thirty-ought-six rounds, fired at fifty per second, would carve them up like Swiss cheese.

The Jeltev swung its IR searchlight around them. The beam swept right across the Geckos, temporarily blinding their IR headset.

Josh and Greg held their breath.

The minigun exploded into life, ripping the night open with a blinding muzzle flash, deafening staccato and the metallic "clinking" of hundreds of spent shells bouncing off the vehicle. Dirt and rocks only a few dozen yards away exploded under the onslaught. They were sitting ducks as they watched the glowing orange tracers sweep the desert floor like a laser beam.

Josh was about to make a run for it, when he realized the train of bullets was moving away from them. Looking carefully, he saw a young coyote running across the desert floor. The bullets quickly caught up and ripped the coyote apart. The gun stopped. In the silence, they heard laughter coming from the Jeltev.

Within seconds, the decrypted radio transmission said, "We neutralized the threat ... a dangerous coyote."

The base replied, "Coyotes don't create that big of a radar return."

As the Jeltev started moving again, they heard, "Maybe you need to recalibrate your radar. We're heading back."

39

CONSPIRACY

Josh waited until the Jeltev was a football field in front of them and then followed them back to the compound.

Greg said, "You're keeping them between you and the radar?"

Josh nodded.

As they followed it into the compound, Greg asked, "Where are we going to park these things?"

Smiling, Josh turned the adaptive camouflage off and drove the Gecko right onto the well-lit parking lot, pulling into an empty space reserved for electric cars.

Tim pulled in next to him.

Josh got out and plugged the Gecko into the charging port. Tim did the same with a nod of approval.

"Hide in plain sight." Greg smiled and then looked around. "This place looks just like a university campus."

Tim, looking around, added, "They clearly don't want their people going in and out much. Because of the extreme security required to get in, I'm hoping it's more relaxed inside."

They were dressed in the same type of casual clothes they saw in Tim's video of the front gate.

As Greg took off his black windbreaker, Tim said, "You're wearing a red shirt."

Greg looked down. "Uh ... yeah?"

Tim and Josh exchanged half-smiles and shrugged.

Greg looked at them questioningly. "What?!"

"Never mind."

They saw only a few people walking outside as they walked toward the largest building. The main entrance was busier so they decided to try a door on the side of the building. Tim tentatively turned the doorknob. It was locked. Greg pulled the blue bracelet out of his pocket, unwrapped the foil around it and held it near the doorknob. They heard a mechanical click and Tim opened the door.

Inside was a set of fire stairs.

Josh shrugged. "Start at the top?"

Tim nodded. "Check your weapons."

They all had gas-fired Tasers, and Josh and Tim had compact nine millimeters. Greg opted out of carrying a pistol, since the only ones he had ever fired were virtual. He had, however, tased himself.

The stairs ended five flights up. Tim carefully peeked out the door and then motioned them to follow. They appeared to be on a maintenance floor. The hall was long and unoccupied, running the length of the building. There were metal doors spaced every 75 feet.

Josh tried the first door. It was locked and the bracelet didn't unlock it.

They went to a door halfway down the hall. It was also locked.

Tim stepped in and in less than 30 seconds picked the lock. They carefully slipped through and closed the door. They found themselves standing on a black metal catwalk 60 feet above the ground. The catwalk was for servicing overhead ductwork and lighting in an industrial ceiling above a room twice the size of a football field. Their vantage point was "midfield."

Looking down, they saw the right side of the room was filled with orderly rows of square cubicles. Each cubicle was about seven by seven feet with seven-foot high walls separating it from the next cubicle. Josh counted 20 rows of 25 cubicles. They could look down into the ones closest to them and see that most were occupied.

They crept slowly out onto the catwalk and pulled out small binoculars with built-in cameras.

Zooming in, they could see that inside each cubicle was a high-tech console with a large display. In front of the console were two nicely padded chairs. In one chair, someone wore a VR headset and operated what looked like a video game controller. It reminded Josh of the stations used by military drone pilots. The second person, who sat next to the "pilot," had a large monitor and a conventional keyboard in front of them. They wore a regular audio headset. The big monitor was divided into three windows: one big one and two small. The biggest display looked like a moving video image from a flight game. Clearly, it was displaying what the nano-drone "pilot" saw in their VR headset. One of the smaller windows displayed a satellite map and a location clearly marked with a seven-digit code. The other window had video and audio controls.

It appeared that one flew the nano-drone while the other monitored the subject via camera and headphone. As Josh scanned across the consoles, he noticed some displays were dark or blank and had only one bored operator. He guessed the individual being monitored was asleep or out of range.

He zoomed in on a display with an active video feed. There was a woman wearing a bathrobe working at a desk. Josh recognized the Prime Minister of France! He hit the record button on the binoculars and systematically scanned as many consoles as he could.

Tim whispered, "In addition to world leaders, I see heads of law enforcement and intelligence agencies."

As Josh continued to scan, he found one of the consoles with a dark screen that read, "Commander Josh Fuze." He noted the seven-digit number next to his name.

Tim pointed toward the left side of the room. There were another 10 rows of 10 cubicles but all had ceilings on top of them preventing them from seeing inside. "Guessing these might be higher level subjects?" Pointing further back to the left, he said, "Supervisors?"

On a raised platform overlooking all the cubicles were stepped rows of occupied consoles looking like Mission Control. There were four rows of ten consoles. Behind the consoles was an even higher glassed-in room that looked like a stadium skybox. It had a commanding view of the consoles and cubicles, but the glass was too dark to see inside.

Greg whispered, "This isn't a terrorist operation; it's an epic conspiracy that probably goes to the White House."

Josh nodded. "We need to find out who's behind that glass."

In their headset, they heard Jen say, "Base security just found your Geckos."

They slipped quietly back across the catwalk and into the hallway. Running down the stairs, they stopped at the exit door and peeked out. Josh saw a Jeltev parked next to their Geckos. Four men are standing around it with automatic weapons.

Josh said, "OK, parking in plain sight was a bad idea."

Greg tapped his chest. "I got this."

Josh and Tim looked at him curiously.

"Look, you guys are too old to pass as one of these gamers. I look the part."

Tim shrugged. "He's right." To Greg, he said, "You distract them and we'll come in from the west side of the parking lot."

Greg said, "West?"

Tim pointed. "Over there."

Greg slipped the blue bracelet on and headed toward the men standing around their Gecko. As he approached, he said, "Those are wicked cool looking. What are they?"

When he spoke, they initially lifted their weapons as they turned toward him, but as Greg moved into the parking lot lights, they lowered them. "Son, you don't need to be here. Move along."

Greg shrugged. "OK, but who were those guys dressed in black?"

"Did you see someone get out of these?"

"No, but they came from this direction. Couple older looking guys, like you, but wearing black shirts and baseball caps."

"Where?!"

Greg pointed behind him toward the main building.

"When?!"

"Just a few seconds ago."

The one speaking said something in his radio, and then to the man next to him, he said, "Stay here."

Three of the four jogged toward the building as Greg moved slowly toward the east side of the vehicles.

Greg said, "Man, I'd love to have one of these things."

The remaining security guard shook his head. "You need to get out of here." With a condescending smile, he added, "Stick with your video games. The real world is dangerous."

As Tim slipped in behind him, Greg said, "You think so?"

The guard turned and Tim tased him, grabbing his weapon as he fell.

Josh pulled the charging cables and popped the canopies, as Tim tossed the M-16 into the bushes. They hopped in but before they could lower the canopy, a head popped out of the top of the Jeltev. The man saw them and yelled excitedly into his radio.

Josh's Gecko was already in motion as the canopy came down.

Strapping in, Greg looked back with his VR headset and said, "Uh oh."

Josh and Tim turned on the adaptive camouflage and accelerated rapidly through the parking lot, but this close, and under the artificial lights of the parking lot, they were still visible.

The Jeltev was pursuing. Its minigun opened up, ripping up parked cars next to them. They were easily outrunning the Jeltev, but they couldn't outrun its bullets.

Over the radio, Josh told Tim, "We both have the data. I'll drag 'em toward the front gate. You head out through the desert."

He got a double mic click.

Josh knew the hybrid Jeltevs were capable of over 90 mph. Resetting the Gecko's suspension for highway, Josh accelerated to 150.

By the time the Jeltev cleared the parking lot, their Gecko was 200 yards down the road. Their active camouflage made them almost invisible, but staying on the road made them predictable.

Sure enough, the 7.6 mm tracers stitched across the road behind them like a red laser, chewing up asphalt and desert in a cloud of debris. It was obvious they didn't have a clear target and were just sweeping the road, but at 50 rounds a second, that could be effective—

There was a loud pop and Josh felt a couple thumps. Two dime-sized holes opened up in front of him as a couple rounds sliced through the Gecko from back to front. Josh jerked the wheel away from the stream of bullets, yelling to Greg, "You OK?"

"I think so!"

Josh's display flashed an "Adaptive Camouflage," "VR" and

"Battery" warning. Looking over his shoulder, Josh realized he'd lost some cameras and their camouflage was failing. The VR display had blank spots and was flickering. "Greg, I want you to put your hand on the yellow and black canopy jettison handle."

"You told me not to touch that!"

"Don't pull it 'til I tell you. The bullets damaged the VR display and we're about to lose it. Without it, we're blind inside and visible outside!"

Once again seeing the world move in slow motion, Josh watched the beam of red tracers stop its sweep off their left side and begin moving back toward the road and them. The gunner had the distance right this time and they'd be nailed by more than just a couple rounds. Just before the stream crossed them, Josh yelled, "Pull it!"

With a bang and whoosh, the canopy blew off into the night, and Josh tore off his headset.

The gunner saw the un-camouflaged canopy rising in front of him and instinctively followed it with the minigun. As the rounds connected, it created a nice little fireball over their heads. Even better, the shredded canopy fell back into the Jeltev's path. As the big vehicle ran over it, it skidded sideways and the minigun fell silent.

Josh flipped the suspension to off-road mode and jumped the road's small embankment. Catching air, they landed hard in the desert still doing 70. Josh squinted through hurricane-speed winds and headed for the perimeter fence. His genetically superior eyes allowed him to see in the dark almost as well as with the headset.

His photographic memory called up a topographic map of the area. He pictured a small hill that sat close to the perimeter and saw it in the distance as a dark smudge obscuring the fence. Heading that way, he yelled back, "You OK?!"

"Yeah! Going to have a nasty bruise but ... apparently, my seat back is made of titanium!"

Josh yelled back, "Hang on!"

As they approached the little hill, he floored the Gecko. They hit the slope doing 90 and flew over the fence. The back tire caught and ripped out a chunk of the razor wire. Landing hard, the Gecko bounced and then slid sideways, kicking up a curtain of sand. They heard the gyros whining, trying to prevent the vehicle from tumbling. Finally, skidding to a stop, Josh turned around to see Greg rubbing his neck. "Ouch!" Then looking at Josh, he grinned. "That was awesome!"

Josh checked the Gecko's instruments. With some of the battery cells damaged, it indicated a range of less than 20 miles and the rear tire was losing pressure. He hoped the engineers built in some reserve. Accelerating toward the highway, he gave Tim and Jen their location.

He saw the Jeltev staying on the access road, but it was joined by conventional security police cars moving at high speed with lights and sirens.

Tim said on the radio, "As soon as you hit the highway, head south."

Josh slid onto the highway, reset the suspension and ran the Gecko as fast as it would go. The range indicator dropped to less than 10 miles. He pressed the emergency reserve button and was able to maintain 90 mph, but could hear sirens approaching from behind.

Squinting through the wind, Josh yelled into his mic, "Is that you ahead?"

"Yup, bring it home."

As they closed on the semi-truck from behind, Josh saw sparks. The truck was running at highway speed but had lowered its ramp to within inches of the road. Smiling, Josh yelled to Greg, "This should be interesting!"

Too late, Josh realized he was coming in too fast. The second his front wheel hit the ramp, he slammed on his brakes. The Gecko skidded up the ramp. It just missed Tim's parked Gecko and slammed into the back of the trailer, mangling the front wheel.

Josh looked back and saw the ramp coming up. Unstrapping, he joined Tim at the back of the trailer and they watched a display from the truck's backup camera. Josh frowned. "Who's driving the truck?"

"Jessica."

Greg joined them and with a shrug added, "She likes NASCAR races and monster truck shows."

On the display, they saw several cars with lights and sirens approaching rapidly from behind. Their truck slowed down as the cars sped on by.

Greg did a fist pump. "We kicked their butt!"

Tim shook his head. "The battle hasn't even started."

V

TEAM

40

RECRUIT

As they sat in the Airstream trailer, Jen said, "I'm still working on decoding the text you pulled out of Solak, but I finished unencrypting the diagrams. I think you need to see them."

They appeared on Josh's tablet.

Tim and Josh studied them. Finally Josh said, "Sheri, take a look at this. It looks more biological than mechanical."

She slipped on reading glasses and took the tablet. After a few seconds, she said, "Hmm. Looks like a surgical placement diagram." She pointed at a branching line and said, "That's got to be a blood vessel." She paused, studying it. "It looks like it's showing these tracking capsules are supposed to be implanted next to a major artery or vein." Looking up, she frowned. "But why?"

Tim pointed at the capsule near where the hooks came out of it. "Look carefully at the picture. See where the capsule touches the vein? What do you see?"

Sheri and Josh crowded closer as Sheri zoomed in.

Josh said, "There's a tiny spring and needle inside the capsule."

Tim rubbed his chin and looked at Sheri, "How much toxin is required to stop someone's heart if it were injected directly into a vein."

"I'm not a toxicologist but there are some potent neurotoxins, and if it went straight to the heart...."

Tim nodded. "The injector could be released on remote radio command." Looking up at them, he added, "*This* is how they killed Davidson."

"And Harrison." Josh whistled softly. "We have the smoking

gun but we still don't know who owns it."

Sheri said, "I wonder how many others have been implanted with these? Inserted next to a vein, they would be too deep to be easily felt under the skin. We might have missed them even on us." She turned to Jessica and Greg. "Can you guys figure out a way to detect these capsules?"

Jessica frowned, thinking. "They should emit some alpha particles that we could detect. We'll get on it."

Tim exhaled sharply. "We need help. A lot of help."

Sheri said, "Yup. Let's start with those in critical positions or that have skills we need: Turan, Meadows, Casey, Kristoff, Elizabeth and Colonel Crow."

Josh frowned. "Elizabeth and Crow?"

Sheri nodded. "We can hold off on Elizabeth for now, but Crow will be launching soon and taking control of the world's most accurate global weapon. We need to get to her before that."

Greg put up his hand.

Smiling, Josh said, "You don't have to raise your hand."

"I think we need someone on the inside. We need to infiltrate the infiltrators." He shrugged. "I'm an excellent gamer. I bet I could get a job with Abadon."

Jessica looked at him with an expression between admiration and irritation.

Tim nodded. "Greg, you got guts. Unfortunately, all of us are recognizable by either the public or the intelligence community, and although you're not quite 30, it looked like those operating the drones were barely twenty."

Greg frowned, thinking. "Wait a minute. I have a close friend who worked with us on the original laser. She's brilliant, an adrenaline junky, killer gamer and a sports drone pilot. She's my age but she's super cute and could easily pass for 20."

Jessica's expression went from admiration to suspicion.

Tim rubbed his chin thoughtfully. "That's actually a good idea ... if she's willing." He shook his head. "But we'll need to make it clear to her this isn't a game and they'll kill her in a second if they suspect anything."

"Tell me about it." He pulled out the blue bracelet. "Jessica and I took this apart." He nodded toward Jessica.

She took over. "It doesn't just open electronic doors. Once

it's on your wrist, it can be electronically locked with a titanium band inside, making it almost impossible to remove. It contains a GPS transmitter, microphone and a built-in Taser plus a toxin injector. It's also powered by a speck of plutonium, so doesn't need to be recharged. Once it's on your wrist, it can track you, tase you and," she raised an eyebrow, "even kill you." Breaking the serious silence, she added, "But think of the savings in employee turnover and retirement benefits."

Sheri and Josh couldn't help but laugh as Greg and Tim shook their heads.

Sheri said, "OK, we need to divide and conquer."

Tim looked at Greg. "Where does your friend live?"

"I think she's working at the National Reconnaissance Office near D.C."

Tim paused. "OK, Greg and I will contact his friend in D.C. While we're there, Sheri and I can try to connect with Carl. Greg, after D.C., can you and Jessica fly to Moscow and scoop up Kristoff?"

They nodded.

"And Josh can go to Houston and do Crow."

Josh corrected, "Recruit."

"What?"

"Nothing. What about Turan and Meadows?"

Tim shook his head. "With their public positions, we can't kidnap them and it's going to be hard to isolate them. Let's get the others first."

Sheri added, "We have to be very careful and assume they've all been implanted and are being monitored. Carl almost certainly has."

Josh nodded toward Jessica.

She said, "We've got some tech that might help. Greg created a cool app that will allow our phones to listen for and localize the high-pitched sound the nano-drones make."

Greg held up his phone so they could see the screen. It looked like it was in camera mode.

Jessica took out and blew a high-pitched dog whistle.

On the phone's screen, they saw a little green box form around her.

Greg said, "I programmed the frequency from the Wraith

specs. It should be able to detect a micro-drone in flight within 15 feet."

Tim asked, "What if it's sitting on someone's shoulder? It won't make a sound."

"I'll turn that over to my beautiful hardware genius."

Jessica patted Greg and said, "I modified everyone's phone. The image chip in your phone's camera can actually see into the infrared, but they put a filter on the lens to block it because it blurs the picture. I replaced the lenses of your phones — sorry about the smeared glue on the back." She pulled out a lighter and heated the tip of a pin. "This should be roughly the temperature of a stationary drone, a little over 150 degrees."

Greg held up his phone again and they saw the tip of the pin glowing brightly with a floating green box around it.

"We also modified your encrypted text app. By hitting this button here, it will embed your text into a picture. You'll see the message but a micro-drone looking over your shoulder will see only the picture due to its limited color resolution."

Jessica added, "We're also trying to find some small very sensitive radiation detectors that can help locate the plutonium powered implants."

Josh said, "Great job!"

Tim added, "Don't forget there are still conventional video cameras and microphones everywhere. Pick your meeting locations carefully."

Tim met Judy Lanier in a coffee shop with Greg. Tim remembered her as one of the optics engineers on the Resurrect Project. Along with Greg, she was part of Dr. Garrett Cho's team that developed the laser. Judy was short and a little stocky with dark hair and eyes, but Greg was right; although the same age as Greg, she *was* extremely cute and looked like she was 20.

Greg introduced her. "Judy, remember Tim Smith from the Resurrect Project?"

"Yes, I think so."

Tim could tell she was being polite and didn't remember him. Not surprising. He cultivated invisibility and it was particularly easy around engineers. When consumed by a project or problem, they were lucky to avoid walking into walls.

As a trainer at The Farm, he evaluated candidates and began assessing her suitability. Being cute was both an asset and a liability. It gave her an advantage when dealing with men, but also made her memorable. The first thing he noticed when he shook her hand was that she was shy and self-conscious. They sat down and Tim proceeded to ask her a series of normal conversational questions about her background and childhood.

"I was born in the U.S. but my father was from the Seychelles and my mother from Pakistan."

"What do you enjoy doing?"

"I like tennis and snowboarding, but I'm not good at either. I've tried skydiving and I'm going to learn how to fly."

Her preference for individual sports, specifically ones that require rapid decision-making, was a positive. Skydiving meant she had the thrill-seeker gene, which indicated a level of physical courage.

"Judy, how did you get into your current career field?"

She gave him a small smile. "I really wanted to be in the military or law enforcement, but I have asthma."

Greg, perceptively, said, "Bingo."

Judy looked at him questioningly.

"Greg's been working with me on a project that involves national security. I think you would be a great candidate, but it could be dangerous." He shook his head. "Let me rephrase that. It could be extremely dangerous."

She didn't hesitate. "I'd like to know more."

"Let's go someplace where we can talk privately."

Once inside the Airstream, Tim said, "What you're about to hear you must never tell anyone. If you decide not to get involved, which is perfectly fine, you must pretend we never had this conversation and forget everything we tell you. Is that clear?"

She nodded and then asked Greg, "Is he like Commander Fuze, like James Bond?"

Looking at Tim, Greg said, "Us engineers nicknamed Commander Fuze, James Bond." He turned back to her. "Tim's like totally the real thing. Ever heard of the CIA Distinguished Intelligence Cross?"

Tim interrupted, "Greg! Have *you* ever heard of OPSEC?!"

"Sure ... that's like, uh ... uh, Operational Secrecy, right?"

"No! It's Operations Security. It means you don't go around telling everyone everything you know."

Judy looked at Tim with awe. "OMG, I know what the Distinguished Intelligence Cross is. I read a lot of spy novels."

Greg looked at Judy, looking at Tim, and said to her, "He's already married."

"Oh wait!" She nodded her head rapidly. "Now I remember. You were married to that beautiful TV star, doctor, uh—"

"Sheri Lopez," Greg finished.

"Yes!" Then, with a puzzled expression, she added, "Uh ... until you were killed in a car crash."

Looking at Greg incredulously, Tim threw his hands in the air.

Greg smiled at him. "Just trying to give you some street cred."

"Greg ... if you say another word ... I may have to shoot you."

Greg winked at Judy, "He's really a way good guy."

Shaking his head in resignation, Tim slowly began to explain all that transpired and their suspicions.

After an hour, she looked at both of them and said, "Wow. This is incredible and scary."

Tim nodded. "At this point, there's no shame in walking away from this and forgetting everything we told you. In fact, it's probably the smartest thing you could do."

"I know, but I'd always regret it." She took a deep breath. "What do I need to do?"

"We need eyes inside. You not only have the intelligence and technical skills, you fit the profile they're looking for. Please understand, we're talking about making you an undercover agent in an organization with no compunction about killing you if they find out."

Tim turned to Greg. "Explain to her about the bracelets."

Greg pulled the blue bracelet from his pocket and told her about the plutonium powered transmitter, Taser and toxin injector.

Tim looked her in the eye. "What these kids don't realize is — it's the last job they'll ever have because no one can ever know what they're doing." He pointed at the bracelet. "I got this one from the morgue."

Greg dropped it. "Eww."

She let out a lungful of air. "Mr. Smith, when I was young I used to pretend I was an international spy. I never pursued it because I knew my asthma would prevent it and it wasn't … practical. The closest I got was helping design secret spy satellites. I do understand. If they find out I'm a spy, I die. Even if they don't, if I try to leave, they'll kill me. Is that a reasonable summary?"

"Yes."

She nodded. "But aside from protecting the world from these lunatics, someone needs to save those kids. I'm in."

Tim shook her hand. "Welcome aboard. I don't have time to take you through a training course at The Farm, so I'm going to give you a crash course in a few days. In the meantime, we'll give you a new identity."

Greg pulled out his tablet. "Jen hacked the website Abadon used for employment so we could see all the job applications."

Judy asked, "Jen?"

Greg smiled. "We'll introduce you to her later. Although we can't see Abadon's selection criteria, by looking at the questions on the application and seeing which they accepted, we know what they're looking for." He pulled up the online application and handed her the tablet. "They're looking for people between 18 and 23. Add seven years to your graduation date and leave out the advanced degrees. Under hobbies, be sure to mention that you're a competitive sports drone pilot and gamer. Oh, Jen did a social media background check on the accepted applicants. One thing they had in common was no immediate family. So … you're now an orphan."

Tim added, "They seem to be collecting smart but disenfranchised kids with no families or those that are estranged from family and friends."

She frowned but nodded. "That makes sense."

"We'll keep your first name. What was your mother's last name?"

"Khan."

"Good. It's a common name but also a warrior name." Tim

smiled and shook her hand. "Welcome to the team Judy Khan."

With a half-smile, Greg pulled out his phone and said, "I'd like you to meet a good friend and another member of our team. Jen, say hi to Judy."

41

EXAM

Standing inside his hotel room near the door, Josh heard a knock. Cracking the door slightly, he saw Wendy knocking on the door across the hall from his room — the wrong room number he purposefully gave her. He didn't hear any nano-drones but scanned with his phone. Confirming it was clear, he opened his door. As she turned and saw him, he grabbed her hand and pulled her into the room.

Looking surprised but smiling, she said, "Uh ... that was interesting."

Josh said, "Please take off your jacket and turn around slowly." She shrugged and then removed her jacket and threw it on the bed. She was wearing jeans and a simple blouse. His sensitive vision didn't pick up any hot nano-drones riding on her or her clothes, but he followed it with a scan using his phone in IR detection mode.

As she completed the turn, she said with a slightly provocative smile, "So, how do I look?"

"I'm sorry. I just had to make sure you weren't bugged."

She frowned. "Bugged? The media attention has been incessant, but I don't think they've stooped to that yet."

He motioned her over to two chairs. "Wendy, are you familiar with the Wraith program?"

She shook her head.

They sat down and he explained the nano-drones and implants.

When he finished, she said, "Wow! This is kind of terrifying, but it explains a lot."

"May I see your hands?"

She held them out.

He took them one at a time and carefully inspected them visually. Then he gently rubbed the skin on the top of her hand.

"I'm worried about what you may find but that actually feels really nice. Been a long time since a man massaged my hands like this."

"I didn't find anything." He smiled and added, "Let me check in with the rest of our team."

He called Sheri using Jen's encryption app. When Sheri answered, he told her, "Her hands are clean. No implants."

"That's good, but … surprising. We've got Carl here…."

He heard conversation in the background.

Finally Sheri said, "Carl says hi and thanks for getting his message." She paused. "He confirmed Davidson died of a neurotoxin-induced heart attack. We found one of the passive RFID chips implanted in Carl's scalp but I'm getting a signal from the radiation detector. I'm pretty sure he also has one of the active transmitters implanted in him." She paused again. "Tim expects Wendy to have one or both. You're going to have to check her all over."

Glancing at Wendy, Josh said, "Uh … that's a *very* bad idea. You'll need to do this one."

Sheri said, "We're in D.C. Don't be such a wuss. In addition to looking for insertion scars, use the radiation detector Jessica gave us. Pay particular attention to areas where the major veins are close to the surface: jugular, subclavian, brachial and femoral."

"Sheri, I don't even know where those are."

"Google it. Let us know what you find." She hung up.

Seeing his face, she said, "What's wrong?"

He took a deep breath. "I'm afraid I need you to take off your clothes."

She gave him a half-smile. "Guess you're not much into foreplay."

"I'm sorry, Wendy. They were very surprised that I didn't find one in your hand and think there's a real possibility they must have implanted one elsewhere."

She nodded and began to undress.

Josh went to the bathroom and got her a bath towel, then

turned around. As she undressed, he googled a map of the human circulatory system.

After a minute, she said, "OK."

He turned back around. The bath towel was actually a bad idea. It displayed less than the ball gown but was somehow sexier. He had her stand near a lamp. He started with her feet as Sheri did with him and looked for insertion scars. Using the radiation detector's probe, he slowly worked his way up to her calves.

"Josh, last time we were together, I asked you to join me on the space station. The offer still stands but now that I'm the Commander, I'd like you to be my deputy, which, by the way, would put you in line for command too. I told you we would make a phenomenal team, and that's true, but ... but I think we could be much more than that." She paused.

As he moved up to her knees, she quickly said, "Josh, I'm an engineer and I'm very logical. I have an IQ of 155 and I'm still young enough to have children. Our kids would be both intelligent and beautiful."

Josh stopped and looked up. "Wendy, I'm married."

"I *know* that. I also know that you two are—" She stopped. "Look, I'm just suggesting that if for whatever reason you mutually decide it's time to ... move on...." She sighed. "Josh, when was the last time you were intimate with her?"

"You're making it very hard for me to concentrate."

"I'm sorry. I know I'm pretty direct but..."

As he moved up her thigh, she opened her towel. "I don't like to play games. I'm an open book."

Kneeling in front of her, sans towel, her comment couldn't have been timed worse. He shook his head and said, "Focus."

"What?"

"Nothing." He was about to stop when he saw what might be an insertion scar. "Wait!" He pressed the little radiation probe firmly against her skin at the junction of her thigh and torso. The digital display indicated a signal. It was right over her femoral vein. "There it is." Pressing in gently with his finger, he felt a tiny bump. He brought her hand down and let her feel it.

She shook her head. "How could it have gotten there?"

He shrugged. "I don't know how or when they put one in my

hand either."

"Is there a chance I could have more than one in me?"

"Sheri said Carl also had an RFID chip implanted."

"Then let's make absolutely sure we know."

He took another deep breath and continued. As he was working his way up her torso, she gave him a puzzled look and said, "Wait a minute. If whoever modified the ISLO's software was behind these neurotoxin capsules," she paused, "why didn't they just kill me with a heart attack like they did with Davidson and Harrison?"

Josh shrugged. "They probably wanted your death to look like an accident. I'm guessing that using the capsule is a last resort since an autopsy could uncover it."

He finished with her scalp. "I'm afraid you have an RFID chip just above your forehead." He gave her back the towel and said, "I know this wasn't easy."

Wrapping herself in the towel, she gave him a wry smile. "I'm sorry, Josh, it just wasn't that good for me. I don't even feel like a cigarette."

He laughed.

She put a hand on his arm. "I *am* a little freaked out by this … but if I had to go through it, I'm glad it was with someone I trust. And," she smiled, "the process wasn't all unpleasant."

With a sheepish smile, he shook his head. "Nor for me. You have a rather spectacular fuselage and empennage."

She laughed. "A compliment only an aerospace engineer can appreciate." Smiling, she added, "Thank you." She took a deep breath and then said, "So … Josh, will you be my deputy … and will you marry me?"

42

PROPOSAL

Immediately after he left the hotel, Sheri called. Before answering, he listened for the telltale hum of the drones and scanned visually. When he was sure that he was clear, he answered.

She said, "Well?"

"You were right. She has an active transmitter attached to her femoral vein and she also has a chip in her scalp." He paused. "And she proposed to me."

There was silence on the other end, and then, "Marriage?!"

"Yeah."

"But you're married."

"Yes, Sheri, I'm aware of that."

There was another pause and then, "Wow, you must give *really good* exams." She burst out laughing.

"It's really not funny."

Still laughing, she barely got out, "Sorry, but actually ... it really is." She finally stopped laughing, and more seriously, asked, "Umm, you guys didn't ... uh...."

"No! Of course not."

He heard Tim say something in the background and then heard Sheri reply, "I am *not* being insensitive." She cleared her throat and said, "OK, sorry. The femoral vein is the same one we use for cardiac catheterization because it gives a fast, clear path to the heart. The capsule implanted there unquestionably has the toxin in it. They probably put the chip in her scalp as a backup for tracking. Josh, depending on the dosage in that capsule, she could be in cardiac arrest within seconds after they initiate release."

"What about Carl?"

"Same. He's got an RFID chip in his scalp but his toxin capsule was attached to the jugular vein in his neck."

"What about Kristoff?"

"Tim just got off the phone with Greg and Jessica. I'll let him tell you."

Tim said, "Jessica said Kristoff is clean. Oh, and he owns a small island in the Caribbean. It's off the grid and EMP hardened. Recommend we all get together there as soon as possible. We're going to check out a few more things here with Carl. Then he's going to come with us to the island. Greg and Jessica will meet us there later. Make sure Colonel Crow comes too."

"There's no way she can come after taking command of the ISLO. She'll be going back up to the station soon and the ISLO's boosting to L2 in a few weeks."

"OK. Will send you the details. See you at the island."

Sheri jumped back on the line. "Wait. I'm sorry, Josh, but I've got to know. What did you say after she proposed?"

He blew out a lung full of air. "I don't think she really meant it but just in case I let her down gently."

"What did you say?"

"I just told her she was brilliant and drop dead gorgeous, but I was still hoping to work things out with Elizabeth."

"Hmmm."

"What?"

"Josh, she's a task oriented personality like you and I. If I heard that, it might suggest I'm still in the game."

"It doesn't matter. That's the last time we'll see her for six months. She's going to be a million miles from Earth. By the time she gets back, she'll forget she even knew me."

She gave him a cynical laugh. "We'll see."

Changing the subject, Josh said, "Now that we have everyone else, we need to figure out how to bring Meadows and Turan in."

He could hear Sheri and Tim talking. Then Sheri said, "Davidson knew there was a high-level security breach. Think about it. They killed him, infiltrated the astronaut core, tried to shoot down our plane in Turkey and built a massive facility in Nevada. There's gotta be a high-placed mole in the U.N. too."

"What do you suggest?"

Tim said, "Why don't you accept Turan's offer to be his deputy. You'll have closer access to him and Meadows, so we can bring them in easier, and you might be able to sniff out a mole."

"OK."

Josh went straight to Turan's office.

Turan said to his executive assistant, "Joann, please send my regrets to the senator and ask if we can reschedule."

"I'm sorry. I shouldn't have just shown up unannounced."

Turan shook his head. "Actually, the delay will help with this particular negotiation. What can I do for you?"

"If the position is still available, I'd be honored to be your deputy."

Turan grinned as he shook his hand with real enthusiasm. "Splendid!" He pulled him into the office and closed the door. "I can't tell you how pleased I am. There are so few people around me who are my intellectual equal." He frowned. "Guess that didn't sound very humble, but I think you know what I mean. Plus, we have the same dry sense of humor." He rubbed his hands together. "We'll need to get you up to speed on all the programs and initiatives before we announce this officially." On his fingers, he ticked off, "ISLO to full operational status, nuclear weapons command and control negotiations, securing the new currency, replacing passports with implanted RFIDs *and*," looking more serious, "ferreting out the organization that killed Davidson and infiltrated the astronaut core." He paused, frowning. "Give me a few days to have my staff set up some briefings for you and some time for me to figure out what I want to dump on your head first."

Josh nodded. "Sounds good. Is it OK if I visit a friend in the Caribbean for a couple days while you're planning my death by PowerPoint?"

Turan slapped him on the back. "See that's the kind of humor we need around here. My executive assistant can set up reservations at the finest resorts and we'll pick up the tab for your trip."

Josh smiled. "Thanks but I think I'd like to keep this a low profile trip."

Turan gave him a curious look and then smiled. "No problem. Have fun with your *friend*."

As he left, part of him wanted to dislike Turan because of Elizabeth, but he knew that was illogical. Turan clearly went out of his way to look after his team. Which was, undoubtedly, one of the reasons Elizabeth found him attractive.

43

ESPIONAGE

"Congratulations, Ms. Khan and welcome to the program."

Judy shook his hand. "Thank you. I'm excited to get started."

"Once you sign here, you'll be flown to the facility by helicopter." He looked at his watch. "We will need your phone and any other electronic devices. After being inspected for viruses, they will, of course, be returned to you at the facility. You may want to let your friends know you're about to start an extended training program and will be out of touch for some time." He smiled. "So they don't worry."

She endured an extensive screening process before boarding, including a full body x-ray, as well as finger, handprint and retina scans. As she surrendered her phone, she knew they'd check all the apps and data. It was clean. She hoped they won't notice the physical modification to the phone's camera lens.

Before she left, Tim and Jen showed her a radio frequency map of the facility. There would be no cell signals there and active jamming covered most of the normal communication spectrum. However, they found some holes. Her only concern was the tiny pico-memory card hidden in the circuit board of her sports drone. The small competition drones were one of the few electronic devices they allowed — actually encouraged — to help them maintain their proficiency. The memory card contained all the apps she'd need and could hold a ton of data. Both were quantum encrypted, but she knew their discovery could still spell her demise.

As the helicopter took off with her and nine other candidates, she was both excited and terrified. There was no going back.

After a 40-minute flight, they made their approach to what looked like a modern college campus. Tim showed her on a map that Abadon was truly in the middle of nowhere. Watching carefully, she saw that there was one very large central building surrounded by a dozen smaller ones. All the buildings were covered in solar panels. She smiled wryly. They might have no regard for human life ... but at least they were environmentally conscious.

They landed on a helo pad where they were met by a young woman wearing jeans and a golf shirt. She wore the same bracelet Greg showed her, except hers was red.

The woman took them into a small building where they did another finger, hand and retina scan. They were then issued bracelets, but theirs were yellow. Quite high-tech and good looking, they were custom fit. The bracelet felt snug on her wrist and also ... warm to the touch, but that might have just been her imagination.

The woman said, "We recommend you keep these on 24/7 for security reasons and for your own protection. They're totally waterproof, so you can even shower with them."

Judy took hers off and put it back on to make sure it didn't lock. So far, so good.

They received a tour of their new home, an impressive apartment complex with inside and outside swimming pools, large common areas and an extensive gym. Her one bedroom apartment was completely furnished and much nicer than her condo in LA. It also had the largest, highest definition TV she'd ever seen.

Twenty of them met in the lobby an hour later to start their orientation. The first session covered the importance of their work. The instructor, not much older than her, said, "You are the first line of defense against a sophisticated conspiracy that's quietly sweeping the globe. You're the new warriors of the 21st Century..." It was pure propaganda but he was a great motivational speaker.

After the class, their instructor said, "From here, we'll divide you into the drone and hacker training groups." He called out six names and said, "OK, you guys go with Joanna, and the rest come with me." The group she was with jumped right into familiarization with the VR technology used to fly the drones.

During the lunch break, one of her classmates said, "Those are the most awesome VR headsets I've ever seen. They're incredible!"

Her engineering side kicked in. "Yeah, they're state of the art with fast processors and outstanding optics." Smiling she added, "Love to try these playing PZang 4." She couldn't help but think that if she got out of here alive, she was going to snag a set.

Their instructor, eating lunch nearby, overheard them and said, "These are *your* VR headsets. You can take them with you when you're not working. Feel free to use them to play games if you wish. We have the most extensive game library in the world, and have beta versions of almost everything in development, including PZang 5. It's all free to play anytime." He smiled. "We encourage game play and participating in the sport drone tournaments to sharpen your skills."

Her classmate shook his head. "This place is like a dream come true. Unlimited game play, free energy drinks, even the pizza is awesome and the cafeteria's open 24/7."

Judy realized this *was* a gamer's idea of Heaven. They believed they were using their skills to defend their country as modern day warriors while getting unlimited, guiltless gameplay on the best equipment in the world. It was a clever strategy. It kept smart kids from closely examining what they were *really* being asked to do. She said softly to herself, "Welcome to the opium den."

Judy started training on the drone simulators and quickly discovered why they needed talented operators. The nano-drones were too tiny to have automatic stabilization. On top of that, the aerodynamics of insect-sized vehicles were weird. It was true seat-of-the-pants flying and took practice to master, but she enjoyed it and caught on fast.

After several hours, her session was over. Her instructor, a skinny, twentyish guy with big eyes and blond hair, named Dustin, said, "You're learning very fast. You'll be a great pilot."

"Thank you. You're an awesome teacher." She gave him her best smile and said, "I'm hungry. Would you like to go get a pizza with me?"

He grinned. "That'd be great."

As they ate, Judy asked him a lot of questions about himself. After he was comfortable with her, she said, "I feel kind of sorry for the hackers. That can't be anywhere near as much fun as flying drones. What do they do, anyway?"

He shrugged. "They kinda do the same thing we do but instead of using drones to track suspects, they use existing infrastructure."

Judy gave him an innocent questioning look.

He continued, "Cameras and microphones are embedded everywhere in our world today, from phones to TVs to traffic cameras. They can tap into all that."

"Wow." She paused. "So, after we master the simulator, what's next?"

"In a few days, we'll let you fly a real nano-drone around the campus for practice." He smiled. "It'll be a piece of cake for you."

She pointed at his red bracelet. "I know yellow bracelets are for us students and that we'll get green ones when we're qualified, but I'm a little confused by the other colors, the blue, red and black ones. Is red the highest level?"

"You can think of them as security or access levels. Red is the second to the highest. Black is the highest but it's reserved for the facility director and his staff. You know, the old folks. The security guards have orange bracelets. As a student, your yellow bracelet only allows you into training areas. The green one will give you access to where you'll work, flying and monitoring basic subjects. Once you've demonstrated proficiency in a real world environment and can be trusted to monitor higher level subjects, you'll get a blue one."

She touched his bracelet, but left her hand resting on his arm. "So is the red one only for instructors?"

"Yes, all instructors have red ones, but," he leaned forward, "It's more than that."

Still touching his arm, she raised her eyebrows.

He leaned closer. "When you've proven your proficiency and loyalty, you get to fly the new tactical drones." His eyes lit up. "I mean these things are as big as a car and carry lasers and missiles." He shrugged. "You also get to monitor special subjects."

Glancing around, he added quietly, "I'm not supposed to tell you this yet, but we're allowed to monitor some very high-level *Americans* that are part of the terrorist conspiracy."

She gave him her best look of awe. Then, with a shy smile, said, "I would so love to be able to do that and work with you. I know we're not supposed to start flying real drones for a couple days, but you said I was pretty good. Is there any chance we can accelerate the curriculum?"

Smiling benevolently, he said, "I don't see why not. You really are a natural and I'd be glad to give you some private coaching."

"Could we start tomorrow?"

Frowning, he said, "Uh...."

With an inviting smile, she gently squeezed his arm.

"Yeah, OK. I gotta switch some shifts with someone. I'll text you."

"Text me?"

"Oh, I keep forgetting you're new. Abadon lets us keep our phones, but there's no cell signal and the Wi-Fi is completely controlled. So, after finishing training, pretty much everyone under 30 here uses an underground network one of us created. We call it BadChat." He shrugged with a smile. "Our hackers are better at creating apps than naming them. One of the hackers figured out how to tap into our phone's walkie-talkie feature to allow all of us to send text and pictures around campus. Give me your phone."

She handed it to him.

He pulled out a charging rock and plugged it into her phone. "This will load the app." He changed a couple settings and handed it back. "It looks like an asteroid game — actually it really is one — but you'll be able to figure out how to operate the texting function inside it."

She frowned. "Do those in charge know about this?"

"Probably, but I think they realized there's no way hundreds of twenty-year-olds could survive without digital communication. We'd lose our minds." He laughed. "Or, maybe they figured that with hundreds of gamers and hackers, there's no way they could *stop us* from communicating. We know a lot more tech tricks than they do. Besides, it's not a security risk. The phone's signal isn't strong enough to travel past the compound."

"Cool. You're quite the maverick."

With a little swagger, he said, "Yeah, sometimes you just have to say WTF."

Trying not to laugh at the irony of him using the acronym instead of the real phrase, she asked, "So, what's your user name on BadChat?"

He smiled sheepishly. "Uh ... actually it *is* Maverick."

As soon as she got back to her apartment, she took her sports drone out to fly. It was not uncommon for the kids to fly them at night, complete with crazy flashing lights. Abadon actively jammed cellular and most other radio frequencies, but left the drone control frequencies open. Working with Jen, they modified her drone controller to transmit a short text piggybacked on the sport drone's control signals. She hoped Jen was able to tap into a SIGINT satellite. It was cumbersome using the controller's joystick to compose a text message, but it worked.

44

ISLAND

Flying on a fake passport, with his chip shielded, Josh caught a flight to Marsh Island Airport in the Abaco Islands.

From the small airport, Josh went to a nearby dock to meet a chartered seaplane Kristoff had arranged. He saw Jessica and Greg already waiting there.

After a quick greeting, they boarded and took off. The island was a 60-minute flight from Abaco, truly off the beaten path.

As they made their approach, he got a good look at Kristoff's island, Bobber Cay. Shaped like a giant comma, it was two miles long. The thick part of the comma had an almost 200-foot tall peak with a cliff dropping to a rocky shore. The steep shoreline wrapped around the outside curve of the comma. On the inside curve was a natural harbor with a beautiful white sand beach. The beach merged into heavy tropical vegetation, which rose gradually toward the island's peak.

Sitting directly under the peak, right on the beach was a large, turquoise Mediterranean-style house. The back of the house disappeared into the tropical vegetation. Extending from the front was a long dock with a small yacht tied to it.

As the plane circled to land, they flew right past the island's peak and caught a reflection. Greg pointed. "Look! Near the top! That almost looked like there was a window embedded in the cliff." Grinning he said, "Finally! A secret hideout in an extinct volcano!"

Jessica shook her head and with a slight frown, said, "Hmm, I don't think it's an extinct volcano. I believe most of these islands are actually made of limestone and—"

"Shhh. Don't ruin it for me."

The seaplane landed and taxied to the dock. They hopped out with minimal bags and headed down the dock toward the house.

Kristoff met them halfway. Barefoot, wearing a Hawaiian shirt and shorts, he had a drink in his hand. After giving each of them a traditional Russian bear hug, he motioned to a very cute blonde woman following him with a tray of drinks. "Help yourself to anything you want ... as long as it's Jack and Coke." He laughed, adding, "And this is Alina."

Jessica grabbed one of the drinks and downed it. "Love the Caribbean. Hate little planes." To Alina, she said, "Thank you."

Alina just nodded and smiled.

Kristoff said, "She's my niece and only speaks Russian."

Jessica gave him an obviously raised eyebrow.

Kristoff shook his head with a smile. "Seriously, Jessica, she really *is* my niece."

As Josh picked up a drink, he smiled at Alina and said, "Zdravstvuyte," and taking a sip, added, "Spasibo."

She gave him a shy smile and said, "Pozhaluysta."

Greg, trying to imitate Josh, casually picked up a drink and nodding at her with his best debonair smile, said, "Spastico."

Josh and Kristoff laughed and Jessica almost spit out her second drink.

Grabbing Greg's shirt, Jessica pulled him along. "Come on, Spastico. You don't even like Jack Daniels."

The house looked even more impressive from the ground. The dock ended in a travertine patio that extended right into the house. They followed Kristoff inside.

"Inside" was a relative term. The side of the house facing the beach had a set of large glass-panels folded accordion-style into the walls, opening the house to the ocean and a gentle tropical breeze.

Jessica did a 360. "Wow! This place is absolutely beautiful."

Inside, they found Tim, Sheri and Carl in beach garb sitting on plush furniture.

After a quick greeting, with a little back pounding between Josh and Carl, Kristoff said, "Alina will show you to your rooms. I have a couple of things I need to check on. Just relax, grab something to drink and we will reconvene."

After changing into beachwear, they joined Tim, Sheri, Carl and Kristoff.

Tim asked, "Is this place secure?"

Kristoff held up a finger to his lips and said, "Follow me."

They walked toward the back of the house. He opened a large but conventional looking door to a hallway. As they walked through, Josh noted the door was thick and made of solid metal. The hallway was a good 50 feet long and must have been cut deep into the island's rocky interior. At the end of the hall were two doors. Kristoff pressed a button and an elevator door opened. He pointed at the other door. "Or you can get some exercise and take the spiral staircase to the island's peak."

Everyone followed him into the elevator.

At the top, the door opened and they found themselves in a large, beautiful, contemporary living room. The walls and carpet were dark tones of gray with muted lighting. The reason became clear as they looked across the room. On the far side, a bank of large windows and a sliding-glass door opened onto a shallow balcony cut into the rock.

They walked toward the windows, which provided a breathtaking view of the ocean below.

Greg turned to Jessica and said, "Told you so."

Jessica ignored him and said, "This is incredible. How on earth did you build this place inside the rock?"

Josh said, "Kristoff Bobinski is one of the world's leading experts in extreme construction."

Kristoff shrugged. "In addition to natural shielding of rock, even windows have metal film, making them impervious to EMP and ... eavesdropping. We can also lower a door over the windows and balcony. From outside it looks like rock."

Jessica said, "So you can make this place invisible. Any *defensive* measures?"

Kristoff smiled. "Above us I installed a Phalanx CIWS, camouflaged of course."

Jessica's eyes got big. "You got a flippin' radar-guided 20 mm Gatling gun on the roof?!"

"Not as fancy as new laser systems ... but I'm *old fashioned,* and it was easier to, uh, procure."

With a big smile, Jessica said, "Nothing says *private island* like a stream of depleted uranium bullets coming at you at 75 rounds per second. That's effin' awesome."

Greg looked at her. "You know, sometimes you scare me."

Kristoff added, "We are secure up here and we also have a fully stocked kitchen and bar."

Alina brought out heavy hors d'oeuvres and positioned herself behind the bar. As they ate, sipped and caught up with each other, they saw the seaplane returning to land.

In Russian, Kristoff told Alina to go down and check.

They gathered around a set of very plush leather sofas and chairs. Kristoff went to a small console and pushed several buttons. Large garage-door-like shutters lowered over each of the windows and balcony. At the same time, movie screens deployed from the ceiling and covered the now shuttered windows. On the screens, high-resolution video images of the outside appeared as if the window were still uncovered.

Kristoff nodded toward the screens. "They are displaying live images from outside so we can see 360 degrees, but we are now completely secure and can talk freely."

Josh said to Kristoff, "I'd like to invite our AI friend, Jen, to participate. She's been instrumental in uncovering the plot and supporting our investigation. She's a powerful resource and ally."

Sheri added, "We told Carl about her."

Kristoff nodded, "There's no cell phone reception anywhere near this island."

Josh said, "Not a problem. She can use the Iridium satellites."

Kristoff said, "OK, I will connect your phone to an external antenna." As soon as they established the connection, Josh introduced Jen to everyone.

The elevator dinged and they heard two women speaking in Russian. Alina came out followed by ... Wendy Crow.

45

AFFAIR

Elizabeth wrapped up the video conference with her team. Smiling, she said, "You guys have done an outstanding job, and it looks as if this fix will take care of the bandwidth problem once and for all. I'll fly to Houston tonight so I can be there for the test tomorrow. If all goes well, we'll just need a quick demo and sign off with Admiral Meadows and the ISLO Commander."

Her project manager in Houston nodded his head. "Yes, I'm positive it will work this time." He frowned. "However, we were just informed that Colonel Crow won't be available." One of his eyebrows went up. "Apparently, she's taking a short vacation in the Caribbean and we'll have to wait until she returns to get the final sign off."

Elizabeth was pissed. Crow was happy to jerk them around, but when they finally had a solution, she was nowhere to be seen. Careful not to show any emotion, Elizabeth said, "No problem. We'll be ready for her when she returns."

After Elizabeth got back to her office, she found a nice surprise. On her desk was a big beautiful bouquet of exotic flowers and a huge basket of chocolate-covered fruit. With ripe dark-chocolate covered strawberries, bananas and pineapples, it must have weighed five pounds. She was starving and immediately stuffed a juicy strawberry into her mouth, then opened the card.

It read, "Heard you pulled it off. You've been putting in crazy hours and working beyond the call of duty. You're doing a great job moving the TELEMED program forward and I believe in you! Keep up the great work. With admiration, Doruk."

She smiled. How someone with the security of the world

resting on his shoulders had time to do random acts of kindness was beyond her.

She went to Turan's office. His executive assistant just nodded when she arrived. Turan told her that as long as his door was open, she could come in anytime.

Elizabeth knocked softly on his doorframe.

He looked up from behind one of the three monitors on his desk and smiled. "Come in."

She shook her head. "You really shouldn't have gotten me those flowers and that incredible fruit basket. I don't know how you knew, but those are my favorites and they're absolutely delicious. Thank you!"

"Pleasure's all mine. You're doing an outstanding job and I'm very proud of you."

"You're an amazing boss." She smiled. "Just wanted to thank you. Well, I better get moving. I'm flying to Houston tonight to oversee the final bandwidth fix."

"Excellent. I'm sure it will go well." Turan came around his desk, sat on the edge and said, "With Josh accepting the position, this has turned out to be an exceptional day."

Elizabeth frowned and with a slight headshake asked, "Position?"

"Deputy Director of Global Security."

She was speechless. Finally she asked the obvious, "My Josh?"

He frowned. "Yes, yes of course."

Shocked, she was not sure how she felt, but said, "That's, uh ... great."

Seeing her face, he said, "I'm sorry, Elizabeth, I thought you knew. I should have let him tell you."

Without thinking, she said, "That'd never happen." She sighed. "I'm sorry ... things are still a little tense after the ball and we haven't been talking ... much." She hadn't heard from him in over two weeks.

"I see. Is there anything I can do to help?"

She shook her head. "No. You've been nothing but awesome." She took a deep breath. "You know what. This is just silly. Josh and I just need to talk this out. Do you know if he's still here?"

Turan shook his head. "I told him it would be a few days before we could set up staff briefings to bring him up to speed. He said he was going to spend a couple days in the Caribbean."

Inhaling sharply, she felt like she'd been punched in the stomach. She managed a, "Oh. OK.... I ... I better go."

Turan gently put his hand on her shoulder. "Are you OK?"

She nodded her head but tears rolled down her cheek.

He gently pulled her in and hugged her.

Josh got the "I told you so" look from Sheri. He stood up to introduce Wendy. "This is—"

With a grin, Greg interrupted, "Colonel Wendy Crow, the new commander of the International Space-based Laser and Observatory!" He jumped up to shake her hand. "It's been all over the news."

She shook everyone's hand and then sat down next to Josh.

Josh said, "OK. Tim, you want to kick it off?"

Tim nodded and looked at Sheri and Carl. "We should probably get the bad news out of the way first." Glancing briefly at Josh, he said, "Sheri checked Kelly and Caitlin, Carl's wife and three-year-old daughter. They've also been implanted with the neurotoxin capsules."

Josh shook his head but kept his face expressionless.

After a deep breath, Carl said, "If you're going to try and force someone to do what you want them to do, there's always the possibility they'll refuse, even if it means their life." He shook his head. "It's very different if they can kill your family." He paused with a frown. "But I honestly don't understand why I and my family were targeted. It's not like I hold a top decision-making position in the agency, and so far, no one's threatened me or told me to do anything." He shook his head again. "All I can think of is that it has to do with Davidson. Somehow he discovered he'd been implanted and figured out he was being watched. He sent a text to me, and others, warning us the Wraith program was being used against us and we were under surveillance. He was killed shortly after. Later, I thought I saw a nano-drone in my house and brought it down with bug spray."

Sheri asked, "That actually works?" She turned to Josh.

"Aren't you an aerospace engineer?"

Josh shrugged, "Probably just gummed up the wings."

Carl said. "I smashed it to be on the safe side. When I looked at it with a magnifying glass, sure enough, it was a Wraith drone." He shook his head. "Finding it in my house changed everything. I had to find a way to communicate with fellow CIA officers without endangering my family or theirs, but didn't know who to trust or how to get the message to them. Then Josh dropped by."

Tim said, "Sheri, can you go over what we know about the implants?"

"By now, everyone's familiar with the basics. The tiny chips placed under the skin — usually in the hand or scalp — are simply passive RFID tags. They allow the victim to be identified and tracked, but only within a range of a couple hundred meters. So, the tracking system has to be close by. Tim, Josh and Wendy were all chipped. We removed Tim's after his untimely death. For Josh, Wendy and Carl, metal impregnated Band-Aids or gloves easily block the signal." She paused. "The larger powered capsules are a much bigger problem." She passed around her tablet with the schematic on the display. "Jen's only been able to unencrypt the graphics so far, but it tells a lot."

Jen inserted, "I'm getting close and I think I will have the text unencrypted in a few days."

"Thanks Jen. If you look closely at the diagrams of the capsule, you'll see they're designed to be attached to a major vein. Like the drones, they're powered by a speck of plutonium-238. This powers a tiny transceiver that, upon encoded command, can release the toxin, which will induce a fatal heart attack within seconds. So far we've found them attached to the femoral vein in Wendy and the jugular vein in Carl." She frowned. "To insert them, I suspect they either tranquilize the victim, or possibly slip it in during a normal medical procedure. The location may simply be a function of the medical procedure they're piggybacked on."

Carl nodded. "I went in for a physical and a few days later got a call. They said I needed to come in and have my carotid artery checked for possible blockage."

Sheri asked, "You went back to your doctor?"

"No. They sent me to another clinic that *specialized* in this type of procedure. They appeared to do a real sonogram—"

"It probably *was* real," Sheri interrupted. "It helped them place the capsule in the right position on your jugular vein."

He sighed. "Kelly and Caitlin were called in for special exams shortly after."

Sheri nodded. "A fake call from your doctor's office and they send you to *their* clinic."

Wendy added, "In the case of astronauts, we're examined and poked so often, we don't even question it when they send us out for tests. They could do it almost anytime and put it anywhere and we wouldn't think twice about it."

Sheri looked at Josh. "We haven't done the exam with the radiation detector on Josh, but he went through an extensive astronaut exam. I'll bet we'll find he has one too."

Tim said, "Think of what that means. If an enemy agent was inserted into the astronaut core and they were able to implant astronauts during physicals, they must have highly placed agents in NASA, the U.N. or both."

Carl asked, "Can we remove them?"

"I could probably take them out under local anesthesia." She sighed. "But they're attached directly to the vein. There's a possibility they're booby-trapped and trying to remove them could trigger the toxin. Until Jen unencrypts the specs, we can't risk it."

Jessica said, "For Josh, Carl and Wendy, we should be able to block the capsule's active signal using a special fabric woven with metallic fibers."

With a cynical smile, Wendy said, "Metal underwear — sounds stylish."

Jessica added, "The material actually feels normal. It *will* block the outgoing signal because the capsule's transmitter is weak." She shook her head. "But without wrapping your entire body in metallic material, the capsule may still be able to *receive* an incoming signal if it's strong enough."

"Meaning they can't track us but ... may still be able to kill us."

Jessica nodded.

Josh said, "Let's review the suspect list. There are multiple terrorist groups with the motive, but not the means. This involves major facilities, the ability to assassinate the DNI, implant chips and capsules, infiltrate the astronaut core and intercept us with a fighter. The U.S., Russia, China, India, Japan, Iran, Korea and Western Europe all probably have the means to do that. Thoughts?"

Carl glanced at Tim. "Tim and I have spent our entire career in the covert world, and we've seen plenty of conspiracies … but not on this scale."

Tim nodded. "There have to be people involved at high levels of government across the world including the U.N. The question is — who are the ringleaders?"

Kristoff said, "Their largest facility appears to be located in the U.S."

Jen inserted, "I just received an encrypted text from our agent inside Abadon. It said that more experienced and loyal operatives get to monitor high-level American subjects."

Carl added, "And, clearly, Davidson wasn't involved." He shrugged, "But that doesn't mean someone high up in the U.S. government isn't."

Wendy glanced at Kristoff. "Sorry, but of all the players, the government that's the most hostile to the new U.N. and what it stands for is Russia."

Tim added, "And we know that Russian intelligence had Josh under conventional surveillance in New York."

46

PENETRATION

Kristoff nodded. "Colonel Crow is right. In addition to President Volkov's nationalism, he despises the Secretary-General."

Josh added, "Probably not all Volkov's fault. Turan shared that General Von Stein is a bit of a loose cannon. Tim, you're the expert here. What's the next step?"

"We need to work independently both to cover more ground and to protect each other's identity. Josh, you try to find out who in the U.N. is involved, and bring in Turan and Meadows. Carl and Jessica, you're in the best positions to figure out who's involved in the U.S. government. Colonel Crow will keep the ISLO's trigger secure from enemy agents. With Jen's help, I'll stay close to our operative inside Abadon. Jen can keep working on the encrypted capsule specs, but I think the key is in Russia."

Kristoff said, "Dah, but I don't have any contacts in this administration."

Sheri said, "I do. When I wrote my last book on global disasters, I interviewed the head of the Russian version of our FEMA, Pasha Antonovich. With the new administration, he's now a cabinet member, Minister of Emergency Situations."

Tim frowned and quickly said, "You don't speak the language and if Russia turns out to be directly involved, you're walking into the lion's den."

"Thank you for worrying about me sweetie, but I have some immunity by being," she dramatically swept her hair back, "a celebrity. Be awkward to knock me off and I can get access where others can't. Besides, I'll have Kristoff there and Jen in my ear."

"Being a celebrity will only carry you so far. You don't want to have an *accident* like your late husband."

She just looked at him.

"I know that look ... but I need you to stay in touch and stick with Kristoff."

Kristoff nodded. "It would make sense she would travel with an old friend from the Resurrect Program." He smiled. "And it wouldn't be unusual for me to be seen hanging around beautiful women." More seriously, he added, "I will make sure she is safe."

"Thank you." Tim looked at Josh. "I think it's time to bring Elizabeth in. We could use her access and insight."

"I'll take care of it."

Finally, turning back to Kristoff, Tim gestured around the room. "This place is impressive. Can we continue to use it as our operational base?"

"Of course. We are only an hour flight from Miami. I will lease fast amphibious plane that can fly us between here and mainland."

Josh said, "Great. Jessica, Greg and Jen, could you please make sure everyone has the apps and hardware mods on their phones?"

They nodded.

Tim added, "Remember, do not discuss any of this in the open with anyone ... including each other."

After the official meeting broke up, Josh noticed that despite taking on the greatest conspiracy in history, the mood was light. They were a group of combat-tested friends with a purpose. After sharing a few pizzas and some more drinks, Tim yawned and nodded to Sheri.

She said, "Go ahead. I'll be right down."

He gave her a meaningful look and headed to the elevator with Greg and Alina.

Kristoff moved behind the bar, and said, "Colonel Crow, what can I get you to drink?"

In Russian, she said, "It's just Wendy and my favorite drink is actually Stoli Elit."

Kristoff, looking surprised, said, "Your Russian is excellent, as is your taste in vodka."

"Most U.S. astronauts learn Russian."

Josh couldn't resist. "Kristoff believes Single Barrel Jack

Daniels is the best liquor in the universe and the *only* American contribution to global culture."

Kristoff shrugged as he poured her a shot. "But ... a good Russian vodka is a close second."

Wendy downed the shot. "Thank you Mr. Bobinski. Could you tell me where the bathroom is?"

He pointed down a hall on the far side of the room. "Call me Kristoff."

After she left, he nodded approvingly. "I like her."

With a wry smile, Sheri said, "Kristoff, you like all beautiful women."

"Dah, but she has spirit and good taste."

Sheri turned her attention to Josh. Punching him in the arm, she said, "I told you! You are *such* a knucklehead."

Josh looked at her with surprise. "Me?! It's *your* fault."

"How is it my fault?"

"Sheri, I told you my examining her whole body was a very bad idea and that *you* should do it. You called me a wuss and hung up."

Kristoff and Jessica leaned in with interest, trying to follow the conversation.

Sheri said, "It had to be done and it was no big deal."

With an incredulous look, he said, "Uh ... *yeah*, if you're a doctor—"

Kristoff tapped them both on the arm.

Wendy came back from the hall. "Kristoff, this place is nothing short of amazing."

He handed her another shot. "Thank you." They clinked glasses and downed them together.

Sheri turned to Josh and said, "OK, we need to check you for the toxin capsule with the radiation detector."

Josh frowned. "You and Jessica need to be re-checked too."

Sheri pulled a radiation detector out of her purse.

Josh said, "What ... here?!"

Jessica shrugged. "It's not like Sheri and I haven't already seen you in the buff."

Wendy helpfully added, "I haven't, but turnabout's fair play."

Josh opened his hands and gave them all a "you can't be

serious" look.

Trying not to laugh, Sheri said, "Sorry Josh, but you've developed a reputation for two things: crashing airplanes and getting naked with the women on the team, so...." She held up the radiation detector.

Shaking his head, he snatched it from her hand. "*I'll* do it." He headed for the elevator. As the door closed, he heard them all laughing and smiled.

Sheri watched Kristoff top off their drinks.

He said, "Josh is smart man. When faced with three formidable women ... he ran away. I shall follow his lead." He set the bottle, representing each of their drinks of choice, on the bar and said, "Goodnight ladies."

After they wished him a goodnight, Sheri realized with "just the girls" and social lubricant onboard, it was an opportunity to learn more about Wendy. Before she could engage her, Jessica said to Sheri, "You know, it's not just that it's fun to embarrass Josh," she smiled, "it is, but I just realized something."

Sheri looked at her with minimal interest as Wendy frowned trying to follow her.

With filters gone, Jessica plowed ahead, "Not only does it make him seem human but you and I are totally task oriented and Josh ... well, he has a pathetic streak of thoughtfulness." She laughed. "Teasing him is like shooting fish in a barrel."

Wendy, frowned, asked, "What do you mean ... *make him seem human?*"

Sheri gave Jessica a "shut up" look.

Jessica missed it as she poured herself another drink, and said, "He's missing like *half* his DNA."

Wendy shook her head. "Wow ... that might explain some things...."

Sheri inserted, "That's just a rumor. It was probably a botched genetic test." Changing the subject, she said, "So, tell us what happened on the station."

Wendy downed her third shot and quickly recounted the events. "After it was over, I went back and reviewed all the videos and time logs." She looked at Sheri. "I'm in excellent aerobic condition. After the module was flooded with CO_2, I was able to maintain consciousness for over three minutes."

Sheri nodded. "Impressive, particularly with strenuous activity."

Frowning, Wendy added, "Yeah, but from the data logs, the time between opening the pod hatch — when I lost consciousness — to when the pod's emergency oxygen was activated was another six minutes. That means Josh was without oxygen for *nine minutes!* Sheri, you're a doctor. Is that even possible?"

Sheri sighed. "Wendy, everything about Josh is at the ... *outside* limit of human capability."

Eyes unfocused, Wendy said softly, "There's just *something* about him...."

With a slight slur, Jessica inserted an irrelevant, "Yeah, and he has a nice bod."

Ignoring her, Wendy continued, "I've never met anyone like him." She glanced at Sheri. "So, what's the story on him? Who *is* he?"

Sheri gave her a small shrug. "Josh's a walking, talking miracle and we all love him, but the real question might be," she took a sip of her wine, *"what* is he?"

Jessica lifted her drink in a mock toast, "Welcome to the Twilight Zone."

Wendy said, "No, I mean I really want to know his story."

Sheri frowned. *"None of us* know his whole story, not even Elizabeth, but I do know ... he's dangerous."

Wendy looked surprised. "Dangerous? He saved my life. He was instrumental in saving the world!"

Jessica added, "Twice!"

Sheri said, "He would never hurt you or any of us. In fact, he'd give his life to protect us," she shook her head, "but he's a lightning rod."

Wendy gave her a questioning look.

"Think about it. He saved your life ... but would you have been a target if he hadn't gone to the station? Where he goes, destruction and mayhem follow." She paused. "Wendy, I don't know what your belief set is." She shrugged. "I don't even know what *mine* is, but there's no way you can convince me he just happens to show up when the world's in trouble. He's not here by accident. He's on a mission. Our job is to support him and," she looked at her pointedly, "not *distract* him." She patted Wendy gently on the hand. "Honey, he's married."

Wendy set her shot glass on the bar and stood up. "It was great to meet you guys. I think I'm going to turn in."

As they watched the elevator door close, Sheri blew out a lungful of air and shook her head.

Jessica, holding her glass up like a microphone, imitated a documentary narrator. In a hushed tone, she said, "On the Serengeti Plain, the defenseless chimpanzee is ruthlessly stalked by the lioness."

Trying not to laugh, Sheri thumped Jessica on the back. "Let's go."

Josh finished running the detector next to his major veins. Sure enough, it alarmed near his right femoral. Remembering how many times he was poked during the physical, he wasn't surprised. Not sleepy and needing exercise and time to think, he went out for a night run on the beach.

There was a sliver of a moon, but his exceptional night vision dark-adapted quickly. It was a humid 80 degrees with a soft ocean breeze. He ran along the strip of sand, bracketed by softly waving palm trees on his left and the gentle whoosh of surf to his right. Running barefoot, he loved the firm but cushioned feel of wet sand under his feet. The pristine island was beautiful, but at night, it took on a haunting and mysterious feel.

After a mile and a half, the beach ended in an aggressive outcrop of rock. Blocking his path, it rose toward the island's ridgeline. He jumped into the cooler water. Swimming away from the beach as hard as he could, he quickly covered a half mile at an Olympic pace. He finally stopped. Treading water, he caught his breath and looked out to sea. It was beautiful. Something in him wanted to keep swimming away, but he was pulled back.

He swam back with a relaxed sidestroke. As he left the water, he carefully climbed up the rough rocks and found a place to sit just above the crashing waves. As his breathing slowed and he dried off, he sucked in the ocean air, absorbing the tropical calm. After a few minutes of Zen, he said aloud, "Jesse, you there?"

He heard no reply, but sensed attention.

"I need to ask you about Doruk Turan. He appears remarkably similar to me and seems to have my abilities. Is he … GMO?"

Yes.

"I knew it! I wish you had shared that with me sooner. Are you in contact with him too?"

No.

He was about to ask more when he caught movement in his peripheral vision. He glanced back down the beach toward the house. His exceptional night vision picked up someone approaching. In the dark, all he could see was the outline of a body … a female body. The silhouette was immediately recognizable; one he was only *too* familiar with….

47

COLLIDE

Kristoff saw Josh, Jessica and Greg off the next morning. Standing on the end of the dock next to a sleek new seaplane, he said, "I wanted to lease a plane but couldn't find any on short notice. Had to buy this one and pay extra to have pilot fly it here this morning."

Josh nodded. "It's a beauty. I'll have the pilot check me out in it on the way back so I can fly us here next time."

Kristoff nodded. "It's fully insured."

Josh shook his head with a smile. "Very funny."

Kristoff gave them all a good Russian hug and kissed their cheeks before they boarded the plane.

As he walked back down the dock, he met Alina and asked, "Have you seen Mr. Smith, Dr. Lopez or Colonel Crow yet?"

She said, "Mr. Smith went for a run on the beach and I think Dr. Lopez and Colonel Crow are still sleeping. Would you like me to wake them?"

"Absolutely not." With a smile, he added, "I've learned that women such as these look like cute fuzzy kittens. Wake them early and you discover they are actually Bengal Tigers only after you've lost your head."

Alina laughed.

Back at the house, Kristoff grabbed a carafe of coffee and a couple cups. He sat outside on the travertine deck that wrapped the front of the house. As he faced the ocean, Sheri's room was on his far left in one wing of the beach house, and Wendy's just to his right. Wendy's room faced the ocean with a private patio angled slightly away from the dock.

He sat pondering their upcoming mission, when he heard a

soft, "Good morning."

Turning to his right, he saw Wendy peeking around her room's patio wall.

He smiled and said, "Good morning," and then pointed to the coffee.

With her long black hair in beautiful disarray, she joined him. "That would be great." She was still wearing pajama bottoms and a tank top, which did nothing to disguise her exceptional physique. Her small smile transformed her from scary to breathtaking.

As she pulled up a chair next to him, he poured her a cup of coffee. Not wanting to poke the tiger, he sat quietly, letting her absorb caffeine.

After a few minutes of silence watching the ocean and sipping, she finally said, "I love the sound of the surf. I kept my patio door open to the beach all night and slept like a rock." She gave him a sheepish smile. "Of course, the Stoli probably helped."

"You hold vodka like a Russian."

"Debatable. I don't drink often," she shook her head, "which is good, because lately, when I have, it's gotten me and others in trouble."

She didn't elaborate and he didn't ask.

Finally she said, "Where is everyone?"

"Most of them left early this morning."

"Josh?"

He nodded

Her gaze shifted to the horizon and her eyes unfocused. After a couple minutes, she said, "In a few weeks, I'll be taking the space station out to L2. We'll be further away from Earth than anyone has ever been. It's the pinnacle of my career, and I wouldn't trade it for anything in the world." She glanced at him with a wistful smile. "But now I realize, for the first time in my life, there are ... *things* ... I don't want to leave behind."

After Sheri woke up, she did research on the current Russian administration. She also checked the news to see what was happening in Moscow and then called her old friend, Minister Pasha Antonovich. "Hi Pasha, it's Sheri Lopez."

In excellent but heavily accented English, he said, "Sheri, it's so good to hear from you. I was so sorry to hear about your husband. Please accept my condolences."

"Thank you. It has been hard." She added the appropriate pause. "Congratulations on your new cabinet position, that's fantastic."

"Thanks Sheri, it's been exciting but challenging." He paused. "Is there anything I can do to help you?"

She sighed. "I just can't sit at home, I'll go crazy. I've decided the best way to deal with this is to get out and work. I'm writing another book."

"That's a great idea."

"I could really use your expertise, particularly from your new vantage as a member of the cabinet."

"Of course, Sheri."

"And I think just getting out of the country and meeting new people will help."

"I think that's a great idea and I would love to see you." He paused, "I remember that you enjoy social events. There's a state dinner in two days if you can make it. I'm sure I could get you an invitation."

"Thank you Pasha, that would be great. While I'm in Russia, Kristoff Bobinski, the Russian construction expert is going to be hosting me. Would it be OK to bring him?"

Sounding a little less enthusiastic, he said, "Yes, yes of course."

After finishing their conversation, Sheri found Kristoff and shared the invitation.

He responded in a monotone, "A state dinner; how exciting." Smiling, he added, "I understand. The Russian government is still dominated by men, and men with vodka inside and a beautiful ear outside…."

"You're a smart man, Kristoff."

He shook his head. "It took me two wives to figure any of this out."

Josh flew back to New York City and went to the U.N. He was excited to see Elizabeth but also nervous. He hoped his new position would at least help her understand that *others* didn't think he was paranoid, and would give him an opportunity to explain what happened on the space station. He'd have to figure out how to get her alone first.

As soon as he arrived at her office, he learned she was in Houston with Turan shepherding the TELEMED program fix but would be back late that afternoon.

He turned himself over to Turan's staff and ended up sitting through 10 hours of briefings with the promise of two more days of the same.

Although he wished they could talk faster, he found that the projects Global Security was working on were extensive and impressive. The only one that gave him pause was the passport initiative. They were promoting the voluntary use of RFID chips, similar to the chip surreptitiously injected into his hand. They wanted the chips to completely replace passports and even have them carry emergency medical information. The idea wasn't new but in a world where country boundaries were fading, the argument was getting stronger. It would speed up international travel and make it easier to catch criminals and terrorists on the move. He knew only too well, however, it also made it easier to track law-abiding citizens.

As for getting the U.N. veto authority over nuclear weapon strikes, it was a great theory. He had a hard time imagining any nuclear capable country agreeing to it, and an even harder time seeing how it could be enforced.

During the meetings, he was introduced to many of Turan's high-level staff as well as the Deputy Secretary-General. Hassan Batusura, from Indonesia, was a small, nervous man and not particularly friendly, but he was supposed to be an exceptional administrator. Josh saw or heard nothing from him or any of Turan's staff that raised suspicion.

After the briefings, he got word that Elizabeth was back from Houston and went to her office. He knocked on her open door.

She looked up. Her face was a mask as she said, "What do you want?"

He was taken back by the cold response and actually stumbled. "I ... umm. We need to talk."

"Is it in regards to telemedicine?"

He frowned. "Uh, no."

"Then I'm not sure we have anything to say to each other." She looked back at her computer monitor.

He was so surprised, he didn't respond initially. Finally he took a step into her office and said, "I'm still your husband! We need to get things straightened out."

She looked back at him. "I think you've made your choices very clear."

"What?! Elizabeth, I know there have been some awkward situations, but I can explain all of it, if you'll just give me the chance."

Still cold as ice, she crossed her arms and sat back. "I'm listening."

He shook his head and with real frustration. "I can't talk about it *here*!"

She shook her head. "I don't have time for this. Our program is under a critical time line, and I have to be back in Houston tomorrow. I don't need distractions."

Now he was mad. "So, I'm just a distraction?!"

Her eyes flashed. "Let me save you some time. I know you were in the Caribbean with Wendy, so let's not pretend anymore."

Again, he was surprised. "Uh ... yes but I can explain." His hands were tied. Even if there were no nano-drones around, he was standing in her office doorway where other people could hear.

"I think you already have. You need to leave now and let me get back to work."

"I..." He shook his head. "Damn it, Elizabeth, you're being unreasonable." He pointed at the giant flower and fruit basket near her desk. "Is it because of those?"

She closed her eyes for a second. When she opened them, he could see tears, but she maintained steel in her voice as she said, "Just leave. Now."

He threw up his hands and opened his mouth but nothing came out. She wouldn't even make eye contact. He turned and left.

As soon as Josh was clear of the U.N. and nano-drones, he called

Sheri and explained what happened.

When he finished, Sheri said, "Yeah, I can see how that would look to her. Glad I'm not in your shoes."

"Sheri, that's not real helpful."

She sighed. "Elizabeth is clearly not of a mindset to let you explain right now and that's not logical or fair to you." She took a deep breath. "Our only chance is to get her alone."

"Any ideas?"

"Yes ... Kristoff and I are scheduled to fly out of New York to Moscow. Let me see if I can meet with her. I'm sorry, Josh, I know this is causing both of you a lot of pain."

"Yeah, and we need to move quickly."

"Why?"

"We need her on the team and ... I'm about to be traded in for a better model."

48

ELIZABETH

That evening, Elizabeth's phone rang.

It was Sheri Lopez. "Hi Elizabeth, how are you doing?"

"Hi Sheri! I'm doing fine but I've been a terrible friend. I'm so sorry about Tim."

"You sent beautiful flowers and Josh told me right after it happened that you'd both jump on an airplane and be there anytime."

"I know but I should have kept in closer touch." She sighed. "How are you doing?"

"I'm doing OK. It helps to reconnect with friends. I'm going to Moscow tomorrow for some research on a new book, but I'll be flying through New York City and have a few hour layover in the morning. Know it's short notice but any chance you might be available for an early breakfast?"

"Absolutely! That would actually work great. I have to fly to Houston tomorrow at noon. Just name the time and place."

"I'll have a driver while I'm there, so I'll pick you up and we can figure out a place to eat."

Dustin led Judy into a small room. It was a mockup of a regular drone operation cubicle. She recognized it from the pictures Tim showed her.

He brought out a small, flat metal box, opened it and gave her a magnifying glass.

She looked inside. "Weird. I've seen pictures but in real life it looks like the offspring of a mosquito that slept with a Transformer."

He laughed. "OK, sit down in the chair and put on your VR headset."

As her headset came alive, she saw what the nano-drone saw. She saw herself sitting in the chair and Dustin handing her the controller. She immediately tried to bring the nano-drone to a hover with Dustin coaching her.

"Easy with it. A little less power. OK, keep it away from the wall."

The real thing was different from the simulators. It was both easier and harder. She flew it into a wall.

He said, "No problem. They're pretty tough. Just give it a little power and work on hovering."

After 10 minutes, he said, "You've got it. I'm going to open the door and I want you to take it for a spin around the campus very carefully. There's a light breeze which you'll have to accommodate for but these things can handle up to 15 knots."

She flew it just outside the room for a few minutes to get used to open spaces and the breeze.

"The next step is flying patterns, but you've got it down pretty well, so I'll teach you some tactics. Take it up to about 20 feet and pick someone with a yellow bracelet walking across campus."

She saw one of her classmates and headed toward him.

"Good. Now come up behind him. We avoid flying in anyone's forward vision area. Although, we're hard to see, we're not invisible and many nano-drones have been smashed by flyswatters."

She flew behind him.

"You want to be a little higher, so if they turn around you won't be in their face and you can see what they're seeing."

She flew it just above and behind his head and kept it there.

"Great job tracking. You really are a natural. OK, now let's try something a little more advanced. This won't be easy. You want to try and land on his shoulder near his collar."

She made several passes but with the video pointed straight ahead, it was difficult to see below and judge distance to the landing.

After several attempts, she finally did it.

"Congratulations! It usually takes days to master that! It's like you've been flying drones for 20 years."

"I feel like I have." He had no idea of her real age. She asked, "Why do we want to land on their shoulder?"

"It's the easiest way to follow them into a building, car, etcetera. There's a good chance that the suspect will enter an area that will block our signal. Not only can't we monitor them, we lose control of the drone. The bottom of each drone has a sticky landing gear, kind of like a real insect, and it'll stay attached even when we lose contact. Then we just wait until we get a signal again and off we go."

"Can the drone record while it's offline?"

He shook his head. "We wish. There isn't enough room in them to record data. They can only transmit what they see and hear."

"Why do we park them near the collar?"

"We tried the hair but people comb it or brush it. People also brush their shoulder for dandruff, or get patted. By keeping it close to the collar, there's less chance of being knocked off or seen."

After the session, they went to the cafeteria for dinner. Smiling Judy asked, "Would you teach me some more of the advanced tactics in after-hours sessions?"

"We're really not supposed to do any after-hours training. I don't want to get us in trouble."

"No, I wouldn't want that but it would be kinda fun ... Maverick." She put her hand on his arm and added, "Then maybe you can come over to my place ... after?"

"Well ... guess it wouldn't hurt if we just took one out for a short flight, and you'll need to know how to operate at night." He looked around with a conspiratorial smile. "Meet me back at the training building tonight at ten."

Judy went straight back to her place and flew her sports drone so she could text Jen the tactics she learned. When she finished, she returned to her apartment. It was possible that her apartment was bugged but it was unlikely she, or any of the drone pilots and hackers, were being regularly monitored. They couldn't monitor all the monitors. Eventually, they'd run out of people. On top of that, they had them contained inside the facility and could kill them quickly with an electronic command.

She disassembled her sports drone on the coffee table in front of the TV. Among drone racers, it was not uncommon to soup up or trick out the drones. With parts scattered all over the table, she knew that even if she was being watched, it would be hard to catch her inserting a circuit into her VR headset. The circuit would save whatever the headset saw to a tiny removable memory card.

The next morning, peeking out her apartment lobby windows, Elizabeth saw a blacked-out limo pull up. She stepped outside.

The driver, a Sikh with a turban, beard and sunglasses, got out and opened the car door for her.

As she slipped inside, Sheri hugged her and said, "I know a nice quiet place to eat in the Hamptons overlooking the ocean."

"That would be great."

"Before we go, is it OK if we get a picture together?" Sheri handed her phone to the driver.

She was a little surprised but said, "Of course."

The driver never took off his sunglasses but swept the phone around the interior as if trying to get it to focus, then took several pictures. He handed it back to Sheri, closed the glass panel between them, and pulled out.

Sheri looked intently at the pictures and then, turned to her and said, "Oh, hold still. It looks like you might have a little bug on your right shoulder. Don't move." She took an empty metal coffee thermos, held it against Elizabeth's shoulder and gently brushed something into it with a tissue.

Elizabeth frowned as she watched Sheri cap the thermos and set it in the limo's cup holder, wondering if the stress of Tim's death might have something to do with her odd behavior. She wasn't sure if Sheri wanted to talk about Tim, so she just let Sheri drive the conversation.

Sheri asked her a lot of questions about her new job. After several minutes describing her program and the challenges, Sheri finally nodded and said, "Wow. Sounds like you've been very busy." She paused. "Oh, I ran into Josh recently. Sorry to hear you guys are having some struggles."

Elizabeth nodded. "I'd rather not talk about that right now."

"Why?"

"Sheri, you have enough on your plate."

With a slight smile, she said, "Remember, I am a psychiatrist and I like to help people, particularly, people I love."

Elizabeth bit the side of her lip and sighed. "Look, I really don't want to talk about it because ... Josh's having an affair."

Sheri frowned. "Are you sure? Was that why you haven't returned his calls?"

Elizabeth matched her frown. "I don't know what he told you but I haven't heard anything from him since he started this..." she exhaled sharply, "...this juvenile conspiracy stuff and began sleeping with Colonel Wendy Crow."

"Hmm ... Josh told me he called you many times and you never responded to his calls or texts."

Elizabeth pulled out her phone and showed Sheri the call log and texts. "Last time he tried to contact me was almost three weeks ago."

"That's interesting." She frowned. "Elizabeth ... I'm afraid you're operating under some significant misinformation."

Elizabeth shook her head. "I hope he hasn't got you caught up in his crazy conspiracy theories."

Sheri paused. "The reason I wanted to meet you was so that we could talk without risk of being overheard or observed."

"You're starting to sound just like him."

"There's a good reason for that. You know those little RFID chips that the U.N. was promoting to replace passports?"

"Yes?"

"Well, Josh and Tim were unknowingly implanted with them so they could be tracked. You probably have one too."

Elizabeth started to object but Sheri continued, "I need you to listen very carefully. Your life depends on it. The conspiracy is real and spans the globe, possibly including the United Nations."

Elizabeth said, "I don't think—"

Sheri held up her hand. "Please ... I know you asked Meadows to help Josh and believe that's why he was sent to the space station. What you don't know was that Wendy discovered the ISLO's software was modified to allow it to destroy targets on Earth. When Wendy tried to tell Josh, whoever was behind it, attempted to shut her up by starting a fire in the space station module she was working in. Josh dove in at the last minute and almost died saving her."

Elizabeth's eyes got big. "OK, I'm listening but saving her life doesn't excuse him for *sleeping* with her or taking her to the Caribbean!"

Sheri gently shook her head. "Please let me finish. After almost burning up and then being asphyxiated, Wendy not only lost consciousness but stopped breathing. Josh was able to get her into one of the pods, restore emergency oxygen and perform CPR. The killer ejected the pod they were in from the space station. With some fancy flying, they got it back to the station before they were asphyxiated again. *Then* Josh faced the killer in a zero-g knife fight. Before they could interrogate him, he died of a heart attack."

Elizabeth shook her head. "This can't be for real."

"The autopsy showed it was caused by a neurotoxin; the same neurotoxin that killed Brian Davidson. It was injected from a capsule surgically implanted inside them. Elizabeth, it's the same capsule Wendy and Josh have inside them, *and* ... there's a possibility you do too. Josh couldn't talk to you except in private because it could put both of your lives in danger."

Elizabeth exhaled slowly. "I'm sorry but this sounds like the plot of a crazy spy movie."

Sheri picked up the coffee thermos, took the top off and carefully poured the contents onto a white tissue. She gave Elizabeth a magnifying glass. "Take a look at what's been riding on you."

She peered at the insect. "What?! It's ... it's a machine!"

"It's called a nano-drone and it's been watching you 24/7."

"Wait ... like in the bedroom and bathroom?"

Sheri nodded.

"Eww." She paused. "I wonder if that's what Toto's been chasing in my apartment."

"Dogs can hear higher frequencies than we can."

Elizabeth put her hand on her forehead. "Dogs and ... *Josh!*"

Sheri nodded. "Elizabeth, you're a nurse. Let's say you have a patient that's been awake for over 30 hours. During that time, they're almost killed twice. They're asphyxiated to the point that they stop breathing. They also watch a man die. What state would you expect them to be in?"

"Emotional shock, exhaustion — PTSD."

"Elizabeth, the only place on the space station that isn't monitored with video and audio is the crew compartments. That's where Wendy told Josh about the software modification in the first place. After it was all over — 30 hours later — she asked Josh to come back to her compartment to talk. Josh said she began shaking uncontrollably."

Elizabeth nodded reluctantly. "Delayed shock."

"And?"

Elizabeth sighed. "Josh ... held her."

"Until she fell asleep. He stayed with her through the night."

Nodding her head slowly, Elizabeth added, "Josh needs very little sleep but even he can't stay awake forever. They *slept* together."

"He did the same thing you or I would have done in that situation. Does this begin to make sense?"

"Yes, yes it does ... but what about the Caribbean? They were there together, right?"

"Yes they were, but so was I, so was Kristoff Bobinski, Greg Langlois, Jessica Lee and ..." she knocked on the glass between them and the driver, "so was Tim."

He opened it, turned around and took off his sunglasses. "Hi Elizabeth."

Speechless, she grabbed his hand with tears in her eyes.

49

REVEAL

Dustin met her at the building. As soon as she had the nano-drone airborne, she headed straight for the main building and followed some students inside.

Dustin said, "Uh, following people through doors is advanced stuff. Good work," trying to sound casual, he added, "but probably need to head on back."

She nodded, but asked, "Will the drone work inside the main building?"

"The campus is blanketed with drone receivers and transmitters for training, so it should but I don't think anyone's ever tried it."

She flew it down the hall, into the main room with all the cubicles and consoles, and then went straight toward the supervisor's area.

"Uh, Judy, you really shouldn't be in here...."

She flew past it to the director's area, up to the "skybox" at the back of the room. It was separated from the supervisor's consoles by a wall of dark glass.

Dustin's voice rose. "Uh, you, you really need to bring it back now."

"Sure. Just want to try one quick thing and I'll come straight back." There was a glass entrance door. It had a gap at the top. She carefully slipped the nano-drone through and saw a man and a woman in their forties with black bracelets sitting behind a large console.

Dustin's voice cracked. "OMG! You can't be in there!"

As she flew over their heads and behind them, she calmly said, "Come on, *Maverick*, aren't you just a little curious what goes on back there?"

With her nano-drone hovering behind them, she saw three large monitors. Two displayed video feeds from the consoles below, but the man on the right was talking to the third monitor. It was a three-way video conference. She moved the drone closer to get a better look. On the screen, she saw two video windows open. On one was the face of an older man talking. The other window had the video turned off but she could hear a woman's voice. They were discussing something about a general's orders.

Hyperventilating, Dustin said, "You've *got* to get out of there!"

"Relax!" She wanted to stay and record but he was approaching hysteria.

"You're going to get us fired!"

"OK, OK." She deftly flew it through the glass gap and followed someone down the hall and out the front door. As she brought the drone back to their room and in for a landing, she could see herself and Dustin standing behind her. His hands were on both sides of his face in a **Home Alone** pose. She landed it perfectly in the metal box. Pulling her headset off, she smiled and said, "That was such a rush! Thank you so much, Dustin."

Looking pale and continuously shaking his head, he said, "You're crazy! You could have gotten us in sooo much trouble."

She leaned in and kissed him on the cheek. "*That's* what makes it fun ... *Maverick.*"

"But what if someone saw us?!"

"Who? Dustin ... *we* are the spies. *We* are the ones who monitor people." She paused, looking directly into his eyes. "No one will ever know as long as *neither of us* say anything. Our little secret?"

He nodded his head rapidly.

She couldn't resist. "So, still want to come over to my place?"

"I ... I'm sorry, I just remembered I have to be somewhere. Umm, maybe some other time?"

She smiled and winked. "Sure."

For the first time, she felt like a real spy.

Back at her apartment, she carefully slipped the pico memory card from her headset and stuck it into her sports drone.

Modified, the sports drone could *transmit* what was on the card, piggybacked on the drone's control frequency.

She took it outside and flew it until it ran out of power, hoping the video made it through. *Who were the people on the monitor?*

They all sat in the back seat of the limo, eating take out. Elizabeth continued to shake her head in amazement as Tim explained why they faked his death.

Still wiping tears from her eyes, Elizabeth just said, "Wow."

Tim gave her a rare smile. "It's good to see you again too. I'm sorry we couldn't tell you but everything Sheri said was true and we didn't want to put you at greater risk."

"I understand."

"Speaking of which," he frowned, "do you still have your concealed carry permit?"

She nodded. "Yeah … but I don't have a gun."

With a disapproving headshake, he pulled something small out of a bag and handed it to her.

She looked at it with a puzzled expression and then gave him a wry smile. "Tim, I didn't know you were into cosmetics."

Sheri laughed. "I'll show you how to use it later." She took a deep breath. "OK, before we get to what happened in the Caribbean, I need to bring you up to speed. We had to check everyone involved to see who'd been implanted with the tracking chips and neurotoxin capsules. We split up. Jessica and Greg went to Moscow and examined Kristoff. I went to D.C. to check out Carl Casey and his family, and Josh, who was the only one who knew Wendy, was supposed to examine her."

Elizabeth frowned.

"The nano-drones and neurotoxin capsules are powered by a speck of plutonium. Jessica got us portable radiation detectors before we left. When I examined Carl, I found a chip but I also found one of the neurotoxin capsules." She paused. "Elizabeth, if you want to get a neurotoxin to the heart quickly, where would you inject it?"

"A major vein of course."

"We found that the capsules are attached to the femoral or

jugular."

Elizabeth's eyes narrowed. "Don't tell me, Wendy's capsule was...."

Sheri nodded. "Look, it was my fault. Josh called me and told me he didn't find a chip in her hand. After finding a capsule in Carl, I told him he needed to look everywhere."

"Sheri!"

"Josh told me on the phone that would be a very bad idea and that I needed to do it. I told him we were in D.C., he was being a wuss." She shook her head. "I was thinking these are practical engineers. He hadn't shared with me all that transpired on the station. Thought he was just being prudish. Had no idea that after he saved her life she *imprinted* on him."

Elizabeth narrowed her eyes and slowly asked, "Did ... *something* happen during the examination?"

"Yeah, but not what you think. She proposed to him."

"Marriage?!"

"That's *exactly* what I said! Then I busted out laughing."

"Sheri, that's really not funny."

Obviously trying not to laugh again, she added, "Yeah, that's exactly what Josh said." Trying to look serious, she continued, "I thought Wendy was kidding, but apparently she asked him to be her deputy on the station and really wanted to marry him."

Elizabeth shook her head. "But she knows he's married!"

Sheri shrugged. "I think Josh pointed that out as well, but Wendy is direct and pragmatic. To be fair to her, when they met on the station, she asked him what Mrs. Fuze thought of him being in space. Josh correctly — but stupidly — said he didn't think you even knew he was up there." Sheri gave Elizabeth a direct look. "If you heard a guy say that, what assumption would you draw?"

Elizabeth exhaled slowly. "Yeah, I get what she thought ... but he never called or even texted me. I had to find out he was on the station from Turan!"

"May I see your phone again?"

Elizabeth frowned but handed it to her.

After a few seconds, Sheri said, "Elizabeth, Josh's number is blocked! You couldn't have gotten any calls or texts from him."

"Wait ... what?!"

Sheri handed it back.

Elizabeth looked at it carefully and finally said, "I didn't do this! I don't understand how this could have happened."

Sheri shrugged. "Well, at least that explains the problem. Let's bring you up to speed on the rest. We told Josh to invite Wendy to the island. He thought she couldn't come due to the upcoming launch. She surprised all of us."

Elizabeth nodded. "Yeah, I get it. She's been implanted with a neurotoxin capsule and she's about to take the space station a million miles away with an enemy agent onboard. I guess I misjudged her intentions."

"Uh, yeah ... *mostly*. After the meeting was over, it was late and Josh went back down to the beach house where our rooms were. Jessica, Wendy and I stayed and talked and had a few drinks. Shortly after we headed down, I noticed neither Wendy nor Josh were in their rooms. I later confronted Josh."

"And?"

"He told me he went for a night swim and run on the beach, *specifically*, so he wouldn't be around when Wendy — who had a few shots — came back down."

Elizabeth shook her head with a frown. "Yeah, I've seen her with a few drinks onboard."

"Josh ran to the end of the island where the beach ends. Said he was just sitting there on the rocks thinking when he saw Wendy coming down the beach."

Elizabeth tilted her head slightly. "So ... what happened?"

"He told me he took the high-ground."

Elizabeth nodded approvingly. "You mean he explained to her that she had no chance with him."

"Uh ... no." She gave her a half-smile. "He literally took the high ground. He climbed up the rocks and hid until she left."

Despite her best efforts, Elizabeth burst out laughing. Finally, shaking her head, she said, "He's not big on emotional confrontation. I can totally see that."

"To be fair, Wendy may have been sans bathing suit."

Elizabeth took a deep breath. "OK, I admit I've been pig-headed, but why the hell didn't he just grab me and say we gotta talk? I would have listened. It just seemed like he ... didn't care."

"He was trying to protect you, but later..." She paused

thoughtfully. "Elizabeth, this psychology stuff is what I do for a living. Josh told me that Turan was just like him," she raised her eyebrows, "only better. See it from his eyes. Turan's every bit as good looking and talented as Josh, but he's also charismatic and holds an incredibly powerful position. With you not returning his calls, Josh believed you'd lost confidence in him and were trading him in for a better model."

"That's ridiculous! Josh is one of the most intelligent, capable men on the planet. He's a genius, intuitive and practically indestructible. I love him. He knows that."

Tim nodded slowly. "Elizabeth, my friend, Congressman Bob McEwen has a great analogy. The M1 Abrams is the most powerful heavy battle tank in the world. It can shrug off bullets and rockets and keep on rolling. Josh is like that M1. He can survive without air, falling off mountains and can literally leap between buildings." He paused. "But open the M1 tank's hatch and get inside ... and you can totally incapacitate it with a couple, well-placed kicks." He paused again. "Elizabeth, you have access to his hatch."

Sheri finished, "You're the only person who can shut down Superman."

"But I love him."

"I know that ... but he doesn't." Sheri shook her head. "And that's *not* a healthy place for your husband to be. Particularly when he's being stalked by a hot astronaut who's offering him the job of his dreams ... among other things." With a challenging expression, she added, "Comprende?"

50

MOSCOW

After staying an extra day on the island, Wendy flew back to Houston and went straight to the Planetary Defense Headquarters. Well-rested and sporting new eagles on her uniform, she stopped in to see Admiral Meadows.

He shook her hand. "Congratulations Colonel, it's well deserved."

"Thank you, sir."

"The administrative change of command will happen tomorrow, but of course Colonel Dale will remain on the station as long as needed for the turnover."

"Sorry about missing the TELEMED demo."

"You deserved some time off before your six-month tour. The demo went well. I authorized them to start making the modification, but this afternoon's meeting will give you one last opportunity to approve it before you boost."

"Thank you, sir."

"Turan's still here in Houston but leaves for New York tomorrow. Recommend you see him before he departs for a face-to-face to cover the," he paused for emphasis, "*other issue* before you launch."

"Yes sir." She paused. "Is Elizabeth Fuze still in Houston?"

"No, she left right after the test but she'll be back for the wrap up meeting tomorrow."

"Thank you sir, I'll try to catch Dr. Turan."

Sheri liked traveling with Kristoff. They flew first class and stayed in a five star hotel in Moscow. Arriving just in time for the state dinner, Sheri chose an elegant cocktail dress, one that highlighted her assets.

Kristoff offered her his arm as they entered the state hall. Elegant and lavish, it looked more in line with the old imperialist Russia. The cocktail party prior to dinner was in full swing with a live band and bar. As they came down the steps, Kristoff said, "You're very beautiful. I'm sure even in Russia, however, someone will recognize you." He frowned. "And seeing you with me, this soon after your husband's death might generate gossip."

Sheri gave him a small smile and quietly said, "We'll either be vindicated when this is all over, or," she shrugged, "we'll be dead. I couldn't care less what the tabloids say."

"Sheri, you are a formidable lady. Tim is a lucky man." He smiled. "And you, Sheri, are also a lucky woman to have him."

She winked. "Regardless of what they say about Kristoff Bobinski, you *are* a gentleman."

"Quiet, you will ruin my image."

Scanning the room, Sheri saw Pasha Antonovich headed their way. A retired Air Force general, he wore his dress uniform replete with medals. He also looked the part. In his early 60s, he had a shock of white hair on a well-weathered face with a burned in frown.

The frown turned to a smile as he took Sheri's hand and kissed it. With a discreet cleavage check, he said, "You are much more beautiful than the actor that portrayed you in the docudrama."

"Uh, thank you ... I guess."

She introduced Kristoff.

Antonovich shook his hand. "Of course, you were responsible for building the Antarctic base. Very impressive."

Kristoff said, "Thank you. Dr. Lopez, her late husband and I were colleagues on the project. I'm simply hosting her while she's visiting."

Sheri smiled. General Pasha Antonovich was divorced and Kristoff subtly but effectively made it clear she was fair game.

After some small talk, Kristoff wandered off and Sheri asked, "As Minister of Emergencies, Pasha, what are your greatest concerns?"

Antonovich thought for a moment and then said, "My job is

to determine how to prevent disasters or mitigate them. Most of the threats I worry about are weather, earthquakes and epidemics."

"What about technology?"

"Yes ... that is a concern," he gave a wry smile, "*particularly* with this administration."

Dinner was announced and Sheri sat next to Antonovich. She asked him many questions, mostly about himself and his rise to the cabinet. As expected, it was a very interesting story, and in the process, she knew he was interested in her. Finally she returned to the technology question.

He responded, "Although I haven't read your books — I promise I will — I have read many books like George Orwell's **1984**." He paused. "Sheri, that technology is here. President Volkov is very interested in these issues." He smiled. "Would you like to meet him?"

"Yes!"

After dinner, he brought her to Alexander Volkov. "Sir, I'd like to introduce Dr. Sheri Lopez, one of the original members of the Millennium comet deflection team."

In excellent English, he said, "It's good to meet you and thank you for your work."

"It's an honor, sir." She noticed that he was guarded and the first man who hadn't noticed her cleavage. He was polite but it was clear he wasn't interested in talking to her. "Mr. President, I understand that you're quite the outdoorsman. I enjoy camping too ... except for those tiny flying insects." She paused. "They seem to be everywhere now-a-days." She raised an eyebrow. "Don't you think?"

He stopped scanning the room and looked at her. "In your country, I believe they call the smallest, most irritating insects, 'no-see-ems?'"

"Yes, they're practically invisible and follow us everywhere, almost as if ... they're being controlled."

"Dr. Lopez, I'm glad you were able to come to Russia. Are you working on a particular project right now?"

"I'm doing ground work for a new book about *dangerous* technology. I know you're extremely busy but I would love to have a few minutes of your perspective, and maybe I could share some things I've *uncovered* as well."

He looked at her and almost imperceptibly raised an eyebrow. Then, loud enough for those around him to hear, he said, "I'm sorry, Dr. Lopez, affairs of the state and my schedule prevent me from granting personal interviews, but it was a pleasure to meet you."

He shook her hand — a clear dismissal.

After he left, she excused herself from Antonovich and found Kristoff.

He said, "I saw you talking to the president."

"Interesting man. I tried dropping a hint and thought I saw a reaction but our *conversation* didn't go very far."

Kristoff smiled thoughtfully. "Just as beauty can open doors, professional politicians, particularly married ones, must be careful about whom they're seen talking with publically."

As they were about to leave, Antonovich came by. "Sheri, I would like to give you a tour of the Kremlin this evening. I have to be over there anyway to meet briefly with," he gave her a meaningful smile, "the president."

"Yes, yes, I would love that, thank you, Pasha."

He nodded. "Let me say some good byes and I'll be right back."

After he left, Kristoff said, "You sure you want to go alone?"

"The invite's pretty specific and I don't want to risk missing this opportunity. If it turns out to be nothing but a date," she smiled, "I can handle myself."

"I'll stay close by and listen in through Jen and your earbud."

Antonovich directed her to a waiting S-class Mercedes. He opened the back door for her. After they were inside, he instructed the driver in Russian where to go. Jen translated perfectly in her tiny earbud with little delay.

On the way to the Kremlin, Antonovich gave her a short history lesson of the Kremlin with some fun and bawdy asides that would never make it into the history books.

After they arrived, he gave her a badge to wear and took her through several security stations. The last one required an airport-like body scan and she had to give up her phone and earbud.

Once inside, he said, "It's safer to talk in here. I really do want to give you tour of Kremlin and ... maybe take you to dinner some time? But you made President Volkov curious and he would like to talk to you briefly."

"Yes, of course."

"Follow me."

They went on a complex route ending in a small but plush conference room. They sat down and made small talk until a door on the other side of the room opened and Volkov came in.

As he sat down, he said, "Dr. Lopez, I apologize for the secretive meeting. My political opponents would love to hear about me meeting privately with a beautiful woman."

She smiled. "I completely understand. I assume this room is secure?"

"Yes. I'm sorry I don't have a lot of time, so you will forgive me if I get right to the point. You spoke of bothersome insects...."

"I was referring to the Wraith nano-drones."

He nodded. "I thought that was the case. What do you know about them, who do you represent and why do you want to talk to me about them?"

Running on her intuition, she decided to go for broke and watch his reaction. "We know the nano-drones are now being used for more than counter-terrorism. Along with RFID chips and active tracking capsules, they're being used to spy and potentially kill world leaders."

Volkov and Antonovich looked at each other, then Volkov asked, "And who would be behind this?"

"We were hoping you would know."

Volkov spoke briefly to Antonovich in Russian. Without Jen, she didn't know what they were saying, but it was a calm conversation.

Finally Volkov said, "We're aware of the implanted chips and nano-drone spying. We don't know who is behind it." He paused. "You still haven't told me who you represent and why you are here. I, of course, checked your background. You've worked directly for the U.S. government and hold a high level security clearance."

"Yes, but I represent a group not associated with any country or the United Nations. I'm here because we have our suspicions about who might be behind this, and … I'm afraid Russia, or some organization inside Russia, is on the list of suspects."

Volkov frowned. "Why would you think we were involved? The Wraith technology is American."

"Yes, but the U.S. Director of National Intelligence believed he was being monitored by nano-drones before his death. We recently learned he was killed by a neurotoxin, which was developed by Russia. We're also aware of your secret development of concealable EMP devices and your rejection of a U.N. brokered elimination of nuclear weapons."

Volkov sat back in his chair and calmly said, "The toxin you refer to has been around for decades and used by several intelligence agencies. As for the EMP devices," he raised an eyebrow, "what do you think its purpose would be?"

She shook her head.

With a slight smile, he said, "Nano-drones are controlled by tiny microprocessors."

Sheri nodded her understanding.

"As for our policy toward the U. N.," he paused, "we have a short list of suspects as well. At the top of our list is … the United Nations."

She frowned. "Why would you think the U. N. was involved?"

"I can't share that. It would put ongoing operations at risk. Suffice it to say, we have evidence that someone — someone probably highly placed inside the U.N. — is involved."

"Then why don't you release it to the press?"

"We still don't know the identity of the individual and the evidence isn't sufficient to make a public accusation."

51

DISCOVERY

Sitting outside Turan's Houston office, Wendy didn't have to wait long.

He came out and shook her hand with a smile. "Congratulations, Colonel. In a few hours you'll officially be the ISLO's commander."

She smiled. "Thank you, sir."

"How was your short Caribbean vacation?"

"It was *mostly* relaxing."

He smiled again. "What happens in the Caribbean stays in the Caribbean." He got up and closed the door to his office. "This room is shielded so we can talk about the Harrison investigation. I wish I could tell you we had some definitive answers but the best the CIA and British SIS have been able to determine is that Harrison *was* connected to Russian intelligence. Don't forget that Josh was under conventional surveillance by Russian agents in New York." He handed her some personnel files and said, "Wendy, I'm going to recommend that before we boost, we replace the following three individuals."

She flipped through the folder. "Just because they have a Russian connection?" She looked up. "You think they're involved?"

Turan shook his head. "We have no evidence of that, and I still have trouble believing the Russian government is directly involved, but *someone* over there is ... and right now I'm afraid they're guilty by association."

"This really sucks for them." She sighed. "But you're right. We can't take any chances."

"I'm glad you agree. You'll need to approve the

replacements." He paused. "Now it's your turn. Is there anyone you want removed or added to the crew before you boost to ensure the mission and protect the station?"

She looked at him for a few moments and finally took a deep breath. "Yes. Yes, there is."

"We'll make it happen. Who do you need removed?"

She said very slowly, "I want to replace my current deputy with Commander Josh Fuze."

Turan looked surprised and then leaned back in his chair. "Wendy...." He stopped and then continued slowly, "Taking him a million miles away from Elizabeth," he gently shook his head, "won't guarantee he falls in love with you."

She blew out a lung full of air. "Look, I admit I like him ... a lot, but I also saw him in action against a trained opponent. I need someone deadly like him. Someone I can trust ... someone *we* can trust. And," she raised her eyebrows slightly, "it might help you as well."

Turan frowned.

She looked down. "You don't have to be a rocket scientist to see that you and Elizabeth have chemistry."

Turan shook his head. "Even if that were true, the same thing applies. Taking Josh a million miles from Elizabeth won't change how *she* feels."

With a wry smile, she said, "Actually, I *am* a rocket scientist, and ... it certainly improves the odds."

He laughed and then shook his head. "Wendy, you're not going to turn me into a King David. Setting aside for a moment that I need him here as *my* deputy ... space station duty is voluntary. I can't order him to go. He's not even a U.N. employee yet." Turan looked at her intently. "Tell me truthfully, how much of this is a real fear about a threat to the station?"

She leaned forward and spoke quickly. "Look, there's no way Harrison acted alone and no guarantee removing those with Russian connections will protect us. Sir, I'll be taking a tin box filled with a nuclear reactor and the world's most powerful laser further from home — and help — than anyone's ever been in history." Matching the intensity of his expression, she finished, "*And* I'll probably be doing it with at least one enemy agent onboard. What would you do?"

He sighed and then nodded. "OK. I'll offer it to him but it will be totally his call. The event on the ISLO is just the tip of the iceberg and we need him here too." He shook his head. "If he agrees to go, I can't spare him for the full six months."

She nodded. "I'll take him however I can get him. Thank you."

Frowning again, he looked at her a little suspiciously. "Wendy is there anything else you're not telling me? I chose you specifically because I need someone I can trust completely. I know, with the infiltration of the astronaut core, we're all afraid that whatever we say might get leaked. Wendy, we're sitting in a secure room and I promise anything you share will be kept private." He paused. "I need to be sure my new Commander can trust me ... and I her. Is there anything else you haven't told me?"

She took a deep breath and finally said, "You're sure this room is secure?"

Josh was finishing *still another* staff briefing when Turan poked his head in the conference room. "Just got back from Houston. How's it going?"

"They're doing a great job, but I had no idea how many programs this department was into." With a smile he added, "I'm thinking maybe a janitorial position would be a good way to start and work my way up."

Turan smiled. To his staff, he said, "May I borrow him for a minute?"

As Turan sat down next to him, his staff collected their briefing material and left.

Josh asked, "How's the ISLO's boost window looking?"

"There will be a delay but it's looking good." He paused. "Which is why we need to talk. While I was out there, Colonel Crow came by to talk to me about two matters."

Josh waited.

Turan exhaled sharply and with a small headshake said, "Wendy wants you to be her deputy aboard the ISLO."

"Yeah, I know." He shook his head. "Being an astronaut was my dream since I was a child, but in this situation ... I think it would be a bad idea for multiple reasons."

"She admitted she likes you … a lot, but she made a strong case that she needs some eyes and muscle onboard after the incident." He frowned. "She also shared something else."

Josh nodded in question.

"I just came from the Secretary-General's office. I'm concerned."

Josh nodded again.

Looking around nervously, Turan added, "We can't talk about the other topic here." He exhaled slowly. "Anyway, you probably heard Jupiter sucked up another planet-killer comet this week. I could really use your help as my deputy here … but there's nothing more important than protecting the Earth from another impact." He paused. "It's your call but if you accept the position on the ISLO, it could be just for a month and instead of being *her* deputy, you could maintain your status as *my* deputy. That way you wouldn't have to work directly … under her."

With a shared look, they tacitly agree *not* to touch that comment.

Judy woke up when she felt a pinch on her left wrist. Still mostly asleep, she tried to rub her wrist with her right hand and hit the bracelet. Waking up suddenly, she sat up and tried to remove the bracelet. It was locked. Afraid of being monitored, she had waited to hack it. Now, it was too late. Her chest began to feel tight.

After leaving the building, he got a call from Jen. "Are you alone?"

He heard his usual nano-drone companion. "Uh, no."

"OK. I finished that crossword puzzle you gave me."

She must have broken the encryption. He asked, "Did, uh, any of the *words* surprise you?"

"Yes. We missed one that has historic impact and ties the whole crossword puzzle together."

He wasn't sure what she meant but it sounded important. He needed to get clear of his drone and find out what she knew. "Can't wait to hear all about it. As soon as I get a *clear spot* on my schedule, we'll talk more. Love you."

He waited for the usual response but heard nothing.

"Hey Jen, you there?"
Nothing.

Sheri and Kristoff were on their way to the Moscow airport when three black SUVs surround their taxi. One pulled in front, one beside them and one behind. They slowed down, forcing the cab to stop. Men in black windbreakers jumped out with automatic weapons. The cab driver just held his hands in the air.

Kristoff said quietly to his phone, "Jen, we're being arrested or kidnapped, please track us as best you can and let Tim and Josh know."

He got no response.

The men opened the doors on both sides. One of them said very calmly in Russian and English, "Please step out of the vehicle."

Kristoff nodded to Sheri and they both slid out. The man motioned them toward one of the SUVs.

Kristoff politely asked in Russian, "May I ask who you are?"

"We are the Russian Federal Security Service and you are under arrest for espionage."

VII

UNCOVER

52

CONFRONT

Elizabeth was in Houston in a session with her technical leads. They were preparing for the final meeting with Meadows and Crow. She glanced down and saw a picture-embedded text. "Need to talk ASAP. Make sure no bugs."

She excused herself, took the elevator down to the building's basement level and went into an empty woman's room. She quickly scanned for nano-drones around her and then turned the phone toward herself. She found a bright spot sitting on her shoulder near her collar. In the basement, it should be dormant. She went into one of the stalls and unwrapped a piece of gum. Popping the gum in her mouth, she took the foil wrapper, scooped up the drone and flushed it down the toilet. She scanned herself again and then found an unlocked janitorial closet.

Inside, she quickly scanned the closet with the bug detector Tim gave her and called the number from the text.

Tim answered immediately, "Are you clear?"

"I think so. I'm in the basement. Found one riding on my shoulder and flushed it. The phone's signal is weak so it should be under the nano-drone threshold."

"Good. We have a problem. The Russians arrested Sheri and Kristoff."

"What?!"

"The press just implicated Russia in sabotage of the space station. The source claimed the information came out of a recent Russian state dinner that Sheri and Kristoff attended. On top of that, Jen disappeared and I lost contact with our agent in Abadon."

"How did they know about Sheri and Kristoff?"

"Only two possibilities. They somehow overheard our plans, or...."

"Or?" Elizabeth prompted.

"Or, someone gave us away. The only place our plans were discussed in the open was on Kristoff's island. As far as surveillance, that place is as airtight as it gets. The probability of someone breaching our meeting is small."

Elizabeth frowned. "Who would betray us?"

"The press said the information came from a high-level U.N. source. Carl, Jessica and Greg all flew straight back to D.C. Greg has a hard time grasping operational security, but he's not stupid. I don't think he'd talk about this in the open. The only people left are the ones in direct contact with U.N. personnel. Aside from you and Josh—"

"Wendy!" Elizabeth interrupted.

"Hold on. We don't want to launch into a witch-hunt. It's circumstantial but we need to find out quickly one way or the other. You and Wendy are both in Houston right now. Could you arrange a private meeting with her in a safe location?"

"I got this."

Tim, obviously hearing the determination in her voice, added, "No lead pipe interrogation."

"Tim, I'd never use a *lead* pipe."

As soon as they finished talking, Elizabeth headed back up to the conference room where the meeting was about to start. Elizabeth couldn't help but notice that Meadows sat her and Wendy on opposite sides of the table.

The meeting went smoothly and the program received its final sign-off. There were several technical discussions going on among the engineers as they wrapped up.

Elizabeth said to Meadows, "I need a private conference room to talk to Colonel Crow."

His eyebrows went up. "Umm. Are you sure that's necessary?"

"We just have a few small items left we need to iron out ... but I would feel more comfortable doing it in one of the maximum security conference rooms." She added casually, "They have the most soundproofing."

Frowning, he quickly asked, "Would you like me to be

present?”

"No."

He saw the look on her face. "OK, uh … conference room 107 in the basement is probably available."

She just smiled at him.

He nodded. "Uh … I'll take care of it."

As he left, Elizabeth went to Wendy. "It was a good meeting."

Wendy nodded. "Yes, it was. Was there anything we missed on the agenda?"

Talking very calmly, Elizabeth said, "I think we covered it pretty well, but there are one or two details I'd like to discuss with you briefly."

"Of course."

"Admiral Meadows scheduled room 107 for us to talk."

She just nodded.

"Meet you down there in about 10 minutes?"

She was clearly trying to read Elizabeth's face but nodded again.

Elizabeth went straight to the conference room. As before, she scanned the hall, the room and herself with her phone. Then she pulled out the bug detector and scanned for wired bugs. It was clean.

She was standing at the door when Wendy walked in. As Elizabeth closed the door, Wendy said, "Just us?"

Elizabeth pulled out her phone and scanned Wendy. Finally she said, "You and the room are clear of nano-drones or wired bugs. We can talk."

As they sat down, Wendy nodded. "So you know what's going on and you're not planning on hitting me with a chair?"

With a small smile, Elizabeth said, "Probably not." Rolling a lipstick tube between her fingers, she continued, "I owe you an apology. I jumped to conclusions about what happened on the space station and unfairly accused you and Josh. I now know what happened."

Wendy, still guarded, nodded. "Apology accepted, and I'm sorry that the situation caused so much trouble."

"Thank you." She paused. "Knowing that you'll soon be in

orbit where you won't be able to talk without being overheard, Tim wanted me to ask you some questions. He figured that since we were together for a meeting and there are enough rumors going around," she gave her a wry smile, "nobody would be surprised if we had a *private* conversation."

"True ... so, what are the questions?"

Elizabeth bit the side of her lip and looked at Wendy closely. "They just need to know who you talked to about the plans from the island."

Too quickly, she said, "I didn't talk to anyone."

Elizabeth could see it on her face. Tilting her head slightly and with a calm voice, Elizabeth said, "You look nervous."

"I'm *not* nervous, and I don't need to be answering to you. Elizabeth, I'm sure you're a wonderful person, but you're not an intelligence operative and you have no military or law enforcement background. No offense, but this is way out of your league and I'm finished talking to you."

Elizabeth's expression never changed and her voice remained utterly calm. "You're right, I'm none of those things, but I know when someone isn't telling the whole truth. We're not finished."

Wendy shook her head with disdain. "Actually, we *are* finished. You're a nurse. Go back to working in a hospital before you get hurt." She leaned forward to get up.

Still calm, Elizabeth stopped rolling her lipstick tube and said, "Sit down."

Wendy laughed as she stood up. "What are you going to do, *defibrillate* me?"

Elizabeth pushed the button on the side of the 'lipstick tube.' There was a popping sound as two barbs shot from the tube and struck Wendy in the chest. Arcing with high voltage, Wendy fell backwards over her chair.

With the wires still connected to the tube, it continued to tase her as Elizabeth walked around the table and sat down on the floor next to her. Turning it off, she said, "Yup."

As Wendy recovered, she slowly sat up. With a look of total disbelief, she said, "What the hell's wrong with you?! Is this still about Josh?"

"No." She shrugged. "Well ... maybe a little. What this is

really about is you lying to me and putting Josh, Sheri and Kristoff's lives in danger."

Wendy reached down to pull out the barbs from her blouse.

Elizabeth held up the Taser with her finger over the button. "Not yet."

Wendy finally shook her head. "I didn't tell anyone except Turan."

Elizabeth's eyebrows went up as she calmly repeated, "You told Turan."

"Yes, we were going to bring him in any way. I saw an opportunity to talk to him in a secure room."

"You heard the press reports. Someone in the U.N. leaked that Russia may be involved in sabotage of the space station and that the information came from a high-level state dinner, *which* Sheri Lopez and Kristoff Bobinski attended. They were just arrested by the Russians. At the same time, Tim lost contact with our agent in Abadon and Jen has disappeared. We need to know *exactly* what you told Turan."

Wendy looked surprised. "Oh my God." Shaking her head, she said, "I ... I can't believe that could have gotten out. I can't believe Turan is involved."

Elizabeth shook her head. "He probably isn't. Did you check for nano-drones before you talked to him?"

"No, he said the office was secure."

"You didn't confirm it? I've had one riding on me all day. Even if there were no nano-drones, did it occur to you that there could still have been wired bugs in that room?" She held up the bug detector Tim gave her.

Wendy took a deep breath, "OK, the only thing I shared in his office was that we thought his life was in danger, and Josh and I were taking action to determine who was behind it. I did say Sheri was going to Russia to investigate, and I did say we were investigating the facility in Nevada."

"What else?"

Frowning, she said, "I didn't say anything about Kristoff, Greg, Jessica or Tim. I never shared that we met in the Caribbean or that we even met."

"Did you tell him we believed there were people involved at high-levels of government across the world?"

Wendy shook her head.

"That may be the only reason that you and Josh aren't dead right now." Elizabeth sighed. "My office is bugged and I'm followed by nano-drones 24/7. I'm sure Turan is too. Or it may be simpler than that. Josh said Turan and the Secretary-General don't see eye-to-eye, but that doesn't mean Turan wouldn't report something this important to his boss, who we know hates the Russian president." As Elizabeth pulled the barbs from Wendy's chest, she said, "Either way, you could have gotten Sheri, Kristoff, Josh and yourself killed." Elizabeth stood up and offered Wendy her hand. Helping her to her feet, she added, "I'm sorry for tasing you but you shouldn't have told anyone."

"You're right."

As they moved toward the conference room door, Elizabeth added, "Oh, and … you also shouldn't mess with married men."

Opening the door, they saw Meadows standing outside.

Wendy walked past him without saying a word.

He turned from her to Elizabeth. "Did, everything go—" He stopped when he saw the office chair tipped over and then finished weakly, "…OK?"

Elizabeth smiled. "Quite well, thank you."

53

EXPOSED

Sheri and Kristoff were taken to Federal Security Service headquarters where they were placed in what was obviously an interrogation room. The room had cameras, a one-way mirror on the wall and a TV.

A senior officer came in and without saying a word, turned on the TV. It was a live English-speaking news network. "Details are still coming in, but we know that an undisclosed, high-level source from the U.N. reported that the astronaut who recently died aboard the International Space-based Laser and Observatory may have been involved in sabotage. Even more disturbing, the astronaut, John Harrison, has been linked to the Russian Intelligence Service. This information appears to have been leaked from the highest levels of the Russian administration during a recent state dinner."

The officer turned to them and in a very calm voice, asked, "Why would you implicate our country in international sabotage? This is how you repay this administration's trust ... by lying?"

Sheri put her fist down on the table. "We had nothing to do with that!"

The Russian officer, in perfect English, repeated, "The highest level of the Russian administration at a recent state dinner?!"

Sheri shook her head emphatically. "First of all, no one in your government, including President Volkov, said anything about Harrison, nor did I ask. I didn't have to. We already knew about Harrison. One of the members of our team, Commander Josh Fuze, saved the life of the astronaut he tried to kill. She discovered he'd modified the laser's aiming software. Fuze was the man who fought and subdued Harrison. All we knew for sure was that his mother was a Russian immigrant to the U.K."

With a half-smile, Kristoff calmly added, "If we were going to incriminate you, we would have waited until we were out of the country first."

Sheri jumped back in, "So, you tell me, was the report right … was Harrison your man?"

The door behind them opened and President Volkov came in and stood next to the officer. "I know who Commander Fuze is. My predecessor briefed me on the meeting at NATO Headquarters regarding … Jen. Yes, Harrison worked for us, but he didn't modify the software, *he discovered* the modification *long* before Colonel Crow did."

Giving him a skeptical look, she asked, "And how do you expect us to believe that?"

"Because the laser has already been fired at a ground target."

"What?!"

"Yes. It was labeled a test *misfire*, but you will find that at that exact same instant, the head of the terrorist group Antiqam — Abu'l-Fadl Haddad — died. Media reports quoted an eyewitness who claimed he was completely incinerated in front of dozens of men."

Kristoff frowned but said, "Couldn't have happened to a nicer guy. Haddad was a butcher that bragged about torturing women and children."

"I agree, but he was incinerated three months ago." With emphasis, he added, "*One month* before Harrison arrived on the station. *That* was why we sent him up."

Sheri looked surprised and then nodded. "Commander Fuze said that Harrison was about to throw a knife at him, but stopped when the station commander yelled Josh's name. Before Harrison died, Josh said that Harrison told him, 'You don't understand.'"

Volkov nodded. "Harrison also knew who Commander Fuze was. My predecessor warned me of his abilities and we had him under surveillance."

"Why?"

"The former president saw him as a genetic super soldier and a dangerous threat, similar to the AI." Volkov shrugged. "I saw him as a potential ally."

She shook her head. "Then who killed Harrison?"

Volkov crossed his arms. "Now *that* is the real question, isn't it? Whoever tried to kill Colonel Crow almost certainly killed Harrison. All we know for sure is that he was killed by that neurotoxin, but we don't know how it was administered."

Sheri said, "We do. It was injected into one of his veins by an implanted plutonium powered capsule. The capsule can be triggered on radio command. We know this because several members of *our* team, including Colonel Crow, have been implanted with them."

Volkov frowned. "Can they be removed?"

"We don't know yet. We're trying to determine if they're booby-trapped."

Volkov paused and then raised an eyebrow and slowly said. "Who would be able to surgically implant astronauts — assigned to the U.N. — without their knowledge?"

Frowning, Sheri nodded. Then tilting her head slightly, she looked directly at Volkov and said, "I don't mean to pry but we also heard that you might secretly belong to an extremist religious organization?"

Volkov looked surprised and then puzzled. With a small laugh, he said, "Russian Orthodox...?"

"Oh ... never mind."

Kristoff said, "We have another problem. The press release was obviously worded specifically to implicate us and ensure we were persona non grata."

Volkov nodded. "Which means ... *they* know you're here."

Judy slowed her breathing. She realized if they triggered the neurotoxin, she wouldn't be feeling tightness in her chest; she'd be dead. It was just anxiety. To be fair, well-deserved anxiety. She got up and took a shower. In case they were monitoring her, she wanted to act normal and the shower would help her relax.

As she closed the shower curtain and turned on the water, she carefully inspected her bracelet. It was very tight, and she knew it was impossible to remove without a diamond tipped saw. Her life depended on finding a way to counter the injector without removing the bracelet. She had an idea but it required materials she didn't have.

After the shower, she used the technique Tim taught her to hide the pico-memory card. As she arrived at her morning class, her classmates were gathered around a senior instructor. She breathed a sigh of relief as she realized they were asking why all their bracelets were stuck on their wrists. She joined them to hear the instructor's explanation.

"I'm sorry, but the bracelets are expensive and many of them have been lost by our newest teammates during orientation. Don't forget, too many infractions during the first 90 days and you'll be sent home and forfeit your pay per the contract. To reduce that risk, they decided to lock the bracelets for new candidates during training." She smiled. "Of course, if you want them off, just report to the infirmary. They'll take it right off, but you will be sent home."

Judy added softly to herself, "In a body bag." They must have found out that they'd been breached, but they didn't know who ... or she'd already be dead.

54

RESCUE

Josh got an embedded text from Tim. "Wendy told Turan about you, Sheri, Kristoff and Abadon. Sheri and Kristoff were arrested by the Russians. Lost contact with Abadon and Jen. Come to D.C. ASAP. Meet us where you met Brian. Be invisible."

Josh put on his newly acquired metallic fiber underwear and shielded glove. He then rented a non-descript car from an underground parking garage using one of his alternate identities. After disabling the car's GPS, he drove to D.C.

He went to the lowest level of the parking garage where he met Davidson. Climbing into a large black SUV, he saw Tim and Carl in the front seat; Jessica and Greg were in the back with him. With a wry smile, Josh said to Tim and Carl. "So, do rental car companies offer like a special spy discount for large black SUVs?"

Turning around, Carl matched his smile. "I once rented a white one."

Tim summarized what Elizabeth told him and then said, "Here's the video Judy transmitted before we lost contact with her and Jen." As he played it, he added, "She's impressive. She figured out how to fly a nano-drone into the monitoring room."

They watched the choppy but recognizable aerial video. The picture moved rapidly over the top of the supervisor consoles and into the glass command room. Inside, they saw a man and a woman in their forties sitting in front of three giant monitors. As the drone flew behind them, they could see the displays. The drone shifted its view to look closely at the third monitor. From the conversation, they could tell it was a three-way conference, but only one of the video windows was active. Tim froze the picture. Although grainy, the image was clear enough.

Josh said, "Hassan Batusura!"

Jessica inhaled sharply. "The Deputy Secretary-General?!" She looked up. "We knew there had to be someone in the U.N. I was beginning to think it was Turan … *never* thought it would be the Secretary-General himself."

Frowning, Carl added, "And the voice of the person we can't see … I know I've heard it before," he shook his head, "but can't quite place it."

Josh said, "I wouldn't have guessed General Von Stein was behind this either, but look at his actions. His priority is to get veto authority over everyone's nuclear strike capability, and Turan said Von Stein talked the General Assembly into giving him direct control of the space-based laser."

Tim added, "With that and the ability to monitor and kill key leaders, he'll soon be the most powerful man in the world."

Frowning, Jessica nodded. "The most powerful man in history. This isn't a conspiracy; it's a global coup. We have to stop him, but first we need to rescue Sheri and Kristoff."

Tim said, "I was able to talk to Sheri briefly. They're OK and she said they have an important piece of the puzzle to share. Hopefully, they'll be allowed to leave soon."

Greg said, "Then the priority is to rescue Judy and figure out what happened to Jen."

Jessica tapped her finger on her chin. "I think I know what happened to Jen. After The Great Tech Out, every new phone had to have a hardwired button that would stop it from communicating directly with other phones. It was a way to put Jen in timeout if she went rogue. *Someone* learned how to secretly initiate that across the globe."

"How did you figure that out?"

"The same time Jen disappeared, the global data network massively slowed down."

Greg frowned. "But I thought the idea behind a *hardware* shutoff is so it *can't* be controlled by Jen or any software."

Jessica rolled her eyes. "Yeah, but to save money and avoid adding another phone button, they made it so you just press and hold the power button for 30 seconds. Someone must have figured out how to spoof that. That time we thought Jen went to sleep … was probably a test. The good news is Jen's not dead …

just sedated."

Josh said, "How do we wake her up?"

"Don't know yet. I have to reverse engineer the process. It won't be easy, but I'm pretty good at finding backdoors."

Greg added, "You mean *creating* them."

"Whatever."

Greg frowned. "If anything happens to Judy, it's my fault for bringing her into this."

Patting Greg on the shoulder, Tim said, "Greg, she volunteered, *and* she volunteered for the right reasons. We'll get her out."

Josh added, "No one in the world's better at exfiltration than Tim. The biggest challenge is how do we communicate with her without Jen?"

Jessica inserted, "Jen showed me how to access the SIGINT satellite. I already sent her a message."

Nodding, Tim said, "We'll probably have to do a smash and grab to get her out."

Josh asked, "Geckos?"

"Yeah, but you broke one and the same trick rarely works twice. We'll need a diversion."

Greg nodded. "Would that involve explosives?"

"Probably."

Jessica held up her hand. "Before we start blowing stuff up, there's a message coming in from Judy." She paused as she read it. "She's got gonads. I like her."

Greg impatiently said, "What?!"

"Hmm, she doesn't want to be rescued, at least not yet. She believes she needs to stay to protect the kids. Instead, she's asking if there's any way we can smuggle stuff *into her.*" She showed them her tablet. "Here's what she wants."

Greg frowned. "Huh. Epoxy, aluminum foil, picture of a bracelet with the neurotoxin injector exposed?" He skipped to the last one and pointed at it. "Not sure how we can get those."

Josh shook his head, but then said, "We can't, but maybe Kristoff can."

Carl added, "I'm scanning the records of the security people at Abadon. We might be able to turn one of them."

"Yeah. Wait ... what?!" Greg shook his head. "The same guys

who tried to shoot us?"

"The security people are prior military who believe they've been hired to defend a Top Secret government facility. They have no idea what's going on inside. I'm trying to find someone we, or the CIA, worked with in the past."

Tim looked at Jessica. "Tell her we'll figure out a way to get the stuff she needs to her as soon as we can, but she needs to be ready to bug out at any time."

Greg nodded. "We've *got* to get this to the press."

Tim shook his head. "A fuzzy video of a video isn't enough and we now know nano-drones are watching the heads of the two largest news networks." Tim looked down at his phone. "Sheri just texted, she's flying back to New York City under a fake ID and I know Elizabeth's returned from Houston. We need to know what they know." He looked at Josh, "Why don't we reconvene in New York while Jessica and Greg work on reviving Jen."

Josh nodded. He was excited to see Elizabeth, but also nervous.

55

DEPUTY

Josh drove back to New York City with Tim. Sheri and Elizabeth met them at the safe house where Tim and Sheri first took Josh.

Tim immediately hugged Sheri, who was still wearing a blonde wig and sunglasses.

Josh and Elizabeth approached each other tentatively, pausing at arm's length.

She reached out and put her hand on his arm. "I'm sorry. I … I jumped to conclusions and never gave you a chance to explain. I just didn't understand. I'm really sorry."

He grabbed her and pulled her in to a hug and kiss. The kiss continued.

Tim cleared his throat.

Sheri punched him. "Let 'em be."

Finally Sheri said, "OK, rent a room."

As they broke lock and sat down, Sheri said to Elizabeth, "So, what exactly happened when you confronted Wendy about spilling the beans, and…." she nodded toward Josh.

Frowning, Tim said, "Is that really important right now? We have some serious things we need to cover."

Sheri said, "Yeah, yeah. Hold your horses." She just looked at Elizabeth.

Elizabeth bit the side of her lip and slowly said, "Well, initially, she was … a little shocked."

Tim burst out laughing.

Sheri looked at him like he'd grown another head. "You *never* laugh. What's going on?"

Tim cleared his throat, trying not to laugh. "She … she tased Wendy."

Josh's eyes got wide.

Sheri turned to Elizabeth. "What!?"

Still biting the side of her lip, Elizabeth shrugged. "When I asked her who she told, she said she was done talking to me and I should go back to nursing. She was going to leave, so...."

"Wow." Sheri grinned. "Remind me not to piss you off."

Josh carefully studied his tablet.

Tim, still smiling, said, "OK, enough backstory. Sheri, what happened in Russia?"

Sheri went through a detailed description of their meetings with President Volkov. She finished with, "I came back here on a fake passport and Kristoff went back to the island."

Josh shook his head. "I feel bad for Harrison, but that explains some things and opens new questions. Wendy said it took at least two people to modify the software, but I'm sure it took more than two to rotate the entire station and fire the laser. We have to get this information to her ASAP."

Tim nodded. "The cat's out of the bag, we need to approach Turan directly and find out where he stands."

Sheri added, "And, until we know, we need to keep the status quo."

Josh frowned in question.

"I mean ... you and Elizabeth need to continue to appear at odds with each other."

Josh and Elizabeth looked at each other sadly.

Sheri rolled her eyes. "You look like kicked puppies." She pulled the radiation detector out of her purse and tossed it to Josh. Nodding towards Elizabeth, she said, "She needs an exam. A *thorough* one. Bedroom's that way."

Josh smiled and offered his hand to Elizabeth.

As they stood up, Sheri added, "Take your time."

The next morning, Josh went to Turan's office.

Turan's executive assistant said he was in an important meeting.

Josh waited outside, but it was only a minute before Turan's door opened and he came out with another man.

Turan saw Josh and said, "Wait, Dan, this is my new deputy I was telling you about, Commander Josh Fuze. As I mentioned,

Josh was a U.S. Navy fighter pilot."

As Josh shook hands, he realized it was Dan Pierre, the Secretary of Defense, and said, "Good to meet you, sir."

Pierre nodded approvingly. "Good to see more U.S. military in the U.N. family, particularly now."

After some small talk, the Sec Def left and Turan motioned Josh into his office, closing the door. "That was an important meeting. The U.S. finally decided to lead the nuclear countries and allow the U.N. veto authority on nuclear strikes. The geeks are going to figure out how to connect us with the nuclear football, so it will require three people to turn the key." He looked at Josh meaningfully. "It helped to be able to tell him that a former U.S. Navy officer was my new deputy. The rest of the countries will fall in line now that the U.S. has agreed."

Josh nodded but said, "Except Russia."

Turan looked disgusted as he shook his head. "Yes, that's going to be *very* difficult after the Secretary-General leaked the information implicating the Russians."

Josh frowned. "We need to talk about that."

Turan nodded. "Yes, but ... not here." Without saying a word, he motioned for Josh to follow him.

They took the elevator down to the lowest basement floor. From there, they went to a small conference room that required a badge swipe to access. Once inside, Turan closed the door and they sat at a small table. "This room is shielded from any electromagnetic signals. We created it right after we learned about Jen ... as an emergency contingency."

Josh did a quick sweep of Turan and the room with his phone. They were clear.

Turan gave him a puzzled look but said, "Wendy told me the two of you were concerned for my life and thought I was under surveillance by nano-drones. I know all about nano-drones. I used them to combat terrorism in Europe." He paused. "I was very skeptical that they could be used against us ... but I discovered Wendy was right. I confirmed there is a secret facility in Nevada operating them."

"How did you find out?"

"The Secretary-General."

Frowning, Josh asked, "You told him about all this?"

"Yes, of course. He's my boss and as a former NATO general, Von Stein was aware of the facility. He said he'd investigate any illegal use."

Josh tilted his head slightly and asked, "You can hear them, can't you?"

Turan nodded. "You?"

"Yeah." It confirmed their genetic similarity. He had to convince Turan that the Secretary-General was behind the conspiracy or anything he told him would go straight to the enemy. "Did Wendy tell you that Sheri was going to Russia to investigate their involvement?"

Turan nodded. "That was a good idea. As a celebrity, she can get access to people that we can't."

"Were you aware that after the Secretary-General leaked the information implicating Russia, Sheri was arrested?"

"What?!"

Josh just nodded and waited.

Frowning, Turan put his hand on his forehead. "It's my fault. I should have known that when I shared that with Von Stein, he'd release it to the press. He and Volkov are enemies and continue to cross swords. The leak had to be retaliation."

"Maybe ... but you don't become a general without the ability to think strategically, and we immediately lost contact with Jen and had to shut down our investigation of Abadon." Until he was sure his conversation wouldn't go any further, Josh's priority was to protect Judy.

Turan slowly said, "And all this happened at the same time," he tapped his fingers on the tabletop, "right after I told ... the Secretary-General."

"Yes."

Turan got up and started pacing. Finally, exhaling sharply, he said, "Josh, I'll level with you. I don't like Von Stein, but ... it's hard for me to imagine him being involved in a major conspiracy, much less behind it. He's a bull in a china shop. I don't think he has the skill or patience to pull something like this off."

Josh pulled out his phone and played the last part of the video from Abadon. They also heard the Deputy Secretary-General talk about following the "General's orders."

Turan shook his head. "This is impossible."

Josh shrugged. "It appears Von Stein is running Abadon through his deputy … unless the Deputy is operating independently."

Turan shook his head again. "No way. The Deputy does what he's told." With a deep breath, Turan added, "It's hard to believe, but the evidence is damning." He paused and looked at Josh. "If this is true, General Von Stein is an exceptional actor."

"Regardless," Josh raised his eyebrows, "Wendy and I have been implanted with the same capsule that killed Harrison and the DNI. It's likely you have too and who knows how many others. We've given Von Stein unilateral control of the ISLO's laser and we're about to hand him nuclear veto authority."

With a half-smile, he said, "Josh, you really know how to ruin my day." He paused, thinking, and then exhaled slowly. "OK, we need to expose him."

"And be ready to arrest him and the Deputy before they can trigger the capsules or use the ISLO."

Turan looked at him intently. "Josh … you're talking about a coup."

"Doruk, the Secretary-General is already in the process of pulling off the greatest coup in history. This is a counter-coup. We've got to shut down Abadon. With their ability to monitor everything we do, they have an incredible advantage, not to mention the ability to kill us."

"I agree. We can prove nano-drones exist, but the evidence that they're spying on world leaders, and that the Secretary-General is behind it, consists of a shaky, low-resolution video." He paused. "Wait! What we *can do* is leverage Von Stein's accusation against Russia. With Volkov's help, we can prove the ISLO was secretly and illegally used to kill the head of Antiqam and that he attempted to frame Russia."

Nodding, Josh added, "We still have to figure out how to prevent his accusers — us — from dying suddenly of a heart attack. We have to find a way to incapacitate him before we expose him."

Turan narrowed his eyes. "I have an idea. Last year, the World Health Organization Director mentioned a virus they were dealing with. It isn't life threatening, but it is a problem because it creates sudden and acute symptoms similar to diseases that are deadly. Maybe Elizabeth could explain what's going on to Dr. Deken and see if we can get a ... sample."

Josh nodded slowly. "When he goes to the hospital, we quarantine him and use our security forces to ensure he remains isolated."

Turan nodded and then blew out a lungful of air. "Josh, there's a lot at stake here. I hope you're right."

56

COUP

Twenty-four hours later, they executed the plan. Within 12 hours, the Secretary-General became extremely ill and was taken to the hospital where he was quarantined. With U.N. security forces guarding and isolating him, Turan called a press conference.

"The Secretary-General has been hospitalized with a serious illness. He is in stable but guarded condition. Due to his recent trip to the Congo, he's been quarantined until they can determine if he was exposed to a dangerous virus." He paused for emphasis. "Unfortunately, I'm sorry to report that the Department of Global Security has also uncovered evidence that General Von Stein secretly and without authority ordered the use of the International Space-based Laser as a weapon."

There was a massive buzz in the room followed by rapid-fire questions.

Turan held up his hand and said, "Let me continue. It appears the charges against Russia are false."

The questions come fast and furious. One yelled out, "What evidence do you have?"

Turan calmly said, "The evidence has been given to the members of the Security Council, and they will decide how it should be released."

Josh admired Turan's ability to handle the press.

"Will Deputy Secretary-General Batusura take over?"

"Unfortunately ... he may also have been involved and is being detained for questioning."

"Then who will be the acting Secretary-General?"

Turan shook his head. "That will be up to the Security Council and General Assembly."

There were dozens of questions shouted at him.

"I'm sorry. This is developing very fast. We're in shock ourselves, but will share what we learn as soon as we can."

Within hours, the General Assembly passed a vote of "no confidence," effectively firing the Secretary-General. With the Deputy Secretary-General under investigation and no specific succession policy in the U.N. Charter, the Security Council appointed Turan as acting Secretary-General. They also nominated him for the permanent position and submitted it for a vote by the General Assembly.

Turan called Josh to his office and said, "I won't pretend I'm not excited about the opportunity, but...." He shook his head.

Josh said, "You'll be great and now you'll be in a better position to track down his co-conspirators. Until we identify them, we're all still at risk."

"Along those lines, I need a new Director of Global Security and a Deputy Secretary-General." He smiled. "I promised you Global Security but I could really use you as my deputy."

Josh shook his head. "I'm barely qualified to be the Deputy of Global Security. I'm certainly not ready to be the Director or the Deputy Secretary-General. Admiral Meadows would be a far better choice."

Turan looked at his desk thoughtfully. "Tell you what. As my existing deputy, you're automatically going to become the acting Director. However, I'm going to propose you to the Security Council as Deputy Secretary-General. When they approve you, we'll make Meadows the head of Global Security."

Josh shrugged. "Whatever I can do to help, but we *really* need to shut down Abadon ASAP and anyone else involved ... or our terms might be very short."

As he left Turan's office, he got an embedded text from Jessica. "Just got to NYC. Can resurrect Jen. Meet at safe house tonight."

Tim, Jessica and Greg were already there when Elizabeth, Sheri and Josh arrived.

Sheri took off her blonde wig. "I hate this thing. Do we really need to keep sneaking around now that we've nailed the Secretary-General and his deputy?"

Tim said, "Until Abadon is shut down and we can remove those capsules, someone can still trigger them. Jen should be able to help us with that if we can bring her back."

Jessica held up her phone. "I figured out how they put Jen to sleep. Someone bribed the chip designers to add a backdoor to the 'off' switch. Then all it requires is an embedded command in a GPS sync signal. Every phone with GPS location on — which is almost all of them — loses its ability to communicate with other phones."

"How'd you figure that out?"

Greg grinned. "Remember, she built a backdoor into the original chip. All the chips are still made in China, and — not surprisingly — Jessica is like a demigod in the chip hacking world. Adolescent hackers probably have posters of her on their wall. I know I would've."

Jessica smiled. "Anyway, I can counter the 'shutdown' command but wanted to talk to you guys before I try it."

Sheri asked, "Why?"

"If I do this right, whoever shut her down won't know I overrode their command, *but* as soon as the world's data streaming improves, it'll be obvious ... *unless,* we ask Jen to restrict the data flow when she wakes up."

Josh said, "Let's do it."

Everyone else nodded.

"Good. I have some other news. Using Carl's contact, we smuggled that package of stuff Judy wanted into Abadon. She sent us a little present back. When I say little...." She opened a watch-sized box with "Solak" printed on the side."

Sheri said, "A nano-drone!"

"Yup and we have its access code to control it."

Sheri nodded. "Hopefully, we won't need it. Let's wake up Jen so we can get those damn capsules out and wrap this thing up."

Jessica jumped on a laptop and connected her phone to an external antenna. "Here we go." She clicked a key on the keyboard and said, "Keep your fingers crossed."

On her cell phone, she pushed the "Jen" button. "Jen, you there?"

Nothing.

"Hey, Jen, you there?"

Nothing.

Frowning, Jessica went back to look at the laptop when they heard, "Jessica, is that you?"

"Jen, you're back!"

"Wow. I've been asleep for a long time. I had some really wild dreams."

"Jen ... Josh, Elizabeth, Sheri and Tim are all here with me."

"Hi everyone."

"Jen, your sleep isn't natural. We discovered that you were put to sleep by our opponents who figured out how to shut off your ability to communicate with other phones."

"Well that sucks."

Jessica smiled. "Yes, it does. Jen, this is important, we don't want them to know you're awake. Can you restrict the data flow between phones so they won't notice you're back?"

"Yes."

Josh said, "It's so good to have you back. We really missed you. I want to hear about your dreams, but first could you share with us what you learned by decrypting the specs on the capsules?"

"Yes. I'm sending the specs to your tablets now. The capsules *are* booby-trapped. Pulling open the clamp that holds the capsule to the vein, will release the toxin. There's a tiny mechanism at the base of the clamp that can be depressed allowing the clamp to be released safely."

"Whew." Elizabeth sighed. "Glad we didn't try removing them."

Josh said, "Can you or Sheri remove them now?"

They both shook their heads and Sheri said, "We need someone with experience in micro-surgery."

Josh said, "Thanks Jen. Just before they put you to sleep, you told me we missed something of historical importance about the capsules."

"Yes, the modified capsules have another ability that we missed. They can not only inject neurotoxin, they can also inject their power source directly into the vein."

Sheri frowned. "Power source?"

Jessica's eyes got big. "The plutonium!"

57

JEN

Jen said, "Yes. Plutonium is very toxic. Even the small amount used to power the capsules will cause organ failure and death within weeks."

Tim added, "Radiation poisoning, It's been used for assassinations before."

Sheri looked puzzled. "But why would they want to kill someone slowly with radiation instead of a fast neurotoxin?"

Frowning, Tim suddenly jumped up and got on the computer. It looked as if he was searching old news articles.

"What is it?" Sheri asked, looking over his shoulder.

Totally focused, he didn't respond, but after a couple minutes, he stopped and swore softly. Shaking his head, Tim slowly said, "I'm such an idiot."

Sheri put her hand on his arm, and asked, "What is it?"

With a sigh, he looked back over his shoulder at them. "Don't you see? The capsules were first used to track terrorists in Europe."

Sheri gave him a puzzled look.

"Two years ago, hundreds of terrorists were found dead from radiation poisoning. Everyone *assumed* they were trying to build an atomic bomb."

Elizabeth put her hand to her mouth. With wide eyes, she said, "They were executed!"

"That's why the program was so effective at eliminating terrorism. Once they located enough of them, any that escaped the raids or air strikes were poisoned."

Tim closed his eyes. When he opened them, he said quietly, "Solak."

Elizabeth and Jessica looked at him with a frown.

Sheri explained, "Solak's the name of the watch company in Turkey that's secretly making the neurotoxin capsules."

Taking a deep breath, Tim turned in his chair to face them. "Four years ago, I was assigned to protect the European Union's head of counter-terrorism. We got a tip that a suicide bomber would try to kill him. One night, someone dressed in black came through the window of his study. I shot them." Looking down, he continued, "I killed a married woman and mother of three. We were told that she was having an affair with the man I was protecting." He looked up. "Her name was Rabia Thomas. Her maiden name was ... *Solak*, the primary heir and future CEO of the Solak Watch Company."

Sheri sucked in a huge breath. "Oh my God! You were protecting Doruk Turan. She wasn't having an affair with him...."

Tim finished, "She must have been trying to find evidence to expose him and protect her family's business." He shook his head. "I was too wrapped up in my failure to look beyond it."

Sheri put her hand on his shoulder. "It was a setup. He used you to eliminate her."

Josh and Elizabeth both shook their heads as Josh said, "This is impossible. There has to be another explanation."

Elizabeth added, "There's no way I could spend that much time with him...."

Sheri looked at Elizabeth and Josh. "You both see things as they can be and look for the best in people. It's one of your gifts."

Tim said softly, "I, on the other hand, am the perpetual skeptic and always look for ulterior motives. I'm the one who should have seen this. I was looking for the classic terrorist motive — destruction."

Sheri added, "We all were. We assumed whoever was behind this was trying to destroy or discredit the ISLO and the U.N. It never occurred to us that this was actually designed to ... *build and strengthen* the U.N.'s control under Turan." She slowly looked around the room. "It all begins to make sense. No one can rise to power without opposition. Yet, those who should be Turan's opponents and competitors always seem to go away or end up supporting him. I know he's a certified genius but apparently ... he's also an incredible chameleon and has Josh's knack for understanding people and predicting outcomes."

Elizabeth looked at her questioningly.

"He defeated terrorism in Europe not just by killing terrorists, but by using psychology. Turan knows Islamic culture. Incinerating their leader in front of them, along with the plutonium poisoning, propagated the belief that they were cursed. Al Qaeda and ISIS referred to him as a Jinn of Shaytan or The Beast."

Elizabeth looked surprised. "They think he's like a minion of the devil or an antichrist? They don't really believe that, do they?"

Sheri shrugged. "There are interesting parallels, like his origin."

"But the antichrist is supposed to come from the Assyrian empire not Turkey."

"I was raised Catholic and never read the Bible. I don't really know what an antichrist is except what I see in horror movies. I *am*, however, a history buff. In biblical times, Turkey was part of the Assyrian empire."

Tim frowned. "Let's stick with what we know. After the discovery of Jen, it was Turan who organized the meeting at NATO Headquarters in Belgium." Looking at Josh, he added, "We stuck our hands into that *new* handprint scanner. That must have been when we were tagged with the RFID chips."

Josh, rubbing the top of his hand, said, "I remember a sting and telling the operator the machine was broken."

Tim continued, "It wasn't just us. Almost all the world's leaders were at that conference and stuck their hands in that machine." He shook his head. "And I don't know if Turan expected you to uncover the ISLO's use as a weapon, but he brilliantly used it to shift control of the laser to the Secretary-General *knowing* he'd soon have the job."

Frowning, Jessica added, "All the ISLO's laser needs to destroy anything or anyone on Earth is a way to identify and locate them. The plutonium powered capsules can transmit a strong enough signal that they can be tracked from orbit."

Tim shook his head. "Carl thought he recognized the voice on the Abadon video that Judy recorded. Jen, can you check the video and see if you can do a voice match?"

"Yes, but I can only compare it to voices that have been

recorded, mostly public figures. It could take quite a while."

Sheri started to say something when Jen interrupted, "Found it."

"Wow. That was fast."

"It was easy because it's Carl's boss's boss — the new Director of National Intelligence, Diane Buller."

Tim asked, "Are you sure?"

"There's a match probability of 99.87%."

Jessica said, "That's just great. One of Turan's *minions* is the new flippin' DNI." Sighing, she added, "Turan has the ability to secretly monitor the world's leaders. As the Secretary-General, he controls the ISLO laser and it, along with the neurotoxin capsules, allows him to kill or hold hostage almost anyone." She paused. "But it may be worse. With access to our country's nuclear strike system, his team of hackers can break into it. They'll be able to *initiate* a launch before anyone knows what's happening." She shook her head. "He's brilliant, ruthless and holds all the cards."

There was a depressing silence.

Looking down with his hand on his forehead, Josh closed his eyes. "I just framed an innocent man and gave Turan the world."

Tim said, "*We* all did. He played *all* of us."

Finally Sheri said, "He's not omnipotent. He's got to have a weakness. Jen, what can you find out about Turan prior to his rise to power?"

"His biography said he was raised in a small village in Turkey near the Syrian border. Just before he started college, his parents were killed and their village destroyed. It was overrun by Islamic Jihadists and became a battle ground for several weeks."

"Can you corroborate his bio with independent references?"

"From college forward, yes, but before that there are no childhood or school pictures of him. They were, presumably, destroyed with their house and village. A news article identified the man they believed led the attack on Turan's village."

"Let me guess," Tim interrupted. "It was a young Abu'l-Fadl Haddad."

"Yes."

Josh closed his eyes. When he opened them, he said, "I just realized when we were planning the coup, Turan said we could prove Von Stein secretly used the ISLO to incinerate Abu'l-Fadl

Haddad." He shook his head. "I never mentioned that to him."

Tim nodded. "Who better to test the laser on … than the man who killed his parents?"

Jen added, "I also found a forensic police report from after the village was liberated. It positively identified the bodies of Turan's parents, but it mentioned a third body found nearby. It was so badly burned, it couldn't be identified beyond being a teenage male that had been shot in the back."

Sheri looked thoughtful. "Haddad killed Turan's parents … but maybe not just his parents." Tilting her head slightly, she glanced at Josh. "An unidentified body and an early life that can't be documented." She stood up and looked around. "Carl couldn't figure out why he, his wife and *daughter* were implanted with the capsules. It's the same reason Elizabeth was implanted and assigned to work with Turan — insurance." She paused and frowning at Josh, said, "You and Turan are connected somehow. He seems to be going to great lengths to recruit or control you. He must need you or … you would've been dead long ago."

With all eyes on him, Josh sighed. "Maybe we can use that." Looking at everyone, he added, "And he *doesn't* hold *all* the cards. He doesn't know Jessica and Greg are involved or that Tim is alive. He thinks Sheri and Kristoff are being held in Russia, and he doesn't know we still have an agent in Abadon or access to a nano-drone and EMP devices."

With a wry smile, Jessica said, "Oh, I feel so much better."

58

RECOVER

Josh took a deep breath and stated the obvious, "We need a plan."

Tim nodded and looked around. "How do we take down the most powerful and popular leader in history?"

Shrugging, Jessica said, "At the risk of sounding insensitive, why the hell don't we just shoot him?"

Tim nodded. "I wouldn't have a problem with that ... but it's not as easy as it sounds. Remember, I was assigned to protect him. He has the world's best technology and talent. Two of his bodyguards are with him whenever he leaves his office. Four more circulate unseen in the background. They're heavily armed and use the latest tech, including, no doubt, nano-drones. He wears ceramic fiber bulletproof vests. His suits and even his ball cap are made of the new reactive titanium nanofiber."

Elizabeth nodded. "Even his underwear's made of it."

They all looked at her.

"What!? He gets hot wearing all that stuff, so sometimes in his office...." She shook her head. "They're like *Long Johns*, OK?"

Tim added, "On top of all that, assassinating the world's most *popular* leader might make us a tad *unpopular*."

They threw out and debated a series of ideas. Finally, after an hour of discussion, they settled on a plan.

Josh sighed. "I have a weird ability to see future probabilities. It's what puts me in the right place at the wrong time." He paused. "But it doesn't work with Turan. For whatever reason, I'm blind to his future actions." He shook his head. "I'm sorry but I can't predict what he'll do."

Frowning, Sheri said, "Maybe ... maybe that applies to his ability to predict your actions as well. This plan could work, but it's very dangerous, especially, for you, Elizabeth and Judy."

Josh looked around. "This has to be unanimous. If there are any reservations, this would be a good time to walk away. I wouldn't blame you for a second." He waited.

"OK then. Do we all understand what we need to work on?"

Sheri said, "Elizabeth and I will find some vascular surgeons."

Jessica nodded. "Soon as I get back to D.C., I'll get the chip from Carl."

Shrugging, Greg said, "I'll learn to fly a nano-drone."

Tim nodded slowly. "I'll work with Judy."

"OK ... and I'll figure out how to create a secure link to the ISLO and talk to Wendy."

Narrowing her eyes, Sheri asked, "Josh, are you sure about that? There's no guarantee she will...." she left the sentence hanging.

"Yeah, I know," he exhaled slowly and shook his head, "but I don't see an option."

She glanced at Tim and then said, "OK.... Then I'll get with Elton and my industry contacts."

Looking around, Josh finished with, "It's an honor to work with all of you again. Please be careful."

As everyone headed out, Jessica, Greg and Josh stayed behind.

Jessica pulled out the nano-drone box.

Josh asked, "I assume you're both gamers?"

They nodded.

"Have either of you flown sports drones?"

They both shook their heads.

"OK, as the resident test pilot and instructor pilot, I'll give it a go first."

Jessica opened the box and with a wry smile, presented it to Josh. "Your fighter, sir."

Greg handed him a VR headset and added, "And your flight helmet."

Josh gave them the two-finger engine start signal. "Light it up."

Greg initialized the nano-drone to the VR headset.

Josh slipped the headset on and picked up the controller.

Gently, he brought the nano-drone up to a wobbly hover.

Jessica reminded him, "This is the only one we got."

Greg said, "Don't worry. He's an awesome pilot."

He heard Greg whisper, "But watch his landings."

The flight response was different from any aircraft he'd ever flown and even odd compared to sports drones he'd played with. It felt like flying through thick but slippery air. As he got a feel for it, he was able to stabilize it in a hover. Then he started flying it in circles, followed quickly by climbs and dives. "OK, this thing is impressive but not easy to fly. Greg, you're next."

The next morning, Josh went up to the roof of the new U.N. building. It was divided into two sides with the elevator bank in the middle. On the south side were a series of conference rooms, used for high-level meetings. The north side was an open space, with railings on three sides and a spectacular view of Manhattan and the East River. In the center of the open area was a 50 by 50 foot formal courtyard with granite tile. Around the perimeter of the courtyard, were trees in large concrete planters spaced every 15 feet. The courtyard was used for personnel recognition events and parties, and required special access, so there was usually no one there.

It had become one of Josh's favorite places to go and think. He'd never detected a nano-drone up here. They weren't needed since the perimeter of the roof was surrounded by conventional surveillance cameras. During his staff briefings, he received a tour of the building's security system. The equipment was state of the art with high-resolution color cameras, but he knew if he stood at the railing and looked outward, his face wasn't visible on the cameras.

He took a deep breath. "Jesse, if Turan is GMO like me, why can't you stop him?"

He has free will ... like you.

Frowning, Josh said, "I always thought the idea of 'good and evil' was just for fairy tales and horror movies." He paused. "But it's hard to imagine anything more *evil* than entropy. The slow, inevitable slide toward darkness, chaos and death." He gently shook his head. "It seems like the path we're on."

What can oppose it?

"Nothing."

Nothing?

Josh thinks for a moment. "Life appears to reverse it by creating order from chaos, but it's an illusion. Life dies and stars burn out. The darkness always wins."

Conscious life can change the rules.

"You mean someday we'll figure out how to reverse entropy?"

Perhaps.

Josh shook his head. "Yeah, but it's almost impossible to imagine anyone or anything reversing the most basic law of the universe."

And how do you think you got here?

He paused. "You mean me ... or the universe?"

Yes.

Josh shook his head again and retreated to the problem at hand. "I can't see any future probabilities with him. It's nothing but a black hole. Can you at least tell me where the hell he came from?"

59

CONVERT

Josh knocked on Turan's doorframe. "Do you have a minute?"

"Of course. Come in."

Josh said, "Congratulations. I heard the General Assembly made it official."

"I couldn't have done it without you and congratulations yourself. They approved you as my deputy."

As they sat down, Turan looked at him carefully and said, "Josh, for having the number two spot in the world, you don't look very happy."

Josh sighed and slowly said, "You definitely had me going with Abadon. I was quick to assume Russia or the U.S. government was behind all this."

Turan got up and shut his office door, then sat back down. With a wry smile, he said, "Never know who's listening." He took a deep breath. "So, you finally figured it out."

Josh nodded. "What you did at Abadon was *very* clever."

"Thank you. Building a fake classified program and convincing people they were working for the U.S. government *was* a brilliant idea." Smiling, he looked directly at Josh with a raised eyebrow. "Thank you."

"Ouch."

Leaning forward, Turan added, "Look Josh, I owe you. If it weren't for you and your crazy laser project, at best I'd be ruling a burned out world of cockroaches and reptiles. I need you and I want to repay you by having you rule at my side." He smiled. "Come on, Josh, with your humbleness, you have to love the irony of your new title. You're just the Deputy Secretary ... of *the entire world*. If you'd like, you can also be governor of the United States."

"You mean president?"

"Sure, whatever you want them to call you."

Josh continued to frown.

Turan leaned back in his chair. "Caitlin must be … what, three, three and a half? She's so cute and has her mother's hair and eyes."

Josh knew his former identity was no longer a secret. He casually said, "Yeah, probably has her mother's temper too."

"No doubt. Because you're my deputy, she will always be protected and her safety will be my highest priority."

Josh just nodded. With Caitlin carrying a neurotoxin capsule, Turan's warning was clear. Changing the subject, Josh asked, "Do you know how you came to be?"

Turan exhaled slowly. "Probably the same way you did. One day you're somewhat dead. Next thing you know, you wake up Superman. My demise wasn't as spectacular as riding an ejection seat into trees." He looked down, eyes unfocused. "As a teenager, I was just shot through the spine by an Islamic Extremist and left to burn alive in my parent's house." Looking back up, he added, "But what goes around comes around."

"Abu'l-Fadl Haddad."

Turan nodded.

"You've harnessed some seriously scary technology."

Still leaning back in his chair, Turan said, "Technology isn't the problem … we are." He tilted his head with a slight smile. "Josh, we're in the Golden Age of information. Do people use it to learn, entertain new ideas or see the world from a different perspective? No. They watch puppy videos, or use it to *reinforce* or *broadcast* their narrow views.

"That's probably true but where are we taking the world?"

Turan smiled. "I'm glad you came to me and we can talk about this openly. I have to admit I was afraid you might go rogue on me when you found out, but I promise, from here on, I will *always* tell you the truth." He paused. "Where are we taking the world? That's a lot to cover. Would you like a cup of coffee?"

Josh nodded.

Turan got up and poured two cups. "Governments all fall on a spectrum from no control — anarchy — to total control — totalitarianism. On one side, you have the American Wild West in the 1800s. On the other side, you have China under Mao, where they determined how many children you could have and what you wear." He shook his head. "Of course, those are extremes, but most lean toward one side or the other." He handed Josh the coffee.

Walking to the window, Turan continued, "The minimal government side believes people are basically good and if unencumbered by government and regulations, they'll do the right thing and prosper." He shrugged. "It's true that productivity and creativity flourish — as illustrated by the past rate of patents and copyrights in your country — but there's a catch. It was summed up by your Benjamin Franklin. When asked if they had a republic or monarchy, he replied, 'A republic ... if you can keep it.'" Turan turned back to Josh. "Limited government only works if people are willing to regulate *themselves*. If they believe it's OK to beat or cheat the system ... it fails."

Josh looked at him pointedly.

Turan laughed. "Touché. Yes, people like me." He shrugged. "On the other side, *they* believe people are basically weak, defective and morally corrupt. They need to be taken care of and heavily regulated to keep them from hurting themselves and each other. That mindset champions large, powerful governments." He gave Josh a wry smile. "Which makes it a lot easier for me — at the risk of sounding immodest — to take over the world."

Josh gave him his wry smile back. "The problem with that philosophy is it assumes whoever's making the decisions for everyone else is not ... 'weak, defective or morally corrupt.'"

Turan smiled. "It's our job, as superior beings, to make sure that doesn't happen."

"So ... *ultimately*, it's about control. *Our* control."

Turan shook his head. "Not at all. If someone wants to drive their motorcycle without a helmet or eat Twinkies all day, I don't care." He shrugged. "If they have a severe head injury, or go into sugar shock, however, I don't think society should have to pick up the bill."

"You'd just let them die?"

"No, that would be cruel. We should euthanize them on the spot. It would reduce health care costs and clean up the gene pool." Seeing Josh's face, he started laughing. "I'm kidding."

Josh shook his head. "OK ... but you do have the ability to kill almost anyone, anywhere, anytime."

Turan paused and looking serious, said, "Yes, but I rarely use it. Most presidents and prime ministers also have that capability." He shrugged. "Ours is just a bit more *extensive* and higher tech."

"Davidson was a good man."

Turan sighed and looked down. "Yes, and I feel bad about that. Unfortunately, he figured out what we were doing and was going to share it with others ... including you." He looked up. "If you were on our team, I'm sure together we could have figured out how to work with him." He paused and with a slight frown, added, "Josh, you believe that most people, if given the chance, will usually do the right thing, don't you?"

He nodded.

"Well ... I don't." He paused. "*That* is one of the reasons I need you with me. We are Yin and Yang. Together we can provide balance." He looked out the window. "I'm not sure you understand how different you and I are from the masses." He looked back at Josh. "You can see the future, can't you?"

"I can see probabilities."

"So can I, but I bet you can't see anything related to me, can you?"

"No."

"And I can't see anything related to you. Do you know why?"

Josh shook his head.

"Because we are humanity's wild cards! We operate outside the normal probabilities." Sweeping his hand across the cityscape, he said, "Together, we can radically alter the course of history ... of humanity. That's why I've spent so much effort to make you part of my team."

Josh nodded thoughtfully.

"As I told you before, I'm working on an epic genetic project." His eyes lit up. "Ever since I came back as a superhuman, I've been trying to understand the process. In a secret lab, we're applying the next generation of Gene Drive and CRISPR technology."

Josh frowned. "To make future generations like us?"

"That's possible, of course, but I'm talking about going

beyond that. Even though we're genetically perfect, we represent a compromise. Josh, imagine what we could accomplish as a species if we could create individuals with highly specialized skills and abilities like extremely intelligent scientists or powerful warriors."

Josh asked, "Like bees and ants?"

"Exactly. Using Gene Drive to insert CRISPR into the code, we can make any gene sequence *absolutely* dominant. Within a few generations a trait would be universal." He raised his eyebrows. "*But we're* going beyond even that. Josh, what if a genetic change could be pushed in one generation to … *everyone!*?" He smiled. "I need to get you to the lab so you could see it for yourself!"

Josh nodded with interest.

Turan took a deep breath. "Sorry, I get excited every time I think about it. Back to the present. As compensation for the responsibilities you will hold, you'll have unique privileges. I know about your interest in space exploration. You can visit the space station whenever you wish. While you're there," he winked, "you can enjoy some *extra-curricular* activity in zero-g." Looking serious, he continued, "Look, I know you've got a talented team working with you. If the situation was reversed, I'd be doing the exact same thing. I also know they're your friends." He paused for emphasis. "So, let's work together and gently disassemble this counter-conspiracy. We'll do it gradually so they have time to adapt. That way we can make sure no one gets hurt."

60

DISASSEMBLE

Dustin said, "Wow, I've never taken a shower with a girl before."

Whispering, she said, "Sorry Dustin, but that's all we're going to do. I needed a place where we can talk without being overheard."

He looked disappointed.

Judy smiled. "You're cute and if we get out of this alive, who knows."

He smiled and then frowned. "Wait, what?! Get out of *what* alive?"

"Things are not as they seem. Abadon is—" She stopped. Putting her finger under his chin, she lifted it. "Dustin, I need you to focus. Looking at my *face* would be a good start."

After she explained everything, his eyes got bigger and he exclaimed, "We're all going to die!"

"Shhh! No. No, we're not, not if we work together. We have a chance, if we can communicate this to the others."

"I have to take showers with everyone?"

She laughed. "No. But somehow ... we have to do this without being discovered."

As the new Science Advisor to the President, Jessica's office was in the Eisenhower Executive Office Building. It was an old, decrepit structure but from her window, she could look down on the White House roof. Her phone beeped an alarm. It was time for her meeting and she didn't want to be late.

She arrived early, but it was 40 minutes after their scheduled meeting that she was finally ushered into the office of the Director of National Intelligence.

Diane Buller shook her hand and said, "It's good to meet you. I'm sorry for the wait," she looked at her watch, "and I'm afraid I don't have much time. You asked for this meeting, what can I do for you?"

Jessica said, "I know you're busy so I'll get right to the point. Jen, the artificial intelligence, has disappeared."

Diane Buller nodded, not looking impressed. "That's too bad. I understand she's been helpful with several science projects, particularly, the development of quantum encryption." She shrugged. "But between you and me, having a child with an IQ in the thousands that can hack practically anything ... is an intelligence nightmare. I can't say I'm sad to see her go. Was there anything else?"

Jessica shouldn't have been surprised by her disinterest. "Are you having any trouble with your phone?"

Buller looked surprised and then gave a short laugh. "I'm *always* having trouble with my phone. I'm from the pre-gizmo generation. Why do you ask?"

"With the loss of Jen, we want to make sure that nothing else dangerous comes in to fill the vacuum. We strongly recommend that the phones of all government leaders have their interphone communication disabled manually."

"I don't know how to do that but I'm sure someone on my staff does."

Jessica shrugged. "If you have your phone with you, I can do it right now. It'll only take a second."

Buller pulled her phone from her purse and handed it to Jessica.

Elizabeth went to Turan's new office. His door was open, so she knocked on the doorframe.

He smiled. "Elizabeth, please come in."

"I haven't seen you since the General Assembly election. I just wanted to congratulate you, sir." She offered her hand.

He came around his desk and took it. "Thank you. Just because I'm the Secretary-General now, you don't have to go all formal on me." He held on to her hand for an extra second.

"Elizabeth, you did an outstanding job with the TELEMED surgical suite, but that program is complete." He paused. "I'd like you to come and work directly for me. You would maintain your position as Special Envoy, but you would be attached to the office of the Secretary-General."

With a slight frown, she said, "Without the TELEMED program and with Jen's disappearance, I'm not sure I'd be of any use to you, and it might be *awkward* with me working for you and … Josh."

Looking serious, he said, "I think we both know he has *other* interests. As my deputy, he will spend a lot of time traveling, including in space." He raised an eyebrow. "And I'm sure we can find something interesting to work on together."

She nodded with a Mona Lisa smile.

He smiled back and then glanced at his phone. "I don't want to be late for my first press conference as Secretary-General." He put his hand on her shoulder. "Maybe we can have dinner some time and discuss your new position?"

"That would be great." She frowned. "Oh, your collar's folded, let me fix it." She went behind him and put her fingers on his collar. Pulling it up from under his bulletproof vest, she straightened it. Then she gave his neck a little rub and patted him on the back. "There you go."

"Thank you." He kissed her on the cheek and left.

61

BETRAY

Floating inside her command office onboard the ISLO, Wendy watched the news report. The reporter said, "The new Secretary-General officially apologized to the Russian government for the reprehensible actions of his predecessor. He thanked President Volkov for helping uncover the conspiracy and promised he would take steps to prevent any future abuses of authority. One of the measures was a new requirement for all employed members of the U.N. to have RFID chips implanted in order to increase security and accountability. He also encouraged the members of the General Assembly to participate."

"The Russian government, in turn, thanked Dr. Turan and said they looked forward to closer ties and productive discussions about nuclear weapons.

The latest polls indicated Dr. Turan held the highest public approval rating of any Secretary-General in history."

Wendy shut off the news and hit the intercom button.

She heard, "Ward here."

Wendy asked, "How's it going?"

"The system's working but it's going slow."

"OK. Keep me informed." She looked at the clock and engaged the communication link to U.N. Headquarters. When they answered, she asked to speak directly with Turan.

After a couple minutes, he answered. "Hi Wendy, how are you doing?"

"Fine sir. Is this communication link secure?"

"Just a second." After a minute, he said, "OK, the line is secure. Is everything OK on the station?"

"Yes sir. The new cooling system is online and we're fully

operational."

"Great. What can I do for you?"

"Sir … I just got a call from Josh Fuze." She hesitated and then with a heavy sigh, continued, "I'm afraid he's gotten back together with Elizabeth and is still working with Sheri Lopez. They haven't given up on their counter-conspiracy. I believe Elizabeth and Sheri are a bad influence on him."

"Oh! That *is* concerning."

"Sir, we have to convince Josh that the battle is over and the new world order has arrived. *Intellectually*, I think he knows it, but hasn't accepted it emotionally. If he could actually *see* a demonstration of the laser's power, I think he'll come around."

"What do you have in mind?"

"On top of the new U.N. building is a large open courtyard. What would you think about putting one of the tracking capsules on a dummy target? Then we could vaporize it in front of him so he understands both the power and reach of this technology. Josh is a good man and I don't want to see him hurt. We have to nip this in the bud for his own good."

"You're absolutely right." There's a pause. "And Wendy…?"

"Yes sir?"

"Thank you for bringing this to my attention. I knew I picked the right person to command the ISLO."

"Thank you, sir."

"I reward those who are loyal and I know sharing this wasn't easy. I have to admit Josh's behavior, particularly, after we had an extensive discussion about being open is," she heard him sigh, "*very* disappointing. After the demonstration, I'm going to put him in timeout."

Frowning, Wendy tentatively asked, "Uh, timeout?"

"Take him out of the game for a while so he can't do any damage. Give him a chance to think about his future. What would you think if I assigned him to the ISLO under your command for the full six month tour?"

"Oh … that would be great."

"Good. Now what details do you have on what they're up to?"

Josh received an invitation from Turan to meet him privately on the roof of the U.N.

At 9:00 p.m., Josh took the elevator up to the top of the building. As the doors opened, he saw Elizabeth standing 15 feet in front of him with one of Turan's personal security agents holding her by her arm.

As he stepped out of the elevator, he was flanked by two more agents. Both were holding .45 semiautomatic pistols.

One said, in accented English, "Place your hands behind your back." As he said that, the man holding Elizabeth displayed a pistol casually held near her kidney.

Josh knew he could take out the men standing next to him, but he couldn't reach the one holding Elizabeth in time. He also noted they were all wearing bulletproof vests. He put his hands behind his back.

After they handcuffed him, they holstered their weapons. One agent held Josh by the arm and the other held Elizabeth. They led them out to the brightly illuminated courtyard with the third agent walking behind them. Leaves on the small trees around the perimeter of the courtyard rustled in a light breeze, carrying the hint of an approaching storm.

At the center of the courtyard, they had installed a raised platform, a two-foot high stage fifteen feet across. On the left side of the stage were three giant monitors. On the right side, sat Turan in a comfortable chair wearing his cyber glasses and playing with his phone. Turan's executive assistant sat right next to the stage at a small desk with a laptop. Another security agent stood beside her.

They brought Josh and Elizabeth in front of the platform, 20 feet from Turan. Releasing them, two of the agents stood directly behind them. The third moved to the side of the platform. Josh noted that the two bodyguards now flanking the stage and facing him had MP5 submachine guns slung over their shoulders.

Josh glanced to his right. In the shadows, just outside the courtyard's illumination, five people sat in chairs. He couldn't see their faces but it looked like three men and two women in business attire.

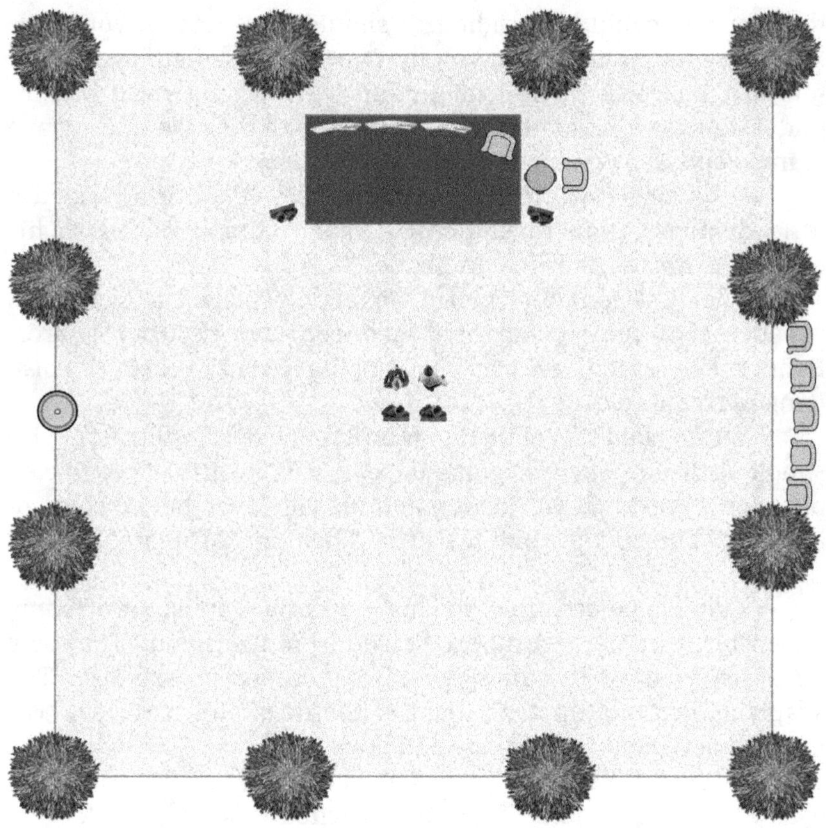

Looking up from his phone, Turan said in a deadpan, "Resistance is futile. We will assimilate you."

Elizabeth shook her head. "*That's* not funny."

With a short laugh, Josh shrugged. "*Actually* ... it *is* pretty funny."

As Elizabeth looked at Josh like he was insane, Turan laughed and said, "See! That's why I don't want to have to destroy you. We have the same sense of humor."

Josh shook his head gently. "I hope you're not going to tell me you're my father."

Still laughing, Turan took his cyber glasses off and put his phone in his pocket. He leaned back in his chair. "Well, work before pleasure." He paused. "By the way, I really am impressed. You got a lot further in your counter-conspiracy than I ever thought you could." He sighed. "I should have known you were humoring me in my office; you don't even *like* coffee." He leaned forward and looked at Josh intently. "Now ... I need you to understand that no matter what you do, with the resources I have at my disposal, I will always be one step ahead."

Gesturing toward the monitors, he said, "I've arranged a little demonstration to emphasize that." Turan nodded to his executive assistant. "Bring up Abadon."

The first monitor turned on and displayed a live video broadcast of Judy being held between two security guards. Behind her, stood six nervous looking twenty-year-olds, also flanked by guards.

Turan said, "We finally found our little infiltrator." He shook his head. "She was going to send out all sorts of terrible — but true — texts about Abadon and me. She even pulled some of our best young people into her little rebellion. Fortunately, one of them turned her in."

Turan glanced toward his executive assistant. "Joann, please bring up the tactical drone feed from the island." They saw an aerial view of Kristoff's island on the second monitor. The seaplane was tied up at the end of the dock and the yacht was moored between the seaplane and house.

"A secret hideout on a ... Caribbean island?" He rolled his eyes with a slight smile. "That's a bit clichéd, don't you think?"

The drone's camera swiveled left. A black quad-copter drone the size of a small fighter was hovering in formation.

"These are two of our brand-new U.N. tactical drones. I actually started building my own *conventional* air force." He paused with a frown. "Oh, I forgot. You met one of my Migs over Turkey." He shook his head. "But conventional fighters are so twentieth century, and, no offense, fighter pilots can be a bit unpredictable. They've been known to hesitate or violate orders they don't like. My Abadon kids just see this as another video game with more points for a higher body count. So, I decided to go with an all drone fleet." Pointing at the monitor, he added, "These little beauties carry a smaller version of the lasers we use on the ISLO, plus some good old fashioned missiles. Nothing like high-explosive warheads for a house renovation project."

The camera view swiveled back and zoomed in on Kristoff's

beach house. They could actually see him in a Hawaiian shirt and flip flops sitting on the patio. He was looking at a tablet but glanced up and appeared to look right at the drone.

Turan nodded to Joann, and the third monitor came alive. It displayed a picture of a large, beautiful brick home.

Josh recognized it.

The picture zoomed in on a window. Inside, they clearly saw Sheri Lopez sitting on a couch in her bathrobe, reading from a tablet.

Turan shook his head. "I really thought after we framed her, the Russians would make sure she met with an unfortunate accident. Somehow, she talked her way out of it."

The picture zoomed in further until Sheri's profile filled the screen along with clearly illuminated crosshairs.

Turning back to face Josh, he said, "As you know, I love movies, but I think there will always be a place for live performance."

On cue, two more security agents led Carl and Kelly into the courtyard. Carl was handcuffed. Josh's heart sank as he saw Kelly carrying a drowsy Caitlin, clutching a little teddy bear.

They led them to the far left side of the courtyard. Detaching one side of Carl's handcuffs, they reattached it to a steel cable anchored to a concrete fountain.

Turan nodded toward Carl and Kelly. "They say a picture is worth a thousand words, so I thought a demonstration would be appropriate, not just for you," he gestured toward the people sitting in the shadows on the other side of the courtyard, "but also for my leadership team."

Jessica looked through binoculars at the illuminated courtyard below. "What the hell?!" She was looking out an apartment window on the 72nd floor of Trump World Tower, the only building with an unobstructed view of the U.N. roof. Handing the binoculars to Elton, she looked through the more powerful telephoto lens. Shaking her head, she exhaled sharply and glanced at Greg. "Are you seeing this?!"

62

DEMO

Josh shook his head and with a puzzled look, said, "You *really* don't have any problem killing people?"

Turan narrowed his eyes. "Actually, I *hate* wasting good resources. That's why you're still alive and why we're on the roof this evening."

Elizabeth shook her head sadly. "You're a psychopath."

He raised an eyebrow. "Now Elizabeth, that's not a politically correct term. We prefer *ethically unencumbered.*" Looking serious, he added, "Our society is sliding toward the belief that everything is relative and there is no right or wrong. It makes it easier for me to consolidate my power, but even without a conscience, I understand there *is* right and wrong, darkness and light, good and evil. A jihadist shoots a teenager in the spine and leaves him to burn alive, but that's OK because it's just his world view?" He shook his head. "Killing children is wrong and always will be." He pulled out a candy bar and held it up. "Caitlin honey, would you like some chocolate?"

Caitlin turned toward him and smiled, then looked back at her mother.

Carl said something to Kelly. She nodded and with tears in her eyes, kissed her and set her down.

She ran to Turan and climbed up on the platform.

Picking her up, he gave her the candy bar and kissed her on the forehead. As she happily ate it, he looked intently at Josh. "I told you I would protect Caitlin and I meant it. As long as I'm alive, she'll be under my protection." He nodded toward the security agents standing behind Carl and Kelly.

They brought Kelly over to the platform, leaving Carl

handcuffed to the fountain.

Turan set Caitlin down and after Kelly scooped her up, the agents took them both to the right side of the platform.

Turan took a deep breath. "Josh, I'm still hoping you'll join me. I need your help with the genetic project. We can change the face of our species!" He nodded toward Caitlin. "Because the cells in the bodies of children are still differentiating, we may even be able to apply it to them and not wait a whole generation!"

Elizabeth shook her head. "You can't do that!"

Turan rolled his eyes. "You're going to throw out some religious nonsense about how humanity shouldn't meddle in the creation of life."

She shrugged. "No, I was just going to say, *you* shouldn't."

He gave her an appreciative nod.

Josh tilted his head, frowning. "You don't believe in the slaughter of innocent children, but you do believe the ends justify the means. You know what you're doing is wrong, is ... *evil*, but *you* feel you're exempt?"

"Exactly! But I do have boundaries."

Looking at Elizabeth, Turan said, "I brought you onboard as insurance in case Josh didn't see things my way, and to get access to Jen so we could shut her down ... thank you by the way. Surprisingly, you really helped with the TELEMED surgical suite." He looked at Josh, "I have to tell you, after spending time with her...." He whistled softly. "Wow. She's intelligent, upbeat and fun, and did you see her in that ball gown? Of course, she's also beautiful sans gown."

Josh glanced at Elizabeth.

Turan gave a short laugh. "Josh, relax. Nano-drones, 24/7 video surveillance ... remember?" He shook his head gently, "You guys really need to work on your trust issues. After I implanted your daughter, I realized keeping Elizabeth as a potential hostage was overkill."

Josh noticed Kelly looking at him with a frown.

Elizabeth's jaw dropped. "*You* tried to drive a wedge between us!"

"Actually, you were doing a pretty good job without my help, *but* I admit I did invite Colonel Crow to the ball and might have suggested that Josh was looking forward to seeing her." He laughed. "I'm sorry, I know I shouldn't laugh, but that episode was priceless." He looked at Elizabeth. "Oh, and I might have deleted some texts *and* blocked Josh on your phone." He shook his head. "Elizabeth, you really shouldn't leave your phone lying around, It's just bad OPSEC." Looking serious, he added, "I generally take what I want, but I think I've exercised remarkable restraint." He looked right at Josh. "And will continue to if—"

"OK! I get it!" Josh sighed. "If I agree to be loyal to you, you will let these people go?"

Turan tilted his head. "Elizabeth yes, and those who are innocent," he nodded toward Kelly and Caitlin, "of course." Then, frowning, he shook his head. "You had your chance to disassemble the counter conspiracy. These people," he swept his arm to include Carl and the TV monitors behind him, "are a threat to the state and to me." With a shrug, he added, "Which are now pretty much one and the same. I'm sorry Josh, but there is a price to pay for disloyalty and what would it say to my team if I let them live?" He leaned forward and quietly added, "This demonstration is also for *them*." He nodded toward the people sitting in the shadow to Josh's right.

Glancing over, Josh thought he saw the Director of National Intelligence leaning forward with a smile. Josh shook his head and in a calm voice said, "You can't rule by fear forever. There's one of you and billions of people out there."

"You're absolutely right, but I'm the benevolent leader that's ending terrorism and protecting the planet. I have my hand on the pulse of the world."

Elizabeth frowned. "Nano-drones."

"Oh, goodness no. They're way too expensive to waste on sheep." With a slight smile, he added, "And I don't need them." He paused. "Think about it. Most people leave their phone in listen mode all the time. How many households have digital assistants or chatbots? Every new game platform and most TVs have cameras and microphones built in.

Smiling he continued, "People were worried about the NSA spying on them. Believe it or not, the NSA has legal and ethical limitations. They should have been worrying about *Big Data* with a commercial incentive. We use the same sophisticated software originally developed by advertisers, but we use it to interpret the responses of billions of people 24/7. We're not peeping toms, although you'd be surprised at what people do in front of their TVs." He shook his head. "All *we* want is their reaction to what they see and hear. It tells us what makes them happy, sad and angry. It tells us what they fear," he paused, "*and* what they're willing to *tolerate* in the name of security. Once you know what drives people—"

"You can *inspire* them?" Elizabeth finished sarcastically.

He shrugged. "Actually, I was going to say manipulate." He put his hands together. "Well ... I've really enjoyed our talk and hope it has been educational, but Josh — as movie fans — we both know long monologs can be dangerous." He glanced at his phone. "*And* the ISLO is coming over the horizon and will be in firing position shortly."

Pointing at the first monitor with Judy, he said, "Joann, please turn on the two way link to Abadon."

Turning to face the monitor, he said, "Hi Judy, I'm Doruk Turan. I gotta say you're very cute but fomenting a rebellion among our kids is not acceptable behavior." Addressing the six standing behind her, he added, "Your bracelets are permanently locked on your wrists. There they will stay for the rest of your lives. At this point in our operation, we're shorthanded and upon the recommendation of your facility director, I'm going to allow you to live." He gave them a slight smile. "Consider yourself on double-secret probation. Any infraction, no matter how small, will result in this." Holding up his phone, he touched a button on the screen.

Judy's eyes got big and her mouth opened as she tried to grab her chest. The two security agents, looking surprised, let go of her arms. She slowly dropped to her knees and with a gasp fell on her side facing away from the camera.

Turan simply said, "Next."

As all eyes shifted to the second monitor, he added, "This should be more cinematically satisfying."

The video zoomed in on Kristoff who was still looking at his tablet. He looked up. Staring right into the camera, he flipped off the drones and walked inside.

Turan shook his head with a disapproving frown. "There are children present." Turan nodded to his executive assistant.

The drone's first laser pulse hit the seaplane, which immediately exploded. Another pulse created a secondary fireball as the fuel ignited. The next few pulses hit the yacht, blowing pieces off into the water and engulfing it in flames.

Turan nodded. "There went any means of escape."

Finally a series of pulses in rapid succession struck the house and it began to burn fiercely.

"He *might* have lived through that."

Four missiles slammed into the house simultaneously. The jungle was incinerated on all sides as a huge orange fireball ballooned up to the top of the island.

Turan shook his head. "Umm ... probably not now. While the tactical drones finish up, we'll demonstrate Light Amplification by Stimulated Emission of Radiation — or in simpler terms — laser cremation." With a wry smile, he added, "Safety first," and put on a pair of yellow tinted laser safety glasses.

The security agents and observers followed his lead.

Turan held up his phone. "Hi Wendy, it's time for that demonstration we discussed. You have a lock on the transmitter capsule code I sent?"

They heard Wendy on speakerphone. "Yes sir, but our system is showing that there are other transmitters in close proximity. It could be dangerous for them."

Turan said, "Yes, I'm also near the target, but we're wearing safety glasses. If you please, fire the laser."

Josh yelled, "Wendy! He's targeting Carl Casey!"

Wendy said, "Did I hear Commander Fuze?"

"Fire the laser, Colonel."

"No sir, not until I know what the target is."

Turan's voice never rose. "Colonel, we discussed this. I'm giving you a direct order as the Secretary-General. *Fire* the laser."

"I'm sorry sir. I can't do that until I have target clarification."

Turan pulled the phone away from his ear and humming to himself softly, pushed an icon on the phone's screen.

After a few seconds, they heard a choking sound from the phone.

Turan shook his head. "You learn so much about people when they're under pressure." Sighing, he added, "I'm sorry Josh, but it looks like we're going to need another Wendy."

Josh noted the position of all six agents as he slowly twisted the handcuffs and found the chain's leverage point.

Turan continued, "I made sure that during their physicals each astronaut was implanted with a neurotoxin capsule, and I have a trusted agent onboard." He held up his phone again. "I also had them wire in a remote override for the laser. So ... while they're busy sorting out the change of command, I can initiate the firing from here." He smiled. "Man, I love my phone."

63

INCINERATE

Kristoff felt the vibration through the metal steps and heard muffled explosions as he jogged up the spiral staircase. He probably shouldn't have flipped off the drone when he saw himself on the monitor.

Stopping to catch his breath, he looked at his tablet and saw the final destruction of his beautiful house. Shaking his head, he selected an app called "Sea Whiz." Inside the app, there were several choices. He selected the flashing red icon that said, "Fully Automatic." A second page appeared that read, "Are you sure?" He smiled and selected, "Yes."

Judy heard Turan talking and the sound of the drones destroying the island. She opened one eye to a slit and saw the feet of her friends and Dustin looking down at her. She opened her eye and winked at him.

With the slightest of smiles, he slowly slipped a hand into his pocket.

Jessica said to Greg, "You've got to get closer!"

Greg worked the controller. "I'm trying!"

Squinting at the screen, she added, "Keep it steady!"

Elton looked up from his monitor. "They're receiving and hopping between feeds."

All eyes focused on Carl, still handcuffed to the concrete fountain.

Turan pushed the button on his phone.

There was a blinding flash and deafening thunderclap, but it was nowhere near Carl.

On the opposite side of the courtyard from Carl was a ball of swirling smoke. As it cleared, the DNI was gone. Those sitting next to her had been blown off their chairs and were obviously singed. One man was trying to pat out a fire on the arm of his suit. Where Diane Buller sat, nothing remained except small charred bone fragments and a deep burn in the shattered granite tile.

"Oops." With raised eyebrows, Turan tapped a finger on his lip. Then, frowning, said, "Hmm ... could I have mixed up the capsule codes again?" He shook his head and sighed. "Oh well, looks like we're going to need another DNI. Lots of turnover in that job." Looking back at Josh and Elizabeth, he added, "You can't expect everything to go perfectly during a live performance. I'm afraid we'll have to try that again, but the ISLO's capacitors need a minute to recharge. In the meantime...." He nodded to Joann.

Sheri frowned as she watched the destruction of the beach house on her tablet. The focus moved to the monitor displaying her profile. As it zoomed in, she casually slipped her hand under her chin. Gently pulling the skin back toward her neck, she frowned and said to herself, "Hmm, need to tighten that up a bit."

Turan pointed at the third monitor. "There's nothing simpler than a good old fashioned head shot to wrap up a television career."

Engrossed in the TV show, Turan's bodyguards violated the most basic rule of personal protection. Taking a deep breath, Josh slowly tilted his head forward.

On the third monitor, the crosshairs carefully centered on Sheri's temple. Then ... her picture disappeared as the scope's view swung skyward. They heard several muffled shots. Finally a face appeared in the scope — smiling.

Turan inhaled sharply. "Tim? Tim Smith?! That's impossible!"

The picture tumbled and came to rest upside down in the grass.

On the first monitor, they saw a tall skinny blond pull something from his pocket and slide it across the floor to Judy's body. At the same time, a very loud ripping sound came from the second monitor. The drone's camera — focused on the smoking crater where the house used to be — suddenly shifted to the left. A stream of bullets interlaced with bright orange tracers was ripping the second drone apart. It disintegrated into burning fragments that fell toward the ocean.

With his body in hyper-drive, Josh slammed the back of his head into the face of the guard behind him. He simultaneously twisted the handcuff chain at its leverage point and snapped it with almost inhuman strength. Spinning right, he used the stunned man behind him as a pivot point for a blindingly fast round kick to the second man's head.

The man was pulling the .45 from his holster when Josh's shin struck him with a knockout blow. The pistol flew straight up in the air.

Josh continued his spin and used his momentum to drive his knee into the first agent's jaw and then caught the pistol. In less than two seconds, both men slumped to the floor unconscious.

All eyes were still glued to the monitors as the drone's camera followed the glowing stream of bullets to its source. On the island's central peak, the camera zoomed in on what looked like R2-D2 on Viagra. A large, rapidly rotating Gatling gun, spewing 75 20mm rounds per second, swiveled toward the camera. The monitor flashed and then displayed static.

Simultaneously, on the first monitor, Judy pulled the pin on the EMP grenade and tossed it. With a bang, the monitor went black.

Sliding the pistol across the floor to Carl, Josh pulled the .45 from the second guard's holster.

At the same time, the two guards holding Kelly turned and saw Josh standing over the bodies of their fellow agents. They immediately let go of Kelly and drew their pistols.

Josh beat them to the draw and put two shots in the dominant shoulder of the nearest one. The impact spun the man and his weapon flew loose as he went down. Josh fired two more shots at the second agent, but the bullets struck his vest as he dove behind the stage.

Turan's personal bodyguards jumped up on the stage unslinging their MP5s.

Josh pointed the .45 right at Turan's head and yelled, "Freeze!"

Seeing the agents still moving, he yelled louder. "Don't even twitch or Turan gets a .45 in the face!"

They froze.

With his peripheral vision, Josh saw that Carl picked up the other pistol and was aiming it at the stage.

Josh yelled, "Put your weapons down, now!"

Turan, not looking the least bit afraid, said, "Forget it. They only follow my orders." He exhaled sharply. "I've told you I don't do well when my plans get changed. I'm very angry with you right now." He shook his head. "And after all I've done for you."

Josh gave him an incredulous look. "You mean like not killing me or stealing my wife?!"

"Exactly!"

Josh just shook his head. "Doruk Turan, you're under arrest. Tell your men to drop their weapons now!"

Turan gave him a slight smile, "Under arrest? Seriously?"

Josh nodded. "Seriously. *Someone* made me the Director of Global Security, which — among other things — authorizes me to arrest any member of the United Nations." He glanced at Turan's bodyguards. "Drop your weapons or face 20 years in prison!"

They didn't move.

With a deep frown, Turan said, "You still don't get it. Sheep need a strong shepherd. I'm superhuman and I *am* their future."

"The world needs good leaders not an emperor. It's over. We used the EMP devices at Abadon. The nano-drones are dead."

Turan shook his head with a slight smile. "I never put all my eggs in one basket, Josh. That's why I will always win. The neurotoxin capsules aren't controlled from Abadon, and I can make more nano-drones."

Josh narrowed his eyes. "I'm only going to give you one more chance."

Turan laughed. "I know you too well. Although you *shouldn't* shoot me because you'd be destroying the most perfect genes in humanity's gene pool ... the reason you *won't* shoot me is because you *can't* shoot an unarmed man. It's just not in you."

Josh tightened up on the trigger and said, "Are you sure?"

Ignoring him, Turan's expression hardens. "I — on the other hand — have no problem killing *you*."

"Doruk, it's over. *Everything* you've said and done on this roof has been broadcast live to the world."

Turan shook his head. "You're bluffing."

"We used one of your nano-drones, the rooftop cameras and telephoto video from the building across the street. Your performance is live!"

He looked at his executive assistant. "Joann?"

Frowning, she typed on her laptop and looked closely at her screen. Then, eyes wide, looked up at him and nodded.

The veins on Turan's neck and forehead began to bulge, as his face contorted in rage. Through clenched teeth, he said to his agents, "Kill him!"

Turan was right. He couldn't shoot an unarmed man and re-aimed at the agent with the .45. He got only one shot off before taking multiple .45 and MP5 rounds in his chest.

64

CHECKMATE

Carl, using the fountain for cover, shot the agent with the .45, hitting him in the hip and leg and continued firing rapidly at the agents with the MP5s.

The bodyguards stopped shooting and tackled an enraged Turan to protect him. Dragging him off the back of the stage, they pulled him back toward one of the concrete planters at the edge of the courtyard.

Carl shot through the cable holding his handcuffs and rushed to Josh's side.

Josh sat up. "Oww."

As Carl grabbed extra magazines from the unconscious guards, he said, "Yeah, hurts even with a bulletproof vest." Glancing at Josh's bleeding arm, he added, "And provides no protection against badly aimed shots." He helped Josh to his feet and they ran for cover behind a planter on the opposite side of the courtyard from Turan. Elizabeth and Kelly were already there.

Turan's executive assistant and the singed observers were nowhere to be seen. It was now Josh, Carl, Elizabeth, Kelly and a crying Caitlin on one side of the courtyard, with Turan and his two bodyguards 50 feet away on the other side.

Josh peeked over the planter and yelled, "It's over! Drop your weapons! There's no place to run!"

Turan's bodyguards answered with a liberal spray of automatic fire. The concrete planter wasn't big enough and Josh and Carl were the bookends. One round grazed Carl's calf.

When the firing stopped, Turan looked over the concrete planter. Sounding manic, he yelled back, "You're right. There *is* no place to run. I still control the neurotoxins." They saw him push a button on his phone.

Elizabeth pulled out a small, capped vial containing Josh and Elizabeth's capsules. She threw them across the courtyard. "Looking for these?!"

Turan frowned and then yelled back, "Congratulations Elizabeth, but I forgot to tell you why your TELEMED system wasn't working. We were secretly testing a powerful microwave beam that could identify and track RFID chips from orbit. Unfortunately, it used the same frequency as your telemetry." Turan stood up.

His bodyguards stood nervously in front of him with guns ready. "Elizabeth, we don't need the plutonium powered capsules anymore! We can now track any RFID chip in the open, *and* I just set the laser to track Josh's chip! To be on the safe side, I programed it to fire a 20-foot-wide beam! Even he can't outrun that!" He laughed. "You might want to give him some *space*!"

Turan tapped his bodyguards and they fired bursts on both sides of the concrete planter to keep them pinned down. He yelled, "Guess you're going to have to ride it out with him!" He looked at his phone. "Only a couple seconds left." He shook his head. "Goodbye Josh! Goodbye Elizabeth!"

Elizabeth poked her head over the planter and yelled back, "And *you* should really pay more attention to *your* RFID chips! It's just bad OPSEC!"

Turan frowned and then his eyes got big as he touched the back of his collar. Dropping his phone, he turned and sprinted toward the edge of the building.

His bodyguards, looking confused, followed, walking backwards to cover him.

Turan didn't stop when he reached the edge. He grabbed the railing with one hand and swung out over—

The blinding flash and deafening thunderclap was accompanied by a powerful shock wave.

Crouching behind the concrete planter, ears ringing, Josh waited several seconds and then peeked over the top of the planter.

Smoke swirled everywhere. Anything flammable within the 20-foot beam was gone or burning. Half the stage was incinerated, along with two trees. Tiny bits of exploded floor tile were falling back down, sounding like rain in the relative silence.

As the smoke cleared, Josh and Carl slowly stood up. They swept the roof with their pistols. The two agents Josh knocked out were still unconscious where he left them. The two they shot were propped up against one of the planters to the side with their hands in the air, but there was no sign of Turan or his two bodyguards.

Josh said to Carl, "Stay here with them." He jogged across the smoking courtyard, feeling the heat still radiating from the floor. As he approached the last place he saw the bodyguards, there was nothing but charred, smoking pieces of bone along with the melted metal of their guns.

Moving carefully toward the railing, he went to the place he last saw Turan. Much of the metal railing was melted. The outer perimeter of the beam clearly went past the edge of the building. Stretching, he peeked over the red-hot metal. He could see the lit concrete deck at the base of the building 600 feet below. With his exceptional vision, he confirmed there was no body. There were, however, many police cars converging on the U.N.

Looking carefully at the railing, he saw something embedded in the smoking metal.

Elizabeth joined him. "I'm sorry. I shouldn't have mentioned the RFID chip, but he made me so mad."

Josh shook his head. "Doesn't matter. He was right. There's no way I could outrun a 20-foot-wide beam." He pointed at the railing. "Neither could he."

Partly embedded in the melted metal were four charred finger bones.

Elizabeth grimaced. "Eww." She shook her head. Then, looking at Josh with a wicked smile, shrugged. "Looks like we're going to need another Secretary-General."

65

BROADCAST

After Dustin helped Judy to her feet, he stood between her and the three security guards.

One of the guards had Colonel insignia on his collar. All three had their pistols drawn, but they weren't pointing them at Judy, Dustin or their fellow conspirators.

Instead, the Colonel was looking at the two men standing near the monitor with black bracelets. His expression wasn't friendly as he asked, "Were you aware he intended to kill her and the others?"

One of them said, "Uh..." as the other one ran out the door.

The Colonel nodded to one of his men, who immediately took off after him. To the other agent, he said, "Lock this one up." On his radio, he told all his security guards to detain everyone with black bracelets.

The Colonel holstered his weapon and then pulled his orange bracelet off and dropped it on the floor. Looking at Judy and Dustin, he said, "We'll get those damn things off you as soon as we can."

Dustin turned to Judy and said, "You were amazing!"

"You didn't do too bad yourself." Frowning, she added, "There's *something else* you need to know."

His eyes get big. "OMG! What is it now?"

"I'm actually 28."

Looking relieved ... then worried, he asked, "Does that mean we can't—"

She pulled him in and kissed him.

Pulling his VR headset off, Greg blew out a lungful of air.

Elton set his phone down and smiled. "All the networks carried it. It went global." With a frown, he asked, "Did you know Turan was going to incinerate Carl Casey with the laser?"

Jessica shook her head. "No, but after Sheri and Elizabeth got a surgeon to pull the capsules out of Josh and Carl, they carried them in their pockets, so Turan wouldn't know we'd removed them."

With a puzzled expression he said, "How did the DNI…?"

"Carl took the implanting of neurotoxin capsules in his wife and daughter pretty seriously. When we found out the DNI was in charge of Abadon … well, what goes around, comes around. As the President's Science Advisor, I just *helped* her with her phone," she shrugged, "and left Carl's capsule inside it."

"What about Turan?"

"We *did* expect Josh to be targeted. It was Tim's idea to plant Josh's RFID chip on Turan. We knew he never went out without his bulletproof vest, so Elizabeth just glued it to the top of the vest."

Greg said, "I only saw what the nano-drone saw. How'd the rest of it look?"

Elton nodded toward the telephoto camera near the window. "Between that, the rooftop cameras Jen tapped into and your excellent nano-drone close-ups," he gave them a wry smile, "I think we set the bar for reality TV."

Watching the police cars approach, Sheri looked at the three bodies on her lawn. "Are they dead?"

Tim shook his head. "No, but they all have holes in them."

Behind the police cars, a large black SUV pulled up.

Tim said, "I notified my old friend Lafferty."

A man got out of the SUV and flashed his ID to the local police. He came straight to Sheri and Tim. "Dr. Lopez, are you alright?"

"Yes, I'm fine, thank you. However, I'd appreciate it if you could get," she waved at the three men on the ground, "these off my lawn. They're bleeding on my freshly mowed grass."

The Deputy Director of the FBI smiled. "We'll take care of

it." Then he shook Tim's hand. "You look remarkably good after a 200 foot plunge in an Audi. Oh, and nice cameo by the way."

Sheri turned and headed toward the house.

They both frowned and Tim asked, "Where are you going?"

"Want to see what kind of network ratings we got on our broadcast."

Wendy and most of the station crew were crowded around a monitor in the central hub. As the transmission ended, she floated in front of the screen and said, "First, we need to find and eliminate that remote control circuit. Then we need to shut down and disassemble the microwave RFID scanner."

There were nods all around.

"We also need to thank Dr. Ann Ward."

There was a round of applause.

Ward shrugged. "Can't take credit. It was all TELEMED robotic surgery. Elizabeth Fuze rounded up some of the best vascular surgeons on the ground and they worked fast. I just applied the topical anesthetic and Band-Aids."

Wendy shook her head. "It was a three-ring circus trying to get all our capsules out. Without you orchestrating it, we wouldn't have finished in time, and several of us," she raised an eyebrow, "would have suffered cardiac arrest."

Ward gracefully bowed to another round of applause.

One of the engineers looked around and said, "What about the others onboard who modified the targeting software like Harrison?"

Wendy nodded. "Harrison was an agent but he was actually a good guy. Turan's people set him up to take the blame for the fire. There were several involved but after they discovered what was going on, all but one of them came forward. Turns out, they were under strict orders given to them directly by Turan. They assumed it was simply a classified program. They couldn't have known what was really going on. None of us did. After they learned that the fire in the module wasn't an accident, they immediately helped us figure out who was responsible. That individual *was* truly an enemy agent."

Ward added, "And is now heavily sedated in sickbay

awaiting a return flight *where* he'll be charged with sabotage and attempted murder."

Wendy finished, "We boost in a week. Let's get back to saving the planet."

EPILOGUE

Josh stood on the balcony cut into the island's rocky peak with Tim and Kristoff. Leaning over the railing with drinks in hand, they looked down the 200-foot cliff.

Tim pointed at the burned beach below and said to Kristoff, "You could rebuild the house but the missiles really messed up the beach."

Kristoff nodded. "Vegetation will return, but have to transplant palm trees and replace sand."

Josh added, "The U.N. should really pay for—"

"With my *home defense* device on roof," Kristoff interrupted with a smile, "last thing I want is government *assistance.*"

Behind them, they heard Sheri asking Judy how she organized the rebellion. Turning around, they leaned back on the railing and listened.

Sitting inside with Sheri and Judy were Elizabeth, Jessica, Greg, Carl, Kelly and Joe Meadows.

"... so then I used 'BadChat', the backchannel communication system the kids use. I sent out a picture of the bracelet with the injector exposed. It went to all the drone pilots and hackers. After that, it was easy to enlist their help. *Of course*, not everyone believed the picture was real. Someone shared it with the facility directors and traced it back to my phone."

Jessica asked, "How did you avoid being killed by the bracelets?"

She pointed at her wrist. They saw a patch of rough red skin encircling it.

"We used the stuff you guys smuggled into us. We just slid the bracelets up our arm as far as we could and then applied the epoxy in a thick ring around our wrists. We stuck strips of aluminum foil on top of the epoxy and when it hardened, slid the bracelets back down over it. We hoped the injectors couldn't penetrate the epoxy and the Taser would short circuit on the aluminum foil." Rubbing her wrist, she grinned. "It worked but I'm still trying to scrape the dang epoxy off."

Nodding, Jessica smiled. "Way to go MacGyver. What about

the EMP devices?"

Judy nodded. "I sent two people into the nano-drone control building and two more to the hacker building."

"How did you signal everyone to detonate them?"

"The hackers tapped into the video signal and broadcast my," she smiled, "academy award winning *demise* to everyone's phone."

Jessica nodded and asked, "So, did the EMP devices work? Did they shut down all the nano-drones?"

"Totally fried them along with the bracelets and all the control consoles. None of that equipment will work again." With a half-smile, she added, "They also fried most of the cars in the parking lot."

Elizabeth asked, "What about the radioactive nano-drones that are still out there?"

"The hackers downloaded the geographic positions of all nano-drones before we fried everything and uploaded the data to Jen."

Jen added, "The half-life of plutonium-238 is 87 years, but I sent the location information to the FBI and Interpol. They should be able to find most of them."

Josh nodded. "Thank you, Judy. You displayed phenomenal ingenuity and courage. Without you, the outcome might have been disastrously different."

She smiled. "It was kinda terrifying most of the time, but I've never felt more alive. I'd do it again." Turning to Sheri, she added, "I want to hear about how you discovered the capsules and escaped from Turkey."

As Sheri began her colorful version, Josh turned around and stared out over the ocean. It was beautiful and peaceful. For the first time since Davidson called him ... he was relaxed.

Sheri finally wrapped up with, "Then after Josh ditched the jet in the river, we hiked—"

"Wait, what?!" He heard Elizabeth ask, "Did you say *ditched*?"

As he slowly turned around, he saw Elizabeth with hands on hips. "You crashed *another* one?"

"No ... I ... did not. I landed it perfectly."

Sheri helpfully added, "*Technically*, I think a perfect landing involves wheels." She shrugged with a smile. "Just saying."

Tim offered, "It was a remarkably smooth belly landing."

Elizabeth nodded. "So, it's repairable?"

Sheri, clearly enjoying herself, added, "Actually, it blew up."

"What?!" Elizabeth shook her head, but he caught the smile crossing her face.

As he came inside, the party shifted to the food table. After heavy foraging, Meadows said, "It's amazing that all of you were able to pull this off without anyone getting shot."

Josh pointed at Carl's bandaged leg.

Carl pointed back at Josh's bandaged arm.

Josh frowned. "All we knew for sure was that if we could broadcast most of what Turan said," he shrugged, "it wouldn't matter if he killed all of us."

Into the solemn silence, Carl added with a half-smile, "Actually ... it would have kinda mattered to me."

Jessica and Sheri, frowning and laughing at the same time, added in unison, "Uh, yeah, kinda mattered to us too."

After more stories, Meadows looked at Josh. "It's still hard to believe *you* are the Secretary-General of the United Nations."

Josh corrected, "Acting. General Von Stein has been exonerated. The General Assembly reversed their vote of no confidence and we need to restore him to office as soon as he's out of the hospital."

With an embarrassed smile, Elizabeth added, "The *supposedly* safe virus almost killed him. He was so sick; he didn't know he'd been fired until he'd already been cleared. I heard he doesn't want the job anymore." She laughed. "Said it was more dangerous than being a general and he wants to spend more time with his grandkids."

Meadows patted Josh on the shoulder. "Four of the five members of the permanent Security Council — China, Russia, the U.S. and U.K. — want to nominate you to be the permanent Secretary-General."

Josh gave a wry smile. "France doesn't like me?"

Sheri shrugged. "They don't know you. They weren't involved in the last minute negotiations when you helped stop WWIII last year."

"Doesn't matter." Josh shook his head. "The Secretary-

General can't be from any of the Permanent Security Council countries."

Meadows put his hand up. "Actually, that's a tradition not a rule. There's nothing in the charter that forbids it. Besides, *technically*, you don't show up as an American citizen anyway."

"*Technically*, I don't show up as a citizen of *any* country. Which is the other reason I can't be Secretary-General; I have no identity, no history."

"Maybe ... but the entire world saw your performance *live*. You might be surprised."

With a mischievous smile, Sheri offered a toast. "You could start a new world order where airplanes are expendable and clothing is optional."

With a short laugh, he rolled his eyes. While they debated the pros and cons, he stepped back out on the balcony.

After a few minutes, Meadows joined him.

Before Meadows said anything, Josh preempted, "I don't *want* to be Secretary-General."

"What does that have to do with anything? I didn't want to command the Antarctic base." He paused. "I'm sorry, but I believe you still have an obligation to use those abilities, particularly, now that we know there are *others* who have them and aren't afraid to use them to kill or destroy."

Tim, Sheri and Elizabeth joined them.

Overhearing Meadows' comment, Sheri added, "I'm *very* concerned about the genetic program Turan was working on. It was cutting-edge terrifying."

"I agree," Josh shrugged, "but Turan's dead."

There was a pause and Tim quietly said, "Carl noticed that the windows on the floor immediately below the roof were shattered."

Josh nodded. "Of course. The beam came in at an angle. The heat took them out."

Tim just looked at him.

Josh shook his head. "We saw what was left of him on the railing. He couldn't have survived."

Tim shrugged. "None of the cameras recorded his incineration and there were no charred bone fragments at the base of the building."

Elizabeth grimaced. "All we know for sure was that ... we got his *hand*." Then, looking out over the ocean, she recited, "For I am going to raise up a shepherd over the land who would not care for the lost, or seek the young, or heal the injured. May his arm be completely withered, his right eye totally blinded!"

There was a pregnant silence.

Sheri broke it with, "Well ... *that* was creepy. Thanks for sharing, Elizabeth."

With some nervous laughs, everyone headed back inside except Josh. Left staring at the ocean, he tried to use his prescient ability to sense the future ... but got nothing.

After a few minutes, Kelly joined him.

He gave her a small smile and said, "I'm glad you could make it."

She put her hand on his arm.

As he looked into those laser green eyes, she said, "I guess part of me always knew."

Josh took a deep breath and exhaled unsteadily. "Kelly," he shook his head gently, "it wasn't my choice. I ... I so wanted to tell you—"

"I know," she interrupted gently and smiled through tears.

"Does Carl...?"

She shook her head.

Sighing, he said, "We need to keep it that way."

"I ... I know. I just want *you* to know you're welcome to be with Caitlin whenever you want."

He barely got out, "Thank you."

Her eyes unfocused as she added, "Josh, you need to keep that position. It's ... it's not over." With that, she kissed him on the cheek and left.

He stood there for several minutes feeling both happy and sad. Looking around to be sure he was alone, he quietly said, "Jesse, thank you once again." He frowned and gently shook his head. "But I don't understand ... how could you let Turan do this?"

Free will.

Josh shook his head again. "But how could he do it?"

Maybe you should ask him.

The trilogy is finished as originally envisioned several years ago. Yes, another story is foreshadowed, but it's your fault … lol. One of our readers pointed out a new technological threat, one that didn't exist when the trilogy was outlined. This new threat pushed its way into the top five. Unfortunately, there are more than three apocalyptic and preventable threats facing us. The next story may be considered an addendum or *possibly* the start of a new series. Thank you for your patience. An excerpt from IMMUNE follows.

Unlike most novels, the Fuzed books will be updated each year with the latest science and technology. Love to have your help updating and improving these stories. Please give us your feedback, corrections and ideas at FuzedTrilogy@comcast.net or via text. Text **"Fuzed"** to **46786.** We'll keep you informed of imminent threats, release of the next book, movie and game development. We'll also enter you into a drawing to have a future character named after you and an invite to the set during filming. We won't share your information and you can shut it off at any time.

Or register by email at www.Fuzed.org (preferably, not with the email you give to car sales managers).

Follow us on Facebook at www.Facebook.com/FuzedTrilogy

HOW REAL WAS THIS?

Not since the industrial revolution has humanity faced such a monumental change. No one could have imagined that the exponential growth of digital processing power would turn telephones into cherished digital assistants, or that we would have autonomous cars, houses and lives. With this gift, however, comes a price. Almost everywhere we go and everything we do leaves a digital footprint, a record of not just our path but our thoughts, beliefs and fears. Add the inevitable rise of machine intelligence and we must choose our destiny ... while we can.

The other apocalyptic threat is not a result of our actions, but our inaction. Asteroid and comet impacts aren't a *potential* threat. There is a 100% probability that an impact will obliterate almost all life on Earth. It's happened before and it's statistically guaranteed to happen again. The problem is — it could be in the far future or tomorrow. For the first time in human history, we have the ability to prevent it. Organizations like the B612 Foundation lead the effort to identify the Earth-orbit-crossing asteroids. However, we still need to develop a strategy to deflect asteroids and comets, particularly, those discovered within a couple years of impact. Our current strategy is Russian Roulette.

In this story, we propose a phased array laser deployed to a position beyond the moon's orbit called L2. The story is fiction but the concept is not. The DE-STAR program is a first step in this direction. Phased array lasers exist and we already have space telescopes deployed to L2. This is one of those rare situations where one concept could be the solution to multiple problems. L2 is not only a perfect place to park a defensive laser system, it could also serve as a gateway to the outer solar system and a waystation to launch crewed and un-crewed missions to Mars and beyond. The phased array could do double duty, boosting spacecraft faster and more efficiently than any propulsion system in existence, and its location in Earth's shadow makes it the ultimate Goldilocks zone for humanity's most powerful observatories. Unfortunately, neither this nor any other project to deflect asteroids or comets discovered within a few years of impact is being actively pursued. Let's change that.

Can fiction really impact reality? The idea of launching communication satellites in orbit around the Earth was first proposed by science fiction author Arthur C. Clark.

IMMUNE

Book Four of the ... Fuzed Trilogy

1

THE END

Josh answered the phone, "Hi Kelly. How are you?"

He heard stress in her voice. "I'm fine. It's … it's Caitlin."

"What's wrong?! Is she sick?"

"Yes, I mean no. I mean … I don't know."

"Kelly, what's going on?"

"She's been running a high temperature for several days. We took her to the doctor. They couldn't find anything wrong with her, but she still has the fever and…."

"And what?"

He heard her sigh. "Josh, she's … she's changing."

"What do you mean *changing*?"

There was a pause. "It's her appearance. Her skin, her hair, even her eyes…."

"Kelly, you're not making sense. How's she changing?"

He heard her take a deep breath. "Josh, she's beginning to look like you."

GLOSSARY

CIWS – Close-In Weapon System. Fully automated, radar-guided, 20 mm Vulcan cannon shaped like R2-D2. It is a last ditch, defensive system used on most warships to destroy incoming missiles or aircraft.

CRISPR - Clustered Regularly Interspaced Short Palindromic Repeats. Cutting-edge genetic engineering tool that can quickly and efficiently edit (remove, add or alter) the DNA or genes of an organism.

DE-STAR – Directed Energy System for Targeting of Asteroids and exploRation. University of California project designed to use a space-based, phased array laser to deflect asteroids and comets.

ECM – Electronic Counter Measures. Device used to detect and spoof or jam radar signals to prevent detection or tracking.

EMP – Electro-Magnetic Pulse. A burst of electromagnetic energy that can induce an electric current in conductors, potentially damaging or destroying equipment with electrical circuits.

EVA – Extra Vehicular Activity. Crewed activities outside of a spacecraft or space station such as space walks or pod flights.

FIS – Russian Federal Intelligence Service. Successor of the KGB and similar in mission to the CIA.

Gecko – an enclosed off-road electric motorcycle with adaptive camouflage. Although fictitious, it is based on the C1 design by Danny Kim, founder of Lit Motors.

Gene Drive – A technique that guarantees the dominance and inheritance of a particular gene in a population. Seen Gene Drive TED Talk by Jennifer Khan.

GMO – **G**enetically **M**odified **O**rganism

IFF – **I**dentify **F**riend or **F**oe. Aircraft radar repeater system that helps Air Traffic Controllers identify aircraft on radar.

ISLO – **I**nternational **S**pace-based **L**aser and **O**bservatory. New space station with a phased-array laser for deflecting asteroids, giant space-based telescopes and a future waystation to Mars.

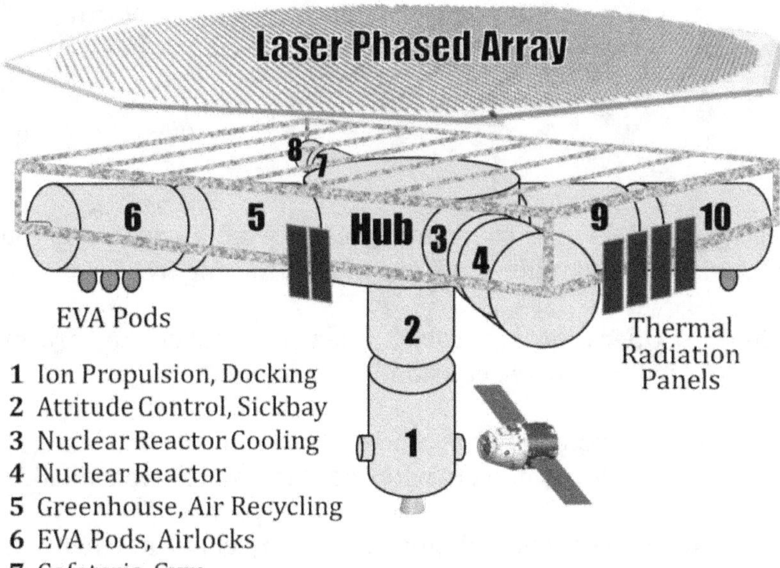

1 Ion Propulsion, Docking
2 Attitude Control, Sickbay
3 Nuclear Reactor Cooling
4 Nuclear Reactor
5 Greenhouse, Air Recycling
6 EVA Pods, Airlocks
7 Cafeteria, Gym
8 Dorm, Bathrooms, Water Storage and Recycling
9 Communication, Support Equipment and Storage
10 Fabrication and Repair, Backup EVA Pod Dock
HUB Control Center for Reactor, Laser, Propulsion and Telescopes

ISS - **I**nternational **S**pace **S**tation currently in low Earth orbit.

L2 – **L**agrangian Point Two. A gravitationally semi-stable orbital point four times further away from Earth than the moon. It remains in Earth's shadow (the Earth eclipses 80% of the sun).

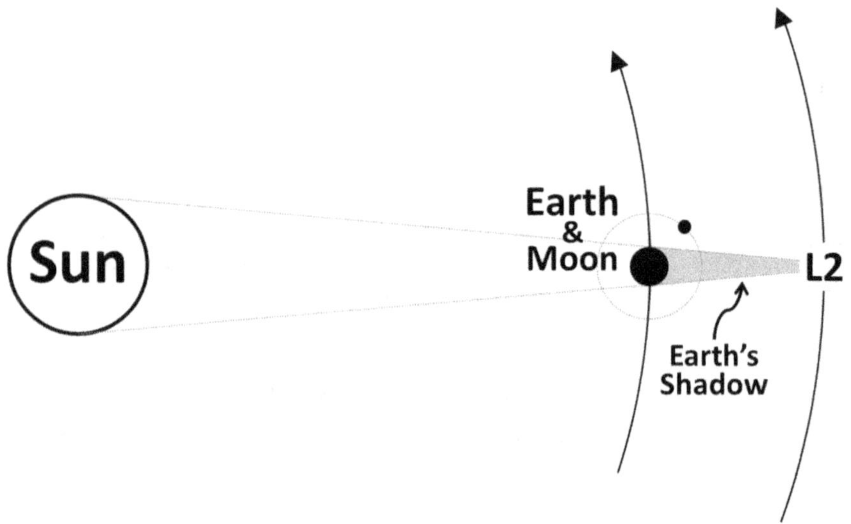

MacGyver – TV series character who successfully used everyday materials like paperclips to escape or beat the enemy.

OPSEC – Operational Security. Measures taken to prevent unintentionally exposing classified information.

Red Shirt – an expendable character. From the original Star Trek series where security officers with red shirts were often killed.

RFID – **R**adio **F**requency **Id**entification. Tiny chips attached to or inserted in an object that when interrogated by a radio signal, emit a unique code allowing identification and tracking.

SIGINT – **Sig**nals **Int**elligence. Intelligence gathering by intercepting electronic signals such as radio or data communications. Often done by satellites.

TELEMED – **Tele-Med**icine. The ability to diagnose and treat illnesses and injuries virtually using telemetry and tele-robotics.

TS/SCI – Top Secret/Sensitive Compartmented Information.

CHARACTER REVIEW

Josh Fuze

Appearance: Late-thirties, omni-racial, but with a body that looks like a 20-year-old Olympic athlete. His eyes are unique — steel gray with flecks of multiple colors.

Background: With mixed heritage, he received an Ivy League education by getting a Navy scholarship. He graduated as an aerospace engineer and became a Navy fighter pilot. After test pilot school, he chased the astronaut program, but never made it. He was promoted to Commander and given the Navy's robotic fighter development program. A year after he married, he was fatally injured while ejecting from a burning jet. He woke up a year later with a new omni-racial body — a genetic blend of humanity's best genes with one-in-a-billion abilities. Good at understanding people and the "big picture," he sucks at details and struggles with the loss of his past life.

Elizabeth Fuze

Appearance: Mid-thirties mix of Scandinavian and East Indian, she has blonde hair but with olive skin. She is the cute "girl next door" with an athletic build and exotic eyes.

Background: Raised in Texas, she grew up in a strong Christian home. Her father owned a computer shop and she became a tech whiz. She studied computer science in college and played collegiate soccer, but switched to nursing and became a neurological nurse. Her husband died in a motorcycle accident shortly after they were married. She is intelligent, intuitive, outgoing, kind and trusting.

Jesse

Appearance and Background: Unknown.

Kristoff Bobinski

Appearance: Looks like a 60-year-old Sean Connery.

Background: He grew up under the Soviet regime, specializing in Siberian construction. He became a U.S. citizen and an expert at building in extreme conditions but still loves his mother country of Russia. A friend of Elton Muske, he is capable, confident and calm but doesn't suffer fools lightly.

Carl Casey

Appearance: In his late-thirties, tall with dark hair and eyes, his expression always makes him appear amused by life.

Background: With a degree in International Law, he was a Navy intelligence officer, squadron mate and good friend of Josh. Joining the CIA after the Navy, he worked as an operative but was an exceptional analyst and rose to upper management. After Josh's "death," he married Josh's widow, Kelly. He's quiet, intelligent and skeptical with a dry sense of humor.

Kelly Casey

Appearance: Mid-thirties, she is a cute, freckled redhead with smiling green eyes.

Background: Married to Josh for only one year, she discovered she was pregnant just before his "fatal" crash. After Josh's "death," she married Carl. She knows no stranger and is gregarious, intuitive and passionate.

Brian Davidson

Appearance: Late-fifties, he is average height with the body of a long-distance runner. He always wears a coat and tie.

Background: He chose the CIA because he believed he could make a difference. Beginning as an operative, he worked his way up in the intelligence community to Deputy Director of the CIA. He is a quiet, intelligent, soft-spoken professional.

Dr. Steve Katori

Appearance: Mid-sixties of Japanese descent, he has bushy white hair and looks a bit like Dr. Michio Kaku.

Background: Boeing's lead engineer, he worked for several aerospace corporations and has a formidable reputation as a no-nonsense, get-the-job-done engineer, smart but tough.

Greg Langlois

Appearance: Late-twenties, he is a handsome but geeky-looking African American engineer with badly matched clothes.

Background: Recruited out of college by Northrup Grumman, he worked on the latest spy satellites. After joining the Blaster team, he solved several major technical challenges. He is brilliant but socially awkward and a little naïve.

Jessica Lee

Appearance: Early thirties, cute, petite Chinese-American.

Background: Her father was a Chinese general, her mother a genetic scientist. They sent her to the U.S. for education when she was a child. She stayed and became a U.S. citizen. A brilliant, arrogant engineer, she invented the BOTIC chip that allows cell phones to share processing power and memory, resulting in the artificial intelligence, Jen. Pragmatic and irreverent, she has a dry sense of humor.

Dr. Sheri Lopez

Appearance: Mid-forties, petite and curvy, she looks similar to Jennifer Lopez.

Background: A competitive tomboy as a child, she became a psychiatrist to understand why she was different. She started a private practice, but had little empathy for her patients and shifted into psychology of the masses, working with the government on mass disaster scenarios. She wrote a bestseller and had her own TV show. Josh originally recruited her as the team's social psychologist. She is strong, intelligent and task-oriented with some serious attitude.

Admiral Joe Meadows

Appearance: Mid-fifties, bald, African American, he looks like an intimidating 250-pound linebacker.

Background: A history major, he is divorced with grown kids. He was Josh's first fleet Squadron Commander and was managing the Navy's aircraft development programs, including robotic fighters. Josh recruited him to lead the comet deflection program. Although his size and face are intimidating, he has a ready smile and booming laugh. A great leader, he puts people first and takes care of his team.

Tim Smith

Appearance: Average height with brown hair, brown eyes and no remarkable features, he blends in well.

Background: With an MS in psychology, he served in Special Forces and became a CIA agent. His specialty was exfiltration and protecting high-visibility political leaders. He left the CIA after accidentally shooting an innocent woman while protecting a European Union Commissioner from a terrorist death threat. Although exonerated, he felt responsible and planned to use his life insurance to take care of the woman's children by "retiring" himself ... until he met Josh and Sheri. Quiet and good at being invisible, he is confident, loyal and extremely deadly.

Jen

Appearance: None

Background: An artificial intelligence accidentally created when all the world's phones were linked by the BOTIC chip. She was "born" when the comet grazed the Earth creating a powerful electromagnetic pulse. She lives in the world's network of phones. Her IQ is in the tens of thousands but she has the innocent personality of a child. She considers Josh and Jessica her parents.